NOGALES PASS

NOGALES PASS

A SEAN WYNN THRILLER

KEITH J. WEBER

ISBN(ebook): 979-8-9898229-4-2

ISBN(print): 979-8-9898229-5-9

Cover design by GetCovers.com

For my Dad, the real inspiration behind Sean Wynn.

Author's Note

THANK YOU FOR PICKING up *Nogales Pass*. If this is your first Sean Wynn novel, welcome! Go ahead and skip this note and go straight to the Prologue. I hope you love it.

However, if you've read the two previous installments of the Sean Wynn series, *Night Rules* and *Intentional*, then you might enjoy the free short story, *The Interviews*, available on my website at keithjweber.com. While *Nogales Pass* is a completely stand-alone story, *The Interviews* takes place between the events of *Intentional* and *Nogales Pass*, and provides a little more background and insight into what makes Sean Wynn tick. It is certainly not required to enjoy *Nogales Pass*, but if you want more Sean Wynn, consider this your chance for a little bonus material.

And if you're a first-time reader who's bothered to read this far, you too, are welcome to download *The Interviews*. You deserve it!

To be kept up-to-date on all things Sean Wynn, visit:

www.keithjweber.com

PROLOGUE

ALL HIS LIFE, TERRANCE had known only one kind of luck, and it wasn't good.

Tonight will be different, he thought. *She's into this.*

The crowded Las Vegas club swirled around them, Creedence Clearwater's "Bad Moon Rising" blared in the background. The tattooed brunette's eyes sparkled as they met his, her full lips wrapped seductively around the straw of her White Russian.

She lowered her drink. The fourth he'd bought her in the last hour. "Your s-sister did all that?"

Terrance wasn't sure if she was slurring her words or if the alcohol was affecting his own hearing. "Swear to God." A twinge of guilt pierced the back of his brain, warning he'd already said too much. He knocked back the last of his Jack and Coke to wash the feeling away.

"She sounds like a badass. I think I'd rather go home with her." The brunette swayed on the barstool.

Terrance laughed and clutched his chest. "Ow, that hurts." He leaned in, shouting to be heard over the din. "I wish you could. She died. Her and her kid. Car accident. Guess you'll have to settle for me."

The brunette's eyes popped wide. She plunked her drink onto the bar, splashing a few drops onto the sleeve of the man who'd been eavesdropping on their conversation. "Whoa. Wait a minute. Your sister brought down a crime boss only to end up being killed in a car accident? No way. You're full of shit."

Terrance smiled as a wave of relief washed over him. It was the reaction he'd been counting on. The one that made this story so perfect. It was just too outrageous to believe.

Even if it is true. Now to play it up before delivering the coup de gráce.

He put his hand to his chest, trying his best to sound serious. "Cross my heart." He held the stoic stance for a moment, then allowed the corners of his mouth to curl upward, before bursting into laughter and leaning into the brunette.

She wrapped her arms around him. "Poor baby." She could barely get the words out between bouts of drunken laughter. "You must be heartbroken. Way too distraught to entertain a woman. I should let you go home. Alone."

"Oh, no. That would be way worse. I need the company."

"What about your sister? Wouldn't that be disrespectful?"

Terrance drew close, putting his lips next to her ear. "Can you keep a secret?"

The brunette leaned back, brushing into the man beside her. She looked at Terrance expectantly.

Terrance lowered his mouth to her ear, but spoke loudly. "She's not really dead. She's in witness protection."

He drew back, holding her gaze for a silent moment, until they both burst out laughing. Neither noticed the man sitting next to them, snapping their picture in the mirror behind the bar.

CHAPTER 1

THREE WEEKS LATER

SEAN WYNN EASED back on the throttle as he swung his new Harley Davidson Road Glide off Interstate 5 into San Diego's Gaslamp Quarter. Friday afternoon traffic was heavy through L.A., turning the normal three-hour ride from his home in Ventura into almost five, making him late for his unit reunion.

If they're anything like they used to be, the real party won't start until after midnight anyway.

A shiver of hesitation coursed down his spine as he pulled into a parking garage a block away from the Marriott. He looked forward to reconnecting with the thirteen guys from his MARSOC Raider team. Guys he considered—and who considered him—brothers. He'd stayed in touch with many of them over the years, until his wife was murdered three years ago. Then he'd dropped off the map.

Explaining his disappearance to them would be easy. And unnecessary. They'd understand.

It was the roughly fifty other people attending tonight, members of the other three Raider teams that made up his MARSOC Company, the Marine Forces Special Operations Command, that he could do without. Not that they were bad people, but they weren't brothers. More like distant cousins.

Steeling himself, Wynn slung his duffle over his shoulder and strode to the Marriott. He checked in, then stopped in his room long enough to change his shirt and wash his face before taking the elevator to the rooftop bar where the reunion was in full swing.

"Spider-Man!" a voice yelled as Wynn pushed through the glass door into the cool spring evening. A bear of a man with red-dish-blond hair and rosy cheeks barreled through the crowd and engulfed him in a powerful embrace.

When the guy finally let go, Wynn asked, "How you doing, Jonesy?" Art Jones had been an assistant rifleman in one of the other teams in Wynn's company eleven years ago. So, a cousin, but a close one.

"I'm good, I'm good. I was hoping you'd be here." Jonesy turned and extended his hand to a woman following in his wake. "I want you to meet my fiancée. Claire, this is Sean Wynn, better known in the unit as Spider-Man."

"It's nice to meet you, Sean. Or do you prefer Spider-Man?"

Wynn smiled. "Sean is fine."

"Why do they call you that?"

Wynn shrugged. "I used to do some rock climbing. Someone saw me on a wall one time and the name stuck."

"No way, man. That's only part of it." Jonesy turned to Claire. "Wynn here's got a spider-sense. Tells him when things are gonna get dicey. One time outside of Ghazni, we were about to walk right into an ambush. Wynn stops, says something doesn't feel right. So we send the dog up and sure enough, there are IEDs all over the place. Even Taliban on the rooftops. Saved our asses that day."

"Oh my God!" Claire said, her eyes wide on both of them. "What'd you do?"

Wynn jumped in. "I seem to remember Jonesy here running like hell."

"Just following you," Jonesy said with a grin.

Wynn laughed, then glanced at Claire. "Our missions are classified."

"Yeah, right. Classified." Jonesy winked at Claire. "I'll tell you later." He turned back to Wynn. "Where's that gorgeous wife of yours?"

The question, although anticipated, stopped Wynn in his tracks. Hearing it out loud for the first time since he'd discovered and avenged the truth of Nicole's murder barely six months ago, struck hard. The pain was still raw.

"She passed."

Jonesy deflated like a balloon. "Oh my God, man. I'm sorry."

Wynn smiled sadly. "It's okay. You didn't know."

The three of them stood awkwardly for a moment until Wynn nodded at the beer in Jonesy's hand. "Where do I get one of those?"

Claire turned and pointed to the bar across the rooftop. "Over there."

"Let me get a drink," Wynn said. "We'll catch up later."

Jonesy paused, then wrapped his arms around Wynn and squeezed, letting go after a long moment.

Wynn tapped the big man on the shoulder. "Thanks, man." He slipped away toward the bar.

That's gonna take some getting used to.

Wynn worked his way through the crowd, chatting with several old friends along the way. More than an hour later, twilight had faded to dark before he finally got a beer and made his way to the roof's edge.

He leaned his elbows against the railing on top of the half wall, twenty-two stories above the street, and looked down into Petco Park, home of the San Diego Padres. Huge banks of LED lights illuminated thousands of fans enjoying the early April home opener against the Dodgers.

"Hell of a way to watch a game, isn't it?" Danny Kovacs, a spotter from back in the day, and someone Wynn would classify as a distant, distant cousin, rested his elbows against the railing next to Wynn. He wore a dark suit over an open-collared, white shirt, and cradled a whiskey tumbler in his hands.

Still a pretentious asshole. "It doesn't suck. How are you, Danny?" The two men clinked their drinks.

"I'm good. What do you ride?"

Wynn cocked his head to the side. He'd left his jacket in his room, and in the last few months had cut his hair and trimmed his goatee. Now in his late thirties, six-one, and a solid one-nine-ty, he didn't think he gave off that "biker" vibe. "A Harley Road Glide. How'd you know?"

"Left toe."

Wynn looked down. He was still wearing his heavy riding boots, the area above his left toe black from the bike's shifter. "You still don't miss a thing, do you, Danny?"

"I try not to," Kovacs said. "Besides, we all have our skills. You still got that... what did we use to call it? That spider-sense?"

Wynn realized he hadn't felt the familiar tingle in over six months, not since he'd killed those responsible for Nicole's murder. "Not as much need for it when you're not carrying an M-16."

"No, I suppose not. What are you up to these days?"

Wynn hated that question. Most guys his age were deep into their careers. After Nicole's death, he'd sold his cybersecurity firm and had done well enough to make work optional for a long time. He'd spent much of the last three years with his Harley on the road. How do you say you're not working without appearing to be either a bum or a snob?

"I'm between gigs right now. I do a little I.T. consulting, but looking for the next thing. How about you?"

Kovacs took a sip. "A little of this. A little of that. Working the family business. Nothing special."

"What kind of business?"

"A couple of nightclubs over in Vegas. Just little things."

"Sounds interesting," Wynn said, more to be polite than out of any real interest. "What's the name? I'll have to stop by next time I'm there."

"The main one's called Pink, but don't bother. They're more for the younger, single guys, if you know what I mean."

"Strip clubs?"

Kovacs shrugged.

"How's Krista feel about that?" Krista Hampson and Wynn had been fast friends in the Corps. At one time, long before he met Nicole, Wynn had hoped they might become something more, but Kovacs had leaped in and swept Krista off her feet. They married a year after Wynn was discharged.

"I wish I knew," Kovacs said. "She was killed in a car accident a few years ago."

A cold shiver sliced through Wynn's chest. "Wow, Danny. I'm sorry. I had no idea."

Kovacs waved his hand dismissively. "No worries. Besides, I heard what happened to your wife. If anyone could understand, I figure it's got to be you."

"Yeah. That I do."

They leaned silently against the railing, side-by-side, looking out at the skyline. A bat cracked in the ballpark and the crowd rose to its feet as a long fly ball dropped into the right field seats. The crowd roared as the runner jogged around the bases.

"Padres' homer," Kovacs said.

"Yeah," Wynn whispered.

The silence stretched between them, each consumed in their own thoughts. Kovacs straightened up. "Well, just wanted to say hi."

"I'm glad you did. You take care now."

The two men shook hands, then Kovacs wandered off into the crowd.

Wynn hung around for another few hours, catching up with his former teammates and reliving stories from their glory days, but the conversation with Kovacs dampened his mood. Shortly before midnight, when small groups began peeling off to go to more serious bars for more serious drinking, Wynn discreetly slipped into the elevator and went down to his room.

Inside, a light was flashing on the phone next to the bed. He picked it up and pushed the message button.

Mr. Wynn, this is the valet downstairs. The parking garage has indicated a problem with your vehicle. Could you please come down as soon as you get this message? Thank you.

"Shit," Wynn muttered. He grabbed his keys and took the elevator down to the lobby. Pushing through the glass doors, he approached the valet stand where a young guy in a hotel uniform stood talking with two others.

"Can I help you, sir?"

"I'm Sean Wynn. You left a message about my bike?"

The guy hesitated as he glanced over Wynn's shoulder. Tires squealed behind him. Wynn turned as two large black SUVs screeched to a stop. Three men in dark suits climbed out of the first vehicle and circled around him, the one in front pulling open his suit jacket to reveal a badge attached to his belt.

"Mr. Wynn. I'm Deputy Todd, with the U.S. Marshals. We'd like to ask you a few questions. Would you mind coming with us?" He motioned to the SUV, its rear door still hanging open.

Dormant for six months, Wynn's spider-sense re-awakened. His gaze roamed back to Todd, then over to the other two. "What about?"

"Routine questions. You're free to leave anytime you want, but we'd like to speak with you in private."

Wynn raised an eyebrow. "Routine? At midnight?"

Todd smiled and held up his phone. "I can get Lieutenant Akins on the line to verify if you like."

Lou Akins was the commanding officer of the Ventura Police Detectives. Wynn had become friends with him over the last few months.

"Do it." Wynn said.

Todd searched his contacts and was about to hit the call button when Wynn said, "Wait."

Don't want to wake the old man if I don't have to. "Let me see the number."

Todd flipped the phone toward Wynn. The number was Akins'.

Wynn turned to the two men behind him. Their suit jackets hung open, maybe a little tight around the shoulders. Probably fit great five years and fifteen pounds ago, but now not so much. Their shoes were scuffed, their pants wrinkled as if after a long day of sitting. They looked tired. Wynn nodded and they pulled open their jackets, revealing their badges. And sidearms.

Wynn held out his hand.

With an exaggerated sigh, one of the men handed over his badge wallet. The leather was creased with the badge's imprint, the plastic window over the ID yellowing with age. Wynn examined the picture. It also looked like it was taken fifteen pounds ago. Not good. Not taken with the care someone would exert if they were trying to forge an ID, but rather with the callousness of someone bored with a government job. He didn't bother with the others. If one was fake, they all would be. And they'd all be this good.

He glanced at the license of the second SUV.

Government plate. Elaborate set up if it's not legit.

Beside the building, the valet and his buddies were fixated on the scene. A few other people had stopped and stood watching.

Todd glanced nervously at the small crowd. He motioned toward the vehicle. "Mr. Wynn, please."

With a nod, Wynn eased himself into the back seat.

Todd climbed into the front and another man jumped in behind the driver, while the third remained outside and closed the door. The SUV accelerated away.

"You want to tell me where we're going, Deputy Todd?"

"Not far. Special Agent Ruiz will answer all your questions when we get there. Just a few minutes."

They traveled in silence less than two miles before the SUV pulled into the driveway of a gated government building. The driver showed his badge, then rolled through when the gates swung open. He drove around the side of the building and down into a nearly empty underground garage.

They parked and everyone stepped out, then waited as the second SUV pulled in beside them. Three more men spilled from the second vehicle.

Wynn looked at Todd. "Six guys for routine questions?"

Todd shrugged.

Wynn scanned the six men. "You said I'd be free to go at any time."

"You are," Todd replied. "But since you've come this far, why not come up and talk to Ruiz?"

Wynn leveled a look at the marshal. "Why don't you tell me what this is about? Then I'll decide if I want to talk to him."

"I'm afraid I can't do that."

"Then I'm out of here." Wynn took a step to go between two deputies, who initially moved to block his path, but on a look from

Todd, stepped back and cleared the way. Wynn brushed past the deputies and started up the ramp toward the exit.

When he was about ten steps away, Todd called out, "Whose side are you on, Wynn?"

Wynn stopped and turned back. "What the hell are you talking about?"

"Why don't you come upstairs and find out?"

Wynn paused for a moment, then tramped back to the group. "This better be good."

Todd smiled, then led Wynn and two deputies to an elevator where they rode up to the fourth floor. When the doors opened, they strode down a carpeted hallway, eventually stopping in front of an open door. Todd motioned Wynn inside a large conference room where another agent waited.

The man was trim, Hispanic, in his late forties. He sat in a chair on the far side of an oak conference table, a manilla file folder open in front of him. He flipped it closed when Wynn walked in.

"Mr. Wynn." The Hispanic guy rose from his chair and stepped around the table. "I'm Special Agent Mark Ruiz. Thank you for coming in."

Wynn shook his hand and nodded.

"Can we get you something to drink?" Ruiz asked.

"You can tell me why I'm here."

Ruiz raised his eyebrows. "A man who likes to get down to business. Please, have a seat."

Wynn pulled out a chair and sat down. Ruiz took a seat across the table while Deputy Todd sat next to Wynn, leaving an empty chair between them.

"I hear you attended a reunion of your old Marine company tonight, is that right?" Ruiz asked.

"Yeah."

"Have you attended any of these reunions before?"

"Company-wide? No."

"Why did you decide to go tonight? Why this one?"

Wynn wasn't about to explain himself to these guys. He felt the first hints of his patience being tested. "What difference does that make?"

Ruiz ignored the question. "When was the last time you saw anyone from your unit?"

"Anyone?" Wynn thought back. "I had a few guys from my team working for me a few years ago. A couple more came to my wedding."

"When was that?"

"Almost seven years ago."

"What about Art Jones?" Ruiz asked. "When was the last time you saw him?"

"Not since my wedding."

"Bob Crofton?"

Wynn's patience lost another step. He'd agreed to talk, not to be interrogated. It was clear these guys were investigating someone, but rather than tell him who, they felt the need to play games. But Crofton was a team member. A brother. *They ain't getting shit about him from me.* "He was one of the guys who worked for me. Maybe a couple of years."

"Danny Kovacs?" Ruiz asked.

"Not since I got out."

"You sure about that?"

Wynn paused. He hadn't been invited to Danny and Krista's wedding, that much he was sure of. He hadn't seen either of them since. "Yeah. I'm sure."

"How well do you know Mr. Kovacs?"

"Now?" Wynn said. "Not at all. Ten years ago, we were in the same company, different teams."

"Were you close?"

Wynn shook his head. Asking about Jonesy and Crofton was a decoy. *Kovacs is the one they're interested in.* "Why don't you just ask whatever it is you want to know?"

"Just trying to understand if you and Mr. Kovacs were friends, is all."

Wynn well remembered how Kovacs had made the move on Krista that he'd been too hesitant to make. He also remembered Kovacs as an entitled douchebag, but had to admit, the episode with Krista may have colored his memory. "We didn't hang out, but he was in my company, so yeah, we were friends."

"What about Krista Hampson?"

Wynn leaned forward and put his elbows on the table, buying time. He hadn't expected them to ask about her. Krista had been in a combat support role. Not a direct operative, but she was a Marine, meaning a badass, nonetheless. "What about her?"

"Were you friends with her also?"

"Yeah. So?"

Ruiz sat back, his movements slow and deliberate, as if pondering a hypothetical. "So, if the two of them were in a burning building and you could save only one, who would it be?"

Wynn leaned back, not bothering to hide his annoyance. "What kind of a question is that? Krista's already dead, as I'm sure you know, so I guess that leaves Danny."

"What if she weren't?"

"If she weren't dead? Krista."

"Why?"

Wynn laughed grimly. "I liked her better."

"No unit loyalty to Kovacs?" Ruiz asked.

"Sure there is. But it's relative."

Ruiz paused. "So, if you could do something to help Krista, or her memory in this case, that might not be in Danny Kovacs' best interest, would you?"

Now we're getting close, Wynn thought. "Has Danny done something wrong?"

Ruiz returned Wynn's gaze.

"To Krista?" Wynn pressed.

Ruiz remained silent.

Wynn thought back to six months ago, to what he'd done in pursuit of his wife's killers. Would he do it again?

In a heartbeat.

"Yeah," Wynn said. "If Danny had something to do with Krista's death, you bet I'd help."

Ruiz stared at Wynn for a long moment, then looked at Todd, who shrugged.

Ruiz motioned his chin toward the door. Todd got up and opened the door, allowing two deputies and a woman to enter. The woman had her head down, her face hidden by dark sunglasses and the brim of a baseball cap pulled low. But there was something familiar in the way she held herself, the curve of her figure, the way she moved. She reached up and took off the hat and sunglasses, then raised her face to Wynn. Something he thought was long dead stirred deep inside him.

"Hi Sean," said Krista Hampson.

CHAPTER 2

WYNN SWALLOWED THE LUMP in his throat. Krista's brunette hair was longer than she'd worn it twelve years ago, with soft curls resting on her shoulders. She was thinner than he remembered, and a few slight wrinkles creased her face, but her eyes still shimmered, her smile still infectious. A butterfly fluttered in his stomach.

He pushed the feeling down. Seeing Krista very much alive, flanked by a pair of U.S. Marshals, generated all kinds of questions. He picked the wrong one.

"Who'd you rat on?"

Her eyes turned hard. "I didn't *rat* on anybody."

"Sorry." He cleared his throat, instantly regretting his choice of words. "I didn't mean it that way. But with Danny telling me you were dead, and all this," Wynn motioned around them, "it's witness protection, right?"

Krista's voice softened. "Yeah."

"Who are they protecting you from?"

Krista glanced at Ruiz, who said, "Gentlemen, can you give us the room?" The two deputies shuffled out the door, leaving Wynn with Krista, Ruiz, and Todd. Krista took a seat next to Ruiz, across the table from Wynn.

When she was settled, Wynn said, "So what does this have to do with Danny?"

Krista opened her mouth to speak, but Ruiz laid a hand on her arm.

"We're keeping an eye on Mr. Kovacs," Ruiz said. "We had a team set up in the building opposite the Marriott tonight. When we saw you talking with him, we thought you might be able to help us."

"With what?"

"We'll get to that in a minute..." Ruiz said.

Wynn sighed, knowing a direct answer would be too much to hope for.

"...But let's start from the beginning," Ruiz continued. He placed his elbows on the table. "What do you know about Mr. Kovacs' business?"

"Only what he told me tonight. His family runs a couple of strip clubs in Vegas."

"Oh, they do more than that." Ruiz tapped the folder in front of him. "Drugs, trafficking, money laundering. You name it, they're into it."

"Okay."

"They'd kept a pretty low profile when Danny's grandfather ran things, but he died about ten years ago and Danny's father, Bennie, took over. Bennie was—hell, still is, forgive my language—one mean son-of-a-bitch. Had no problem killing anyone who got in his way. And not just murder, but torture. I won't go into details, but it's fair to say most of his victims were probably begging to be put out of their misery."

"You're using past tense. Did something happen to Bennie?"

Ruiz sat back. "Ms. Hampson happened. She provided the FBI with information that secured multiple murder convictions. He's now serving consecutive life sentences in Victorville."

Wynn's lips formed an "o" as he blew a silent whistle. Victorville was a well-known high-security penitentiary for the worst of the worst. It took guts to go against anyone who could wind up there.

Wynn looked at Krista; she stared back at him. "Provided information?" Wynn said. "Did you testify?"

"No need," Ruiz said. "The information led to evidence that was more than sufficient."

"And yet you still wound up in witness protection," Wynn said, his gaze still on Krista. For a moment, her stare faltered.

"There were... extenuating circumstances," Ruiz said.

A silence fell over the table as Wynn waited for further explanation. When none came, he asked, "Like what?"

The two marshals turned to Krista. She glanced away and bit her lip, then looked Wynn in the eye. "I have a son." She paused. Her voice grew stronger. "To be accurate, Danny and I have a son. Joshua. He's seven now, but was less than a year when all this went down. If Bennie knew I was alive, he'd realize it was me who gave him up. He'd have no problem killing me, but knowing him, he might also go after Joshua. I couldn't risk that."

"He'd kill his own grandson?" Wynn asked.

Krista shook her head and laughed humorlessly. "You have no idea. Even if he didn't, the idea of Josh growing up in that family, in that environment? No way I could let that happen."

"So, you provided information that put Bennie away, faked a car crash that supposedly killed both you and Joshua, and went into witness protection." Wynn paused. "Why am I here?"

Krista looked away as Ruiz picked up the story. "Three weeks ago, Ms. Hampson's parents received a package in the mail. In it was a note demanding Ms. Hampson's son, Joshua, be returned to his father."

Frowning, Wynn turned to Krista. "How'd Danny find out you're alive?"

"We'll get to that in a minute," Ruiz said.

What could be more important? Wynn paused as he thought it through. "What else was in the package?"

Ruiz slid the manilla file in front of him over to Todd, who opened it and passed three eight-by-ten photographs to Wynn. "A human eyeball packed in dry ice, and a flash drive with a video on it, showing the eyeball's removal from its owner," Todd said.

Something cold slithered down Wynn's spine as he examined the photos. "Whose was it?"

"Terrance Hampson," Todd said. "Ms. Hampson's brother."

Wynn glanced at Krista. The façade of a former Marine was still there, but barely. Behind it, she looked ill. "The video's that clear?"

"We tested the DNA," Ruiz said. "It was conclusive."

Wynn paused as the icy cold reached his fingertips. "What else did the note say?"

Todd glanced at Krista, her eyes vacant, as if bracing herself. He hesitated, then said, "That a piece of Mr. Hampson would be returned to his parents every week, until Joshua Kovacs is returned to his father."

Wynn's stomach churned. He had no doubt the threats were real. He was also keenly aware that Ruiz had said *three weeks ago*. "What else have they sent?"

"His right pinky finger, left big toe, and left ear. We expect something else on Wednesday."

"Have you traced the packages?"

"They were sent via overnight mail through different carriers dropped at different locations in the southwest U.S. The first came from Vegas, then from Phoenix, the last from Tucson. They're taking him south."

"Or parts of him," Wynn said.

"We don't think so, no," Todd said. "Our medical examiner says the tissue hasn't been separated from the body for long. He thinks they're cutting, packing, and mailing right away. They want us to know he's still alive."

Krista's face turned pale. She bolted to the corner of the room; a soft, retching noise emanated from her shaking frame as she dry-heaved into a wastebasket.

Wynn started to rise, but Todd put a hand on his arm. Instead, Ruiz got up and waited next to her until the heaving subsided, then handed her a handkerchief and a bottle of water. He shot Todd a glaring look as he led her back to her chair.

"Sorry," Todd said.

When they were all back in their seats, Wynn asked, "Why don't you just arrest Danny?"

"We brought him in," Ruiz said. "But we had nothing to hold him on. Legally we have no proof, which is all the reasonable doubt he needs. His lawyer argued that he was a victim, too. That it might be someone with a grudge, trying to set Kovacs up. Remember, Joshua is legally dead. All Kovacs had to do was play the grieving father. We had no other evidence, so the judge let him go. The next week, the finger and the ear showed up. That's how we got four parts with only three packages. It was a message: Don't do that again."

Wynn sat back, steepled his fingers in front of his lips, his mind racing to put it all together. "So, it is *possible* that it's not Danny?"

Ruiz and Todd exchanged a look. "Technically, yes," Todd said. "But c'mon. Who else is going to make that ransom request?"

"Or send us that message," Ruiz said.

Wynn shook his head. "No argument here, but that makes it that much more important to understand how they found out."

Ruiz leaned forward. "Honestly, we don't know. Terrance was last seen in Vegas a month ago, with some girl in a bar. Her body was found the next day, which immediately made him a person of interest. Until that package showed up at the Hampson's. We're guessing either someone recognized him, or maybe he shot his mouth off to the wrong people. She was collateral damage, and he hasn't been heard from since."

"Obviously you can't meet their demands," Wynn said. "I mean, there's no way you'll hand over Joshua, so what's your next move?"

The two marshals looked at one another, and then to Krista. Finally, Ruiz said, "To answer your original question, that's why you're here. We'd like you to go undercover and help us rescue Terrance."

CHAPTER 3

WYNN LET OUT A single, derisive laugh. "That's the best plan you've got?"

"Actually," Ruiz said, his voice even. "I think we got pretty lucky."

"How do you figure that?"

"When our investigation revealed Kovacs' intention to attend tonight's reunion, it was suggested that someone from his unit might be a good candidate. We did background workups and vetted several people until we narrowed it down to a few, including you. When you told Kovacs you were between jobs, well, we couldn't have set it up any better."

How the hell... then Wynn remembered the surveillance Ruiz mentioned earlier. *They heard everything.* "You picked me because I told him I'm unemployed?"

"That, and a couple of conversations we had with Lieutenant Lou Akins of the Ventura Police Department, as well as Agent Will Parker from the FBI."

Wynn rolled his eyes. He knew where this was going.

Six months ago, Akins had overseen the re-opening of the investigation into the murder of Wynn's wife, while Parker had been in charge of a multi-agency investigation into a sex-trafficking ring last summer. Wynn had played a minor role in solving both cases, but for some reason, Akins and Parker tended to exaggerate his contribution.

"Whatever they told you, don't believe it," Wynn said.

"They said you had a real problem following orders," Ruiz countered.

"That you can believe. Which by itself should be a disqualifier. Why me?"

Ruiz leaned forward. "First of all, Kovacs knows you. He knows you're not a cop, meaning he'll be more willing to let you in as compared to a stranger." Ruiz exhaled heavily and leaned back. "And second, are Akins and Parker. Besides not taking orders, they both said that if one of their family members was in trouble and needed help—outside of law enforcement—you'd be the first person they'd call."

"Bullshit."

"It's true. They think very highly of you."

Wynn sank back in his chair and shook his head.

"Sean?" Krista leaned forward. Wynn could tell she was trying to put on a brave face, but her eyes glistened, betraying her fear. "I know we're asking a lot, but would you at least hear us out? You might be Terrance's last hope."

Damn. He could feel the perspiration rise to the surface of his skin. *She's making it personal.* He sighed and looked to Ruiz. "What's your plan?"

"You'll ask Kovacs for a job," Ruiz said. "He knows your wife has passed, and that you're currently not working. It won't take much to make it look like you've fallen on hard times."

"Kovacs isn't going to buy that. If he does any checking—which he will—he'll blow that hard times cover in a heartbeat."

"We have ways to make it believable," Ruiz said.

"How's that?"

"We'll have the IRS freeze all your accounts and put a foreclosure lien on your house," Ruiz said. "We'll remove it when the job is finished, but if he checks while you're undercover, he'll see exactly what we want him to: that Sean Wynn is destitute."

The room shifted as Wynn realized the reach of the people he was talking to. *They might actually be able to pull this off. Getting me in, anyway.* "What kind of job am I supposed to ask for? I told him I did computer consulting."

"He knows your military background," Todd said. "In his line of work, he'll always have need for people with your skills. Tell him you'll do anything. He'll find a place for you."

"Even if he does, he's not going to show me where he's holding a kidnap victim. Besides, you said you think they've moved him south. If I'm stuck in Vegas, it could be months before I learn anything about Terrance. If ever."

"We realize it's not a perfect situation, Mr. Wynn." Ruiz said. "It seldom is. And let me be clear. We're not asking you to rescue Terrance. We need you to get us some actionable information. Kovacs didn't do this alone. We need you to find someone who knows something. Someone we can put pressure on. At least some of those people are likely in Vegas. You find them, and we'll take it from there."

"Even that's gonna take some time."

"Agreed. But I doubt Kovacs has the patience to run through eighteen more fingers and toes. The fact that he knows you gives you a head start. If that's all the advantage we can muster, we'll take it."

"How long are you thinking this little op will run?"

Ruiz sat back and sighed. "Honestly, that's difficult to say. It might be better to think in terms of potential outcomes. The first, ideally, is that you're successful in gathering some information, and we're able to rescue Terrance within a matter of weeks. The second is that you come up dry with no prospects at all. In that case, we'll pull you out whenever you decide there's nothing more to be gained."

Ruiz paused and glanced at Krista. "The third," he continued, "is that they kill Terrance, nullifying your need to be there."

A silence settled in as Wynn looked around the table. He stared at Todd, who looked away. Krista's eyes were downcast. Only Ruiz returned his gaze.

"There is a fourth potential outcome," Wynn said.

Ruiz nodded. "There is."

The silence returned. There was no need to say it.

Kovacs could discover why I'm really there. Then kill me.

———

Wynn allowed the uncomfortable moment to linger, making it very clear he was well aware of the risk they were asking him to take. Finally, he asked, "What about getting me out?"

Ruiz sighed. "If all works as planned, when we put Kovacs in jail, the rest of his crew, including you, will scatter. You'll want to keep a low profile, but you should be able to resume your life as normal."

"And if it doesn't go as planned?"

"We have a contingency plan. It does require a bit more... commitment... on your part, but it'll work."

Wynn listened while Ruiz explained the contingent exit plan. He was right; it wasn't ideal. When Ruiz finished, Wynn sat silently as he considered all he'd heard. The marshals stared at him expectantly.

A sane person wouldn't just tell them, no, but hell no.

But the words wouldn't come.

There was just something in his DNA that wouldn't let him. It was the same thing that spurred him to commit to the Marine Corps as a high school senior after 9/11; the thing that prompted him to pursue MARSOC, the Marine equivalent of the Navy Seals or Army

Rangers; the thing that drove him to blow up a sex-trafficking ring almost a year ago; to avenge Nicole's killers.

Krista's voice broke the silence. "Can I talk to Sean alone?"

No need. His decision was made, but he was curious what she had to say.

When the door clicked shut and they were alone, Krista's shoulders dropped a little. Gone was the all-business, no-bull-shit attitude she carried as a Marine. In its place was a vulnerability he had sensed and had been drawn to more than a dozen years ago.

"I want you to know it's okay if you don't want to do this," Krista said. "It's asking a lot and obviously very dangerous, so if you don't want to, I'll understand."

Wynn nodded, acknowledging the way out she'd provided. "I know. How are your parents holding up?"

Krista paused at the sudden change in topic. "I haven't spoken to them directly, but I'm told Mom's a mess. Outwardly, Dad's a rock, but I'm sure it's killing him inside."

"They know your death was faked?"

"Yeah. I blew it. I couldn't bear seeing what it did to my mom. She couldn't get over it." Krista paused as a tear formed in her eye.

"One day I followed her. I thought she was going to hurt herself, so I revealed myself." She laughed sadly. "I thought she was going to have a heart attack right there."

Wynn smiled.

"Anyway, I told her exactly what happened. When Dad noticed the change in her attitude and started asking questions, she told him. One of them must have told Terrance. So all of this is really my fault."

Wynn shook his head. "Do you agree with Ruiz's assessment of how Danny found out?"

"I don't know. I mean, yeah, probably. Terrance was always bragging about his badass big sister in the Marines. It's not a stretch to think he might've said something to the wrong people."

"Then it's not your fault. He's a big boy. He should know how to keep a secret."

Krista glanced away, unconvinced.

"I assume your parents are still toeing the line, responding to the kidnappers by saying you and Joshua are dead, so there's no way they can meet the demand, right?"

"Yeah."

"Who are they communicating through?"

"It's a kidnapping, so the FBI."

"Protection?"

"They've moved Joshua and me to a safe house outside of Vegas. Agent Todd and a few of his guys have been staying with us. The FBI's got a couple of guys stationed at my parents' home in Phoenix in case Danny tries to get to them."

Wynn nodded. "That's good. Have the marshals been over to your parents' house?"

"I don't think so. Why?"

"Danny's probably got people watching them. If they see marshals show up, that'll confirm you're alive."

"They seem to know what they're doing," Krista said.

"Let's hope. In the meantime, we'll operate under the assumption Danny only suspects you're alive. We can't do anything that'll confirm it for him."

"You don't have to do this," Krista said.

"I know," Wynn said. "But I will."

CHAPTER 4

Wynn spent all day Saturday with Ruiz's team going over everything they knew about Danny Kovacs and his organization.

Including the video showing the removal of Terrance Hampson's eyeball.

It wasn't pretty.

Terrance had been tied to a chair, in what appeared to be a dingy, dimly lit basement with cinderblock walls. To the side, a workbench sat beneath a set of wooden stairs, a dark hallway in the background.

Four men inflicted the torture. Three dressed in hooded, black, long-sleeved coveralls, while the fourth remained unseen behind the camera. Two men held him still while the third made the extraction using a pair of Stanley long-nose pliers. The screams had turned Wynn's stomach. Not the kind of details he enjoyed seeing, but important, nonetheless.

When the video finished playing, Wynn asked, "What are the rules?"

"Rules?" Ruiz asked.

"Of engagement."

If half of what Ruiz had said about Kovacs' were true, Wynn may well have to get his hands dirty to get close enough to learn anything useful. He needed to know how far he could go without losing Ruiz's support.

"Your job is to get information only, remember?" Ruiz said.

"And to do that," Wynn countered, "I'll have to earn Kovacs' trust. Which may mean bending the rules."

Ruiz nodded, conceding the point. "Don't harm civilians; try not to kill anybody."

Wynn nodded. *Try* was the operative word. He hoped it wouldn't come to that, but it was good to know the line was drawn fairly wide.

Later that evening, Wynn found himself alone with Krista in the conference room. Despite the gravity of the mission at hand, his pulse danced a quick little two-step.

"Now that you see what Danny is capable of, are you sure you still want to do this?" Krista asked.

"Do you have a better idea?" Wynn replied.

Krista raised her eyebrows and shrugged. "No. But it's dangerous."

"I know what I'm getting into," Wynn said.

They sat in silence for a few moments.

"Go ahead," Krista said. "Ask it."

"Ask what?"

"How I could have been so stupid to marry Danny in the first place."

Wynn smiled. She was right. He'd wondered exactly that many times. Before he met Nicole, of course. "I'm guessing you fell in love."

Krista smiled regrettably. "That damn Brigadier's Ball. That was our first date. I had seen Danny around. Truthfully, I wasn't all that interested. Thought he was an arrogant, privileged prick. But he was persistent. I thought maybe if I said yes and it was a disaster, he'd back off.

"Then he showed up in his dress blues and a fancy limousine, a bottle of champagne. I thought, 'Wow, if this is how the other half lives, count me in.' It was exciting. By the end of the night, I was smitten."

Wynn wasn't at all sure he wanted to hear this, but he smiled and nodded, encouraging her to go on.

"At first, I thought his family's clubs were just fancy bars. By the time I found out they were strip clubs, I was already in love. Whether it was with the lifestyle or Danny, I'm not sure. I tried to justify it by telling myself it wasn't *his* business. Blamed it on his dad. We were married before I realized what else they were into. But when I got pregnant with Joshua, something clicked. The blinders came off. I started seeing Danny differently. As Bennie's son, capable of doing all the same shit Bennie was doing. I knew I had to do something. I couldn't let Joshua fall into the same life Danny had."

"You did what you felt was right," Wynn said.

"No. I got drunk on the excitement," Krista said. "And now, seven years later, my family and I are still paying for it." She shook her head. "Never again."

They were interrupted as Ruiz and Todd entered the room. Ruiz's eyes darted between Krista and Wynn. "Everything good?" he asked.

Krista looked away.

"Just fine," Wynn replied.

"Good," Ruiz said. "I have some things for you." He handed Wynn a small flip phone. "There are two numbers programmed in. The first one is me, the second is Todd. Both numbers are burners, so even if Kovacs does get his hands on it, he won't be able to tie it to us. But to be safe, keep it hidden."

Wynn studied the numbers, committing them to memory. "Will do."

"I want you to check in every day. If we don't hear from you, we're going to assume something's gone sideways, and send in the cavalry."

Wynn nodded. "Good to know."

"You'll also need these." Ruiz handed Wynn two thin, silver disks, each a bit smaller than a Vegas poker chip. "You know what these are?"

"AirTags."

"Good. Put one on your bike and attach the other to your keys and keep it with you. If Kovacs sees it, he'll think you use it to keep track of your keys. In reality, we'll use them to keep track of you. You know how they work?"

"Bluetooth," Wynn said.

"Then you know their limitations."

"Yeah."

Unlike regular GPS trackers, the AirTag used Bluetooth technology to piggyback off nearby cell phones. The result was a much smaller, less expensive device, with a battery that could last up to a year. The disadvantage, was that if there were no cell phones nearby, the device wouldn't work.

Wynn stuffed the burner and one of the AirTags into his pocket, then put the other tag into a small leather case and attached it to his bike keys. He downloaded the app onto his personal phone and made sure both tags were working. When satisfied, he asked, "What about weapons?"

Ruiz hesitated. "What about 'em?"

"You don't expect me to go in there empty-handed, do you?"

"What do you think you'll need?"

"A pair of Glocks," Wynn said, "with extra mags and ammo, at minimum."

Ruiz nodded to Todd. "We'll give you one."

Todd left the room and was back less than a minute later, carrying a Glock 19 and hip holster. No extra ammo. No extra mags. Wynn took the weapon and ejected the magazine, verified it was full, then checked the chamber.

Better than nothing. Wynn re-inserted the mag and placed the gun in the holster.

"Anything else?" Ruiz asked.

"Not on my end," Wynn said.

"Good. Then I think we're done here. Todd will give you a ride back to the Marriott. You can head to Vegas tomorrow."

Wynn got up and turned to leave.

"Sean, wait." Krista rose from her seat and went over to him. "Thank you." She reached up on her tiptoes and kissed him on the cheek. He felt his face flush as her right hand found his left and slipped him a small piece of paper. "Be careful."

She turned and disappeared out the door. Wynn glanced at the two marshals and shrugged, as if to say, *What can I say?*

Todd rolled his eyes. "Let's go."

Wynn stepped into the hallway and turned in the opposite direction Krista had gone. Keeping his head down, he strode ahead of Todd and opened the small paper in his hand. Ten digits had been scrawled across it.

Her phone number.

CHAPTER 5

A SHOT OF ADRENALINE quickened Wynn's pulse when he arrived back at his Ventura home around noon on Sunday. Security vans, police cars, and tow trucks, all with their lights flashing, crowded the street out front. He had to hand it to Ruiz—the man worked fast. Two uniformed police officers stood in the driveway, while a locksmith changed the locks on Wynn's front door.

It was all part of Ruiz's plan to make him appear penniless.

Which was working.

Several of his neighbors gathered in their yards or in small groups on the sidewalk, watching the activity in front of his house.

Time to put on a show.

Wynn wove the big bike through the maze of vehicles, revving the engine to announce his arrival.

His stomach tightened as he squealed to a stop, remembering the contents of the gun vault inside his bedroom closet. He hoped to hell no one had touched those. Jumping off the bike, he hustled up the driveway when the two cops stepped in front of him.

"Hold on, sir," one of the officers said. "Authorized personnel only."

"It's my house."

"Not anymore, sir."

Wynn's mind raced. Ruiz really hadn't given him any time to prepare. "Akins. Lieutenant Lou Akins. Is he around?"

The deputy stepped back and spoke into a radio. "Lieutenant? The property owner is here. He wants to see you."

A voice came back over the radio. "It's okay. Send him up."

Wynn hurried through the garage and into the house, then vaulted up the steps two at a time to where Akins stood alone in his bedroom doorway.

"No one had better have touched my guns," Wynn said as he pushed past the sixty-something commanding officer of the Ventura Police Detectives. Akins closed the door behind them. The man sported short gray hair, a slight paunch, and a fatherly, paternal air. The two had grown close over the past six months, bonding over the shared pain of losing Ty Lenihan, a detective under Akins' command and close friend of Wynn's. Ruiz had agreed to bring Akins in on the deception as Wynn's one link to his real past.

"Relax," Akins said, "I told them everything inside was off limits until further notice."

Wynn entered the huge walk-in closet, which at one time had been a second bedroom, made considerably smaller by a massive steel vault that filled an entire wall. He pressed a code into an electronic lock on the front of the safe and waited until a light turned green and the deadbolts slid back. Wynn swung the heavy steel doors open to reveal his personal arsenal, more than thirty weapons, securely in place.

He trusted Akins, but still let out a sigh of relief. Akins stepped up next to Wynn, admiring an M&P 15 hanging on the wall. "Every time I see this, it's like I've stepped onto a movie set. Are all these properly registered?"

"Most of 'em." Wynn winked as he glanced at the older man.

Akins smiled and shook his head. "I don't want to know." He paused a moment. "You sure you know what you're getting into? Going undercover is serious business, even for someone trained for it."

"I think so," Wynn said. He opened a drawer at the bottom of the vault, one that did indeed contain unregistered weapons he'd purchased off the record. He sure as hell wasn't going into this with anything registered in his own name.

He pulled another Glock 19 from the drawer, then grabbed a backpack and placed the Glock, along with several extra magazines, ammunition, and a couple of holsters into it. "The advantage is that I'm going in as me, not pretending to be someone else. The easiest lies are the ones closest to the truth."

"That's true," Akins said, "But it also makes your real life harder to get back to."

Wynn looked at him quizzically. "Meaning?"

"Meaning not only do you have to get information that can lead to Terrance's rescue, but you have to do it in a way that doesn't point back to you. If Kovacs or his men think you had something to do with it, you're going to be looking over your shoulder the rest of your life."

Wynn nodded. He'd already considered that. "Understood." The more he thought about it, the less thrilled he was with Ruiz's exit plan. It was going to cost him a year of his life. At minimum. Silently, he was hoping to find a better way.

"So why take the risk?" Akins asked.

"If the situation were reversed, I would hope someone would do it for me." Wynn grabbed a seven-inch knife and ankle sheath from a drawer and stuffed them into the backpack.

"You sure that's it?"

Wynn stopped packing and looked at Akins, raising an eyebrow. "What else would there be?"

"Ruiz seems to think you and Ms. Hampson might have a past."

We might have, if Kovacs hadn't butt in. "He's thinking too hard. We were friends. Never a single date."

"Regardless, he's afraid that might be a problem."

Wynn suppressed a smile, recalling how easily he and Krista had picked up their relationship in the last thirty-six hours; how his stomach flipped when she looked him in the eye. "Only if he makes it one."

Akins looked at him. "As long as you're doing this for the right reasons."

Wynn resumed packing. "It's the right thing to do." *Would it make a difference if it wasn't Krista's brother?* He had to admit, if only to himself, *It might.*

A woman's voice came from downstairs. "Hello?"

"Be right down," Wynn called out. He locked up the vault and slung the backpack over his shoulder, then hustled down the stairs. Wynn's attorney, Linda Trilby, stood in the kitchen.

"Linda, thanks for coming," Wynn said. "Do you have the papers?"

Wynn had agreed to Ruiz's little plan about placing an IRS lien on the house and making him appear penniless, but he wasn't about to do it without some legal protection of his own. In his experience, the IRS had plenty of ways to take your property, but very few for returning it. The papers he'd asked Trilby to draw up would ensure his assets were protected.

"Right here," Trilby said, holding up a leather binder. "Although I still don't know why you're doing this." Her eyes flitted to the right as Akins entered the kitchen a few steps behind Wynn.

"Ruiz didn't tell you?" Wynn asked.

"Not a word."

"That's probably for the best," Wynn said.

"Does he know?" Trilby asked, nodding toward Akins.

"He does," Wynn said.

Trilby turned to face Akins head on, arching an eyebrow like a schoolteacher sizing up an unruly student. "And you agree with what he's doing?"

Akins shrugged.

"Well, that's comforting." Her voice dripped with sarcasm.

"I appreciate your concern," Wynn said. "But I know what I'm doing. I just want to make sure I don't get screwed in the process."

"Legally, this'll do it." She opened the binder and pulled out a thin stack of papers. She flipped to the last page and handed Wynn a pen. "Sign here."

Wynn signed the paper.

"Let me go on record as saying I don't like it," Trilby said.

"So noted," Wynn replied.

Trilby stuffed the papers back into the binder. "Well, whatever this is, be careful." She walked out through the front door.

"Second thoughts?" Akins asked.

"No. I'm good." Wynn checked the time on his phone. "I better get going. Still gotta get to Vegas today."

"Before you go..." Akins paused until he knew he had Wynn's attention. "Sean, I know you. When you get your mind set on a task, you push until something breaks loose. But being undercover doesn't work that way. You need to slow down, stay under the radar, and let it come to you. Your main assignment here is to get information, not rescue Terrance yourself. I want you to promise you'll remember that."

Wynn smiled. He placed a hand on the older man's shoulder. "I promise." He paused as his smile turned mischievous. "And bill Ruiz for the new window."

Akins' face screwed up in puzzlement. "What new window?"

"Gotta make it look good for the neighbors." Wynn patted the older man on the back and slung his pack over his shoulder, then jogged out through the garage. Grabbing a hammer from a work-bench, he stomped out to the front yard and flung the hammer through the living room window, sending glass shards flying, all while screaming expletives at the two cops still standing in the driveway. They made a move as if to arrest him, but on a look from Akins, stood back and let him go. Wynn tramped over to his bike, revved the engine, then left a long and smoky trail of burning rubber as he squealed away.

CHAPTER 6

THE ASPHALT'S DASHED WHITE lines and steady thunder of the Harley's big V-Twin were hypnotic as Wynn reeled in the three hundred miles between Ventura and Vegas, his world reduced to a two-tone palette split by the horizon. Blue sky above, a dirty tan below. Even the dried-out scrub brush that covered the desert blended into the sandy landscape, the only relief being the slightly off-tan grayness of the highway, stretching arrow straight to the horizon.

The monotony of the desert allowed his mind to wander. To Nicole. And Krista. To what his life might have been if he'd had the courage to ask Krista out. He almost had. To the Brigadier's Ball, right there in San Diego, between deployments.

He'd been working out in the base gym. Doing an early version of his now almost-daily kata. Krista had been lifting weights. They got to talking. Flirting. But he never manned up the courage to ask, and the moment slipped away.

He pushed the thought aside. Four years married to Nicole was worth a lifetime with anyone else. But that life was over. And now that he'd avenged her death, he felt himself healing, perhaps finally ready to build a new life.

His lip curled into a slight smile. It'd been a long time since he'd felt dopamine flowing through his veins.

It felt good. He'd missed it.

But pursuing it would have to wait. He had a job to do.

Part of which included a continual risk assessment. Danny knew Krista and Wynn were friends, but did he know Wynn had been interested? Danny was always good at picking up on things. Always a step ahead. If he did, Wynn's showing up now could raise suspicion. *Another thing to figure out once I'm in.*

Once across the Nevada state line, Wynn stopped to secure Ruiz's second AirTag underneath the seat of his Road Glide before moving on. Dusk was falling as he arrived in Vegas a little after seven. Millions of neon lights reflected off his chrome tailpipes as he cruised the strip.

Wynn shook his head, once again amazed at the monstrous new properties that continued to pop up, each attempting to outdo the others as "the" place to be. Where starlets and wannabes flashed their black cards, hoping real daddy wouldn't cut them off before they found a sugar daddy to take his place.

That world had never appealed to Wynn.

He was more comfortable in dive bars and cheap motels. Exactly the kind that suited his new financial status. He didn't have to go far off the strip to find one that rented rooms both by the week, and by the hour.

His room was on the second floor of a two-story, L-shaped motel called the All-Nighter. He hoped the name wasn't indicative of its clientele, but knew it probably was.

From his saddlebags, Wynn grabbed his backpack and duffle, which still had a couple of days' worth of clean clothes from his abbreviated trip to San Diego. Taking the concrete and steel stairs up to the walkway, he found his room and was inserting the electronic key when a man in a rumpled suit, shirt tails sticking out from beneath his jacket, stumbled out of a room two doors down.

"Bitch! I paid you!" the man yelled.

"Not for that, you didn't," came a female voice from inside the room. "Get out of here before I call my man."

The guy turned and saw Wynn. "What are you looking at?"

Wynn held up one hand, as if to say, *whatever*. The guy seemed to consider his options, then with a "Hmph," spun on his heels and strode to the stairs at the far end of the walkway.

A young Latina woman with bleach-blonde hair, naked except for a loosely held sheet, appeared in the doorway and watched him go. She turned when Wynn opened his door.

"You okay?" Wynn asked.

Her look of anger changed to seduction when she saw a new prospect. "I'm great, baby. The question is, how are you? Maybe I can help?" She let the sheet drop a little.

It was hard to tell her age. She wasn't a child, but the streets had a way of aging a person. Wynn guessed maybe twenty-five, but he wasn't sure. "Maybe another time." He opened his door and went inside, closing it behind him, then waited for the sound of her door to close.

Wynn glanced around the room. It was a standard cheap motel. A bed, a ratty stuffed chair, a TV on top of a dresser, and a small table with one chair. Nothing else. After tossing his duffle onto the dresser, Wynn placed his backpack on the bed and took out the knife and burner phone.

Getting down on his knees, he pushed the mattress a couple of feet off the box spring, then used the knife to pry out a few of the staples that held the fabric to the spring's wooden frame. He left one Glock and an extra magazine in the backpack, then set the spare Glock and ammo inside the frame. Making sure the burner was off, he set that inside the frame also, then used the knife's handle to hammer the staples back into place.

He pushed the mattress back into position and dug into the backpack. He pulled out the ankle sheath and strapped it to his right leg, then slipped the blade inside. He'd prefer to take the Glock, but Nevada required permits, which he didn't have. Besides, taking a gun when asking for a job was probably never advisable, no matter how well you knew the boss.

Wynn pulled out his personal phone, opened a maps app, and searched for Kovacs' two clubs. The main club, Pink, sat in an industrial area a bit south of downtown, not far from the Circus Circus casino. The second club, *La Rosado Dos*—The Pink Deuce—was further south.

He went back out to his bike and fired it up, the low rhythm rumbling across the parking lot. Glancing toward his room, he noticed the woman two doors down watching him through her window. He dropped the bike into gear and sped away.

CHAPTER 7

TEN MINUTES LATER, WYNN spotted the marquee, the word "Pink" scrawled in cursive neon above the entrance. He parked in the wide lot, relatively empty this early in the evening, and strolled toward the front, studying the building as he approached.

It was a single-story, with pink stucco siding complemented by thick white columns. Large arched recesses, each with a painted silhouette of a nude girl, accented the sides where windows might have been.

A bouncer stood outside the entrance. He was big, maybe six-three, approaching two hundred forty pounds. He had long black hair tied into a ponytail and a thin, manicured beard. His suit jacket hung well over a black t-shirt. The guy worked out.

Wynn nodded as he slid past and pulled open the tinted glass door. Inside the foyer, a slightly smaller man sat on a stool behind a podium.

"Thirty bucks cover," the doorman said.

"I'm looking for Danny—uh, Mr. Kovacs. Is he here?"

"Thirty bucks."

Wynn handed the money over. "Is Mr. Kovacs here?"

"Who's asking?"

"Sean Wynn. An old Marine buddy."

The guy slid off his stool and pulled open one of the double doors leading into the club. Heavy metal music pulsed through the opening. The guy shouted to a leather-corseted young woman inside the club, then motioned to Wynn. "Heather here will show you to a seat while I see if Mr. Kovacs is available."

Wynn followed the woman past the bar and several small tables where maybe twenty guys, most by themselves or in groups of two or three, sat scattered throughout the room. Stopping at a table next to the stage, she pulled out a chair. When he sat, she leaned into him from behind, pressing her chest into his shoulders. "What'll you have?"

He caught a whiff of her perfume. "Corona."

She squeezed his shoulder and left.

In front of him, a brunette wearing only a G-string and high heels swung around a pole on the stage. It took strength, balance, flexibility, and hours of practice to make pole dancing look smooth. Hours this girl clearly hadn't put in. Not that Wynn was an expert. Nicole's gym had offered a class, which led to a laugh-filled—and love-filled—evening when she'd attempted to show him what she'd learned.

Wynn pushed the thought from his mind and examined the girl's face. She looked young. And new. And, beneath all the mascara, scared.

He felt a small tug on his heart strings and quickly pushed them away. Nothing he could do. Not what he was here for.

He hadn't been in a strip club since his bachelor party seven years ago, but they hadn't changed much. Dark, except for the stage and a few accent lights, and loud, playing the same 80s heavy metal they all did.

Behind him, the bar stretched the full length of the room. To his left, a hallway led deeper into the club. *No doubt the VIP and dressing rooms.* To his right, another hallway led off to the restrooms and a private dance room.

"Give it up for Summer!" The DJ's voice came over the loud-speaker as the music transitioned from Def Leppard to Motley Crüe. "And what comes after summer? Welcome to the stage, Autumn!" A long-haired blonde burst through the curtains wearing a cowboy hat and boots, a brown leather vest, and Daisy Duke shorts.

Wynn dropped thirty bucks on Heather's tray as she set two Coronas, the club minimum, on the table in front of him. He nursed the first one through Autumn's three-song set and was starting on the second when Kovacs came out of the hallway and wove his way through the empty chairs to Wynn's table. The big bouncer from outside trailed behind.

"Sean!" Kovacs slapped Wynn on the back and settled into a chair next to him. "Haven't seen you in ten years and now twice in a couple of days. What's up?"

"I told you the next time I was in Vegas I might stop by."

"That was only two nights ago," Kovacs seemed to suddenly notice Wynn's jacket and boots. "Shit, did you ride here? That must have taken all day."

"Yeah, it's been a rough day." Wynn paused and leaned forward. "Is there someplace a little quieter we can talk?"

Kovacs cocked his head, searching Wynn's face. After a long second, he said, "Sure." Getting up, he tapped Wynn on the shoulder. "Come with me."

Kovacs led him past the VIP rooms, to a door at the end of the hall. The bouncer followed. On the other side of the door, the hall continued past a brightly lit opening into a dressing room, where several girls, in various stages of undress, sat in front of mirrors applying makeup.

Kovacs opened a door opposite the dressing room and went into a large office, stepping behind a desk and motioning Wynn to a chair across from him. To one side, a couch sat beneath a 1950s-era framed painting of the Vegas Strip. The bouncer stepped inside, closed the door, and remained standing several feet behind Wynn.

"Rough day?" Kovacs asked as he sat down. "What's up?"

Wynn looked back at the bouncer. He'd taken off his jacket to reveal bulging biceps, pecs, and traps, all threatening to rip right through his tight black t-shirt.

"Don't mind Vaz," Kovacs said. "He attends all my meetings. Boring, but part of his job description."

"Vaz?"

"José Vasquez. We call him Vaz."

Wynn turned in his seat. "Nice to meet you, Vaz."

The big man nodded but said nothing.

Wynn turned back as Kovacs asked, "So, what's going on?"

Wynn sighed heavily. "I screwed up, man."

"How so?"

"I sold my business a couple of years ago; didn't pay the taxes. The IRS foreclosed on my house yesterday and froze all my bank accounts. I'm broke."

Kovacs smiled at him with a hint of condescension. It reminded Wynn all over again why he never liked the guy. "Gotta pay your taxes, Sean. That's what feeds the jarheads."

"I know, I know. It's just... After Nicole died, I wasn't thinking clearly. It got away from me. Then it was just easier to ignore."

Kovacs picked up a pen and sat back, holding the pen with both hands in front of his chin. "My accountants specialize in keeping the IRS away, Sean. I'm not sure they can help once a foreclosure is already in process."

"No, that's not it."

"So how can I help?"

Wynn paused and looked down. "I was wondering if I could get a job, come work for you 'til I get back on my feet."

Kovacs tapped the pen on the chair's arm. "Well, we do have an opening for a bartender. Do you know how to fix drinks?"

A bartending job wasn't going to cut it. Those weren't the guys Kovacs would turn to when he needed a little muscle. Not the guys he would call on if he wanted to kidnap an ex-brother-in-law. Wynn nodded toward Vaz. "I was thinking more along the lines of a bouncer."

Vaz bit back a quiet laugh.

Kovacs smiled. "I know you're well-trained, Sean, but that was a lot of years ago. We like our security staff to be younger, and honestly, bigger. Intimidation is the name of the game. Can't have the patrons thinking they could actually beat one of our guys now, can we?"

"I won't get beat," Wynn said.

Vaz laughed again, this time not bothering to hide it.

"I always admired that about you," Kovacs said. "Overwhelming self-confidence." He paused. "I might consider it, but Vaz has the final say. He's in charge of the security staff and his interview is a little more... physical."

Kovacs gave a slight nod toward Vaz, and Wynn's spider-sense flew off the chart. He ducked low as Vaz's huge right fist breezed the air above his head. He jumped up, shoving the chair backward into Vaz and creating space between them, then turned to face the bouncer.

"Seriously?" Wynn asked.

Kovacs shrugged as Vaz flung the chair out of the way, then stepped toward Wynn, using both hands to grab Wynn's jacket by the lapels. Wynn shot his hands up between Vaz's arms, spread his elbows and broke Vaz's grip, then gave a light pop with both palms to Vaz's ears. With any force, the move could break a man's eardrums. But Wynn didn't want to hurt the guy, he just wanted to pass the interview.

What he accomplished was to piss off a much larger man.

Stunned, Vaz took several steps backward and shook his head. Wynn met his gaze, hoping that would be enough. Instead, anger boiled behind the bouncer's eyes.

He's not gonna let this go.

Vaz steadied himself, then circled slowly to the right, stalking. Wynn moved easily with him, maintaining the space between them as they exchanged positions inside the room. Vaz was now in front of Kovacs' desk, Wynn's back to the door.

Watching the big man's feet, Wynn realized Vaz was a brawler, untrained and reliant on his size.

Vaz feinted once, then twice with his upper body, but his feet remained parallel; a dominant, intimidating position. But not a fighting one.

Finally, on the third move, Vaz lunged forward. Wynn pivoted quickly to the side, using his left hand to redirect the big man past him, then chopped his right hand down on Vaz's neck. The crushing blow accelerated the big guy's momentum, shoving him headfirst into the hollow door, shattering it and sending Vaz and splinters of wood flying into the hallway. Several girls, standing in the dressing room doorway, screamed as the debris, and Vaz, landed heavily at their feet. Their terrified faces stared back at Wynn through the remnants of the broken door.

Rage contorted Vaz's features as he rose to his knees. He stopped when Kovacs stepped in front of Wynn.

"That's enough," Kovacs said. Turning to Wynn, he said, "Be here tomorrow. Ten a.m. You can start as a carpenter fixing this mess. Then as a bartender. I'll take the cost of repairs out of your pay. Let's hope you don't break anything else."

Still an asshole. But I'm in.

Wynn nodded and stepped through the broken door as Vaz rose to his feet and blocked the way. Wynn met the taller man's gaze, their noses only inches apart.

"Let it go, boys," Kovacs said. "The girls can't handle that much testosterone."

Vaz's hot breath reeked in Wynn's face, but he held his ground. After a long moment, Vaz stepped aside. Wynn moved around him and past several of the girls as he stalked away down the hall.

————

"You shoulda let me beat the shit out of him," Vaz said.

Kovacs rolled his eyes. *Here we go.*

Vaz slid the chair he had pushed out of the way to the front of Kovacs' desk and sank into it. "Save time. You know I'm gonna do it eventually."

"No, you're not," Kovacs said. "Forget about Wynn. We've got other problems right now. Did you find out when Murano's getting into town?"

"Eddie's got a meeting with him Thursday night."

Kovacs didn't bother asking what the meeting was about. It was well known—in certain circles—that Arturo Murano wanted to take over Kovacs' territory.

"And Eddie's listening to this shit?" Kovacs asked.

"He's Switzerland. In his position he's got to stay neutral. That means listening to everybody."

"I thought you two were friends."

"We are," Vaz said. "But this is business. Friendship is secondary."

Kovacs stewed in silence for a few moments, then asked, "How many men does he have?"

"About twenty so far. More on the way."

Kovacs raised his voice; spat the words, "How *many* more?"

Vaz looked over his shoulder at the broken door. Dancers were coming in and out of the dressing room across the hall. He turned back to Kovacs. "No idea. Hell, Murano probably doesn't even know. He's just gonna keep recruiting 'em 'til he's confident he has enough."

Kovacs glanced at the door and lowered his voice. "The only way he'll know that is if he's got someone here telling him how many we've got."

"You still think we have a leak?" Vaz asked.

"I *know* we have a leak. And I'm tired of paying Eddie for the half-scraps of intel I could get anywhere. He needs to figure out who it is."

Vaz nodded. "I'll put some pressure on him."

"Do it quickly. Murano wouldn't be coming if he didn't think he could make a move. We need to shut him down. Make the bastard wish he'd stayed in California."

"We knew this was coming. It's a little sooner than we thought, but we knew." Vaz paused. "What do you want me to do?"

Kovacs exhaled heavily and leaned back in his chair. "Just find out who's fucking us."

CHAPTER 8

A BROWN HAZE FILTERED the Vegas sun as Wynn swung his Harley into the club's parking lot the next morning. Except for a white, sixteen-foot Ford box truck, the lot was empty. He checked his phone; ten minutes early.

He strolled to the front door and gave a little tug. As expected, it was locked. Casting a quick glance up and down the street, he wandered around to the back.

An eight-foot-tall privacy fence created an isolated, U-shaped space behind the building, open only to the parking lot on the right. The space was paved with asphalt, ample enough for a supply truck to back in and unload, with room to spare. A dumpster and a pile of wooden pallets sat in the back corner.

A flat steel door interrupted the stucco siding about halfway down the width of the building. The sun had bleached the door's once bright pink paint to a pallid color, several shades lighter than the rest of the building. He tried the handle. Also locked.

Wynn ambled back to his bike, arriving just as a white Cadillac CT-5 pulled into the lot. A short-haired brunette—early forties, low-heeled pumps, jeans, and a cream-leather jacket—opened the driver's door. She tossed a cigarette to the ground as she got out. "You Wynn?"

"That's me."

"So, you're the reason I'm here so damn early." She sorted through a large set of keys as she marched toward the front door.

Wynn fell in step behind her. "Danny set the time, not me."

She stopped and turned to him. "Danny?"

"We were in the Marines together."

"Around here he's Mr. Kovacs. You might want to remember that."

"Good to know. Thanks. I didn't catch your name."

Resuming her pace, she said, "I'm Deborah. Office manager, talent manager, whatever manager Mr. Kovacs needs on any given day. Apparently today I'm the construction manager."

Wynn shrugged. "Sorry about that."

Deborah unlocked the door and turned on the lights as she led Wynn through the club and down the hallway past Kovacs' office. The remains of the shattered door leaned against the wall near the end of the hall.

Two doors Wynn hadn't noticed the night before extended beyond the office. A steel door at the end of the hall presumably led outside to the parking lot where he had been moments earlier. The other, on the left, was halfway between Kovacs' office and the exit. Deborah pushed that one open and disappeared inside.

Wynn followed her into a storeroom where rows of shelving held cases upon cases of whiskey, vodka, bourbon, and tequila. A small section held various kitchen and cleaning supplies, while a few forlorn hand and power tools sat on a low shelf near the floor.

"You should be able to find the tools you'll need down there," Deborah said. "Once you figure out what parts you'll need, you can take the truck outside. There's a Lowe's about two miles east of here.

Get what you need, tell 'em it's on the Pink account, and sign for it. Keys to the truck are on the hook beside the door. Any questions?"

"Why's it so cold in here?"

Deborah nodded to a silver door at the far end of the room. "Beer cooler. Only help yourself if you're not fond of your fingers, understood?"

Wynn nodded. "Got it."

"Then get to it. And don't take all day. We open at four." With that, she turned and left.

Wynn rummaged through the tools, which included some Craftsman, Ronix, and DeWalt. But what caught his attention were the Stanley. Unfortunately, there were only odds and ends. No complete sets missing a pair of long-nose pliers like the kind used in the video of Terrance.

He found a cordless drill and battery, which he plugged in to charge. Next, he grabbed a hammer and pry bar, a tape measure and a pencil, then went back to Kovacs' office. Deborah sat behind the desk, tapping on the keyboard.

"Sorry." Wynn wedged the pry bar into the splintered frame. "This is gonna be loud."

"Do what you need to do," Deborah said.

He'd hoped for a few minutes to snoop through the office, but she remained glued to the desk. More than once he felt her eyes watching him.

An hour later, he had the broken pieces removed and hauled out to the dumpster, and a materials list of the new parts needed. With no opportunity to search the office, he grabbed the truck keys and went outside.

The truck looked like it had been driven hard. Small divots in the front fenders were well on their way to rusting through, and long scratches stretched the length of the battered cargo box. He bypassed the oversized pickup cab and went straight to the rear, where the roll-up cargo door was secured by a padlock. Using the lone key attached to the fob, he unlocked the door and rolled it up.

A putrid smell hit him hard. Organic, but not alive.

A five-gallon bucket sat an arm's length away. He grabbed it and pulled it close to look inside, then immediately thrust it away as the stench boiled through his nostrils.

Taking a deep breath and holding it, he tilted the bucket for a quick peek. Maggots crawled over a dark, gel-like sheen on the bottom. The edges had formed a grayish-black crust, while the center remained a shiny, deep maroon.

Blood. But it can't be that easy.

If this was really incriminating, he knew they wouldn't leave it lying around. Regardless, he had to get a sample to Ruiz.

The problem was timing. Even though he'd memorized Ruiz's number, he didn't want to call it from his own phone, and the burner was back at the motel. He didn't want to stop there with the truck and risk someone seeing him. But other than this excursion, he didn't foresee an opportunity to leave Pink until much later in the day.

The other problem was appearance. It wouldn't bode well for the bucket to go missing the first time he took the truck.

Further inside the cargo area, a heavy-duty locker box sat against the back wall. It was eighteen inches tall, maybe thirty inches deep, and roughly six feet wide, stretching the entire width of the truck. Its hinged lid was secured by another padlock that hung from a single clasp in the center of the box.

Wynn took a deep breath and climbed into the cargo hold, then hurried back to the locker box. With only one choice, he inserted the same key into the lock. It didn't turn.

Frustrated, he jumped out and used the fob to unlock the cab, then rummaged through the glove box and beneath the two captain's chairs, eventually finding an old rag and a pen. Wrapping the rag around the pen, he held his breath as he stuck the rag into the bucket and wiped up a sample.

Taking another deep breath, he grabbed the bucket and carried it to the rear corner of the lot, where he stashed it beside the stack of wooden pallets. He dropped the rag behind the dumpster.

Easy to say it stunk too much to take along. Hopefully the rag won't be noticed before Ruiz can get someone over here.

With that taken care of, he climbed in behind the wheel, the seat sagging beneath his weight. Like the outside, the interior had also seen better days. The dash was cracked, the seat slightly torn. A heavy layer of dust coated the instrument panel. He turned the key, half expecting it not to start. To his surprise, it fired right up. He checked the odometer. *A hundred and fifty-seven thousand miles. This thing gets used.*

An hour later, Wynn was back at Pink with a new, heavy-duty door. When he was done unloading the supplies, he retrieved the bucket and put it back in the cargo box. A quick glance confirmed the rag was still behind the dumpster. Satisfied, he returned to the task at hand.

He'd decided to replace the flimsy doorjamb with a solid piece of two-by-six fir and add a deadbolt. From what he'd seen of Kovacs' operation so far, he suspected this may not be the last time someone got thrown against that door.

It also gave him the opportunity to make an extra key.

CHAPTER 9

WYNN WAS FINISHING UP when the first of the dancers arrived. He recognized her as Autumn, the blonde girl with the cowboy hat and Daisy Duke shorts from the day before. She stopped and watched as he gathered the scattered tools.

"You're the guy, huh?" she asked.

"Depends on what guy you mean."

"Did you really put Vaz through that door?"

He shook his head. He didn't need that story floating around. Didn't need Vaz thinking Wynn was challenging his alpha-dog status. "He tripped. It was an accident."

Her eyes narrowed. "Bullshit. I was out front, but the girls told me. Man, I'd have given anything to see Vaz get his ass kicked."

"Sorry to burst your bubble, but nobody kicked anyone's ass. He tripped, and the door was cheap. Anyone would have gone through."

"Too bad. He could use being knocked down a notch or two. I was hoping someone might have finally done it."

"Not me. Sorry." Wynn brushed his hand on his jeans and extended it. "I'm Sean, by the way."

"Autumn," she said, taking his hand. "Around here, anyway."

"And outside this place?"

She smiled coyly. "That'll wait 'til I get to know you better."

Wynn returned the smile. "Fair enough." It'd be easy to learn her real name, but he didn't press it. The important thing was to make friends, whoever they might be.

Just then, the door to the bar opened and Deborah stepped through. "Oh shit," she said when she saw Wynn and Autumn together. "Don't tell me you're one of those."

"One of what?" Wynn asked.

"Remember what I said about the beer? Same goes for the girls. Hands off."

Autumn rolled her eyes. "Relax, Deb. We're just talking." She turned and stepped into the dressing room. "Nice to meet you, Sean."

Wynn nodded, then turned his attention back to Deborah.

"Finished yet?" she asked.

"Just cleaning up."

"Good. Come on out to the bar when you're done, and let's see if you can make drinks as well as you fix doors."

Wynn put the remaining tools away, then placed the new keys on the desk, patting his pocket to confirm he still had the extra.

He closed the door and paused as two more dancers came down the hall. They glanced at him and shared a conspiratorial laugh as they ducked into the dressing room.

Shit. Definitely not what I need. He went out to the bar where Deborah was counting cash from the register.

"Have you ever tended bar?" Deborah asked.

"Not for pay."

"Great," she said sarcastically. "Can you make an Old Fashioned?"

"Bourbon or rye?"

Deborah raised an eyebrow. "Wow. He knows the difference. We may have to send you over to the Deuce."

"Why's that?" Wynn asked.

"More sophisticated clientele over there. Around here we mostly pour beer. But let's not get ahead of ourselves. Go ahead and stock the coolers from the back and familiarize yourself with the layout. I'll stick with you until the main shift comes in at nine. It's usually pretty quiet until then."

Wynn spent the next few hours behind the bar, pouring drafts, opening bottles, and fixing the occasional cocktail, but mostly bored. Deborah was right. It was slow.

He felt sorry for the half-dozen dancers on duty. With no more than twenty guys in the place, tips were scarce. It didn't take long to see the pattern: ten minutes on the main stage, ten minutes on a satellite stage, then thirty minutes mingling with the patrons in hopes of loosening their wallets for a lap dance. Then it was back to the dressing room for a quick costume change before their next turn on the main stage.

A little after eight o'clock, things started picking up. A steady stream of guys, and the occasional woman, began to fill the seats. New dancers joined the rotation, and a third stage opened for more guys to crowd around.

Wynn finished pouring a draft when Kovacs slid onto a stool across the bar. "You're a natural back there."

"We had plenty of practice back in the day," Wynn said.

"That we did. Nice job on the door, by the way."

"Figured you could use an upgrade."

He had barely finished speaking when Vaz stepped up to the bar. "Where are the keys, asshole?"

A quick shot of adrenaline coursed through Wynn's veins as he remembered the copy in his pocket. "What?"

"The truck. Where are the keys?"

Relief flooded over him. "Shit." Wynn had completely forgotten he still had them. He dug into his pocket and, being careful not to grab the office key, pulled out the truck's keys, then handed them to Vaz. "Sorry about that."

"Fucking asshole." Vaz stalked off toward the hallway that led to the back rooms and handed the keys to another of the club's bouncers.

"Good to see you two are becoming friends," Kovacs said.

"Yeah, I've got a little work to do on that one," Wynn replied.

"A lot of work, if I know Vaz." Kovacs paused. "You said you do computer consulting, right?"

"Yeah."

"A man of many talents."

Wynn shrugged. "More than schlepping drinks, but if that's what you need..."

Kovacs nodded slowly. "We'll see. Maybe you'll make head bartender one day."

"A guy can dream." Wynn paused, sensing an opportunity. "Hey, listen. I really appreciate you taking me on, but I was wondering if you know of any other way to make some quick cash? I'm in a serious bind here."

Kovacs' eyes narrowed. "What do you have in mind?"

"Hell, I don't know. But you've obviously done well. How'd you get started?"

"Family business, Sean. I had a head start."

Wynn nodded thoughtfully. "Well, all I know is it's going to take forever to dig out of this thing on a bartender's wage. I'm open to almost anything," he paused for emphasis, "so if something comes up, keep me in mind, okay?"

Kovacs tilted his head ever-so-slightly, giving Wynn an appraising, thoughtful look. After a moment, he tapped his fist on the counter. "I'll let you know." He slipped off the barstool and walked toward his office. Deborah had joined Vaz at the mouth of the hallway.

Kovacs stopped, said something to Deborah, then the two of them disappeared down the hall.

When Kovacs was gone, Vaz locked eyes with Wynn from across the bar, mouthed two words, then turned and followed Kovacs.

Wynn wasn't a lip reader, but was pretty sure he didn't need to be. Vaz's message was clear.

You're dead.

————

Kovacs' mind raced as he strode back to his office. A guy like Wynn could be an asset, especially with Murano making threats. *But can I trust him? Is his story really as simple as he claims? Or is there a reason he showed up now?*

Kovacs settled into his office chair as Deborah took a seat in front of the desk. Vaz closed the new door and remained standing.

"Have you done a background check on Wynn yet?" Kovacs asked.

"Preliminary," Deborah replied. "I only met the guy this morning. So far he checks out."

"How deep did you go?"

"We go next level on all employees, sir."

"Go deeper. Inner circle deep. I want to know everything about him."

"Yes, sir."

"And get a locksmith in here. I want these locks changed."

————

"I'm in." Wynn sat in the chair in his room at the All-Nighter, on the burner with Ruiz.

"Any trouble?" Ruiz asked.

"Nothing serious," Wynn said. "His head bouncer—a guy named Jose Vasquez—doesn't like me, but I can handle him."

"That's good. Any first impressions?"

"Vasquez seems to be Kovacs' right-hand man. Sits in on all his meetings. I'd bet he knows all about Terrance."

"We'll check him out."

"I also found a bucket today with what looked, and smelled, like blood in it. I can't believe they'd be so stupid as to leave it out if it had anything to do with Terrance, but figured we have to check. I put a sample on a rag and stashed it near the dumpster behind the club. Can you have someone pick it up and get it tested?"

"Absolutely. I'll get someone over there tonight. Anything else?" Ruiz asked.

"That's it for now. How's Krista holding up?"

"Ms. Hampson is good."

Wynn paused as he considered his next request. "I'd like to talk to her."

"Why?"

He didn't have a ready answer for that one. At least not one he wanted to share with Ruiz. "Forget it."

"I'll give her your regards."

Wynn disconnected, dropped the phone on the bed, sighed, and lay back. He already had Krista's phone number; could call her any time he wanted. He'd just prefer not going around Ruiz if he didn't have to.

So much for that.

CHAPTER 10

THE NEXT TWO DAYS passed without incident, or progress, as Wynn settled into his role as a bartender at Pink. He found excuses to explore the entire building, and was neither surprised nor disappointed when he saw the new lock on Kovacs' office door.

While the idea of searching Kovacs' office made sense, he really didn't expect to find anything. He doubted there would be a secret doorway leading to a hidden basement, or a random piece of paper or computer file saying, "Terrance is here." That stuff only happened in the movies.

As Ruiz had said, Kovacs' people were the key.

With that in mind, Wynn had paid particular attention to Vaz and his bouncers, many of whom fit the general size and build of the guys on the video. He learned several of their names—Chad, Kevin, Marcus, and Andre—and made an extra effort, without being too obvious, to ingratiate himself and hopefully pick up some bit of information. So far, all he'd gotten were odd glances and rude hand gestures.

He'd also gone the extra mile with his fellow bartenders and wait staff, quietly sharing his tips and taking on the less glamorous tasks.

They had been happy to let him help, but clueless when it came to anything else.

As for the dancers, Wynn had reasoned that Deborah stood a better chance of knowing something about Terrance than any of them. Since there was a "hands off" policy anyway, Wynn worked on developing a relationship with Deborah, while remaining distant from the dancers.

With one exception.

For some reason, Autumn, the blonde he'd met on his first day, seemed to enjoy giving him a hard time. While most dancers, when finished, would head straight back to the dressing room, Autumn always stopped by the bar, to Wynn, and asked for a bottle of water. Considering she'd just come off the stage, she was often, well, exposed.

Harmless flirting, he had thought. *But not what I'm here for.*

What he was here for, however, was going nowhere. If he had hoped for a quick answer, or even a clue, regarding the whereabouts of Terrance Hampson, he was sorely disappointed.

As he prepared for his third night at the club, Wynn strapped the knife sheath to his ankle and inserted the blade. It had become a regular part of his daily apparel. He'd prefer the Glock, but that would be harder to conceal or explain. As such, he kept one locked in the saddlebag of his bike, and the other hidden in the box spring in his room.

The lot was almost full when he parked his Harley behind the club and made his way to the rear door. While most employees came in the front, Wynn wanted to be as visible to Kovacs as possible, even if that meant just walking by his office on the way to the bar.

Unfortunately, wherever Kovacs was, Vaz was never far away. As Wynn came through the door, he spotted the big bouncer talking with one of the dancers outside the dressing room.

Gotta make peace with this guy. If Kovacs does have Terrance, Vaz is sure to know about it.

Vaz turned and squared himself as Wynn approached.

"Hey, listen," Wynn said as he stopped in front of the bouncer. "I know we got off on the wrong foot the other day." To one side, Kovacs was on the phone in his office. On the other, Autumn and another girl were in the dressing room, sitting in front of mirrors, putting on makeup. Autumn looked at him through the mirror's reflection, clearly listening.

"I pushed, and you tripped," Wynn said. "It was a lucky shot. One in a hundred. Ninety-nine other times you'd have kicked my ass. We both know it. But I need this job, so I'm hoping we can put it behind us and just go about doing our jobs. What do you say?"

Vaz remained silent as he looked down at Wynn, grunted once, then stepped past him and pushed through the door leading outside. Autumn appeared in the dressing room doorway.

"I think I saw your balls in the parking lot," Autumn said. She brushed past him toward the bar. "You might want to find them before your shift starts. Nights can get kind of rough around here."

Wynn closed his eyes and sighed.

———

Vaz made sure the door closed behind him, then noticed Wynn's bike parked in the corner. He considered kicking the damn thing over but thought better of it.

Wouldn't hurt enough.

He moved to the corner of the building and scanned the parking lot, ensuring he was alone. Satisfied, he pulled out his phone and dialed a number.

"What's up?" the voice on the other end asked.

"You got a couple of guys who are free tonight?" Vaz asked.

"I'm sure I could rustle up a few. What do you need?"

"Remember that new guy I told you about? Kovacs' Marine buddy?"

"Yeah. What about him?"

"Kovacs told me to leave him alone. Didn't say anything about you."

"He isn't stupid. He'll know you set it up."

Vaz looked thoughtfully back at the door. He spoke slowly as he gathered his thoughts. "Wynn and Autumn seem to be connecting. Bring Nadeem along. He'll provide a spark."

"He'll provide the whole fucking explosion."

"Contain him. Use your guys instead."

There was a pause on the line. Finally, the voice said, "How bad?"

"No hospitals, but make him hurt."

CHAPTER 11

PINK REMAINED PACKED ALL night. Wynn was busy behind the bar as a full staff of dancers and waitresses ran back and forth between the bar, the stages, and the VIP rooms. Vaz and his bouncers milled throughout the club, staying visible, but mostly quiet.

A little before eleven, Vaz led four dancers to a prime, semi-circular booth occupied by four men, next to the main stage. After some discussion, the dancers led the guys one-by-one to the VIP rooms. Once empty, a waitress rushed over and cleaned the booth, while another hurried up to Wynn and ordered five bottles of water and three martinis.

Deborah appeared beside him. "I'll make those. Special recipe for special guests."

"Oh yeah? Who's that?"

"You'll see."

Wynn shrugged, took the next order, and went back to pouring beer.

A few minutes later, Vaz escorted two women and three men to the now-empty booth. One of the women, clearly the group's leader, was a striking Latina dressed in an exquisite white pantsuit. She was shirtless beneath a short-cropped jacket, her caramel skin contrasting starkly with the "V" formed by her lapels that plunged all the way to her bare navel.

In her early thirties, the woman had dark eyes and shoulder-length black hair that slicked down the back of her neck. She slipped into the booth, while one of the men and the other woman slid in beside her. The two other men turned and remained standing on either side, with their hands clasped in front.

Bodyguards. But who's the lady?

For the next forty-five minutes, the woman in white watched as various dancers took the stage, each giving her significantly more attention than they had the guys who were seated there previously. When their set ended, the woman would nod and one of her bodyguards would hand the dancer a bill or two. Wynn had no idea what the denominations were, but guessed they weren't Washingtons or Lincolns. Probably either Grants or Franklins.

Autumn had barely taken the main stage when Deborah appeared beside Wynn. "Looks like the whole gang is showing up tonight." She nodded to the entrance. Six men, three Caucasian, two Hispanic, and one Middle Eastern, had come in the front door.

"Who are they?" Wynn asked.

"Frenemies," Deborah replied.

Wynn looked a question at her.

She shrugged. "Sometimes friends, sometimes not. Depends on the night."

Wynn turned back to the group. One of the Hispanics, a rail-thin man with his hair greased back and a pencil-thin mustache, surveyed the room. He nodded toward the stage where Autumn danced, and the group wove their way through the crowd, stopping at a table next to the stage.

The table was already occupied.

By three guys. Big, like ex-college football players. And drunk.

The newcomers pressed in close, the skinny guy with the mustache and the Middle Eastern man standing in front, blocking the footballer's view, while the others stood behind.

The air in the room was suddenly electric. All eyes, including those of the woman in white, focused on the newcomers. Two bouncers, Marcus, and Kevin, stood at the front door, watching. Near the back hallway, Vaz and another bouncer, Andre, also watched.

The skinny guy with the mustache leaned in and spoke to the footballers. The heavy metal music prevented Wynn from hearing what was said, but it seemed clear he and his friends wanted the table. Unfortunately, the drunk footballers didn't seem keen on giving it up. Men seated nearby got up or scooted back as it appeared the confrontation was about to boil over.

Until the Middle Eastern man, who to this point had barely taken his eyes off Autumn, reached into his pocket and pulled out his wallet, silently placing a thick wad of bills on the table.

The three footballers looked at the guys behind them, then at each other, and finally at the stack of cash. They got up slowly, grabbed the cash, and slunk away, eventually finding a table in the far corner of the room.

"Crisis averted," Wynn said.

"For now," Deborah replied.

As the newcomers took their seats, the Middle Eastern man nodded briefly to the woman in white, then turned his attention back to Autumn.

Interesting.

Like the other dancers, Autumn focused primarily on the woman in white, though Wynn noticed her throwing nervous glances at the new group. When the set ended, she scooped up the stray bills still littering the stage and disappeared behind the curtain.

Odd. She normally comes over here.

Wynn kept an eye on the new group. Especially the skinny guy with the pencil mustache. He seemed to be well-known among the dancers. Every few minutes a dancer would approach, give him an abbreviated lap dance, then hurry away.

Wynn looked closer; tried to get a better look at the guy. *Some kind of celebrity?* If so, Wynn didn't recognize him.

Twenty minutes later, Wynn figured it out.

The guy wasn't a celebrity.

He was a dealer.

Selling little white baggies right there on the floor. Using the dancers as go-betweens. Patrons would slip the cash inside the dancers' G-strings or stockings, who would then deliver it to the dealer. He would replace it with a baggie wrapped in a presumably much smaller bill, that would then be returned to the patron. The dancer, of course, kept whatever bill the baggie was wrapped in as her commission.

Wynn stepped up beside Deborah. "Your frenemies are selling Blow."

"What?" Deborah gasped in mock astonishment. "Congratulations, Sherlock. You solved the case."

Wynn furrowed his brow. "That doesn't bother you?"

"That's the least of the trouble that guy can cause."

"Who is he?"

"His name's Eddie. Call him a necessary evil."

"And Kovacs doesn't mind him selling coke in his club?"

"Forget it," Deborah said, then turned away.

Wynn stared after her and shook his head.

Fifteen minutes later, a commotion stirred in the far corner of the room. Wynn's view was blocked by four of Eddie's companions who had left their stage-side table and now surrounded Autumn as she flirted with the footballers.

Autumn's voice rose above the pounding music. "No! Tell Nadeem I'm busy."

"You heard her, man," the largest—and drunkest—of the three footballers said. "She wants to stay here."

Andre rose from his seat near the back hallway, but Vaz put a hand on his arm and shook his head slightly.

Wynn's spider-sense tingled. Vaz was telling him to stay put even though a big part of their job was to protect the dancers. *Why aren't they doing something?*

One of Eddie's guys grabbed Autumn's arm. "Doesn't matter what she wants."

"Let go!" Autumn yelled.

"Back off, man," the drunk guy said.

Still, neither Vaz nor Andre moved. A quick glance around the room showed the other bouncers taking their cues from Vaz.

"Vaz! A little help!" A tinge of panic colored Autumn's voice as she struggled against the man's grip.

A slight smile appeared on Vaz's face.

"Vaz!" Autumn yelled.

The bouncers remained still.

The three footballers leaped up, spilling their chairs backward, and lunged toward Eddie's guys.

Wynn vaulted over the bar and sprinted across the room, pushing his way through the crowd. When he got there, Eddie's guys turned their attention away from the footballers, one of whom was already bloodied on the floor, and focused on Wynn.

Like water spilling from a dam, the four men crashed down on Wynn with a barrage of fists, knees, feet, and elbows. Wynn deflected a jab from his right and saw the guy on his left winding up for a side kick. Wynn spun in close before the guy could launch his strike and threw his elbow, smashing it into the guy's nose. He ducked beneath a right hook and countered with a quick strike to the stomach that doubled the second guy over.

Behind him, the sound of breaking glass rang out. A set of hands latched onto Wynn's shoulders. He grabbed the wrist and lifted it over his head, ducking beneath the third man's arm and twisting it just short of the breaking point. The guy held a broken bottle in his hand.

Wynn pressed down, forcing the guy's shoulder and face toward the floor, then lifted his heavy riding boot and stomped on the back of the man's arm, dislocating his shoulder.

Wynn pushed the man away, but a sea of hands grabbed at him and closed the space, making it impossible to throw a punch. Now it was all elbows and knees. Wynn threw his left elbow back, connecting solidly with yet another guy's windpipe. A satisfying gurgle came from his throat as he staggered away.

A weak jab grazed Wynn's jaw. He spun around, looking for whoever had landed the lucky shot, when a solid kick landed on his right kidney. The air burst from Wynn's lungs as he stumbled and dropped to one knee. Hands on the back of his head pushed his head down as a knee grew larger coming toward his face. A blur flashed in front of him, and the knee was gone.

"That's enough!" The music stopped as Vaz's deep voice boomed throughout the room.

Everyone stopped. Vaz and five bouncers had entered the fray.

"Back off," Vaz said.

Wynn glanced to his left and saw one of the bouncers, Marcus, holding back the guy whose knee Wynn had almost become intimately acquainted with. Wynn caught his eye and nodded a quick thanks.

Another bouncer, a guy named Kevin, grabbed Wynn and pulled him up. Wynn scanned the damage. One of Eddie's guys was on the floor, gasping for breath, but recovering. He wouldn't talk much for a couple days, but he'd be fine. Another sat in a chair, his arm hanging limp at his side, staring daggers at Wynn, while a third streamed blood from his nose, but otherwise seemed okay. Only the fourth guy, the one Marcus held, showed no outward signs of damage.

His guts are going to feel it tomorrow, Wynn thought.

Autumn stood behind one of the footballers near a secondary stage. Wynn caught her eye, but she quickly looked away, then scampered toward the dressing room. Wynn watched her pass the woman in white, noticing the two bodyguards each had a hand inside their jackets.

Eddie, who to this point had remained out of the skirmish, approached.

"Time for you and your boys to go," Vaz said to him.

Eddie smiled. "Just a little fun, Vaz."

Wynn tried to shake loose of Kevin's grip, but he held on.

"Maybe so, but that's enough for tonight," Vaz said.

"This could be bad for business," Eddie said. His tone seemed to carry a veiled threat Wynn didn't understand.

Vaz nodded toward the Middle Eastern guy; apparently his name was Nadeem. "He can stay. The rest of you need to go."

Nadeem shook his head. "No. If my hosts are leaving, I'll go, too."

"Your choice," Vaz said.

"My uncle will hear about this," Eddie said.

"I'm sure he'll get both sides," Vaz said, holding Eddie's stare for a few seconds.

Finally, Eddie tilted forward at the waist in a mock bow. "Whatever you say, Vaz. I'm sure we'll see you soon."

Eddie turned toward Wynn, still held tight in Kevin's grip. "As for you..." He sucker-punched Wynn in the gut, knocking the breath out of him. Wynn doubled over but stayed on his feet. Kevin held his arms, preventing him from striking back. "Learn your place."

CHAPTER 12

EDDIE AND HIS PACK slowly made their way to the door, while the footballers attended to their friend on the floor. Wynn looked up in time to see Kovacs speaking briefly with Nadeem. They shook hands, and Nadeem followed as Vaz escorted Eddie and his entourage out the door. The music started back up. Two waitresses cleaned up the broken glass and righted the overturned tables and chairs. Wynn shook loose from Kevin and slunk back to the bar where Kovacs joined him.

"Was that some kind of audition?" Kovacs asked.

Wynn breathed heavily, still recovering from Eddie's cheap shot. "I thought bouncers were supposed to stop shit like that."

"Vaz knows what he's doing. He knew how far he'd let it go."

"He'd let your dancers get molested and your customers fight?" The adrenaline still surged through Wynn's veins, making his voice angrier than he intended.

"That would have been over in two seconds had you not jumped in," Kovacs said.

"And you're okay with them selling drugs in your club?"

Kovacs shrugged but stayed silent.

Wynn paused and looked toward the door. "What? You get a cut from that guy?"

"Would that be such a bad thing?"

Wynn cocked an eyebrow.

"You're not the only one who wants to make money," Kovacs said. "You said you'd be open to almost anything, but where do you draw the line?"

"You can run a pharmacy through here for all I care," Wynn said. "Hell, I'll help you. I just think it's bad for business to let the customers beat each other up."

"Maybe it is. But it's worse to have a wild card running around who doesn't understand how things work around here."

"So tell me."

Kovacs said nothing for a moment as he stared at Wynn. "Are you sure you want to know?"

Maybe I'll finally learn something about Terrance, Wynn thought. "I can handle it."

"I have no doubt you can," Kovacs said. "Meet me here at ten o'clock tomorrow morning. Let's see if you really *want* to."

———

Outside the club, Vaz pulled Eddie away from the others. He spoke quietly. "I told you to make him hurt."

"Yeah, but you didn't tell me he was a fucking ninja," Eddie replied.

"I told you he was a former Marine."

"Like that means anything."

Vaz paused. "I suppose not. But we did learn one thing."

"What's that?" Eddie asked.

Vaz turned to go back inside. "Not to underestimate him."

———

Wynn stepped behind the bar, grabbed a towel, and put some ice in it. He put it to his cheek as Marcus approached.

"How you feeling?" Marcus asked.

Wynn winced as he twisted at the waist. "I think my back is gonna feel it worse tomorrow."

"You're lucky that's all it is. You didn't get the memo, huh?"

"What memo?"

Marcus nodded at Vaz, who had just come in the front door. "Vaz told us Eddie was bringing some friends in tonight. Said they needed to blow off a little steam. Told us to stand down unless it got bad. I guess he didn't figure he needed to tell the bartenders, too."

The bartenders? Or just this bartender? Wynn watched Vaz cross the room. *The son-of-a-bitch set me up.*

———

Kovacs stood at the entrance to the hallway and signaled for Vaz to follow him, then made his way down the hall to his office. He eased into the chair behind the desk as Vaz closed the door and leaned against the wall.

"What the fuck was that?" Kovacs asked.

"What?"

"Hands off the girls is rule number one, and you wait until a bartender jumps in?"

"It was Eddie's crew," Vaz said innocently. "Figured they had a little leeway."

"And that had nothing to do with Wynn?"

Vaz smiled. "It was an added bonus."

"I'm telling you, let it go."

Vaz pushed off the wall and stepped up behind the chair in front of Kovacs' desk. He put his hands on the back of the chair and leaned forward. "You knew this guy in the Marines, right?"

"Yeah. So?"

"You met your wife in the Marines, too, right? Did they know each other?"

"Again, I say, yeah. So?"

"You think it's a coincidence he shows up now?"

Kovacs tapped his fingers on the desk. He knew what Vaz was suggesting, but that particular problem was never discussed in this office. He could never be sure who might be listening. He shrugged. "Possibly."

"Possibly my ass," Vaz said. "Until you know for sure, you need to keep him away from everything."

"Your concern is noted," Kovacs said. "Moving on. Did you talk to Eddie?"

"Kevin's the leak."

"Kevin? You're sure?"

"I set up multiple deals. Each with different prices and quantities. Eventually it was Kevin's that got back to Eddie."

"Kevin, Kevin, Kevin." Kovacs sighed, as if disappointed in a child. "How long's he been with us?"

"Three years. Driving for the last two."

"Any irregularities in his deliveries?"

"Haven't seen any."

Kovacs nodded. "And now he's leaking info to Murano?"

"So it would seem," Vaz said.

"Is Eddie's meeting with Murano still on for tomorrow night?"

"As far as I know."

"Where?" Kovacs asked.

"That's still to be determined."

Kovacs paused. "Think they'd do it at the speedway?"

The corners of Vaz's mouth turned up in a slight smile. "I can ask."

"Do it." Kovacs motioned to the door. "Get Deborah."

Vaz slipped out of the office, leaving Kovacs alone with his thoughts. *Murano's recruiting guys, and I'm losing them. Replacing Kevin with Wynn would be an upgrade, if I can trust him...*

Moments later, Vaz returned with Deborah. She slid into a chair while Vaz assumed his usual position against the wall.

"What have you found out about Wynn?"

"So far he checks out," Deborah said. "He owns a house on the bay in Ventura and has a good credit score, so that would indicate he has some assets. But there is an IRS foreclosure lien on his house, so it's possible they've also frozen whatever else he has. He spent a night in a Wyoming jail last summer, but those charges were dismissed."

"Why was he held?" Kovacs asked.

"Traffic charges. Speeding, reckless, and evading an officer. Minor stuff."

Kovacs laced his fingers as he sat back. "Anything else?"

"Not on him. His wife was mentioned in a couple of news stories last fall. Something about her murder being a mistaken hit instead of a random thing, but it sounds like she was collateral damage."

"What about his family, friends?" Kovacs asked.

"No children. His parents are retired in Colorado. In terms of friends, he seems to be a loner. No online presence on Facebook, Instagram, X, or LinkedIn. None of 'em. According to his credit card statements, it looks like he spent a lot of time on the road the past couple of years."

Consistent with his story.

"Sir, you asked me to go inner circle deep and I have, but that can only tell us so much. The reality is this guy comes up neutral. You're going to need something more before you decide to bring him in completely."

Kovacs nodded. *Agreed. Like a loyalty test.*

CHAPTER 13

THE NEXT DAY, WYNN went in early. He still didn't have a key but knew Deborah—despite her complaint the first time they met—was usually in by ten. Her Cadillac was parked in the lot when he arrived.

Kovacs' office door was open when he came up the back hallway. He stopped when he saw Deborah behind the desk.

Motioning to the new, heavy-duty lock on the door, Wynn said, "Danny didn't like my work?"

"Mr. Kovacs prefers custom locks," Deborah said.

Wynn shrugged, a little impressed despite himself, then made his way out to the main club. He was washing glasses behind the bar when Kovacs appeared, settling onto a barstool opposite Wynn.

"You still want to make some extra cash?" Kovacs asked.

Wynn dried his hands on a bar towel. "Absolutely. You got something?"

Kovacs shrugged. "Maybe. You said you'd be willing to do almost anything. What's that mean?"

"Hell, I don't know. Computer work. Manual labor. Whatever you've got."

Kovacs shook his head disgustedly. "I can hire anybody to do that shit. Pay 'em pennies. If you want to make serious money, you've got to do what nobody else is willing to do."

"I'm listening," Wynn said.

"Tell me more about what you've been doing since you got out," Kovacs said.

Wynn shrugged. "Not much to tell. Went to USC on the GI bill, studied computers. Met a girl, got married. You know the rest."

"Not really. Remind me how your wife died?"

Wynn let out a deep breath. *He knows damn well. I'll play along.* "She was murdered. A couple of guys wanted to kill her boss, got her instead."

"I thought the papers said it was a random shooting?"

"That's what we all believed at first. But then the killer came forward with a story about being hired. When I looked into it, the pieces fit. Turns out he was right."

"And the cops never knew?" Kovacs asked.

"Not a clue."

"That must have pissed you off."

Wynn nodded grimly. "To say the least."

"Did they ever catch the guys behind it?"

"The cops?" Wynn laughed sarcastically. "They couldn't catch a cold."

"So, what did you do?"

He shrugged. "I took care of it."

"How?"

Wynn locked his eyes on Kovacs. "I added marks to my tally."

The silence lingered as they held each other's gaze. Finally, Kovacs nodded and said, "I see."

It was a phrase they used back in the Corps to count their enemy kills.

"What about your business? You sold it but didn't pay the taxes?"

Wynn straightened up. *Keep going. Gotta sell it.* He grabbed a towel and a glass. "Yeah. Fucking government. A guy gets a little ahead, and they come and take everything. Better to just do things under the table."

"But that could lead to other problems," Kovacs said.

"Only if you get caught."

"Which, not to point out the obvious, you did. That's why you're here, right?"

"Listen," Wynn said. "You and I both saw it back in the corps. The guys who played by the rules got squat, while those who skirted 'em a little did well for themselves. I should know. I played by their rules. But you get bent over enough times and suddenly playing by the rules doesn't make much sense anymore."

Kovacs nodded slowly, his expression thoughtful. "So, what? Now you're a no-rules kind of guy?"

"Let's say the line has shifted."

"So where do you draw it?"

Setting the glass down, Wynn leaned forward, his elbows on the bar, his eyes unblinking. "Somewhere past wherever it takes to make some serious fucking money."

The weight of his words hung between them once again. After a long moment, Kovacs asked, "Would you add new marks?"

Wynn kept his eyes locked on him. "If I had to."

Kovacs broke into a grim smile. "Then come with me."

He led Wynn out the back door to a black Lincoln Navigator. Vaz stood by the front passenger door and took shotgun while Kovacs and Wynn climbed in the back. Kevin, the bouncer who'd held Wynn back the night before, sat behind the wheel, his eyes briefly meeting Wynn's in the mirror before flickering away.

As they pulled out of the lot and turned north, Wynn asked, "Where are we going?"

"To see if you've kept up your skills these past ten years," Kovacs said.

Wynn nodded.

They sat in silence for a few minutes as they turned onto the 95 and headed northwest, out of the city.

"Last night," Wynn said, "you said I didn't understand how things work around here. Care to enlighten me?"

"Maybe," Kovacs said. "What's on your mind?"

"I'm curious why you let that dealer—what's his name, Eddie?—deal drugs in your club? I mean, I get that you get a cut, but I pegged the guy in twenty minutes and wasn't even looking. You get an undercover cop in here, and he'll be tagged before the first bra comes off. Then you'll be in deep shit, too. You can't make that much off of dime baggies to justify the risk, can you?"

Kovacs sighed. "Eddie's a punk, but he's connected. That makes him useful. And you know what they say, keep your friends close..." His voice trailed off.

Wynn waited a beat for Kovacs to continue, curious what kind of connections were worth risking your business. When he didn't elaborate, Wynn changed tack, turned his comments toward Vaz and threw out a little test of his own. "The other thing I don't get, is why you didn't step in when those guys were hassling Autumn?"

Wynn was well aware last night's scuffle had nothing to do with Autumn; it was all about him. She was just the bait. He was curious how Vaz would spin it.

To his chagrin, Vaz didn't. Kovacs answered for him. "Autumn hasn't been the easiest employee. Sometimes it helps to keep them in line if they know the bouncer's response time correlates directly to the amount of trouble they cause."

"I get that, but isn't it normally off-limits to let the customers manhandle the girls?"

"Nadeem's a special customer. He gets a little more leeway."

Wynn nodded, but was curious what made Nadeem special. He doubted it had anything to do with Terrance. Therefore, unimportant. He looked out the window as Kevin pulled off the highway onto a two-lane paved road that soon gave way to a dirt path winding into the desert. Wynn's spider-sense simmered as they drove several miles through the desolate landscape, climbing over rocky hills and plunging into dusty valleys. Nothing but sand, rock, scrub, and cacti as far as the eye could see.

Topping a small rise, they descended into a wide bowl where the old Ford Cargo truck was parked thirty yards off the road. Marcus, the bouncer who had saved Wynn from a knee in the face, sat on the edge of the open cargo deck.

Kevin pulled the Lincoln to a stop thirty feet away.

"Show time," Kovacs said.

———————

"The AirTag has stopped moving, sir," Agent Todd said.

Ruiz nodded. *I can see that.* He wiped a bead of sweat from his temple. *Damn career is on the line with this one.*

Twenty minutes earlier, Ruiz had been sitting at his desk when he received a call from Todd. *Wynn's AirTag is going into the desert*, Todd had said. *Northwest of the city.*

Ruiz knew the area. It was the most unpopulated region around Vegas. Unless you counted the bodies that had been dumped there.

Is Wynn blown already? Are they taking him there to kill him? Or is he already dead and they're just dumping the body?

Ruiz didn't think so. During last night's check-in Wynn had mentioned a scuffle at the club, but indicated it was no big deal. Other than that, things had been quiet. No reason to think Kovacs might be on to him. Which gave Ruiz a choice.

He could call up the bird and get a team out there within fifteen minutes. But that seemed to be of limited use. If Kovacs was onto him, Wynn would be dead in fifteen minutes. If not, sending in the cavalry would certainly end the operation, and put a target on Wynn's back going forward.

No, he had to let this play out.

He watched the red dot on the monitor and prayed that he was right.

CHAPTER 14

WYNN, KOVACS, AND VAZ spilled from the SUV, while Kevin lagged noticeably behind. They rounded in front of the Lincoln and crossed to the cargo truck.

"Hey, Marcus. Are we all set?" Kovacs asked.

Marcus was about ten years younger than Wynn, and clean cut. He looked more like a prom king quarterback than a bouncer at a crime-ridden strip club. Wynn hadn't spoken to him much, but he seemed like an okay guy. Especially after saving Wynn from getting his face smashed in last night.

"Yes sir, Mr. Kovacs." Marcus stepped away from the open cargo door to reveal a McMillan TAC-50 long-range sniper rifle. The Navy SEALS used a version of this called the Mk-15, but Wynn had never fired one. Next to it lay a Glock 19.

"What's this?" Wynn asked.

"Sean, I'm disappointed," Kovacs said. "I thought you'd recognize a TAC-50."

"I recognize it easily enough. What's it for?"

"To see if you've maintained your skills. I've seen what you can do hand-to-hand. I want to know if you can still shoot."

"We never trained on the TAC."

"No, but it's not that different. And this is what we have, so it'll have to do."

"Okay." Wynn stepped forward and caressed his fingers down the long, black barrel. He'd never fired a TAC-50, but had a Remington MSR in his vault at home that he used to shoot regularly. Kovacs was right; they weren't that different.

The TAC was propped on a bipod and mounted with a Vortex Viper HS-T scope. Rumor had it that one of these had been used to kill an ISIS combatant from over 3,500 meters during the conflict in Iraq. "What's the target?"

Kovacs nodded to Marcus.

"Paper," Marcus said. He indicated a series of targets attached to bushes well off the road. "We'll start with the Glock at ten, thirty, and fifty meters, then move on to the TAC."

"Where are those?" Wynn asked.

"Out there." Marcus pointed across the sand in the direction of a large dune. Wynn squinted, trying to find the target. "These might help." Marcus handed Wynn a pair of binoculars.

Wynn focused down range, eventually finding the small white paper that held the outline of a man. Concentric circles radiated out from both the head and the heart. "How far is that?" he asked.

"Sixteen hundred meters."

"Seriously?" Wynn said. "You want me to hit something almost a mile away?"

Kovacs face broke into a cocky grin. "I seem to remember you were pretty good."

"I was never that good."

"That's why we'll start with something a little closer."

Kovacs nodded to Marcus, who said, "Look about fifteen degrees to your left. That one's eight hundred meters. Another fifteen degrees there's one at four hundred, and another fifteen there's one at two hundred."

"Hell, Sean. That's shorter than most par-three's," Kovacs said. "Even if you haven't fired a single round since you got out, you should be able to hit that."

Wynn handed the binoculars to Kovacs. "Well, let's find out." He picked up the Glock and ejected the empty magazine. "Ammo?"

Marcus glanced at Kovacs, who nodded, then handed Wynn a full magazine, which he inserted into the grip.

"What constitutes passing this little test?" Wynn asked.

"Two parts," Kovacs said. "Two out of three in the kill zone at thirty meters with the Glock, and eight hundred meters with the TAC."

"And the prize?"

"Maybe we'll get you out from behind the bar."

Wynn rolled his eyes. "Do I get a couple of practice shots to test the sights?"

"One."

Wynn glanced up and shook his head. "You haven't changed a bit."

Kovacs laughed. "You have no idea."

Wynn strode away from the truck to where a line had been drawn in the sand. He stepped his left foot forward and extended the Glock in a two-handed grip, closed one eye, and sighted down the barrel.

"That's the thirty you're aiming at," Marcus said.

"That's the test, right?" Wynn asked.

"Yeah," Kovacs said. "Is this your practice shot?"

"I'll save that for the TAC." Wynn breathed slowly, in and out, then fired three times, without pause. He lowered the gun and peered at the target. "Passed that one." He handed the Glock back to Marcus.

Kovacs lips turned up in a slight smile. "Let's see how you do with the TAC."

———

Ruiz hoped that Todd and the other two agents huddled around the monitor couldn't see—or smell—the perspiration rolling down his sides.

Wynn's AirTag had moved very little since stopping. A little movement was good. Could mean he was alive and well and walking around in a small area.

It could also just be the satellites readjusting their readings as they flew through the sky.

CHAPTER 15

Wynn followed Marcus to the rear of the truck, picked up the TAC, then continued around to the front where a four-by-four mat had been laid out in the dirt. Wynn set the rifle down with the bipod a little off the mat, then crawled down onto his stomach next to it. "Ammo?"

Marcus handed him three fifty caliber rounds, big and deadly. Each was nearly as long as a dollar bill and as thick as his ring finger. While the Glock's 9-millimeter round caused nasty entrance and exit wounds, a hit was survivable if the bullet didn't strike any vital organs or arteries. The fifty-cal was a different story. An impact from one of those virtually anywhere on the body created a shock wave so violent it would burst internal organs. Chances of survival were slim, at best.

Wynn donned a pair of earmuffs and plastic eye protection that lay on the mat, settled the butt of the rifle snugly against his shoulder, then pulled back the bolt and inserted a bullet into the chamber.

This won't be as easy.

He took his time as he focused the scope on the two-hundred-meter target. He breathed in and out slowly, deeply, willing his heart to slow and the adrenaline from his veins. Setting the crosshairs on the target, he exhaled and held it, then slowly squeezed the trigger.

The TAC-50 boomed as a shock wave emanated from the tip of the barrel. A small hole appeared slightly right of center on the target.

Kovacs held the binoculars to his eyes. "That was your test shot. Now show me two more."

Wynn pulled back the bolt, ejecting the spent casing, and slipped a second bullet into the chamber, then slid the bolt back into place. Kovacs was right. Shooting a stationary paper target at two hundred meters with no wind was child's play. And after the test shot, he was pretty sure he'd have no trouble at eight hundred meters, either. *But will that fit my cover?* He took his time to think it through as he placed two more bullets in the kill zone of the target, one in the head, one in the heart.

"Let's see how you do at four hundred," Kovacs said.

Wynn swung the rifle fifteen degrees to the right and repositioned his body, then held up his hand for more ammo.

Marcus handed him three more rounds. Wynn loaded one into the chamber. This was the most important shot. The one that would tell Kovacs he still had the skills, but maybe not quite as perfect as they once were. He calmed his breath, lined up the shot, then squeezed the trigger.

A hole appeared in the target, barely inside the line representing the head shot kill zone.

Perfect.

A hit in the direct center would have told Kovacs he'd spent a fair amount of time practicing. A hit that almost missed would indicate he still had the skills, but they were waning. *Exactly what I want him to think.* Wynn placed the second shot just outside the center circle of the heart kill zone.

"Impressive," said Kovacs. "Now the real test."

Wynn scooted himself and the rifle another fifteen degrees and sighted in on the eight-hundred-meter target. A puff of wind stirred the dust across the desert. *Make it believable.* He slowed his breathing and squeezed the trigger. A second later a hole appeared on the target, three inches outside the kill zone.

"You're slipping, Sean." Kovacs said.

Wynn held out his hand and was given two more rounds. He chambered a new bullet and focused on the heart kill zone. He went through his routine, exhaled deeply, and put the round in the second ring.

"Nice," Kovacs said. "Now the money shot."

Wynn ejected the shell casing and inserted the new round, then steadied himself for the final shot. The previous one didn't go exactly where he'd planned, so he took his time, re-assessed the wind, watched the heat waves rise off the desert floor, then gently squeezed the trigger.

Kovacs lowered his binoculars. "Right on the line."

"Tie goes to the runner, right?" Wynn asked.

"That may work in baseball, but it'll get you killed here." There was something menacing in Kovacs' voice. Sensing movement behind him, Wynn sat up. Kovacs was pointing the Glock at Vaz.

"What the—" Vaz stuttered.

"Shut up," Kovacs said. He used the gun to motion Vaz away from the group.

Wynn dropped the ear and eye protectors and scrambled to his feet. Marcus and Kevin took a step back. Wynn stepped back with them.

"Uh-uh. Don't go too far, Spider-Man," Kovacs said, using Wynn's old Marine nickname. "The test isn't over."

Wynn stopped. He eyed Kovacs warily.

"You remember back when we hunted al-Qaida?" Kovacs said. "We'd get tips from the locals. Some were good, but some were bullshit. They tried to ambush us, remember?"

Sweat popped from Wynn's brow, a rush of adrenaline coursed through his veins. "Yeah. I remember."

"Do you remember what we did to those who lied to us?"

"We took 'em prisoner."

"Most of the time. But when we were out in the desert like this, taking 'em prisoner meant we had to guard 'em, feed 'em, watch 'em shit. Had to make sure they didn't run off. Remember?"

Wynn closed his eyes. He knew where this was going. "I remember."

"A lot easier just to kill 'em."

Wynn used his most calming, soothing voice. "But we never did it, Danny. It was just talk."

"I've got a traitor in my ranks, Spider-Man. Someone's been working against me, trying to ambush me."

"How do you know?"

"We've all got our spies, Spider-Man."

The constant use of his Marine nickname triggered Wynn's memory, causing thousands of images to flood through his mind. Many of endless days on patrol, but many more of countless hours spent with his platoonmates, bonding like brothers in the down time between missions. In a fraction of a second, he saw Jonesy, and Crofton.

And Kovacs. He focused on Kovacs. Younger. Smiling. Mischievous. Cunning.

"So, what? Are you just going to kill him?" Wynn asked.

"Not me." Kovacs motioned for Wynn to join him. "You said you were willing to add to your tally. No time like the present." He looked at Vaz. "On your knees."

The color drained from Vaz's face. "Mr. Kovacs, I swear. I didn't—"

"Shut up! On your knees."

Vaz lowered himself to his knees. Kovacs stood in front of him and offered the Glock to Wynn. "Semper Fi."

It was a twisted use of the Marine Corps motto. Latin for "Always Faithful," it represented all the Corps' values—duty, honor, courage, and commitment—all wrapped up in one simple phrase. It was a reminder that as a former brother, Wynn was expected to support and protect his fellow Marine. An expression of loyalty to America, the Corps, and especially to each other.

Wynn looked Kovacs in the eye. "You sure about this?"

Kovacs nodded grimly. "I'm sure."

Ruiz's rules of engagement flashed through Wynn's mind. *Try not to kill anybody.*

Kevin and Marcus shuffled anxiously in the sand.

Kovacs has changed, but maybe not that much. Wynn took the gun from Kovacs and pointed it at Vaz's forehead. "With pleasure."

"Fuck you," Vaz spat.

Wynn pulled the trigger.

Click.

A flood of relief washed over him. Kovacs had had a sick sense of humor back in the day. Wynn had counted on him not having lost it, counted on the gun being empty. Counted on this being another test.

A look of dawning realization spread across Vaz's face. The empty gun meant Kovacs had no intention to hurt him, but Wynn sure as hell showed he would. Vaz launched himself off the sand and drove his shoulder into Wynn's midsection.

Wynn tossed the impotent gun aside and spun as the two men fell to the sand, grappling in a fury of flying fists. Wynn wrapped his legs around Vaz's torso and held him close, battering at Vaz's head, trying to withstand the assault.

Feeling Vaz attempt to roll on top, Wynn struggled and twisted, knowing he couldn't let the bigger man succeed, but in one powerful move, Wynn was dragged under as the big man loomed above.

The TAC exploded next to them.

"Enough!" Kovacs yelled. Marcus held the rifle, its barrel smoking.

Wynn paused, but Vaz took the opportunity to get in one more punch, slamming his fist into Wynn's cheek.

Kovacs put a hand on Vaz's shoulder. "I said that's enough."

Pushing Vaz away, Wynn scrambled to his feet, the metallic taste of blood thick in his mouth.

"Very good, Sean." Kovacs sauntered over and picked up the discarded Glock. "You passed."

Wynn gasped to catch his breath. His eyes darted between Vaz and Kovacs.

"Relax, Vaz," Kovacs said as Vaz climbed to his feet and glared at Wynn. "You were never at risk. But if you're going into battle with someone, you want to know they'll do what needs to be done." He ejected the empty magazine from the Glock and inserted a new one. "But we still have a traitor." Kovacs paused. "Hey, Kevin."

Kevin looked up, his eyes going wide as Kovacs pointed the gun at him and pulled the trigger. The shot exploded across the desert as a bright red hole appeared in Kevin's chest. He stood for a moment, a look of disbelief on his face, then sank to his knees, fell forward, and lay still.

Kovacs lowered the Glock, stuffed it in the back of his waistband, and stepped over to Wynn. "You should know," Kovacs said as he dug into his pocket and pulled out a stack of bills, "I'll never ask you to do anything I'm not prepared to do myself."

Kovacs handed Wynn a neatly wrapped stack of hundred-dollar-bills. "Split that with Marcus. He knows what to do. Vaz, get the keys."

Stunned at the sudden turn of events, Wynn remained silent as Vaz stalked over and dug the car keys out of Kevin's pocket.

Kovacs called over his shoulder as he strode toward the Lincoln. "Marcus will give you a ride back to town. Be back at the club by eight o'clock. In the meantime, get some rest. You're gonna have a long night."

Wynn looked back at Marcus, who shrugged, then watched as Vaz and Kovacs climbed into the Lincoln and drove away.

CHAPTER 16

WYNN STOOD NEXT TO the truck, examining his cheek in the side mirror. A bruise was forming from Vaz's cheap shot, the second he'd taken in the last twelve hours.

No wonder Krista wanted Joshua away from here.

Marcus jumped down from the back of the truck and tossed a plastic-wrapped bundle toward Wynn. "Put this on."

Wynn caught the package. It was thin and rectangular, like a new shirt. He tore open the plastic, shook out the cloth inside, and held it up.

Coveralls. Long-sleeved and hooded. White.

Almost exactly like the guys wore in Terrance's video.

"What's this?"

Marcus pulled a couple of shovels from the back of the truck, then nodded toward Kevin's body. "We gotta bury him," he said as he slipped his t-shirt over his head. "Unless you like your clothes sweaty and dirty."

Wynn shrugged, then stripped off his shirt and pulled on the coveralls.

"I've got gloves for you, too, but your boots are your own," Marcus said.

Wynn paused. *Boots. Did the video show any of the men's boots? Maybe we can ID someone...*

"Get a move on, Wynn. We don't have all day."

Wynn nodded and finished getting dressed, then spent the next hour helping Marcus bury Kevin's body as the sun beat down overhead. Sweat dripped from his nose as his arms and legs, like lead from the post-adrenaline crash, struggled to dig into the rocky desert soil. If there'd been any doubt Kovacs was capable of Terrance's kidnapping, it was gone now. Not only was Kovacs an asshole, he was a murdering, torturing asshole.

When finished, Marcus handed his shovel to Wynn. "Put these away."

Wynn grabbed both shovels and went to the back of the cargo truck. The locker box sat with its lid open. Wynn tossed the shovels into the truck, then climbed in beside them and carried them to the back.

Inside the locker, beneath two more shovels, sat at least a dozen plastic packages of coveralls. Some white. Some black. *Like those worn in Terrance's video.* Several boxes of ammunition, nine-mil for the Glock, 50-caliber for the TAC, among others, sat scattered on the floor of the locker. To one side, a package of zip ties and three rolls of duct tape sat inside a long coil of rope.

His mind racing, Wynn put the two shovels into the locker, then stepped back. Marcus jumped in beside him and placed the heavy plastic case containing the TAC into the locker, then closed the lid and secured the padlock.

"What about these?" Wynn asked, tugging at his coveralls.

"I've got a bag for 'em in the cab."

They hopped out of the truck and stripped out of the coveralls, placing them into a cloth bag that Marcus stuffed behind the seat.

"You got a laundry service for these?" Wynn asked.

"Something like that." Marcus dug further behind the seat and grabbed a couple of bottles of water and tossed one to Wynn.

"Thanks." Wynn took a long drink. "You're surprisingly well prepared. Did you know this was gonna happen?"

Marcus took a long drink and let out a heavy breath. "No. But Vaz insists we keep the truck stocked."

"Stocked? You mean this happens a lot?"

Marcus shrugged. "Depends on your definition. Considering the business Kovacs is in, I'm surprised it doesn't happen more."

"You don't get tired of cleaning up after him?"

"Usually we leave 'em where they lay."

"Why'd we bother burying him today?"

"My guess is we're a little too close to home. Things like this usually happen a bit further south." Marcus tossed the keys to Wynn. "You drive. Let's get out of here."

Wynn took a last look around, committing the view to memory, then climbed in behind the wheel. He turned the key and looked at the fuel gauge, a habit he'd acquired on the Harleys. The tank was a little over half full. He glanced at the odometer.

A hundred fifty-nine thousand. Someone's put nearly two thousand miles on this thing since Sunday.

"What's the problem, Wynn? Let's go."

Wynn started the engine. "No problem. I was just thinking. Kovacs said Kevin was a traitor. Wouldn't he want to keep him alive long enough to find out who he was spying for?"

"He already knows. Arturo Murano."

Wynn pulled a tight U-turn and remained silent, hoping Marcus would continue. When he didn't, Wynn asked. "Who's that?"

"Ask Kovacs."

Clearly, Marcus wasn't going to say anything. Wynn changed tack. "Still, if he kept Kevin alive, maybe he could learn something else."

"Trust me. Better for Kevin this way."

Wynn raised his eyebrows. "He's better off *dead*?"

Marcus paused, looked at Wynn as the truck bounced along. "How long were you a Marine?"

"Eight years."

"How long was Kovacs in?"

"About the same, I think," Wynn said.

"What'd you guys do?"

"Normal Marine stuff. Why?"

"Curious where he learned some of this shit."

Wynn gave a quick, sideways glance. "What shit?"

Marcus shrugged. "Let's just say if you ever cross Kovacs, or he ever thinks you've crossed him, you should hope for what happened to Kevin today."

Instead of what's happening to Terrance, Wynn thought. He took a sip of water. Tried to keep the urgency he was feeling out of his voice. "Why? What do you do when you don't kill 'em?"

"You don't want to know," Marcus said with a shake of his head. His face lightened a shade or two. "And I don't want to talk about it."

Damn. He's spooked. Maybe Ruiz can get him to talk. They rode a few minutes in silence.

After a while, Marcus said, "Eight years, huh?"

"Yeah."

"Why'd you get out?"

Wynn shrugged. "Tired of the bureaucratic bullshit."

Marcus let out a short laugh. "We don't have *that* problem. Here, only one opinion matters. Kovacs controls everything."

"Vaz has no say?"

"Maybe privately. But publicly he does exactly what Kovacs says. Regardless, you need to watch your back. Vaz isn't going to forget this."

Wynn cocked an eyebrow. "You warning me off?"

"Too late for that. You're in."

"How do you figure?"

"That money in your pocket?" Marcus scooted down in his seat and closed his eyes. "That was Kovacs' offer and your acceptance. You're in, whether you like it or not. And if you do have second thoughts, take a look at those calluses on your hands. That's the only way anyone ever gets out of here."

"No problem." Wynn glanced at Marcus, who looked as if he might already be asleep. "As long as he pays me, I'm all in."

———

Kovacs had been waiting for it the past couple of hours. But he had to give Vaz credit; the guy was a pro. He'd put his personal anger aside and made the last-minute arrangements for Eddie's meeting this evening with Murano. When everything was set, Vaz finally let it out.

"Why are we fucking around with this guy?" Vaz asked. He slumped onto the couch in Kovacs' office.

"You saw his shooting," Kovacs replied. "Wynn could be useful."

"You think that little stunt proved anything?"

"It proved he'd kill you."

"Which is why he can't be trusted."

"Just the opposite," Kovacs said. "The fact that he followed *that* order, without question, earned a great deal of trust."

Vaz shook his head. "I'm telling you, he's trying to fuck us."

"Maybe," Kovacs said. But for what Vaz was suggesting to be true, the Feds would've had to have gotten a hold of Wynn before the reunion. *Wynn's not that good an actor. He was totally surprised when I told him about Krista.*

"We should get rid of him," Vaz said.

"You're just pissed he beat you," Kovacs said. "If it turns out he is trying to fuck us, you can have him. But in the meantime, leave him alone. We can use a guy with his skills."

"If he is, we won't know until it's too late," Vaz said.

"So we keep testing him. Keep raising the stakes."

"How do you plan on doing that?"

"Tonight," Kovacs said, a slight smile curling his lip. "With Murano."

CHAPTER 17

THE EARLY AFTERNOON SUN beat down overhead when Wynn parked the truck next to his bike in the Pink parking lot. Marcus mumbled a quick *See you later,* then hopped into an old Chevy Camaro and was gone.

Besides the truck and his Harley, Deborah's Cadillac was the only other vehicle in the lot. He was about to go inside when an early 2000s Audi sports car turned in and pulled up next to him. The tinted window buzzed down to reveal Autumn behind the wheel.

She scrunched her face when she saw the lump under his eye. "Is that from last night?"

Wynn had almost forgotten about that one. "No. Vaz finally got his revenge."

"You're lucky that's all he did."

"If you say so."

She nodded. "Trust me. I've seen him do way worse. Anyway, I wanted to apologize for what I said last night, and thank you for stepping in. I hope you didn't do it *because* of what I said."

"I did it because it seemed like you needed help." Wynn paused as he thought back on the previous night. "What's the deal with that

Middle East dude? Sounded like he was the one giving the orders. You know him?"

Autumn rolled her eyes. "Nadeem. He's a creep. Wish those guys would've kicked his ass."

"Why's that?"

"He's a stalker. And jealous. I went out with him once and he asked me to go away with him. Like he had my whole life planned out. In Saudi Arabia! I said no. Now, every time he comes in, he gets pissed if I dance or even talk to other guys. Which is kind of the whole point of the job, right? I figured he wouldn't hassle those big guys, but obviously I was wrong."

"Does Vaz know all this?"

"Oh yeah. But Nadeem's got money so Kovacs, Vaz, Deborah—they all give him latitude."

Wynn recalled Kovacs comment about giving Nadeem leeway, even shaking his hand after the fight. *Vaz put all the kindling and fuel in place, then threw Autumn in as the spark.* "So, Nadeem and that dealer, Eddie, they're tight?"

"Eddie's tight with anyone who has money. At least he tries to be."

"What's his story?"

"Long and messed up."

Wynn waited for her to continue, but she looked away. "Too long to get into out here in a hot parking lot. Have you had lunch?"

Wynn's stomach growled at the idea. "Not yet."

"I know this great little Italian joint. Let me buy you lunch as a thank you."

Wynn looked down at himself. Even though he'd changed back into his regular clothes, the scuffle with Vaz and the physical exertion from digging the grave left him hot, sweaty, and dirty. "Would love to, but I should probably clean up first. And truthfully, I'm too damn hungry. Let's grab something quick, on me, and I'll take a raincheck on the Italian place."

"Fair enough." Autumn paused. "My name's Jenna, by the way."

Wynn smiled and extended his hand. "It's nice to meet you, Jenna."

She shook his hand. "Lead the way."

Jenna followed as Wynn rode his Harley to an In-N-Out Burger not far away. They went inside and got their food, then sat under an umbrella at a table outside.

When they were settled, Jenna looked at the bruise on Wynn's face. "So, where did you run into Vaz?"

"Kovacs took us to a shooting range. He and I used to be in the Marines together. We spent hours on the range back then."

She rolled her eyes. "Male bonding?"

Wynn smiled. "Something like that."

"Be careful. I don't think that shit works on Vaz."

Wynn touched the bruise on his face. "Obviously. That's twice now you've made comments about him. What's up with you two?"

Jenna took a drink. "We used to date. I'm not proud of it. I mean, I know he used to hook up with other girls, but he told me he'd stopped. He didn't, so I broke it off. The result is I get less protection than the others."

Wynn nodded thoughtfully. "That actually explains a lot."

She smiled. "Sad, right?"

"If it makes you feel any better, I don't think he likes me much, either."

"After a day on the range? I thought you'd be buddies by now."

Wynn laughed. "If it were up to him, he'd fire my ass. Or worse."

"Well, at least you've got Kovacs on your side."

Wynn shrugged and took a bite.

"So, Kovacs was a Marine," Jenna mused. "Weird. He doesn't strike me as the type."

"Why's that?"

She shrugged. "I don't know. I guess I have this image. Some of the things he does don't seem very 'Marine-like,' if you know what I mean."

"Not really," Wynn said, even though he knew exactly what she meant. They were the same reasons that made it impossible to understand what Krista had ever seen in Kovacs. Wynn shook the thought of her from his mind. He'd been doing that a lot lately. "What's he do?"

"Some of the girls they hire." Jenna shook her head. "I mean, I think most of us know what we're getting into when we come work for a place like this. But some of these girls don't have a clue."

Wynn thought back to the girl he'd seen dancing when he first came to the club on Sunday. "Yeah. I've noticed some of them seem a little reluctant."

"Have you been to the other club?"

"The Deuce? No, not yet."

"Go check it out. See if you notice anything."

He frowned, recalling Deborah's comment of a more sophisticated clientele. "Like what?"

"Just go check it out."

Wynn pressed a little further, but Jenna refused to say anything more. Instead, she turned the conversation back toward him. "What's your story?" she asked.

"Got in a little trouble with the IRS. Figured Vegas was as good a place as any to try to make some quick cash."

"It can be. Especially if you don't care how you do it."

Wynn shrugged. "Kovacs seems to be doing well."

"Like I said."

"Oh yeah? What's he into?"

Jenna put down her burger and smiled devilishly. "Did you see that woman in the white pantsuit last night?"

"Yeah?"

"Know who she is?"

Wynn shook his head.

"Her name's Carmen Delgado. She works for Ruben Garcia."

She said the names as though he should know who they were. Wynn shrugged and shook his head.

"Ruben Garcia? The Garcia cartel out of Mexico? She works for him. Pretty high up."

"No shit?" *Ruiz mentioned Kovacs was into drugs.* "Does Kovacs distribute for 'em?"

"The smart money says so."

"But you've never seen it?"

"No, but between that, and Eddie hanging around all the time, I'm sure Kovacs is involved."

"What's he got to do with it?"

"He's Garcia's nephew. Why else would Kovacs let him hang around and deal his shit if he didn't want to stay in Garcia's good graces?"

Wynn shook his head. "How do you know all this?"

"Eddie and Vaz used to be tight. He used to hang around when we were going out."

"Used to be?"

"Yeah, I don't know if they had some kind of falling out or what, but they don't seem as close anymore."

"But Kovacs lets him hang around anyway?"

"Eddie's good for other things. As Garcia's nephew, he's got connections. I know Vaz used to find it helpful, so I'm guessing Kovacs does too."

Wynn recalled Kovacs' comment, *We've all got our spies, Spider-Man.* "You think Eddie might know something about Kovacs' competition?"

"I'm sure he does."

"Like who?"

"Vaz and Eddie used to talk about a guy named Murano, but I know nothing about him, and I don't want to."

"That's probably smart. Still, it seems risky for Eddie. If people find out he's sharing information."

"You'd think so, but most of his contacts are low level guys. A 'word on the street' kind of network. And those guys love him. He keeps them supplied. Besides, as Garcia's nephew he's untouchable. Anyone who hurts Eddie is gonna have the full wrath of the Garcia cartel coming down on them."

Wynn shook his head. "So that's why he acts like he owns the place."

"Yeah. He and Vaz used to talk about how one day they were gonna rule this town."

"Vaz has got ambitions, too?"

"Definitely. Did you see the way he sucked up to Delgado last night?"

Wynn recalled how Vaz had cleared the guys out of that prime booth to make way for Delgado, but then remembered how Jenna and the other dancers seemed to give her extra attention also. "I get why Vaz might suck up, but the dancers seemed to like her, too."

"She tips well. That, and she's gay."

"Really?"

"Yeah. When she's in town she likes to come by. If she sees something she likes..." Jenna wiggled her eyebrows.

Wynn paused. "Wow. Have you ever...?"

"No. She likes darker skin. I haven't been able to figure out if that's a good thing or not."

"Why's that?"

"When the girls come back, they say she treats 'em really well, and pays 'em even better. Which is why we all dance for her. The problem is they don't all come back."

Wynn took a drink, put his cup down, his spider-sense tingling. "Where do they go?"

"No idea. I don't know if she gives them enough money to leave, or if something else happens to them."

"Like what?"

Jenna shrugged. "Use your imagination. Could be anything."

"And the girls who do come back, they don't say?"

"Only that she pays well."

Wynn paused again. "Are any of these girls still at the club?"

"Not at Pink, but like I said, go check out the Deuce."

"I guess I'll have to." Wynn shook his head as he processed everything Jenna told him. "There's a lot of shit going on around here."

"There is. And most of it's not good." She lowered her voice and put a hand on his arm. "A lot of people come and go around here. If it weren't for the money, I'd be gone, too. And I will be. Soon. You seem like a nice guy, Sean. I wanted to warn you. Kovacs scares me."

Smart girl. "I'll be alright. I've known him a long time. Vaz is the variable."

"Yeah, well don't get between them."

"Why? Are they as tight as they seem?"

"Oh yeah. I've seen a couple people try to come between them. They don't last long."

"As employees?"

"As people."

CHAPTER 18

AFTER LUNCH, WYNN RODE back to his motel to shower, then pulled out the burner to check in with Ruiz.

"You had us worried," Ruiz said when he picked up the phone.

"Why's that?" Wynn asked.

"Your little excursion out in the desert. Not sure how familiar you are with the area, but that's where guys like Kovacs dump their trash."

"Well, get a crew out there. He dumped one today."

"What?" Ruiz spluttered.

"One of his bouncers. I don't have the full story, but it sounds like the guy was giving information to one of his competitors. Called him a traitor."

"So we can get him on murder?"

Wynn hesitated. "I don't know. It's complicated."

"How so?"

Wynn explained what happened. How there were more than Kovacs' prints on the murder weapon.

"But with your testimony we could still put him away," Ruiz said.

"And then I'd have to go into witness protection like Krista. No thanks. Besides, that wouldn't get us any closer to Terrance."

Ruiz sighed. "No, it wouldn't. Any progress?"

"Have you found anything on this guy Vasquez? Kovacs doesn't make a move without him."

"We're still looking. Nothing serious so far."

"Well get on it," Wynn said, a note of irritation creeping into his voice. "Not like this is a tea party here."

"I know, I know," Ruiz said. "Anything besides him?"

"This other bouncer, Marcus. You'll want to check him out."

"Why's that?"

"When we were driving back to town, he commented that being killed is preferable to what else Kovacs might do to somebody. I'm guessing he was referring to Terrance, which means he knows something."

"What's his last name?" Ruiz asked.

"No idea."

"All right. We'll look into it. With either of these guys, we'll need to see if we can bring them in and hold them on something else. If we only bring them in on this, they're sure to run right back and tell Kovacs, which puts you at risk."

"I'm already at risk," Wynn said.

"*More* risk," Ruiz said. "What else?"

"There's one more guy who might know something. His name's Eddie. Not sure of his last name, but he's Ruben Garcia's nephew, so maybe Garcia."

"Ruben Garcia?" Ruiz's tone made it clear he knew of him.

"I don't have any proof, but the rumor is Kovacs is distributing for him."

"What's that got to do with Terrance?"

"Maybe nothing, but we're assuming Terrance was taken south, right?"

"Yeah."

"Maybe Kovacs is having Garcia hold him. Out of the country, secure compound. A lot less risky than holding him somewhere here."

"And as Garcia's nephew, odds are good Eddie would know about it," Ruiz said.

"That's what I'm thinking," Wynn said. He paused. "One other thing. Does that video ever show the feet of the guys torturing Terrance?"

"Their feet?" Ruiz paused. "I don't think so. Why?"

"When we were in the desert, Marcus had me put on a white version of the same coveralls the guys were wearing in the video, but they didn't cover our feet. If we could identify the shoes any of those guys were wearing, maybe I could match that up with someone here."

"Good idea," Ruiz said. "I'll check the video and send you pictures if we get something. In the meantime, we'll dig into these names, see if we can't find something solid to hold them on."

"Good," Wynn said. "What about the rag?"

Ruiz sighed. "Good news and bad. The blood was human, but not Terrance's. It was mixed with urine and had traces of endometrial and epithelial tissue."

"Come again?"

"Menses'. Some woman had her period in there. You said that sample came from a bucket found in the back of a truck, right?"

"Yeah."

"The obvious explanation is they're moving people. At least one person, anyway. The fact it was mixed with urine indicates she was likely in there a long time, probably over a long distance. Had nowhere else to go."

Wynn sighed, suddenly tired at the thought. "Sounds like all bad news. Means we're no closer to finding Terrance, and maybe someone else is in trouble, too."

"We've considered that," Ruiz said. "But that's not your issue. Stay focused on Terrance and hopefully this will all be over soon."

Wynn paused, knowing Ruiz was right. He couldn't save everyone. He had to stay focused. "Did the Hampsons receive a package today?"

"Yesterday." Ruiz said, now sounding tired himself. "Another finger. And a warning that the pieces are going to get bigger if they don't hand over the kid."

"I hope you're working this from other angles. At the rate I'm going, there won't be anything left."

"We are, but you're still our best hope."

Wynn's stomach churned at the thought. It'd only been a few days, and he'd identified a few names, but he still felt a long way from anything tangible that might save Terrance. If they were all depending on him, that was slim hope indeed. "I want to talk to Krista."

"Why?" Ruiz asked.

This time Wynn was prepared. "Because I'm risking my ass here. Now that I'm getting to know Kovacs, she might be able to tell me something that'll help."

Ruiz paused. "I'll see what I can do."

Wynn disconnected the call. He didn't need Ruiz's permission to contact Krista, but for some inexplicable reason, he wanted it. It had been four days since he'd spoken to her, but it felt longer. Much longer. He punched her number into the burner, but his finger hesitated over the call button. *What if she's not alone? What if one of Ruiz's men is with her? She won't recognize this number. Might hand it to one of them to answer.*

He erased the digits and pulled up the text app, then punched them in again. *What do I say?* He typed one word: *Hey.*

Once again, his finger hesitated a long moment over the send button. *Real smooth, Wynn. You're supposed to be preventing her brother from getting his fingers chopped off, and instead you're flirting like a lovestruck twelve-year-old.* His finger hovered over the send button, then moved to the delete button. He punched it three times, powered off the phone, and stuck it back in the box spring.

————

At the same time, Vaz stood within the enclosed parking area behind the club, a phone to his ear.

"Change of plans," he said quietly. "Instead of one target tonight, we've got two."

CHAPTER 19

THAT EVENING, WYNN WAS behind the bar at Pink, hoping for an opportunity to continue his conversation with Marcus, but according to Deborah, he was at the Deuce. A little after eleven, Kovacs appeared in the hall and waved him back. Wynn followed him to the office where Kovacs settled in behind the desk.

"What's up?" Wynn slid into a chair.

"You're still here." Kovacs leaned back. "Gotta admit, I'm kind of surprised."

"Why? Because you wasted some guy I barely knew?" He shrugged. "Not gonna say I liked it, but I'm not losing any sleep over it."

Kovacs nodded and paused. "When I asked you to shoot Vaz, did you know the gun was empty?"

"It felt a little light, but I figured if you wanted him dead, he'd be dead whether I pulled the trigger or not. The only question was if I was going to join him."

"Self-preservation?"

"Strongest motivator in the world," Wynn said.

"And if it happens again?"

"You're the judge and jury. I'm just the guy flipping the switch."

Kovacs nodded slowly, steepled his fingers in front of his chin. "That range shooting today, was it luck or are you really that good?"

"I can't promise I'll hit it every time, but nine times out of ten? Yeah, I can do it."

Kovacs' lips turned up in a grim smile. "Then let's go flip a switch."

Shit, Wynn thought. *Hope I didn't oversell this thing.*

Wynn followed Kovacs out of the office and through the back door to where three identical Lincoln Navigators waited. Vaz stood next to one. He saw Wynn and took an aggressive step forward. Kovacs jumped between them.

"Let's get something straight right now," Kovacs said as Vaz and Wynn glared at each other. "You two need to put your personal grievances aside. What happened today was a test. I needed to know that Wynn had my back, and Vaz, you need to know that I have yours. The only question is whether you'll have each other's, and that's no longer a question, because I'm telling you, you'd better. Failure to do so will be interpreted as a failure to serve me, and you saw what happened when Kevin did that. Am I clear?"

Neither of them made a sound.

"Are we clear?" Kovacs demanded.

Both Wynn and Vaz nodded and mumbled, which, given the situation, was apparently enough for Kovacs. "Good. Let's load up."

As they had before, Vaz climbed in shotgun while Kovacs and Wynn piled in the rear. A new driver, another bouncer named Chad, was behind the wheel. When the doors closed, the three vehicles caravanned out of the lot.

"Where are we going?" Wynn asked. Kovacs' earlier comment made it fairly clear he was about to test Ruiz's rules of engagement.

"To take care of a problem," Kovacs said. "A guy named Arturo Murano. He's the one Kevin was spying for. Word is he's coming after me, so it's time to take him out."

"What's the plan?"

"We're meeting under the guise of striking a deal to make peace." Kovacs nodded over his shoulder. "I want you to take your new toy and eliminate the problem."

Wynn glanced into the cargo hold behind them. The TAC and several boxes of ammo sat in the rear. He'd hoped it wouldn't come to this.

"Where are we doing this?" Wynn asked.

"Out by the speedway."

Wynn knew the area. The Las Vegas Motor Speedway was on the northeast side of town, away from the glitz and glamour. Relatively isolated, and close to the freeway, perfect for a quick escape for anyone who needed it.

Kovacs continued. "You'll be positioned on a roof; we'll be down in the parking lot. Just like Afghanistan. Scan the area, let us know if he's got anyone hiding in the weeds. Once we know it's clear, Vaz will identify the target with a laser pen. When you're locked in, wait for his command, then take the shot."

"Distance?"

"Four to five hundred meters."

Shit. Wynn had shown earlier that was well within his range. And shown a willingness to kill. He didn't like it, but he'd painted himself into a corner. "Comms?" he asked.

Vaz handed back a small two-way radio with an earpiece and microphone, while Kovacs explained. "These are set to voice active. It'll transmit as soon as you start talking. You'll be in communication with Vaz, but other than the shoot command, don't expect a lot of verbal instruction. That's why he's got the laser."

Wynn nodded and threaded the wire from the microphone through his shirt, then plugged it into the radio and clipped it to his belt.

"Channel B," Vaz said.

Wynn selected the channel, then pressed the earpiece into his right ear.

"Test one-two," Vaz said.

The voice was clear over the radio. "Confirm comm." Wynn nodded at the vehicle ahead of them. "How many guys are we bringing to this little shindig?"

"Besides us? Six," Kovacs said.

"And how many will they bring?"

"More," Kovacs said. "But don't worry about that. Take out Murano and the rest will scatter. We'll take care of those who don't."

"And once he's down?"

"If any others look like a threat, take 'em out."

Great. Wynn glanced up. Chad looked at him through the rearview mirror. Fear flickered in the man's eyes before he quickly looked away. Wynn's spider-sense trembled. "In that case, can I also get something a little smaller, more maneuverable?"

"You'll be well away from the action."

"Doesn't matter," Wynn said. "You know the motto. Hope for the best, plan for the worst."

Kovacs rolled his eyes. "We've got a spare Glock in back. You can get it when we let you out."

As they approached the speedway, Chad slowed and turned onto a side street. The other SUVs continued on.

"They're going to make sure everything's cool before we go in," Kovacs said. "That'll give you time to get in position."

They turned into a warehouse alongside the speedway and eased to a stop. Vaz grabbed a pair of bolt cutters and headed to a small steel cage that encircled a roof-access ladder, its door secured by a simple padlock. Vaz snipped through the lock, then returned to the back of the SUV where Kovacs was opening the rear hatch, revealing a small arsenal.

"Figured you might need something to carry all this in," Kovacs said, handing Wynn an armament vest. Wynn slipped it on, then put three magazines, each holding five rounds for the TAC, into the various pockets. He picked up the Glock, checked the chamber and the mag, and put it into a holster on his hip. Finally, he hoisted the TAC from its case, checked the action, then slung it over his shoulder.

"Take that ladder to the roof, then head to the east edge," Kovacs said. "You should be able to see the rest of the crew getting in position. Make sure the area is clear, then give us the word, and we'll go in."

"Got it," Wynn said.

"Remember, Vaz will identify the target with the laser. Take the shot on his command. No delay."

"Understood."

"And Spider-Man," Kovacs put his hand on Wynn's arm. Wynn paused again at his old Marine nickname. "Don't let me down."

CHAPTER 20

Wynn held Kovacs' cold stare until the killer finally turned and walked around the side of the SUV. He and Vaz got in, and the Lincoln pulled away.

Wynn hustled to the cage, ducked inside, and climbed the ladder. The rooftop was broad, flat, and covered with a thin layer of pea gravel over tar, still sticky from the day's heat. And smelly. A sharp odor hung over the roof. A maze of thick pipes snaked across the almost acre-sized space, while a waist-high wall enclosed the entire area.

Wynn crouched low as he crossed the rooftop, his footsteps crunching on the gravel surface. At the east edge, he unslung the rifle from his shoulder, knelt on one knee, and peered over the wall.

A quarter mile away, a half-dozen SUVs sat parked under the yellowish glow of the sodium streetlamps. Wynn picked up the rifle, extended the bipods, and peered through the scope.

He immediately recognized the two Lincolns that held Kovacs' men, so instead, focused on the other four vehicles. A driver and passenger were visible in the front of each. No way to tell how many more might be in the rear seats.

Eddie and a heavy-set Hispanic man stood in the glare of headlights coming from two of the SUVs, while four other men formed a semicircle further behind them.

He scrutinized the surrounding area, quickly coming to the realization that the only other reasonable place an enemy could hide was in the back of the grandstands across the lot. He began the slow process of scanning each level of the stadium.

Vaz's voice came through the earpiece. "All clear?"

"Negative," Wynn said. "Give me a minute."

"Copy that," Vaz said.

Wynn quickly scanned the rest of the stands. It wasn't as thorough as he would've liked, but it was enough. He didn't see anything threatening.

"Okay, Vaz," Wynn said. "You're clear." He reached into a vest pocket and pulled out a five-round magazine, inserted it into the TAC, then pulled back on the bolt handle, loading a 50-caliber round into the chamber.

Sensing movement below, Wynn tracked the scope down into the lot. Kovacs' Lincoln pulled in among the other vehicles. Car doors opened and men dressed in jeans and light jackets stepped onto the pavement. Vaz hung back as Kovacs strode toward Eddie and the heavy-set guy, who turned and faced Kovacs straight on.

Wynn scanned the men on the other side. While their hands were empty, a couple had pistols clearly visible stuffed in the front of their jeans.

He turned the scope back toward Kovacs. After a few minutes of quiet conversation, the stocky Hispanic lit a cigarette. His voice rose, allowing Vaz's microphone to pick up a word or two. Wynn strained to decipher the occasional syllable that came through his earpiece, but nothing made sense. He scanned the men on both sides, many of whom were getting restless, shifting their weight back and forth from one foot to the other, hands sneaking close to their bodies. *The moment I pull the trigger, this thing's gonna explode.*

"Vaz, I don't have a target," Wynn said.

Vaz shifted a step to his right. Wynn waited for the red dot to appear, assuming it would land on the stocky guy, but when nothing came, he examined the angle. Or rather, the lack thereof. The stocky guy had moved a couple of steps to his left, keeping Kovacs perfectly lined up between himself and Vaz.

He's not allowing Vaz to light him up... "Vaz, he knows. Could be a trap. You need to abort and get the hell out of there."

An indistinct whisper came over the earpiece.

The big guy—Wynn assumed it was Murano—stepped forward and stood directly in front of Kovacs. Vaz took a cigarette out of his pocket and brought both hands to his face, covering his mouth. "Now," Vaz whispered.

"Negative. You need to abort. It's too risky."

"Now!" Vaz hissed again.

Wynn was about to protest when the crunch of pea gravel came from behind him. He spun away from the rifle, his hands shooting up barely in time to catch the wrist of a man driving a knife toward his chest.

"I've got company!" Wynn yelled as the TAC fell backward onto the roof. Wynn surged upward from his kneeling position, wrapping his left arm around the assailant's elbow. He slid his right hand up and collapsed the guy's wrist, causing the knife to drop.

The guy grabbed the back of Wynn's shirt. With both of Wynn's hands occupied, Wynn was yanked back and spun around. His calf caught on one of the pipes, sending him tumbling backward. He held on tight, making sure his attacker fell with him, then pushed the guy away.

Landing hard, Wynn rolled across the rooftop, reaching for the Glock at his hip. By the time Wynn came out of his roll, the guy was already on his feet, drawing a pistol from behind his back.

Wynn pointed his Glock at the guy and double-tapped the trigger. The man flew back and lay sprawled on the rooftop, two small wounds spilling blood from his chest. After an agonizingly long moment of silence, gunfire erupted from the parking lot below.

Scrambling to his feet, Wynn ran back and picked up the TAC, set the bipod on the half-wall, and looked through the scope. Chaos ruled the lot. Men were running and shooting in all directions. Some hid behind the SUVs, while others lie motionless on the asphalt.

Kovacs and Vaz crouched with two other men behind their SUV as gunfire flared all around. To their left, one of Kovacs' men was down, while Murano was nowhere to be seen. Two of Murano's men had crossed the no-man's-land between the vehicles and now used the left Lincoln as cover to try to flank Kovacs. Wynn sighted in on the left leg of the closest, hoping the rifle's fall hadn't misaligned the sights. He exhaled slowly and squeezed the trigger.

The TAC boomed across the parking lot, and the guy crumpled to the ground, his leg twisted at an unnatural angle. No doubt he'd never walk again. If he survived.

The remaining man crouched behind the Lincoln, looking frantically for the source of the shot. Wynn sighted in on the front tire of one of Murano's SUVs and fired a second time, blowing out the tire.

Sensing their escape window closing, Murano's men ran for their cars as small arms fire popped all around. They piled in, leaving their dead or wounded where they lay, then squealed away as Vaz and some of Kovacs' men fired after them.

"Vaz, what's the situation?" Wynn asked. "Any hostiles left?"

Vaz didn't get a chance to respond; Kovacs pulled the earpiece away and screamed into the microphone. "What happened, Wynn? Why didn't you shoot when you were told?"

"He knew. A guy jumped me—"

"Who knew?" Kovacs interrupted. "Murano?"

Wynn looked back at the body lying on the roof. "Yeah. Either Murano had the same idea, or you've got another leak."

Sirens wailed in the distance. "Fuck!" Kovacs muttered. "Meet us back at the club. And don't get caught."

Wynn watched from the rooftop as Kovacs and his men jumped into the Lincolns and sped away. As the sirens grew louder, Wynn grabbed the TAC and raced to the far edge of the roof, glancing to the southwest. Flashing red and blue lights were barely a mile away. He scrambled down the ladder and jogged away from the building to get his bearings.

Streetlamps lit up everything to the north, west, and south. Cops were coming from the southwest. There was really only one choice: east, into the darkness. He broke into a run, disappearing into the desert night.

CHAPTER 21

AMBIENT LIGHT FROM THE speedway provided just enough illumination to avoid the bushes that littered the landscape as Wynn jogged across the sand, but not enough to reveal the softball-sized rocks that threatened to twist his ankles.

Slowing to a fast walk, Wynn glanced to his right. A pair of lonely headlights slid along Highway 604, barely a quarter of a mile away. A mile to his left, a steady procession of vehicles cruised back and forth along Interstate 15. Several miles ahead, he knew the two highways crossed, putting him in the middle of a long, narrow triangle, the two highways on either side, the speedway behind.

While the most direct route back to the city was south across the more desolate 604, it would also take him near Nellis Air Force Base, and Wynn had no desire to test the alertness of the base's guards. To the north, across Interstate 15, lay nothing but sand and mountains.

It was a longer, more circuitous walk, but considerably safer.

Wynn continued away from the speedway until he came to a dirt road that led north toward the 15, putting the speedway and the cop cars that now filled it far to his left. Two hundred yards from the freeway, the dirt path opened to an abandoned quarry where a large circular pit had been carved into the desert floor.

Circling the quarry, Wynn found a patch of bushes on its eastern rim, then unslung the TAC from his shoulder and removed the magazine from its seat. He pulled back on the bolt, ejecting the spent round from the chamber, then used the butt to sweep a long, 12-inch-deep groove into the sand at the base of the bushes.

Working quickly, Wynn removed the armament vest and his shirt, then used the shirt to wipe his fingerprints from the rifle. He tore a pocket off the vest and stuffed the cloth into the barrel, then wrapped the rest of the vest around the center portion of the rifle, taking extra care to cover the scope, trigger, and bolt. Laying the rifle into the groove, he pushed the sand back on top of it, then found a large rock to place next to it. He slipped his shirt back on and found a tumbleweed to smooth out the sand as he erased his tracks back to the quarry.

Glancing back toward the speedway, he scanned the sky for the telltale flashing lights of a police helicopter. Seeing none, he continued along the dirt road to the far edge of the quarry, then picked his way through the desert. He came to a stop behind a bush ten yards from the freeway shoulder.

More than a mile away, the flashing red and blue police lights were clearly visible, indicating that something had happened at the speedway. Motorists would be more alert because of it, more likely to call in any strange sightings, like that of a man crossing the freeway on foot, not far away.

With that in mind, Wynn waited patiently as the cars zipped by. Ten minutes passed before a lull in traffic allowed him to dash across both lanes and disappear.

Moonlight reflecting off the sand allowed Wynn to navigate his way around the northeastern edge of the city. A direct route back to the club would be a fifteen-mile walk, but he had no desire to draw attention to himself by strolling leisurely through this remote part of town. Better to add a few miles to his hike and get well away from the speedway before taking a straight shot south to Las Vegas Boulevard, and eventually back to the club.

The long trek gave him plenty of time to think. Ruiz had said Kovacs had more going on beyond a simple kidnapping, and Wynn was beginning to see all of it. Barely five days into the assignment, Wynn had already killed one man on the rooftop, maybe a second with his shot down into the parking lot, and witnessed the death of a third.

None of which particularly bothered him. Having been raised in a military family, Wynn had come to terms with existential questions at an early age. As such, he drew a very distinct line between murder and killing. Murder was a crime against the innocent. Something done to someone who had done nothing to deserve it.

Killing, on the other hand, was deserved.

Justified.

Required even, if the target threatened your safety or way of life.

The guy on the roof had clearly been a threat, and Wynn had a hard time believing Kevin or the guy in the parking lot were innocent. Still, the fact that he hadn't witnessed evidence of their guilt niggled the back of his brain.

That was the problem with moral issues. There was always the question of perspective and degree. Thankfully, Wynn's parents had gifted him a strong sense of right and wrong. Kovacs, from any perspective, had proven himself a murderer. Wynn would have no problem taking him out, given the chance. Assuming, of course, that doing so wouldn't jeopardize Terrance.

But what about Murano or his men? Wynn had no idea who Murano was, or what he'd done. Was he, or anyone who worked for him, any more guilty than Kovacs himself? Based on everything Wynn had seen so far, he doubted it.

But that didn't mean they were innocent.

From his perspective, anyone assisting either Kovacs or Murano was likely guilty of something, and therefore on the wrong side of the line.

So he'd taken the shot.

He took no joy in it, nor did he feel bad about it. It was a risk anyone who participated in this world subconsciously accepted. Himself included. He'd known all along that to find Terrance, he was going to have to earn Kovacs' trust. He knew what that might mean. He just hadn't expected it this soon.

Or this much.

So far, he was comfortable he was still on the right side of the moral line. He just hoped Kovacs wouldn't push him any closer to it.

Having sorted it all out in his mind, his conscience was clear by the time he made it back to the club. But that didn't mean he was happy. Being attacked on a rooftop and left to hoof it all night through the desert was no way to build loyalty.

He swung open Pink's back door around six a.m. and made his way up the hallway. A shadow cut through the light spilling from Kovacs' office. Vaz appeared in the doorway, but Wynn shoved past him on his way out to the empty bar.

"Wynn!" Kovacs yelled from his office.

Wynn ignored the summons and continued to the bar. He grabbed a bottle of water from a cooler, took a long draw, and wiped his mouth.

Kovacs and Vaz followed him, each taking a stool while Wynn took another long drink, draining the bottle. He grabbed another and plodded out from behind the bar, slumping into one of the padded chairs at a table behind Kovacs.

Kovacs and Vaz turned on their stools to look at him. No one spoke for a long moment as Wynn's anger simmered.

Finally, Kovacs broke the silence. "What the hell happened last night?"

"You tell me," Wynn snapped.

"Why didn't you take the shot?"

"Murano knew what we were doing. He stepped up close to you right as Vaz gave the signal, then some asshole jumped me on the roof. All that didn't happen by accident."

Kovacs and Vaz exchanged a quick glance, but said nothing.

"Three possibilities," Wynn said. "Either Murano had the same idea, someone followed us, or you've got another leak. Maybe it's time you tell me what the hell's going on. Who is Murano, anyway?"

Kovacs hesitated. "Murano and I do some work for the same person. Murano handles the west coast, we cover the Rocky Mountain region. You may not know this, Sean, but my dad went to prison, and when that happened, Murano thought he would take over our territory. Obviously, I wasn't about to let that happen. He's been trying to take me out ever since."

I'm getting pulled into a damn mafia war, Wynn thought. "And exactly what kind of work is that?"

"Does it matter?"

Wynn exploded. "Damn right it matters! Just like back in the Corps. Some missions made sense. We knew exactly what the objective was and why. Others, we wondered what the fuck we were doing out there. And you remember which ones were successful, right? The ones where we knew what we were fighting for. So far, I've buried one guy for you, and now shot two more, so yeah, I'd like to know why the hell I'm doing that."

Kovacs paused, then reached into his pocket and tossed a neat stack of bundled bills onto the table next to Wynn.

Wynn looked at the money, a brand-new bale, straight from the Fed. A hundred one-hundred-dollar bills. Ten thousand dollars.

"Or," said Kovacs quietly, "you can be a good little soldier, do what you're told, and be paid very well for it."

Wynn looked at Kovacs. "I'm not a mercenary."

"Good. Mercenaries work for the highest bidder, regardless of which side they're on. I want private soldiers. Guys who'll be loyal to *me*. Guys who'll do what I tell 'em, when I tell 'em. If you need a cause, there's the door. Go find one. My business is *my* business, and if you think I'm going to fill you in on everything we do here, then you better ride on back to L.A. because it's not happening. I can use a guy with your skills, but if you decide to stay, you need to understand that I'll tell you what you need to know, when you need to know it. And that right there," he pointed at the money on the table, "better be all the motivation you need. When I tell you to do something, you damn well better do it without hesitation. Understood?"

Wynn paused, thoughts of Terrance and Krista flitting into his mind. He willed his temper down and nodded.

"Good. Where's the TAC?" Kovacs asked.

"In the desert."

"Where?"

"I'm not sure," Wynn lied. "Somewhere north of the fifteen. When you left, I took it and hauled ass. I knew I couldn't stroll down the Strip with it, so I wiped it down and buried it. I might be able to find it again, but it was dark, and I kicked some sand over it. But if I can't find it, no one else will either."

"And the Glock?"

Wynn lifted his shirt, pulled the Glock from its holster, and set it on the table.

"I assume that's what you used on the guy on the roof?"

Wynn nodded.

"It's tainted. Leave it. Vaz will get you a new one."

Wynn leaned forward, picked up the money, and thumbed through the bills. "Am I still tending bar?"

"For the record, yes. But off the record, I need a driver and a gunner. I assume you can drive?"

"Well enough."

"Good. You want to know what we do here? It starts with supply runs. Twice a week. Be back here tonight. Vaz will show you how it's done. When you're not driving or riding shotgun, you can pretend to help out behind the bar."

Wynn nodded again.

"Make no mistake, Wynn, this isn't over. Murano will hit back, and I've still got a business to run. Go get some sleep. It's gonna be another long night."

Getting up, Wynn stuffed the money in a front pocket and made his way to the hallway.

As he got to the hall entrance, Kovacs called out, "Hey, Wynn. One more thing."

Wynn looked back.

"There's one other difference between this and being a mercenary."

"What's that?"

"Here, once you're in, you're in for good."

————

On the ride back to his motel, Wynn stopped at a fast-food joint to fill his stomach before settling into what he hoped would be a long and restful sleep. He rumbled his Harley into the motel's parking lot a little before seven. As he dismounted, he glanced up to his room on the second floor.

Two doors down, from the same room where he'd encountered the bleach-bottle-blonde when he first checked in, a different girl peeked out from the curtained window. Her dark, disheveled hair stuck out in all directions. An oversized t-shirt hung loosely off her shoulder. They locked eyes for a moment before a hand touched her bare shoulder and gently pulled her away from the glass. The curtain fell back into place.

CHAPTER 22

IT WAS LATE MORNING by the time Danny Kovacs got out of bed, showered, and dressed for the day. He'd been up most of the night, but had managed to catch a couple of hours of sleep at the club while waiting for Wynn to return. Now, he stood in his kitchen at home and cranked his neck to one side, then rolled his head in a wide, slow circle, working out the kinks that came from sleeping in his office. There were way more comfortable couches in the VIP rooms, but he knew what went on in there. No way he was sleeping on one of those.

He grabbed a cup of coffee, slipped his phone into a pocket, then carried his laptop out to the patio. He set both the drink and laptop on a table, then pulled out a chair and sat. Across the patio, one of his house staff used a paddle to stir the water on the other side of the large, rectangular pool.

He knew it was an odd demand, but he couldn't stand the sight of a smooth, glass-like surface. Its stillness was a stark reminder that there were no children to run through the three-acre backyard. No one to laugh and play and jump and swim, no one to disturb the perfect tranquility of the water. No one to share the fifteen-thousand-square-foot home; a home that he lived in alone, ever since Krista and Joshua died.

But they aren't really dead, are they?

His mind wandered down a familiar path as frustration welled up inside. Their deaths had come as a devastating blow, but a feeling of uncertainty constantly lingered just beneath the surface. The charred remains he'd been shown in the morgue were roughly the same size as his wife and infant son, but he'd had a hard time believing those unrecognizable shapes were really them.

When his father, Bennie, was arrested two weeks later, he pushed his doubts aside. His attention was required elsewhere. Arturo Murano, Garcia's west coast distributor, was making accusations, saying a mole had infiltrated the Kovacs family.

Then, late one morning, he'd received a phone call from Deborah, insisting he come down to the club right away. Ruben Garcia himself had smuggled his way into the U.S. and shown up at the club, seeking assurances that Kovacs' operation was clean.

It was a make-or-break moment. Garcia was about to pull his business when Kovacs was struck with inspiration. A new venture, one that had the potential to be equally profitable, and could expand Garcia's product distribution worldwide. One that Arturo Murano couldn't match.

Garcia went for it.

And with that, Danny Kovacs expanded the family business. Globally.

Because, after all, that's what it was. A business. It didn't matter that he was dealing in sex and drugs, the rules of business were the same. Not the laws, but the rules. And Danny Kovacs had become a very good businessman.

Calling on contacts he'd made while serving in the United States Marine Corps eleven years ago—contacts the Corps would be very unhappy to know he'd made—he forged new relationships, created new networks, and opened a new avenue of enterprise.

And then, about a month ago, he'd been texted a picture of his former brother-in-law, Krista's brother, Terrance. Drunk at a bar and telling stories about how his big sister had brought down a crime family kingpin, faked her death, and went into witness protection. The guy who sent him the text said Terrance was trying to make it appear as if he were bullshitting, making up the story to get laid. But there were too many similarities, the story a little too close to what he knew to be true.

Anxious to find out, Danny made a mistake. He'd acted rashly. He'd ordered Vaz to pick up Terrance, thinking he could trade Terrance for Joshua. Now he knew that was never going to happen. It would have been better if he'd acted discreetly, gotten someone to befriend the family. Gain their trust. He might've learned where Krista was, then simply taken Joshua. Quietly. Without FBI involvement. Now they all but knew he had Terrance, which was unfortunate.

For Terrance.

He would pay for Danny's mistake.

He'd been able to stash Terrance far away, locked away like a forgotten secret. And while it would be easy to get rid of him, that wouldn't provide any answers.

Or enough suffering.

Kovacs had suffered for seven years, thinking his son was dead. Maybe he should hold Terrance for seven of his own, drop an occasional finger or toe in the mail to Krista's parents, let them know Terrance was still alive, still suffering.

Then Wynn showed up.

Vaz was right. That was one hell of a coincidence. Something Kovacs normally didn't believe in. But it could also be attributed to their conversation at the reunion. Wynn had seemed truly surprised when Kovacs told him Krista had died.

If his story was to be believed, Wynn had experienced a lot since Kovacs had last seen him. The things he'd gone through would change a man, and supposedly they had. They'd made him harder, more callous. Certainly, the test with Vaz and his performance at the speedway indicated Wynn was no longer the boy scout he'd been back in the Corps. And Kovacs could use a guy with those skills. But did people ever really change? Deep down, at the core of their being?

Maybe.

Maybe not.

It was impossible to know.

He needed another test. An ultimate, definitive test. One that would reveal Wynn's true intentions either way. The seed of an idea germinated in his mind.

But that would have to wait.

The events at the speedway created more pressing concerns. Murano was still alive and undoubtedly pissed. This thing was on the verge of all-out war. Whatever his thoughts regarding Wynn's intentions, the events at the speedway had proven Wynn right about one thing. They had another leak.

He picked up his phone and dialed Vaz. "Have you talked to Eddie?"

"It's Chad."

"He's sure this time?"

"Kevin was in on it too, but so is Chad."

Kovacs paused. If Chad was the leak, the supply runs were also at risk. "All right. Here's what we do. Change the pickup location, then take Chad along with you and Wynn tonight. Make Wynn get rid of him before you make the pickup."

"Will do."

"One other thing. Change of plan with our guest down south."

"You want to get rid of him?"

"Just the opposite. Get him a doctor. I want him with us a while."

CHAPTER 23

WYNN SLEPT UNTIL MID-AFTERNOON. A dream he hadn't had in several months jolted him awake. It was of Nicole, and their last night at the restaurant. He heard the gunshots, saw the stray bullet pierce her chest.

He sat for a few moments, allowing the adrenaline to dissipate from his system and his heart to calm. Finally, he got up, showered, and dressed in the last of his clean clothes. The motel had a coin-operated laundry on the first floor. With a little time to kill, he stuffed his dirty clothes into his duffle and headed downstairs.

The room was empty when he walked in. Three stackable washer-dryer units sat along one wall. He chose the cleanest looking and put his clothes in, got it started, then pulled out his phone and settled in to wait.

A few minutes later, the door opened and in came the blonde from two doors down, carrying a small load of clothes in a clear trash bag. She was wearing cut-off blue jean shorts, a loose tank top, and sandals. Her hair was wet as if she'd just stepped out of the shower; her face free of makeup, which, Wynn thought, actually made her dark complexion prettier.

She mumbled a quick hello and Wynn nodded in reply, then returned to his phone as she emptied the bag into one of the washers.

When she finished, she dropped into a chair across from Wynn. "I hate laundry."

Wynn gave a faint smile. "Agreed."

An awkward silence developed.

"That's a nice bike you ride."

"Thanks," Wynn said, not looking up from his phone. He had no desire to engage in conversation; he wasn't a prospect.

The silence returned. The blonde got her phone out, tapped the screen a few times, then set it down.

"Hey, about the other day... I appreciate your asking if I was okay. That guy was a creep. I went into tough-girl mode to get him out. Ended up giving you some of that also. I'm sorry."

"No problem," Wynn said. He glanced up and met her eye. "I'm glad you're alright."

"Thanks. I'm Maria by the way." She extended her hand.

Wynn shook it. "I'm Sean. Nice to meet you."

A relieved smile spread across Maria's face. "Nice to meet you, Sean. What brings you to a dump like this?"

Wynn smiled. "Work. I'm new in town. Need a place to stay until I can find something permanent. You?"

"This is as permanent as it gets for me. At least until I save enough to get out of here for good."

"Oh yeah? Where to then?"

"I'm thinking Phoenix or Tucson. I still have family in Mexico, so I want to stay close."

"Is that where you're from? I wouldn't have guessed."

Maria laughed. "The blonde hair, huh? My father was white. My mother Hispanic."

"No," Wynn said, glancing at the dark roots beneath her blonde locks. "You don't have an accent."

She smiled. "It still slips out once in a while, but I've been here since I was fifteen. Been trying to get rid of it."

"Why?"

"It's a clue I'm not legal. No accent, people assume I was born here."

Wynn nodded. "You've done a good job."

"Thanks. What about you? You were out late last night. Or should I say early this morning?"

"I was working."

Her eyebrows raised. "What kind of job keeps you out until six in the morning?"

"I tend bar at one of the clubs. We had some things to do after closing."

"Bartender, huh? Which club?"

"Pink."

Maria froze as the color drained from her face. "Pink, huh? How'd you... How'd you get on there?"

Seeing her reaction, Wynn spoke slowly. "I know the owner."

Maria's gaze flicked briefly to the washing machines. "It's good to have friends," she said, her voice shaking slightly. She picked up her phone. "Oh, shit. I forgot. I have an appointment. I gotta go."

She jumped up and ran out the door, leaving her laundry tumbling in the washer.

————

When his laundry was done, Wynn went back to his room and dug out the burner for his daily check-in.

Ruiz had texted him two pictures. He tapped the first one and a dark image filled the screen. Wynn recognized it immediately. It was from the Terrance video. A full screen shot of two men holding him to a chair while a third approached from the front. One of the men holding him had his foot on a bracing rail of the chair. The shot was too far away to make out any detail.

Wynn clicked on the second photo. It was a close up of the man's foot. Surprisingly good quality. While the first shot had been dark and grainy, this second picture had been enhanced. Lightened and sharpened. The man was wearing a cowboy boot. What appeared to be a rattlesnake skin texture wrapped around the base, while an intricately sewn upper was filled with swirls and curlicues. Not the most unique design, nor was there any indication of the brand, but it was something.

He punched the speed dial for Ruiz.

"Did you get the pictures?" Ruiz asked.

"Yeah, but it's not what I expected. Haven't seen too many cowboy boots around Pink."

"That's a good thing. When you do, it'll narrow it down."

"We'll see," Wynn said skeptically. "What about Marcus? Did you find anything on him?"

"So far, he's clean. According to the state labor office, his last name is Edwards. The guy barely got a traffic ticket, but we'll keep looking."

"Well, hustle it up. Every day gets sketchier around here."

"Why? What happened?"

"You must have seen me at the speedway last night?"

Ruiz sighed. "We did."

"If you've watched the news, then you know what happened."

"We know what. We don't know who or why."

"Eddie was trying to broker a peace between Kovacs and a guy named Arturo Murano, Kovacs' main competitor. There's a blood-feud between them. Kovacs is afraid Murano's trying to take him out. Last night was a preemptive strike."

"Is Murano one of the dead?" Ruiz asked.

"I don't think so. I didn't see his body after it was all done."

"Which means he's still a factor."

"Yeah. What do you know about him?"

"Nothing. But let me check with the DEA. They might know something."

"See if they can take him off the table," Wynn said. "This thing is tough enough without a mafia war on top of it."

"I'll see what I can do."

"Have you learned anything about Vaz or Eddie?"

"Eddie's been arrested a dozen times, all on nickel and dime stuff. Nothing big. Your guy Vasquez had a couple arrests as a minor but nothing for several years. They don't seem to be players."

"Wannabe's," Wynn said.

"What's that mean?"

"I talked to one of the dancers. She said they both have ambitions, but so far haven't done much."

"Well... watch 'em."

"Always," Wynn said. "One other thing. Kovacs wants me to make a supply run for him tonight. Not sure what that entails, other than I'll likely be going out of town. So call off the cavalry. I don't need him seeing suspicious vehicles every time he takes me somewhere."

"Fine," Ruiz said. "Better for my budget anyway."

CHAPTER 24

JENNA'S COMMENT TO *SEE if you notice anything* about the Deuce had been nagging at the back of Wynn's brain all day. Yesterday, there'd been no opportunity to check it out, and he doubted there'd be anything to see early in the evening, assuming whatever Jenna was referring to wouldn't become apparent until after the place got rolling. He had no reason to believe whatever it was would be related to Terrance, but so far, Pink hadn't revealed anything useful. Maybe the Deuce would.

The challenge was finding a reason to go there. Showing up with no purpose felt like a risky proposition. Thankfully, luck was finally on his side when he rolled into an overflowing Pink parking lot a little before eight.

He parked his bike in the secluded area behind the club and went in the back door, past Kovacs office, which was locked up tight. He made his way out to the bar where the place was surprisingly busy for so early in the evening. Deborah and a couple of new guys were hurriedly fixing drinks.

Sliding in beside her, Wynn asked, "Is Vaz around?"

"He and Mr. Kovacs are at the Deuce," Deborah said, not bothering to look at him as she mixed a cocktail. "He wants you to take the truck over. Do me a favor while you're at it and take a few kegs with you."

"Sure. Which ones?"

"They're marked, back in the walk-in. Three of 'em. The head bartender over there is a guy named Kent. I'll text him you're coming."

"You got it." Wynn went back down the hallway, found the keys and a dolly, then loaded the first of the kegs and wheeled it outside to the truck.

He used the keys to open the padlock and heaved the door up. The bucket, now clean, sat near the lockbox against the back wall. Using a ramp beneath the cargo bed, Wynn loaded the three kegs and twenty minutes later parked near the back door of the Deuce.

Deborah had said the Deuce had a more sophisticated clientele, evident by the cars in the lot. Several Ferraris, Lamborghinis, and stretch limousines were parked throughout. The back door was locked, so he circled to the front of the building, which was larger and more ornate than the original Pink. A bouncer and a doorman, neither of whom he knew, were situated inside the front foyer.

"Thirty bucks," the doorman said.

"Employee discount," Wynn said as he stepped past the guy. "I'm from the other club. Got some kegs for Kent."

The guy nodded and Wynn pushed through the door. He paused and looked around. The Deuce was much larger and busier than Pink. And louder.

Girls mingled with customers on the floor while dancers filled the six stages and rap music blasted over the speakers. To the left, similar to the original Pink, the bar stretched the entire length of one wall, with a hallway leading to the back at the far end of the room.

Three guys were fixing drinks behind the bar. Wynn worked his way over and caught the eye of one who looked to be in his late twenties.

Leaning across the bar, he shouted to be heard above the music. "Are you Kent?"

The guy nodded.

"I've got some kegs for you."

"Beer cooler is in the back, just like the other place. Put two in there and bring the third up here."

Wynn nodded, then meandered through the tightly packed bodies toward the hallway at the back of the room. He stepped aside as two girls, followed by Vaz, came up the hall.

"Did you bring the truck?" Vaz asked.

Wynn nodded. "Brought some kegs over for Deborah."

"Get 'em unloaded. We'll take off as soon as Chad gets here."

"Where are we going?"

Vaz ignored the question and continued out to the bar. Further up the hall, light spilled from an open doorway. Kovacs called out from behind a desk inside. "Sean."

Wynn paused in the entrance.

"You good?" Kovacs asked.

"Good?"

Kovacs leaned back in his chair. "After our little conversation this morning."

Wynn tapped his pocket. "Keep it coming and I'll be great."

Kovacs smiled. "In that case, come by my place tomorrow around six-thirty. I'm having a little get together and need a few more bodies on security."

"Sure. Anything in particular you need me to do?"

"Normal party security." Kovacs wrote his address on a piece of paper and handed it to Wynn. "Vaz will give you your assignment when you get there." He turned back to his computer.

Wynn nodded. *Perfect. Maybe I'll learn something useful.* "I'll be there."

Dismissed, he stepped into the hallway and glanced into the dressing room. Close to a dozen girls sat in front of mirrors touching up their makeup. Nothing unusual about that.

He wedged the back door open and put the first two kegs in the beer cooler. He was bringing the third up the hallway when a stunning Hispanic girl darted out of the dressing room and stumbled into him. Wynn caught her before she fell.

"Cabrón!" the girl mumbled as she pushed off him and hurried away.

Wynn didn't speak a lot of Spanish but was pretty sure he'd just been insulted.

He wheeled the keg behind the bar and waited as Kent removed the old one. Over the speakers, the DJ's voice cut through the din. "Now welcome to the stage, Lola!" Wynn glanced up to see the girl he'd bumped into take the main stage as a Spanish rap tune blasted throughout the room.

Wynn slid the new keg into place and watched as Kent hooked it up.

"You all set?" Wynn asked.

"We're good."

Wynn glanced toward the front door where Vaz stood talking to the unknown bouncer, Chad still nowhere to be seen. He wheeled the empty keg back to the storage room, then went back to the club and sat at the end of the bar.

He scanned the room while he waited, suddenly noticing the ethnicity of the Deuce's clientele. Asian, American, Middle Eastern, European—both eastern and western. A veritable melting pot in a single room.

At a table nearby, a girl was giving a lap dance to a heavy-set white guy. Gold chains lay nestled in the tuft of chest hair sprouting from his low-buttoned shirt. He looked like the poster boy for the Russian mafia as he stuffed a hundred-dollar-bill into her G-string.

Maybe not more sophisticated, but definitely richer.

Another girl came by. Based on the denominations flowering from her garter, she too seemed to be having a good night. Wynn glanced around the room. Six girls danced on the various stages while he counted more than a dozen mingling throughout the club. Add in those back in the dressing room and those he couldn't see in either the VIP or private dance rooms, and there had to be more than thirty girls here.

All of them young. All of them pretty. All of them making decent money.

And almost all of them Latina.

CHAPTER 25

Wynn was still trying to decide what to make of his observation when Vaz stepped up beside him.

"Let's go," Vaz said.

Wynn followed him down the hallway, pausing while Vaz grabbed a large cargo net out of the storeroom. Outside, Chad stood near the truck's open rear cargo door. He held out his hand as Wynn approached.

"Keys," Chad said.

"I'll drive," Wynn said. With only two seats in the cab, someone was going to have to ride in the back.

"You know where we're going?"

Wynn nodded to Vaz, who threw the net into the cargo area. "Vaz can navigate."

"What makes you think he knows?"

Wynn glanced between the two men.

"Hand 'em over." Vaz motioned to the cargo hold.

Wynn sighed in frustration, tossed the keys to Chad, and jumped into the back of the truck. The five-gallon bucket sat against the left side; the cargo net lay sprawled across the floor. He stepped to the back wall and sat on the locker box, wedging his shoulders into the corner.

"Relax," Chad said from the open doorway. "Three-and-a-half, maybe four hours, tops." He pulled on the rope; the rolling door slammed down, plunging Wynn into darkness.

Moments later, the suspension dipped as Chad and Vaz got in the front. The doors thumped closed, and the engine started up. The truck swayed as it rolled out of the parking lot.

They bounced around the city streets for a few minutes until the road smoothed and the truck picked up speed.

Wynn pulled out his phone and opened the maps app, then pinched and zoomed and swiped until he determined they were on Interstate 15 heading south. He followed their progress as they got onto the 215 toward Henderson, then the 11 toward Hoover Dam. Once they hit the 93 South toward Kingman, Arizona, he put the phone away and settled in.

We're going to Phoenix. Four hours away, exactly like Chad said.

Wynn closed his eyes and leaned his head back into the corner. He hoped to catch a little shut-eye, but the steel locker box and constant swaying made sleep impossible. He squinted through the darkness until he could make out the shape of the bucket against the opposite wall.

Ruiz had said Kovacs was into trafficking. While Wynn had helped the FBI take down one cell, there were thousands more. The fact that the blood contained menses meant this is how they moved them, right here in this truck. Odds were good they had used it to move Terrance, too.

The question—as it pertained to Terrance—was where? Hopefully, this little road trip would provide a clue to that answer.

He pulled out his phone every twenty minutes to check their progress. He felt the truck sway through the curves and heard other cars around them as they cruised through Kingman. Though he would have preferred being up front, driving, in some control of where they were going, the map app on his phone told him all he needed to know.

Three hours after being locked in, the truck slowed. Wynn pulled out his phone and checked the map. They were near Wickenburg, an hour northwest of Phoenix. He was pushed side to side as the truck swayed through a series of turns, then battered by the unmistakable sound of small pebbles being thrown from the tires, pounding the underside of the cargo box like a heavy rain.

Looking closer at his phone, he realized they were no longer heading toward Phoenix, but east, into a deserted patch of nothingness well north of the city.

Wynn climbed to his feet and braced himself as the truck bounced along the washboard track. Eventually, the truck turned onto a relatively flat surface and eased to a stop. The engine shut down and the doors opened, the suspension giving a little as Vaz and Chad slipped out.

The cab doors slammed and moments later the back door rolled up. Wynn jumped down and glanced around. They were parked in a desolate patch of desert. Light from the crescent moon peeked from behind a partially cloudy sky, revealing a rocky clearing surrounded by thick scrub and cacti. A dim glow beneath the clouds to his left hinted at the direction of Wickenburg.

"They're late," Chad said as he looked around.

"Don't worry about it," Vaz said. "If you gotta take a leak, now's the time."

Vaz put a hand on Wynn's arm and gestured for silence as Chad hurried over to the bushes.

When the sound of Chad relieving himself splashed across the clearing, Vaz pulled a Sig Sauer P365 from his side holster. He kept his voice low. "Kevin had help." He nodded toward Chad.

"The speedway?" Wynn asked.

Vaz nodded and held out the gun. "Go do it."

Shit! Don't these guys get tired of killing people? Wynn was about to protest when an idea flitted across his mind. Still, he had to make it look good. He nodded toward Vaz. "Why should I have all the fun?"

Vaz stepped back and pointed the gun at Wynn's face. "Because Mr. Kovacs said so. And if you don't, I'll go back alone." Vaz flipped the gun around, holding the butt out to Wynn. "And don't get any ideas. If I don't come back, you're dead."

"Relax. Just thought maybe you'd want to." Wynn took the gun and edged up behind Chad. He extended it in a one-handed grip as Chad turned around.

"Don't you guys—" Chad's face turned pale in the moonlight when he saw the gun.

"Orders," is all Wynn said.

"Vaz!" Chad's voice was shaky. "What the hell, man?"

"Give Kevin my regards," Vaz said.

"Kevin?" Chad sounded confused. "No, Vaz, you got it all wrong. Kevin might've been talking to Murano, but not me. I'm solid."

Vaz turned away.

"Vaz! Come on. Whatever you're thinking, I didn't do it." Chad stepped forward, as if to follow Vaz, but Wynn raised the gun and pointed it directly into his face. Chad stopped. He looked like he might cry.

Wynn motioned the gun into the brush. "Move."

Chad backed away, stumbling through the bushes. "C'mon, Wynn. Whatever they said, I didn't do it. You gotta believe me."

"Shut up." Wynn used the gun to direct Chad through the maze of bushes until they came to a small open space forty feet in. Wynn glanced back toward the truck. Vaz's head and shoulders were barely visible in the moonlight above the scrub. "On your knees."

Tears burst from Chad's eyes. "No, man. You can't do this."

"Shut up, get on your knees, and don't move." Wynn waited until Chad was on his knees then called back to Vaz. "You got the keys?"

Vaz opened the driver's door of the truck and checked the ignition. "Yeah. Just do it."

Wynn pointed the gun at Chad. "Fall over and stay still," he whispered. Moving his hand a fraction to the right, he pulled the trigger. The gunshot exploded next to Chad's head, and he fell to the side, reaching his hand to his ear and squirming in the dirt. Wynn knelt and glanced toward the truck, making sure he was out of Vaz's sight, then leaned down next to Chad's face. "Disappear, asshole." He clubbed Chad in the head with the butt of the Sig. Chad went still.

Wynn dug into his own pocket and pulled out his keys, then unfastened the AirTag Ruiz had given him and stuffed it into Chad's pocket. Hopefully, Ruiz could use it to pick him up and question him about Terrance. Wynn was banking on Chad feeling no loyalty to Kovacs after this. He might talk, give Ruiz everything they need.

Vaz called from the clearing. "What's going on, Wynn?"

"Hold on." He found Chad's wallet and phone, then stood and held them high as he trampled out of the bushes. "Wanted his wallet. It'll be harder to ID him and make it look like a robbery."

Wynn was well aware that without his phone, the AirTag wouldn't work until Chad got close to someone else's phone. But he also didn't want Chad calling anyone, letting the word out that he was alive, and raising the question as to why Wynn didn't kill him.

Wynn pushed the wallet into Vaz's chest as he strode past, found a large rock, and placed Chad's phone on it. He smashed his heel down, shattering the phone and sending small pieces of glass and plastic skittering across the sand.

He picked up the broken phone and heaved it into the bushes, then stalked toward the truck and sat on the rear bumper. "Who are we waiting for?"

Ignoring the question, Vaz trekked into the bushes toward Chad. The moon slipped behind a cloud, creating dark shadows in the brush.

Wynn held his breath. *Stay still, you dipshit.*

He willed himself calm as Vaz paused a few feet from where he'd left Chad. The seconds seemed to stretch into minutes until Vaz came out of the bushes and approached the back of the truck.

"You're driving," Vaz said as he breezed past Wynn and climbed into the passenger seat.

Wynn got off the bumper and rolled the door down, latching it in place. He climbed in behind the wheel. "Satisfied?"

Vaz settled in and looked straight ahead. "Let's go."

CHAPTER 26

WYNN EASED THE TRUCK out of the clearing and back onto the gravel road. Vaz pointed to the left. "That way."

They rode a mile in silence until a light flashed ahead. It went dark, then flashed again.

Vaz nodded. "There."

Wynn slowed until his headlights revealed a man standing beside the road. He'd placed a red cloth over the flashlight and used it to direct Wynn onto a dirt path. A fresh pair of tire tracks set deep in the sand showed the way.

"Running lights," Vaz said.

Wynn killed the headlights, leaving only the dim yellow glow of the truck's running lights to help navigate the way through a thick maze of scrub and cacti. Thankfully, they didn't have to go far. Within a hundred yards, the path opened to a small clearing where another cargo truck, identical to their own, sat with its rear door open.

"Pull past it and back up to the rear," Vaz said. "I'll direct you." He jumped out.

Wynn maneuvered the truck past its twin, then stopped and backed up so that the two rear bumpers were barely a foot apart. He shut down the engine and set the parking brake, then went around to the back where Vaz had already opened the cargo door.

Carmen Delgado, the woman in white from the club the other night, appeared at the side of the truck.

"Ms. Delgado. It's good to see you again," Vaz said.

Delgado nodded at Wynn. "Who's your friend?"

"Sean Wynn. He's new, but Mr. Kovacs has known him for years. They were in the Marines together."

"A Marine?"

Wynn stuck out his hand. "Yes, ma'am."

Delgado regarded his outstretched hand coolly, then turned away. "Be careful with my merchandise, Vaz."

Wynn glanced into the cargo hold of the second truck. Crates, a little larger than office storage boxes, were stacked to the ceiling, giving no clue as to what was inside. But that was okay. Garcia ran one of the largest cocaine cartels in all of Mexico. It sure as hell wasn't coffee in all those crates.

"Yes, ma'am," Vaz said. He climbed into the cargo hold, where Wynn had just spent the last three hours, picked the net off the floor, and began fastening it to some eyehooks on the right wall about two-thirds of the way back. The other man jumped into the back of his own truck.

"Get up here," Vaz said to Wynn. "You're in the middle. Straddle 'em."

The guy from the other truck was already holding a crate, waiting to hand it to Wynn. He clambered up and placed one foot into the bed of each truck, his legs spanning the open space between, then took the crate and handed it to Vaz in an old-fashioned bucket brigade.

Despite the darkness, they worked fast. Wynn couldn't see how many crates were in Delgado's truck, or how much progress they were making. He was just taking them as fast as he could from one guy and turning and handing them to Vaz.

Until he turned back and bumped into a young woman.

"*Pardòn,*" she said as she stepped across the gap between the two trucks and moved deep into the cargo hold.

Wynn felt a nudge on his shoulder. He turned back as another girl ignored him and stepped across the gap. Behind her, four more girls waited. Mind racing, he took each one by the hand and helped them step across the gap as they transferred from one truck to the other.

The brigade stopped for a moment as Vaz secured the cargo net to the opposite wall, essentially trapping the girls in the back of the truck.

The net provides protection in case the crates slide.

The bucket had been pushed back, into the section that now held the girls. *Guess that solves that mystery.*

The girls whispered excitedly. The whites of their eyes, and of their teeth, practically glowed in the darkness.

Odd, Wynn thought, *They don't seem nervous. Or scared.*

Vaz finished securing the net, and Wynn was handed another box as the brigade started up again, crate-by-crate, until a thick wall had been built, enclosing the girls behind.

———

After pulling back onto the dirt road, Wynn's heart pounded as they drove past the clearing where he'd left Chad. *Stay out of sight, you idiot.*

The fact they were transporting a truckload of cocaine and a half-dozen girls illegally were the least of his concerns. Now, it was a race against the clock. *Gotta get back and have Ruiz pick up Chad before he runs back to Murano. Or it gets back to Kovacs that he's still alive.*

The problem, of course, is that he'd told Ruiz not to have anyone follow him. He had no idea how long it would take for Ruiz to get someone out here.

Regardless, Wynn felt adrenaline surge through his veins. Not just from the fear of Chad being discovered, but from excitement. Getting Chad into Ruiz's custody could be a major step forward; a first and potentially breakthrough step in rescuing Terrance. With Kovacs' growing trust, and therefore Wynn's growing access to this side of the operation, any info they could garner from Chad might be enough to pull this thing off.

More immediately, the fact that Vaz hadn't asked for the Sig back was also a minor comfort. He didn't trust Vaz, but it seemed the truce Kovacs had demanded was holding.

For now.

Even so, he dropped the Sig into the door pocket and kept his left hand near the seven o'clock position on the steering wheel, a natural driving position, but still close to the Sig, just in case.

Wynn glanced at the fuel gauge. "We're gonna need gas."

Vaz grunted.

They stopped at a station on the edge of Wickenburg. When he finished filling the tank, Wynn hustled inside to use the restroom. He stepped into a private stall and pulled up the AirTag app on his phone.

Chad's AirTag didn't show.

That could mean several things. Chad could still be lying unconscious in the desert. He could be hiking toward town with no one around. Or he might have found the AirTag and tossed it away. No way to know.

Wynn wanted to text Ruiz, but he couldn't use his own phone to do it. Too risky if Kovacs ever looked at his phone.

Footsteps indicated someone entering the bathroom. Wynn closed the app and stuffed the phone into his pocket. He exited the stall and stopped at the sink to wash his hands. A trucker stood in front of a urinal, the outline of a cell phone showing in his back pocket.

Wynn took his time at the sink while an idea formed. He could simply ask to borrow the guy's phone, but that could lead to a prolonged conversation. He couldn't afford for Vaz to see that. Wynn wasn't the greatest pickpocket, *but maybe...*

Wynn slid over so the only open sink would be between him and the paper towel dispenser. When the trucker finished, he stepped up to the open sink. Wynn shook the water from his hands, then reached around the guy toward the paper towels. He purposefully caught his foot against the trucker's shoe and fell into him, pushing the trucker into the counter.

"What the hell ..." the trucker said.

With one hand on the trucker's back, Wynn slipped his other into the trucker's back pocket and slid the phone halfway out when Vaz burst through the door. Wynn let go just as the trucker pushed off the counter and swung around, sending him stumbling into Vaz as the phone clattered to the floor.

"My bad! My bad," Wynn said as he regained his footing and held his hands up in surrender. "Lost my balance is all."

"Fucking idiot." The trucker took an aggressive step forward.

Vaz did the same.

The trucker pulled up short.

"Normally, I'd be happy to let you beat the shit out of him," Vaz said. "But we're in kind of a hurry, so maybe another time."

The trucker's eyes moved back and forth between Vaz and Wynn. No doubt no longer liking the odds. He took a step back and crouched down to pick up his phone. He pressed a button to turn it on. "You're lucky it isn't broke, asshole."

"Simple mistake, man," Wynn said. "I'm sorry."

The trucker paused, then muttered, "Asshole," as he pushed past Wynn and out the door.

Wynn turned to Vaz. "Thanks."

Vaz shook his head. "He can kick the shit out of you all day for all I care, but we need to get going, so get your ass out to the truck."

Wynn nodded, then exited the restroom. There were a few other customers scattered throughout the store, but there was no time. Nor could he risk a second run-in. He grabbed a cup of coffee from a self-serve station against the back wall, paid at the counter, then hustled outside.

Vaz was already waiting in the passenger seat when Wynn got back to the truck. "Let's get moving."

"No other stops?"

"Just drive."

CHAPTER 27

Wynn fired up the engine and got back on the highway toward Vegas.

Once past Kingman, Vaz started making calls, arranging for people to meet them when they got back.

Shit. Whether he's arranging to get rid of the girls or the crates, that's gonna take time. Wynn suppressed the desire to pull out his phone and check for the location of Chad's AirTag. Instead, his mind ran the calculations like a junior high math problem. *If Chad took twenty minutes to clear his head, then started walking, he could be back in Wickenburg anytime within the next hour. If he finds a phone, word he's alive could be out before I even notify Ruiz.*

Wynn gripped the steering wheel a little tighter and pressed down on the gas.

"Speed limit," Vaz said. "No more."

Reluctantly, Wynn eased off the gas, flexing his fingers on the wheel.

The first hint of dawn was still more than an hour away when Wynn and Vaz hit the outskirts of Vegas. Vaz directed him through a series of quiet streets to an abandoned three-story warehouse about a mile from the club.

Vaz pointed to a gate in an eight-foot-tall chain-link fence. "Pull in here."

Wynn turned in, his headlights splashing over Marcus, who emerged from the shadows to open the gate. Wynn drove through, then followed Vaz's directions down the side of the building and around the corner.

"Kill the lights," Vaz said, then nodded toward an open garage door. "In there."

Wynn pulled into the warehouse, the night becoming even darker inside. Ambient light leaked in through the open door, allowing Wynn to make out a dark SUV parked inside.

"Park next to it," Vaz said.

Wynn eased up next to the SUV, which he could now see was one of Kovacs' Lincolns. He stopped and got out, then was immediately hit in the face with the beam from a flashlight.

"What's he doing here?" Andre asked.

"He'll help Marcus at the gate," Vaz replied. "You got the radios?"

The flashlight's beam swung away as Andre reached into the Lincoln and took out a pair of two-way radio headsets, identical to the ones they'd used at the speedway. He handed one to Vaz, the other to Wynn.

"You'll be manning the gate," Vaz said as he fit the earpiece. "Marcus will cover you. Only let one car in at a time. I'll give you a password for each car. When they repeat it, let 'em in. If they can't... that's why Marcus is here."

Great. They'll shoot me first. "How many cars are we expecting?"

"Six. Five minutes each. In and out in thirty."

Thirty more for Chad.

Wynn inserted the earpiece and ran the wire inside his shirt, then plugged it in and fastened the radio to his belt. He tested the comm to make sure they could hear each other, then grabbed the Sig out of the truck and checked the magazine. Full, minus the one shot he took at Chad. He reinserted it and stuffed the Sig in the back of his jeans.

"Anything else?" Wynn asked.

Vaz shook his head. "First car should be here in five minutes."

Wynn jogged around the side of the building, the urge to check his phone for Chad's AirTag growing with each step. Thirty yards ahead, Marcus leaned against a small shed inside the fence.

Can't stop. He'll see if I pull out my phone. Wynn hustled along until he reached the gate. Marcus handed him a key and nodded to a padlock securing a chain to the entrance.

"Let 'em in one at a time," Marcus said. "Re-lock the gate after they come in, and when they go out."

"Wouldn't it be faster if they all came in at once?"

"Faster. Not safer."

"Why not? Less time for the cops to catch us."

"Cops aren't the only ones we need to watch out for."

Wynn nodded.

Marcus motioned toward the gate. "You're on the outside. I'll be covering you from here. If something happens, get your ass down. That's the safest place."

Wynn walked over to the gate and opened the padlock, then slipped through. As he relocked the gate, Vaz's voice came over the earpiece. "Wynn, you there?"

"Copy that."

"The first one should be showing up any second. A black Cadillac SUV with three guys. The password is blackjack. Have 'em pop the tailgate and take a look."

Wynn felt silly asking for passwords like some cartoon spy, but he could see the logic in the system. No one was going to sneak in, the exchange was controlled, and the dealers remained separated. They could fight their turf wars on their own time.

But each minute allows Chad to get further away.

Thankfully, the first five cars came and went without incident. On time. Like clockwork. It was only when the driver of the sixth car, an Acura SUV, rolled down his heavily tinted window, that Wynn got a bad feeling.

It was Eddie, the dealer who had sucker-punched Wynn at the club.

"Well now, if it isn't our little hero," Eddie said. "You cost me sales the other night."

"I'm sure you did fine."

"I did. No thanks to you. What's your name, hero?"

"Not important," Wynn said. "If you've done this before you know there's only one thing I want to hear."

Eddie stroked his pencil-thin mustache, then tapped his phone and put it to his ear. "The new guy. What's his name?"

He listened a few seconds then lowered the phone. "Sean Wynn. Is that what you want to hear?"

"Not even close."

Eddie smirked. "Yeah. But now I know."

Wynn didn't move.

"Fine," Eddie said. "Roulette."

Wynn remained still.

"What? That's your fucking password. Open the gate."

"I thought since we were getting to know each other, you might want to introduce yourself."

Eddie paused, the smirk on his face evaporating, replaced by a cold glare. "I'm Eddie. You don't want to know me."

"Finally, one thing we agree on." Wynn slid around the front of the car and opened the gate.

The Acura rolled through; Wynn closed the gate behind it. He strolled over to Marcus, who stood smoking a cigarette near the corner of the small building. "Is that guy always an asshole?"

"Eddie? Yeah. Pretty much."

"How often do we do this?"

"Twice a week."

"They move that much?"

"It ain't called sin city for nothing."

Wynn paused. "What about the girls?"

Marcus inhaled a long draw on his cigarette. His face glowed. "You ask too many questions, Wynn. Not good for your health. Keep your head down, do what you're told, and draw your paycheck. That's the key to longevity around here."

Wynn felt a tug on his conscience. As well as the girls seemed to be doing at the Deuce last night, and as excited as these six seemed to be earlier, he had experience with sex-traffickers. It wasn't good. He had a hard time believing these girls were going to like how their journey ended.

But that wasn't his problem. So said his head, anyway. He nodded. "Got it. Thanks."

A pair of headlights appeared from around the corner of the warehouse. Wynn jogged to the gate, unlocked it, and held it open. Eddie slowed, glaring at him as he eased the Acura through and disappeared down the street.

A moment later the cargo truck and the Lincoln appeared around the far corner. Andre stopped the truck long enough for Marcus to jump in, then eased out of the lot, took a right, and drove away. Wynn hadn't seen the girls in any of the cars as they left, so he assumed they were still in the truck.

Vaz buzzed down the window of the Lincoln as he eased to a stop beside Wynn. "Be at Kovacs' place by six-thirty tonight."

Wynn nodded. "How about a ride back to the club?"

"It's only a mile." Vaz pointed up the road. "Get hoofing."

The window buzzed up as Vaz pulled away, the Lincoln's taillights fading in the morning gray.

Asshole. Wynn turned and broke into a fast jog. He had to get back and call Ruiz.

————————

Vaz glanced in his rearview mirror and watched Wynn break into a jog the other direction. Satisfied, he made a left around the corner and pulled to a stop beside Eddie's Acura, which was waiting at the curb. Vaz buzzed down the passenger window.

"What's the deal with that guy?" Eddie asked through the open windows.

Vaz shrugged. "One of Kovacs' old Marine buddies."

"You've told me that," Eddie said. "Is he a player?"

"No, but he could still be trouble."

"How?"

"He's part of Kovacs' past," Vaz said.

Eddie paused as he thought about it. "You think he's a plant?"

"He's trouble either way. We don't need Kovacs listening to anyone but me."

"Kovacs trusts him?"

Vaz shrugged. "Kovacs is like your uncle. They don't trust anyone, but they'll *use* anyone. He seems to think Wynn can help."

"My uncle's a Cabrón," Eddie said.

Vaz laughed. "Like I said."

Eddie laughed too, then paused and turned somber. "So, Chad's gone?"

"Yeah."

"Too bad. I liked him. We could've used him."

"Agreed," Vaz said. "But when things turned to shit at the speedway, he was the only logical scapegoat. Otherwise, Kovacs might've started looking at me."

"Can't have that."

"No shit."

"So what's plan B? When are we gonna take these guys out? I ain't gonna suck up to Kovacs and Uncle Ruben forever."

Vaz glanced over his shoulder. Made sure no one was around. "Gotta let things calm down. Been a lot of killing in the last week. Even for us. Maybe Murano will strike back on his own."

Eddie shook his head, huffing in frustration. "Can't wait for someone else. *We* need to make this happen."

"That's where you're wrong. If we keep stirring the pot, something will break loose. Hell, if we keep feeding Kovacs these bullshit names, he'll take out his own power base without even knowing it. We just need to be patient."

"What about Uncle Ruben?" Eddie said the last two words with mocking contempt.

"Patience, man. Let the opportunity come to us."

CHAPTER 28

TENDRILS OF DIM LIGHT shot up from the horizon, melting the dark sky overhead. Normally, Wynn would pause to appreciate the dawn, but at this moment, his only thought was on Chad.

He was about halfway back to the club, far enough from the warehouse to risk it, when he pulled out his phone and called up the tracker app.

The AirTag was sitting outside a Subway sandwich shop in Wickenburg.

Shit.

Wynn sprinted the half mile back to his bike, now sitting alone in the Pink parking lot. The engine's deep rumble shattered the early morning silence as he hit the ignition, then dropped it into gear and sped back to the All-Nighter.

It'd been a risk—a big one—not killing Chad. The fact that the AirTag was now in Wickenburg told him Chad had at least gotten that far. If he had dumped it there or still had it on him was unknown. Wynn could only hope the guy was dumb enough not to check his pockets, and smart enough to stay out of sight until Ruiz could take him into custody.

Ten minutes later, Wynn was on the line with a very worried and slightly confused Ruiz.

"Where are you?" Ruiz asked.

"In my room. In Vegas."

"Okay. I see one of your tags there, but the other is in Arizona."

"That's why I'm calling. I had to leave it with someone."

"Who?"

Wynn explained what happened, and his hope that Chad could tell them something about Terrance.

Ruiz immediately understood. "The tag was offline most of the night. Came back on about ninety minutes ago. Been sitting still for the last half-hour."

"You need to get someone out there and pick him up, ASAP," Wynn said. "If Kovacs finds out he's alive, my ass is toast."

"Got it. Hang on a moment."

Wynn waited while Ruiz put people in motion to nab Chad. When that was done, Ruiz came back on the line. "So, what were you doing there?"

"Kovacs called it a supply run. After getting rid of Chad, we brought back a half-dozen girls and a truckload of what I assume was cocaine, considering we got it from Carmen Delgado."

"Whoa, back up. I think I missed a few steps. Who's Carmen Delgado?"

Wynn explained what he'd learned from Jenna about Delgado being one of Garcia's top generals and connected the dots for him.

"So, beyond the murder you witnessed two days ago, you've got evidence of both drugs and trafficking?" Ruiz asked.

"At this point I can't confirm either. I've got no proof. As for the girls, I'd lean more towards smuggling. They seemed excited about what was going on."

"They weren't afraid?"

"Not from what I could tell."

The conversation lulled for a moment as they both considered what that could mean. Finally, Wynn asked, "Got anything more on Vaz or Eddie?"

"Only the minor busts I told you about yesterday."

"What about Murano?"

"He's a more interesting story," Ruiz said. "Started as a grunt for Garcia, but was good enough and loyal enough that he rose through the ranks. He was placed in his current position by Garcia himself. Word on the street is he wants all the U.S. distribution."

"Which would explain the feud," Wynn said.

"Agreed."

"Any chance you can pick him up and hold him a while?" Wynn asked. "At least until I get out of here?"

"Not yet. We'll keep on it, though."

"Yeah, do that. While you're at it, get me some info on Garcia and Delgado. If they are holding Terrance, I'd like to know what I'm dealing with here."

"I'll see what I can find," Ruiz said, "but the word is Garcia's a ghost. Very seldom seen in public. Never heard of Delgado, so she might be the same, but I'll see what I can find. Anything else?"

"When can I talk to Krista?"

Ruiz sighed. "We're working on it."

———

Chad sat in a booth inside a McDonalds, directly across the street from the Subway where he'd hidden the AirTag. His first instinct when he'd found it was to ditch the damn thing, but he had too many questions. Someone had pointed the finger at him. Falsely. But who? And why? *And why didn't Wynn kill me? Why tell me to disappear and then put an AirTag in my pocket?*

He'd had a long time to think about it as he trekked through the desert toward Wickenburg. He'd come to two definitive conclusions. Someone—likely Kovacs or Vaz—wanted him dead. And someone else—Wynn?—wanted him alive. Leaving him stuck smack in the middle.

Purgatory, right here on earth.

Shortly after dawn, he bummed a ride and five bucks from a rancher on his way into town. He made up a story about his car breaking down and forgetting his phone and wallet. When the rancher asked how he got the bloody knock on his head, he admitted to wrecking his car and hitting his head on the steering wheel. The rancher looked dubious but helped him out, anyway.

Now it was almost nine a.m., and he was getting hungry again. *Should've bummed twenty bucks from the guy.* Chad was nursing his fourth cup of free-refill coffee, still sitting in the booth that gave him an unobstructed view of the trash can outside the Subway.

He hoped that if the AirTag was stationary long enough, someone might come to check on it. Hopefully, it would be Wynn. Then he could ask him what the hell was going on. But maybe it would be one of Kovacs' other guys. Maybe even one of Murano's guys. Truthfully, he didn't know what to expect.

What he wasn't expecting was the Wickenburg police car making its third pass in the last half-hour.

And he sure as hell wasn't expecting it to stop. Or for a cop to get out and use his phone like some kind of electronic divining rod, and walk right up to the trash can, push it out of the way, crouch down, and pick up the AirTag.

Chad turned away and lifted the cup to his lips, taking a long drink as the officer scanned the area.

Wynn put an AirTag on me and the cops show up. Can mean only one thing. He looked around for someone with a phone he could borrow. *I gotta get back to Vegas.*

———

Wynn slept fitfully until mid-afternoon. The long nights were creating havoc with his circadian rhythm. He dug into the box spring for the burner and called Ruiz. "Did they pick up Chad?"

"Bad news. He ditched the AirTag. Cops kept an eye on the area, but they missed him. He's gone."

Shit. Wynn's earlier excitement disappeared like a breath in the wind.

"Talk me through it," Ruiz continued. "How big a problem is this?"

Wynn paused, thinking it through. "All he knows for sure is that I didn't kill him. He'll assume I put the tracker on him instead. He doesn't know if I did any of that on my own or if it was on Kovacs' orders."

"If he thinks you did it on your own," Ruiz said, "you'd think he'd feel pretty grateful."

"That doesn't mean he won't haul ass back to Murano," Wynn said. "Especially if he is a spy."

Ruiz hesitated. "Maybe it does. Someone in Murano's camp ratted him out to Kovacs. If he's got any brains at all, he's going to keep a low profile until he knows who that is. Hell, if he's smart, he'll disappear permanently."

Wynn stayed silent. In the brief time he'd known him, Chad didn't appear to be that smart.

Ruiz broke the silence. "It's your call. If you want to cut this thing off and get out, no one will blame you."

"You got any other leads on Terrance?"

"Honestly, no."

Wynn sighed. It was like leaving a man behind. No way he'd ever do it. "I'll stay. It's not even been a full week and Kovacs is starting to trust me. He's asked me to help provide security for a party he's having tonight. Let's play this out a little more and see what happens."

"You sure?"

"For now."

"All right," Ruiz said. "In the meantime, take that other tag off the bike and keep it on you."

"Will do," Wynn said. "Any info on Garcia or Delgado?"

"Nothing more than we already know. The DEA isn't being overly cooperative."

Wynn's voice took on a note of agitation. "Why the hell not? They do realize you've got someone undercover here, right?"

"They know. Don't worry, I'll get you something soon."

"Make sure you do."

CHAPTER 29

At six-fifteen that evening, Wynn rumbled his Road Glide into the gated driveway in front of Kovacs' house, the SIG he'd gotten from Vaz in a holster under his shirt; the knife, as always, strapped to his ankle. The gate hung open with two men he assumed were bouncers from the Deuce standing watch. He flipped up his visor to reveal his face and was waved up the drive.

With the sun still an hour from setting, Wynn got a good look at what Kovacs called home. The front yard was roughly an acre in size, not huge by wealthy crime boss standards, but manicured and spotless. Xeriscaped flower beds designed for the Vegas heat flanked the driveway and bordered the property, leaving small patches of grass with towering palm trees in the middle.

The two-lane driveway stretched a hundred and fifty feet from the gate, where it circled a large fountain in front of a sprawling two-story, white stucco home. Several cars, including Deborah's white Cadillac, sat parked near a six-car garage to the left. Wynn eased his bike next to the Caddy.

"Oh, good," a voice dripping with sarcasm said when he shut down the engine and removed his helmet. "Sean's here. We can get started now." Deborah leaned against the garage; her arms crossed with a cigarette held next to her lips. "Do you really enjoy riding that thing or just like how loud it is when you make an entrance?"

Wynn shrugged. "Why don't you come with me sometime and find out?"

Deborah flashed her eyebrows and pushed off the wall, then dropped the cigarette and snuffed it out with her toe. "C'mon."

She led him around the side of the house and into the backyard. He paused a moment to take it all in.

The yard itself was three acres, surrounded by an eight-foot stucco privacy wall. A concrete pool deck with built-in planters and seating areas occupied about a third of the space directly behind the house, beyond which an immaculate lawn was dotted with more palm trees. White columns held up a spectacular pergola next to the house.

An army of men and women in white jackets were setting up round tables with large white umbrellas out in the yard, while smaller tables and chairs surrounded a crystalline blue pool.

A runway and square platform stage had been erected inside the pool, extending a foot above the waterline. Stage lights hung from a network of twelve-foot-tall trusses that lined the water's edge.

Next to a pair of glass doors that led into the house, Vaz spoke to a group of more than a dozen guys, each wearing an identical dark suit.

Wynn leaned toward Deborah and whispered, "Am I late?"

"No. Go listen in. He'll get to you when he's ready."

"I didn't realize there was a dress code."

"We'll take care of that when you're done. Go."

Wynn ambled over to the outskirts of the group, still taking in the scene and only half listening as Vaz talked about working in pairs, communication protocols, and watch rotations.

"Wynn!" Vaz's voice brought his attention back. "I take it you've done security before?"

"Yes, sir."

"Good. You'll partner with Marcus. Just do what he says."

Then to everyone, Vaz asked, "Any questions?"

When none came, he dismissed the group and Marcus approached. "First things first. Go with Deborah and get outfitted. I'll come find you after I talk with Vaz."

Deborah appeared at Wynn's side. "C'mon, biker boy." She led him to the far end of the pool and into a guest suite at the opposite end of the house. Racks of beachwear and women's swimsuits lined the walls. Nearly twenty young women sat in front of mirrors applying makeup or trying on various swimsuits. Four of the girls he'd picked up on the supply run last night huddled around a rack of clothes, chattering excitedly.

Something in Wynn's gut knotted. "What kind of a party is this?" he asked.

With a sweep of her hand, Deborah said, "Welcome to the world of high fashion."

"This is a fashion show?" Wynn couldn't help the note of incredulity that snuck into his voice.

"It actually makes more sense than you would think," Deborah said. "Up-and-coming designers need to showcase their work, and we've got lots of young women who would love to become models. Mr. Kovacs has tons of great connections. Put those three elements together and, boom, fashion show."

Deborah led him through the suite to a large bedroom now converted into a dressing room. Blue jeans and t-shirts hung inside doorless lockers along two walls, while racks full of white shirts, dark slacks, and blazers lined the other two walls. A waist-high cabinet filled with shelves of dress shoes sat in the middle of the room, with a basket of clean socks and belts on top. A second doorway led to a room beyond.

"Pick an empty locker, then find your sizes and get dressed. Marcus will set you up from there." She nodded to the far door, then turned and left.

Curious, Wynn stepped into the second room and stopped, raising his eyebrows.

The room was an arsenal. Racks holding pistols, rifles, and semi-automatics covered the walls. Glass-fronted cabinets containing more pistols, ammunition, clips, and extra magazines created rows through the middle of the room.

He could outfit an army with all this.

Slowly strolling down one row, he found a cabinet with electronic surveillance gear, radios, video cameras, and microphones. Another held knives and brass knuckles. Further along, he stopped abruptly.

Tools.

Hammers, pliers, and shears. Black and yellow. Stanley.

Exactly the kind of stuff used on Terrance. But there's no way Kovacs would be stupid enough to keep him here, unless...

A voice startled him from the doorway. "What makes you so special?" Marcus said.

Wynn's spider-sense jumped. Marcus' tone and demeanor were calm, but the question felt hostile. "In what sense?"

"Most new guys get stuck at the front gate all night, but you get to be a rover. Not that I'm complaining. Vaz told me to stick with you, show you around, answer your questions. But other than that, let you do your thing."

Wynn paused. "My guess is Kovacs wants to see if I still know how to do security."

"I guess we'll find out." Marcus glanced around the room. "See anything you like?"

Wynn moved away from the tools. "Lots."

Marcus smiled. "Well alright, then, Mr. *Marine.* Get dressed and let me know what you need."

Ten minutes later, Wynn was dressed like all the other security guys. He found an extra magazine for the SIG in the armory room, then had Marcus set him up with an earpiece and radio so he could hear the rest of the team.

Next was a tour of the property. Wynn couldn't believe Kovacs would keep Terrance at his home, but the place was big enough. *A secret room maybe?* He hoped for a chance to search.

They made their way through a gauntlet of half-naked women in the guest suite and out to the concrete patio surrounding the pool. They stepped out of the way as workers finished assembling pipe and draping around the entrance to the suite.

As they made their way around the expansive property, Marcus filled him in on the logistics of the evening; how many guests were expected, when they would arrive, the dining and entertainment schedule, and when the party was expected to wind down. Wynn also inquired about the security plan.

Essentially, six pairs of guards would rotate through five fixed and one "floating" station every twenty minutes. The fixed stations included the front gate, the front door, and three positions in the backyard, including a pair of four-foot platforms along the back fence that allowed the guards to see over the privacy wall.

Dusk had fallen by the time they finished the tour and were back beside the pool.

"What about electronic surveillance?" Wynn asked.

"Mr. Kovacs isn't big on cameras. He's got one at the front gate and another overlooking the driveway, but those are more for convenience than security. He likes his privacy."

"What about inside the house?" Wynn asked.

"What about it?"

"Is there a safe room, or a bunker, or basement?"

"Not that I'm aware of. You can ask Vaz."

"You don't know?"

Marcus shrugged. "Like I said, Mr. Kovacs likes his privacy. Nobody goes inside except Vaz."

CHAPTER 30

WYNN AND MARCUS LINGERED on the patio, outside a wall of floor-to-ceiling plate-glass windows. Kovacs was visible inside, pouring himself a drink at a large granite island in the kitchen. He motioned Wynn inside.

"Invited in," Wynn said to Marcus. "Must be our lucky day."

"You go," Marcus said. "I'll wait here."

Wynn shrugged, then stepped through the sliders and closed the door behind him, shutting out the noise from outside.

"What do you think?" Kovacs asked.

"Impressive. I had no idea you were into fashion."

Kovacs smirked as he took a sip. "I'm not. I'm into money. But you'd be surprised how much these idiots pay for a couple pieces of fabric. I get forty percent of everything sold."

"Nice."

"What do you think of our security?"

"Only thing you're missing is a couple of long guns either on the second floor or roof covering the front and back. Happy to check that out if you want." *Would give me a chance to look around.*

Kovacs nodded as he considered it.

"That and a safe room," Wynn said.

Kovacs laughed. "You've been watching too many movies."

Wynn shrugged. "This is a lot of security for a fashion show. Are you expecting trouble?"

"Not really, but you know the motto..."

"Yeah."

A smart speaker chimed from somewhere in the room, followed by a male voice. "First guests arriving now, sir."

Kovacs drained his glass and refilled it. "And it begins. Talk to Vaz if you need anything, but otherwise, just keep your eyes open."

Within an hour, the party was in full swing with more than two hundred guests. Vaz barked orders over the radio while white-jacketed wait staff hurried from table to table serving drinks and hors d'oeuvres. Small clusters of men and women dressed in tuxedos and evening gowns, elegant in the soft light of bamboo tiki torches, mingled by the pool and throughout the yard.

Having never attended a fashion show, Wynn was surprised by the guest diversity. Men and women, young and old, of almost every race, ethnicity, and nationality, circulated throughout the yard. Besides an apparent interest in fashion, the only thing they appeared to have in common was that they all brought their own bodyguards.

"Is that normal?" Wynn asked Marcus, referring to the bodyguards.

"For this crowd it is."

"You've seen these folks before?"

Marcus scanned the yard. "A lot of 'em frequent the Deuce. Maybe a third are new."

"Are they carrying?"

"They're not supposed to, but I'm sure most probably are."

Wynn paused, allowing his gaze to linger on each guest and their bodyguards for a moment, attempting to commit each one to memory before moving on to the next.

Across the pool, Carmen Delgado sat on a cushioned sofa beside a fire pit. She wore a black dress with a sheer silver shawl draped over her shoulders, and dangling diamond earrings that glittered in the firelight.

Leaning casually back into the sofa, she was in a deep conversation with a man whose back was to Wynn. Two bodyguards stood nearby.

"How about Ms. Delgado?" Wynn asked. "Has she been here before?"

"Yeah. She's a regular."

"Who's that with her?"

"You don't recognize Nadeem?"

It took Wynn a moment to remember. *The guy who prompted the fight in the club the other night. The one Jenna called a stalker.* "What's his story? I hear he's loaded."

Marcus smirked. "And then some. His daddy's a Saudi oil baron. The guy's got more money than half these people put together."

Wynn paused as a couple of waiters came by ringing chimes, indicating the show was about to begin. Delgado got up and made her way to a table at the edge of the pool.

"Let's split up during the show," Wynn said. *Maybe I can find a moment to slip inside and look around.* "Better coverage. You stay here and I'll go to the other side."

As Wynn made his way around, the stage lighting, which had been dim, gradually intensified until the runway and stage were brightly lit. Kovacs strode down the runway and onto the platform in the middle of the pool. His voice boomed from the speakers.

"Good evening and welcome, everyone. Thank you all for coming. We've got an exciting evening planned tonight to share the latest inspiration from three of the industry's hottest young designers."

Kovacs paused as the audience gave a polite round of applause.

"If you haven't been with us before, I'll draw your attention to the television monitor above the curtain at the start of the runway.

A number will appear on that monitor for each design as it comes onto the stage. If you see something you like, text the number of the design to the second number on the screen and you'll be entered into the bidding. It's that simple. And with that, let the show begin!"

The lights snapped out, plunging the area into darkness as technopop dance music blasted from the speakers. After a few moments, the lights burst back on as the curtains at the end of the runway flew open and Lola, the dancer from the Deuce who had run into Wynn last night, came strutting down the runway in a little-red-riding-hood cape over a teeny red bikini.

The crowd gasped and broke into applause. Wynn glanced at the monitor, noticing the two numbers on the screen. Movement to his right drew his attention away. He scanned the audience, his gaze settling on Carmen Delgado across the pool.

She was looking at him.

They locked eyes for a moment, then Wynn nodded, and Delgado looked away. Wynn made note of her two bodyguards, then continued his scan around the pool.

For the next forty-five minutes, Wynn circled the perimeter as over thirty young women, including the six that he and Vaz had brought up from Wickenburg last night, continuously paraded down the runway, alternating between swimwear, evening wear, and outfits that Wynn could only describe as barely there.

At one point, Wynn found himself standing behind Nadeem, seated at a small table. To Wynn's surprise, even Nadeem seemed interested in certain pieces as he checked the monitors and worked his phone.

When the show ended, the models strode out in single file and lined the runway, while the three designers, two women and a man, took their bows from the stage.

Once again Kovacs' voice came over the loudspeakers. "Give it up for our wonderful designers!"

The crowd applauded politely.

"Now, as you all know, is the time to get down to business. If you'd like to speak to any of our designers or models, they'll be circulating for the next hour while we finalize the bids. We hope you saw something you like, and thank you for coming."

The stage lights dimmed to a comfortable level as the soft, lilting notes of a classical piano replaced the technopop. The wait staff re-appeared, carrying trays of food and drink, as the guests dispersed to mingle throughout the yard.

Chatter over the radio headset, which had been limited during the show, picked up as the guards rotated positions and confirmed their check-ins. All seemed to be going smoothly until an unrecognized voice came over the radio. "Hey Vaz, it's Hugo. I've got someone down near platform two."

"Who is it?" Vaz responded.

"Don't know. Looks like a bodyguard. He's breathing but unconscious."

"Marcus, are you close? Can you check it out?"

"I'm on it," Marcus replied.

Wynn looked across the pool to see Marcus move away from the house and disappear into the dimly lit yard. Platform two was toward the south end of the property, furthest away from the pool.

Vaz's voice came again. "Everyone stay alert 'til we know more."

Wynn scanned the crowd, checking off each guest as he ran through his mental list.

A minute later, Marcus came over the radio. "Vaz, it's Eduardo, one of Ms. Delgado's guys. Looks like he took a hit to the back of the head. Breathing shallow and bleeding."

"Anyone got eyes on Delgado?" Vaz asked.

Wynn pivoted sharply. He'd seen her get up from the table next to the pool, but others now occupied the couches where she had been sitting before the show.

"She likes to talk to the models in the dressing room after the shows," Marcus said.

Wynn triggered his microphone. "I'm close. On my way."

He hurried toward the guest suite where he'd seen the girls prepping before the show, now hidden by the black curtains at the beginning of the runway. Flinging back the drapes, he was about to rush into the suite when a glint of light reflecting off the concrete caught his eye. It turned dark as he approached, with more spots leading away around the side of the house.

"Vaz, it's Wynn. I've got a blood trail behind the guest suite."

He turned the corner. A male body lay against the side of the building, blood still oozing from a puncture wound to the neck.

"And a body," Wynn said.

A soft scraping sound came from around the corner ahead. Wynn drew the SIG and rushed forward, pausing at the corner to look around.

Darkness engulfed the empty space between the rear of the guest suite and the eight-foot privacy wall twenty feet away. Ambient city light created a faint glow above the wall.

A dark, humped shape extended above the top of the wall, accompanied by the sound of men exhaling, as if lifting something heavy. Wynn took aim as the shape of a man's silhouette, just like the targets in the desert, materialized above the wall.

"Drop it!" Wynn yelled.

The silhouette didn't move, but the sound of guns being drawn cut through the darkness.

Wynn pulled the trigger, the SIG flashing in his hands as the silhouette's head jerked backward and fell out of sight behind the wall. Wynn dropped to the ground and rolled into the grass as whatever the men had been lifting fell heavily to the ground.

Like lightning, bright flashes of gunfire erupted below the wall, sending stucco flying from the corner Wynn had just vacated.

Through the flashes, Wynn saw two men firing back at him, separated by a dark shape on the ground.

Wynn focused on the closer of the two men and squeezed the trigger, then quickly aimed the gun toward the second man and fired twice more. Unable to see the results of his shots, he rolled again, back toward the building, until he was hidden behind the corner.

He held his breath, listening intently. The only sound was a high-pitched whimpering.

"Wynn! What the hell's happening?" Vaz screamed through the earpiece.

Wynn reached up and pulled the headset away, straining to hear any clue if the men were still alive.

After fifteen seconds, the whimpering stopped. No other sounds came from around the corner. Quiet footsteps approached from behind. Wynn put the earpiece back in and triggered the mic.

"I'm on the ground near the back corner. Don't fucking shoot me," he hissed. "We need some light back here."

"What's the situation?" Vaz asked.

"Unknown. I think three hostiles. Two on this side of the wall, one on the other. All potentially hit, but status unknown."

"What about Delgado?"

"Unknown. We need some light."

"Hang tight."

Wynn listened as Vaz positioned guards on either side of the privacy wall, approaching from both the front and back yards.

"I see your light," Wynn said as a flashlight peeked around the corner behind him.

Marcus and another man approached from behind. "You alright?" Marcus asked.

"Yeah, I'm good."

Wynn listened over the earpiece as the other guards arrived. The two on the other side of the wall spoke first. "We got one guy and an SUV out here. The dude's dead."

"You're sure?" Vaz asked.

"Oh yeah. Headshot. I'm sure."

"Can you climb up and shine your lights down the other side?" Marcus asked. "We need to see what we're dealing with here."

As multiple flashlights lit up the scene, Wynn peeked out from behind the corner.

Carmen Delgado lie in the grass, her hands zip-tied behind her back and black duct tape over her mouth, but no visible injuries. Two other men lay sprawled in the grass beside her. Bubbles rose from a gaping wound in the first man's chest, while the second lay completely still.

Wynn got up and approached as Marcus picked up the dead men's guns and moved them away. Wynn knelt in front of Delgado and eased the tape from her mouth. He used the knife from his ankle sheath to free her wrists.

"Are you hurt?" Wynn asked.

"Nothing serious," Delgado replied. "But I've had better days."

CHAPTER 31

Wynn leaned against the granite countertop in Kovacs' kitchen, as Deborah doted on Carmen Delgado in what was technically the living room. In reality, it was all one big open floorplan. Now that her two bodyguards were either dead or incapacitated, Delgado had insisted that Wynn stay with her until her new security team arrived.

When Vaz and his men had secured the scene behind the guest suite, Deborah had taken Delgado inside the main house and helped her clean up. The black dress she wore at the party was replaced by blue jeans and a white, form-fitting t-shirt. A jacket was draped over her shoulders, leaving her arms free. Gauze bandages wrapped around both elbows, which had been scraped when she'd been dropped down the back wall.

The party had wound down after the incident, although not as quickly as Wynn would have imagined. Several of the guests stayed to finish their business once Kovacs assured them the police would not be called.

"Can I get you anything?" Deborah asked of Delgado.

"A cup of coffee, decaf, would be great."

Deborah was about to repeat the request to Wynn, when Delgado continued, "And while you get that, I'd like a word with Mr. Wynn."

Deborah shot a warning glance at Wynn as they passed each other; Deborah on her way to the kitchen, Wynn to a spot on the couch next to Delgado.

"How are you feeling?" Wynn asked as he sat.

"I'm good, thanks to you." Delgado's eyebrow arched as she looked him over appraisingly. "It seems you have a thing for damsels in distress."

Wynn's forehead creased; he shook his head slightly.

"The other night, at the club, when Nadeem's guys got rough with that dancer? You rushed in while Vaz and his boys sat on their asses."

He'd almost forgotten Delgado was there. "They had it under control. But I'm new. I didn't realize."

Delgado nodded slowly, a flicker of skepticism briefly crossing her face. "Sure they did." She was about to say something more when the glass door slid open, and Kovacs and Vaz stepped through. An annoyed look flashed across Delgado's face.

Kovacs paused as he took in the scene, then quickly strode over. "Carmen, how are you?"

Taking that as his cue to retreat, Wynn got up and silently moved back to the kitchen. Kovacs took his place on the couch.

"I'm good, thanks to Mr. Wynn."

Kovacs glanced at Wynn. "Yeah, Sean's been a hell of a find. We're lucky to have him."

"I should say so. Mr. Garcia would not be pleased if something happened to me."

"Understandably. But you can tell Mr. Garcia we have things well under control," Kovacs said, his voice smooth.

Delgado paused. "Uh-huh. Who were those men?"

"They were Murano's guys."

"Murano?" Disbelief etched her features. She shook her head. "He wouldn't dare."

Kovacs stood as Deborah approached and handed Delgado a cup of coffee. "I'm afraid he would. He's been pissed ever since Mr. Garcia allowed me to take over my father's territory. We had a little run-in with him the other night."

"What happened?"

"He bought a couple of my guys. He was maneuvering to take me out. We struck first."

"You must have missed."

Kovacs didn't respond.

"So, what?" Delgado said. "He tried to kidnap me in an attempt to show Mr. Garcia that he's better than you?"

"Something like that," Kovacs said. "It was a high-risk move. He must be getting desperate."

"But thanks to Mr. Wynn, he failed."

Kovacs nodded.

Delgado paused. "From now on, when I come to town, I want Mr. Wynn on my security detail. That includes accompanying me back to Mexico tomorrow."

CHAPTER 32

WYNN SPENT THE NIGHT on Kovacs' couch, then showered and changed back into his own clothes inside the guest suite the next morning. When he came out, Vaz and Deborah were seated by the pool. One of Kovacs' house staff was serving bacon, eggs, and coffee. It smelled great.

The woman stood back, apparently waiting to see if Wynn would join them. When he pulled out a chair, she rushed forward.

"Can I get you something, sir?"

"Coffee." Wynn pointed at Vaz's plate. "And twice what he's having."

She brought the coffee and then disappeared inside.

Wynn took a sip and sat back. "Has Delgado's new security team arrived yet?"

"This morning," Deborah replied.

"Does she still want me to go with her?"

"As far as I know."

Vaz remained silent. Wynn could feel the anger radiating off him. He didn't need another altercation with the big man.

"Hey, Vaz. You want to go instead? Fine with me. I can do without another fifteen-hours in the desert."

Carmen Delgado's voice came from over his shoulder. "I'm sorry to hear that. Although you might change your mind when we're all done."

Wynn's face flushed as Delgado and Kovacs pulled out chairs and sat down. The woman returned and poured coffee, then set full plates in front of each of them.

"I'm sorry," Wynn said. "I didn't mean—"

Delgado cut him off. "Not to worry, Mr. Wynn. I don't like long road trips either. That's why I don't travel like everyone else. From what I hear, neither do you."

Wynn nodded, saved from having to respond as Kovacs spoke up. "Carmen, I wish you'd reconsider, and let Vaz go with you, too. Wynn's good, but I'd feel better knowing you had two of my best."

She looked at Kovacs coolly. "Has something changed since last night?"

"No."

"Then why are you bringing up something that was already settled?"

Kovacs glanced at Wynn. "If you're sure."

"I am."

Delgado and Deborah made small talk as they finished breakfast. When they were done, Delgado got up and said to Wynn, "Meet me out front in ten minutes. Leave your phone. You won't need it."

When she was gone, Kovacs looked at Wynn. "Don't get any ideas. The only thing you two have in common is that you both like women."

Wynn nodded. He handed his phone to Deborah.

"Seriously," Kovacs continued. "Be polite, but keep your mouth shut. Don't volunteer anything. Do whatever she tells you and then get your ass back here ASAP. Don't fuck this up."

————

Vaz watched, still seething, as Wynn hustled away. Deborah excused herself too, leaving Kovacs and Vaz alone at the table.

"You think she'll take him across?" Kovacs asked.

"No idea," Vaz said. "If she does, there's a good chance he'll see your guest."

"I've been thinking about that," Kovacs said slowly. "You've been worried about the timing, that maybe that's why he's here? Maybe we should show him. Maybe that would be exactly the test we need."

Vaz listened, his expression turning grim as Kovacs explained what he wanted to do.

"They'll have to work fast," Vaz said.

"Just get it done," Kovacs said.

Vaz got up from the table and strolled into the backyard. When he was out of earshot, he pulled out his phone and tapped a number. Eddie picked up with a single word. "Yeah?"

"You're lucky," Vaz said quietly, not taking any chances. "He bought it. We told Delgado it was Murano's guys."

"Doesn't feel lucky," Eddie said. "Feels like we're down three more."

"Don't tell me you're getting sentimental."

"Fuck 'em. But we have limited guys here, Vaz. We need to get rid of Wynn before he costs us anymore."

"Kovacs might have a way of doing that. At least a way of determining if he's a risk."

"What's that?"

Eddie listened while Vaz relayed Kovacs' instructions. When he finished, Eddie said, "That's sick." He paused. "I love it."

CHAPTER 33

WYNN EASED INTO THE back seat of a long, black stretch limousine along with Carmen Delgado and her new security team. Two guys. Paunchy. They looked tired.

"Do you have your phone?" Delgado asked.

"Left it with Deborah," Wynn replied.

"Good."

Wynn tapped the keys in his pocket, wishing he'd had time to grab the second AirTag off his bike like Ruiz had suggested. Without his phone or the tag, he was completely off the grid.

They rode in silence for the next twenty minutes, taking the 613 east, then north on Decatur Blvd. Wynn hadn't been expecting that, but he was learning to expect the unexpected from Carmen Delgado.

The limo turned into the North Las Vegas Airport, stopped at one security checkpoint, then drove onto the tarmac. The dual jet engines of a waiting Gulfstream G700 were already humming.

A flight attendant opened Delgado's door a few paces from the forward steps. Wynn followed her out of the limo, then stopped when Delgado paused at the base of the stairs. Another limo pulled up next to a private jet forty yards away.

Wynn tracked Delgado's gaze as Nadeem and one of the girls he and Vaz had brought up from Wickenburg two nights ago emerged from the second limo, each with a champagne glass in hand. Nadeem was dressed in black slacks and a white dinner jacket, while the girl wore dark sunglasses and an expensive-looking silver gown that shimmered in the morning sun. They smiled and laughed as they made their way toward the idling plane.

"Wait here," Delgado said. She called out Nadeem's name, then hurried to catch him.

Nadeem turned and saw Delgado, then sent the girl toward the plane while he stopped and waited. Wynn stepped away from the whine of the Gulfstream's engines as Delgado called after the girl, who turned as she reached the jet.

A sharp word from Nadeem froze the girl next to the plane's stairway. Delgado stopped in front of him, their conversation drowned by the Gulfstream. Wynn took another step forward, curious. Whatever the conversation, Nadeem clearly didn't like it. He became animated, waving his arm as if dismissing Delgado, then strode toward his plane.

Undeterred, Delgado followed and said something that made Nadeem stop and respond. He waved for the girl to join him. When she reached them, Nadeem wrapped an arm around her waist and pulled her close. She reciprocated by putting both arms around his shoulders and kissing him on the cheek.

Moments later, Nadeem and the girl turned and walked toward their plane, while Delgado strode back to the Gulfstream.

"What was that all about?" Wynn asked when Delgado got close.

"Don't worry about it."

Wynn followed her up the short stairway, ducking his head as he entered the Gulfstream. Two pilots were running through the pre-flight checklist in the cockpit.

He made his way into the forward cabin, which held four plush leather seats, two facing forward, two facing the rear. Delgado slid into one of the forward-facing seats and motioned Wynn to the chair opposite. The new bodyguards shuffled past them, collapsing into seats further back. Delgado gazed out the window as the plane taxied into position.

Facing backward, the normally familiar thrust of the plane accelerating down the runway felt oddly unfamiliar as it worked to pull Wynn out of his seat on takeoff, rather than push him back into it.

When they had finally leveled off, Wynn asked, "Where are we going?"

"Nogales."

"Arizona? I thought we were going to Mexico."

A slight smile curled Delgado's lip as she held his eye. She then looked down and turned off her phone.

Wynn shrugged to himself. He looked out the window as the desert scrolled by below.

Delgado's voice broke the silence. "I never got a chance to thank you for saving me last night. So, thank you."

"Of course. I'm glad you're okay. How are the arms?"

She held her arms out, twisting them to see her elbows. She'd removed the bandages, revealing angry red scrapes. "They'll be fine."

"That's good," he said, his eyes returning to the window.

"What's your story, Mr. Wynn?"

"Not much to tell. Former Marine. Widower. In trouble with the IRS and needed a job. Called an old friend, and here I am."

She nodded.

"And yours?" Wynn asked.

Delgado paused, then unbuckled her seat belt and stood. "When we get there, I'll have a favor to ask, and I'll need you to trust me."

"What's the favor?"

"When we get there. We land in forty-five minutes." With that, she strolled down the aisle, past the two bodyguards who slept sprawled in their own leather seats, and into the stateroom at the rear of the plane. Wynn watched her go. She turned and glanced up, making brief eye contact before closing the door.

Forty minutes later, as promised, Wynn's stomach rose to his throat as the plane began its initial descent. When the wheels finally touched down, he glanced through the window, a barren landscape of scrub and cacti dotted a small valley surrounded by rolling hills. A half dozen low buildings, including a small terminal and hangar, sat along the northwest side of the lone runway.

The plane taxied for a minute or two, then came to a stop a hundred feet short of the terminal. The engines wound down as the flight attendant opened the cabin door and lowered the stairs, allowing warm air and bright sunshine to billow inside.

The two bodyguards exited first, but Wynn remained seated until Delgado came out of the stateroom. He followed her out the door, across the tarmac, and through the small terminal building to a waiting SUV. It was a beat-up old Nissan, maybe nice when it rolled off the assembly line, but a considerable step down from the black limo they'd taken earlier.

One of the bodyguards jumped in the driver's seat while the other held the front passenger door for Delgado, then slid into the rear. Wynn climbed in behind the driver. As they pulled out of the tiny parking lot, Wynn glanced back and saw the Gulfstream already taxiing to the end of the runway. It turned a hundred eighty degrees, then accelerated down the runway and lifted into the sky.

So much for getting back quickly.

CHAPTER 34

THEY DROVE SOUTHWEST ON a two-lane highway for ten minutes before the road widened and the driver pulled over.

Delgado turned around. "That favor I mentioned?" She held out a blindfold and a black pillowcase. "Put these on."

Wynn's spider-sense erupted. "Hey, if you don't want me to see where we're going, I'll get out right here. I can make my way back to Vegas."

One side of Delgado's mouth ticked up slightly. "I'm sure you can, but there's someone who wants to meet you, and this is for your own good. Trust me, Mr. Wynn, I'll make it worth your while."

Wynn hesitated as he looked her in the eye. After a long moment, she arched an eyebrow and nodded. "For your own good."

With a sigh, Wynn took the blindfold. He could see no reason she'd want to hurt him. *Unless she knows why I'm really here. But there's no way she could know that. Unless Chad...*

He held her gaze. For some reason, he trusted her. *I must be crazy.* He put it on. Light crept in around the edges.

"Turn around."

He turned toward the window, then felt the pillowcase being lowered over his head. What little light had remained, disappeared.

"You'll notice we haven't tied your wrists, nor have I asked for your gun. Yet. That's because I trust you to leave this on until I tell you. Understood?"

"Understood."

"And since we can hardly be seen driving around like this, you'll need to get down on the floor."

With another resigned sigh, he turned his back to the door and wriggled his way into the footwell, extending his legs across the transmission hump into the bodyguard's foot space.

Deal with it, asshole.

"Keep your hands where I can see them, Cabrón," the bodyguard said.

The car accelerated, and they pulled back onto the road, continuing at a steady speed for five minutes before slowing. He could feel the brakes being applied, then the gas, then the brakes again. The sounds of other cars filled the cab. They were obviously somewhere in town, maneuvering through traffic, turning left and right, again and again, sometimes for a few seconds, sometimes longer. Wynn tried to keep track of the turns, but it soon became hopeless.

Eventually, the road turned rough, and the driver accelerated. Small pebbles flew up into the wheel wells creating a vibration Wynn could both feel and hear. His stomach rose and fell as the car sped over undulating hills. His mind raced, battling alternate scenarios. *They're either taking me into the desert to kill me, or someplace they don't want me to see. But if they wanted to kill me, why go through all this? Why not just do it in Vegas? Why would Kovacs have told me to get back quickly? It's got to be someplace they don't want me to see.*

He didn't normally bet with stakes this high, but he put his life on this one.

Within a few minutes, the car slowed and turned sharply, creeped forward several seconds, then rose onto a smooth surface and stopped. The engine died. Metal squealed on metal, the sound ending with a loud bang. *A garage door being closed.*

They waited a few moments, then Delgado said, "You can get up now, Mr. Wynn, but leave the blindfold on."

He lifted himself onto the seat as the door beside him opened. A strong hand grabbed his arm and pulled him out. The place smelled of oil and grease. Their footsteps sounded hollow, not like the space was big, but as if it were built of hard surfaces, concrete and steel.

The big hand let go of his left arm while a smaller hand took hold of his right. "Stand here," Delgado said.

Wynn stood silently, listening as the remaining car doors slammed shut, followed by a motorized humming sound. It was low-pitched and steady, punctuated by ticks and squeaks. Ten, maybe fifteen seconds, then ended with a solid clunk.

Delgado's hand on his arm nudged him forward. "Take a step and sit on the floor."

He did so. The floor felt hard and cool. Concrete. Other bodies moved around him.

"Straighten your legs and scoot forward."

He did so, feeling the floor disappear beneath his feet, an edge of some kind cutting into his calves. A sound of grinding came from his right, like something heavy being slid across the floor. A blast of cool, stale air followed.

"A little more," Delgado said. "There's going to be a small drop, a couple of feet, but it's solid."

The battle in his mind intensified. *Am I jumping into my grave?*

Pushing the thought away, Wynn inched forward until his legs dangled, his rear end and hands on the edge. He felt Delgado move between his legs, placing her hands on his sides.

"Just a short hop. I got you."

Wynn pushed off and dropped, his feet landing solidly on another smooth floor. Delgado's hands stayed on his sides as she turned him ninety degrees.

"Get on your hands and knees."

Wynn stopped. He'd gone along long enough. He reached up and began to pull the pillowcase off his head. Delgado grabbed his arm and held tight.

"Don't do it, Sean." It was the first time she'd used his first name.

He paused. "How about you tell me what we're doing?"

"Only a little further and you can take that thing off, I promise. But if you do it now, we're going to have big problems."

He paused. He'd bet correctly. *Second scenario confirmed. The only problem comes if I see what they don't want me to.*

"Hands and knees," Delgado prompted.

He got down.

"Back up. You'll be getting onto a ladder."

Wynn crawled backward, felt the floor once again disappear beneath his feet. Kept his weight on his left knee while he stretched his right foot down, searching for something solid. He found it, then transferred part of his weight to it.

"There's a handle by your right hip," Delgado said.

Wynn moved his right hand across the floor. The concrete turned to dirt. He found the handle.

"There you go. Just ease on back."

He eased his full weight onto his right foot, brought his left foot down next to it, found the handle with his left hand.

"See you at the bottom," Delgado said.

The air was cool and stale as he descended, the same as he'd caught a whiff of while sitting on the floor moments ago. The rungs were rough metal, and small, maybe a half-inch in diameter, like rebar.

He counted the rungs as he went, kicking out with his feet to get a feel for the size of the shaft.

It was tight, maybe six inches on either side, making it roughly three, maybe three and a half feet wide. He pushed his butt back and bumped into the rear wall. Same three feet. Not much more.

Ten rungs down, he felt a dribble of dirt land on his hands from above. Delgado's muffled voice trickled down. "You're clear on what to do?"

She's talking to one of the guards. Wynn strained to hear a response, but nothing came.

He descended slowly, continuing to count each step until his foot hit solid ground.

Twenty-six rungs at chest level. Each roughly a foot apart. Add the little jump and he was thirty feet below ground. Give or take.

He swept his foot around, ensuring the ground was solid, then waved a hand around head high. The shaft had opened into a larger room. Not much, but enough for him to step off the ladder and stand upright to one side.

He heard Delgado come down the ladder and step down onto the floor. "You can take that off now."

Wynn pulled the pillowcase over his head and yanked the blindfold off. He scrunched his eyes against the surprisingly bright light. He stood in a dirt cavern the size of a small walk-in closet; large enough for maybe four or five people to stand upright, but no more. The metal ladder fastened to the wall beside him extended upward into the dim chute.

Opposite the shaft, a five-foot-high by four-foot-wide tunnel, lit by bare bulbs spaced every fifty feet or so, led off into the distance. Heavy wood beams in the shape of an inverted "U" occasionally braced the walls and ceiling. One of Delgado's bodyguards, the driver, was already well down the tunnel.

Delgado looked at him and smiled. "Welcome to Nogales Pass."

CHAPTER 35

WYNN RUBBED HIS HANDS together, then wiped the dirt and grime from the ladder onto his jeans as he took in the cramped space.

"I hope you're not claustrophobic," Delgado said as she stepped into the tunnel.

"I'll be fine." Wynn looked up the empty shaft. "Your other guy isn't coming?"

"You want someone here to let you out, don't you?"

Wynn nodded.

"And bring those." Delgado indicated the pillowcase and blindfold. "You're not done with them."

Wynn was forced to crouch as he followed Delgado into the tunnel, which sloped gently downward and curved slowly to the right, making it hard to determine distance. Wynn counted his steps, but knew the length of his stride was off as he crouched through the passage. The step count would yield a rough estimate of the tunnel's length, but nothing precise.

The air was cool and dry. Every so often, a breath of warm air floated across his face. After the third time, he stopped and looked at the ceiling. A four-inch hole rose into the dirt.

Ventilation. And electricity. He was impressed. This was no weekend project.

After nearly a thousand steps, the tunnel leveled off and took a sharp turn to the right. The left wall transitioned from dirt to stone, several smooth, horizontal drill lines visible in the rock.

"They blasted this?" Wynn asked.

Delgado paused, glancing back over her shoulder. "*You* want to try digging through solid rock? C'mon, we're almost there."

Another two hundred steps brought them to another chamber, similar to the one at the other end, but larger. Several wooden crates sat stacked against one wall, while two wheeled garden carts stood upright next to them.

Used to move the drugs, Wynn thought.

The driver clamored up a wooden ladder affixed to the wall and disappeared out of sight. A moment later, a dim light entered the shaft.

Delgado motioned to the pillowcase. "Time to put that back on."

"Is it really necessary?" Wynn asked.

She turned to him and took the pillowcase from his hand. "You saved my life last night. Consider this as returning the favor. If I let you go up there without it, you'll be just as dead."

Wynn sighed and tied the blindfold around his eyes, then leaned forward to allow Delgado to pull the pillowcase over his head. She guided him to the ladder, and he hoisted himself up, almost immediately feeling the flush of warm air from above.

Counting the rungs as he went, he'd only reached twenty-one before a hand grabbed him and helped him out of the shaft. He crawled on his hands and knees until he was clear of the opening, then climbed to his feet.

The air was still musty and dank, but now there was something else. Chemical. *Bleach?* It was faint, but noticeable.

Bodies shuffled around him as Delgado's polite voice rose from the shaft. "*Gracias*." Moments later, a body bumped into him, and Delgado's voice came again. "*Donde esta...*"

Where is... Wynn didn't catch the rest of what Delgado said, but her voice was no longer polite. It was tense. Sharp. A male voice responded, followed by nervous laughter from the group.

A soft hand touched his arm. "Give me your gun," Delgado said.

"Why?"

"I can't take you any further if you're armed. You'll get it back before you leave, but otherwise, this is as far as you go."

Wynn pulled out the SIG and handed it to her, the weight of the situation settling heavily on his shoulders. No backup, no AirTag, and now no gun. He hoped he was right about trusting her—at least for now.

She withdrew a moment, then said, "This way."

Delgado led him up a flight of stairs and across a rough-tiled floor, eventually placing his hand on the back of a wooden chair. "Sit. It's going to be a few minutes."

He sat and listened intently. It was quiet at first, then several pairs of feet lumbered in an adjacent room. Deep voices mumbled an occasional word or two, nothing he could make out. Eventually, several people shuffled into the room and spread out around him. A deep male voice said, "Carmen," then continued in Spanish. Delgado responded, also in Spanish. Wynn didn't understand what they were saying, but sensed a warmth and friendliness between the two.

A slight tug pulled the pillowcase from his head as Delgado said, "You can take these off now."

Wynn untied the blindfold and blinked against the light. He was sitting at a small dining table in what appeared to be a modest Mexican home. Brightly colored tiles lined the kitchen counters, and intricately painted plates hung from the walls. Delgado sat to his right.

Behind her, sunlight filtered through the cracks between blue wooden shutters that covered a large window, preventing any chance of seeing outside. Three hard-looking men surrounded them in the kitchen while Delgado's driver stood at the mouth of a dark hallway.

In the chair opposite, a man in his mid-sixties, his thick gray hair and white beard neatly groomed, stared at Wynn over a cup of coffee. He was dressed well, wearing slacks and a blazer over an open-collared, white button-down shirt. A bulging, twelve-inch square canvas cinch sack sat in the center of the table.

"*Hablas español*?" the man said.

"*Un poquito*," Wynn replied.

"You'd prefer English?" The man's tone was friendly, yet measured.

Wynn eased into a grateful smile. "Yes, please."

"My name's Ruben Garcia. I hear I owe you a debt of gratitude."

"Just doing my job."

Garcia smiled. "Indeed." He took a sip of coffee. "I guess we're fortunate that Mr. Kovacs has such dedicated employees."

Wynn nodded but said nothing.

"How dedicated are you, Mr. Wynn?"

"To what?"

"To Mr. Kovacs, of course."

"He's an old Marine buddy. Gave me a job when I needed it. Whatever that buys, I guess."

Garcia smiled. "So you can be bought?"

Wynn smiled. A slip of the tongue. A twist of the words. *A test of trust.* "I'd like to think my word is worth something."

"I see," Garcia said. "You're a man of honor."

"I'd like to think so."

"I, too, am a man of honor. But everyone has a price."

Wynn shrugged. He needed to tread carefully here.

"What's your price, Mr. Wynn?"

"To do what?"

"Come work for me."

Wynn paused. *Would that help me find Terrance? Or pull me in deeper?* He spoke cautiously. "Doing what, exactly?"

"It's very simple. I find myself in the position of a parent refereeing an argument between children. Your Mr. Kovacs is accusing Arturo Murano of this assault on Carmen, and yet Arturo denies he had anything to do with it. I would like you to help me discover the truth."

Pull me in deeper. No thanks. "While I appreciate the offer, I'm new. No one's going to tell me anything. I'd hate to accept a job and not be able to perform. It's probably best if I stick with where I'm at."

The smile died from Garcia's face. He nodded to the cinch sack on the table.

Wynn's eyes went to it, but he kept his hands down. "What's that?"

"Your starting salary. Plus a bonus. As a way to repay my debt."

"You have no debt to me, Mr. Garcia."

"You don't know how much is in there."

"I'm sure it's very generous, but it doesn't matter. I helped Ms. Delgado because it was part of the job. Not in hopes of any reward or advancement. If my employer thinks I deserve a bonus, he'll give it to me. You don't owe me a thing."

Garcia paused a long moment, the tension between them rising as the silence lengthened. Finally, Garcia said, "Some men of honor..." he nodded to a man who had moved behind Wynn, "... may take offense to the refusal of such a generous offer."

The man behind Wynn drew a pistol from his waistband and pressed it firmly against the back of Wynn's head.

Sitting stock still, Wynn's gaze swept around the room. He locked eyes with Delgado. She shrugged, then nodded. He had no choice.

"After further consideration," Wynn said, "I'd be honored to accept your offer."

"Excellent," Garcia said. He leaned back and took a sip of coffee, his demeanor now completely friendly again, as if he hadn't just threatened Wynn's life.

"So I'm clear," Wynn said cautiously, "exactly how am I supposed to get this information?"

"Stealth, Mr. Wynn. Nothing as heroic as breaking up bar fights or foiling kidnapping attempts. Just keep an eye on some people."

"Like who?" Wynn asked.

"Kovacs and Vaz primarily. Murano, if you get the chance... and Eddie."

"Eddie?"

"When I was a child, whenever my friends and I saw a large mound of dirt, we played a game called King of the Mountain. One person would race to the top of the mound and the others would try to knock him off. We had no idea real life would be so similar."

"You think one of those guys is trying to knock you off?"

Garcia shrugged. "It would be only natural."

"And Eddie might be one of them?"

"He's my nephew, not my son." Garcia shrugged, as if that said it all.

"And if I hear something?"

"Tell Carmen. She'll take care of the rest. And you'll be well rewarded."

Wynn nodded. The two men held each other's eye. Garcia finally gave a short, humorless laugh and stood. "You're an interesting man, Mr. Wynn. I'm glad you reconsidered. I'll look forward to hearing from you." He left the bag on the table and walked out, followed by the three men, leaving only Delgado and her bodyguard.

"Welcome to the team. I guess," Delgado said.

"Did you know he was going to do that?"

"Mr. Garcia seldom tells anyone his plans." Delgado stood. "Come on. Let's get you back."

Wynn raised the blindfold to put it on, but she waved it away.

"Don't bother. You're one of us now."

As Wynn followed her toward the hallway, Delgado nodded to the cinch sack. "Don't forget that."

Wynn picked it up—it was heavier than he expected—and slung it over his shoulder like a backpack.

Delgado led him through a short hallway and down a flight of wooden stairs into a basement. A three-foot-square hole in the floor indicated the tunnel entrance.

Wynn looked around the room. Gray and dingy. The lighting was dim but sufficient; enough to make out a concrete floor and cinderblock walls. A workbench and shelves sat beneath the wooden stairs. A dark hallway led off to his left.

Adrenaline surged through his veins, quickening his pulse. He'd seen this room before.

This is where they assaulted Terrance in the video.

CHAPTER 36

THE SHARP STENCH OF bleach was heavier. Wynn wasn't sure if that was because he was no longer wearing the hood, or if it was just more noticeable compared to the fresh air upstairs.

He licked his lips; tried to keep his voice steady. "My gun?"

Delgado nodded to the wooden workbench beneath the stairs. Several tools littered the bench, including a pair of Stanley long-nose pliers, screwdrivers, and shears, all with darkly stained blades. His Sig sat among them.

A scrubbing sound eked faintly from the hallway toward the back. Wynn glanced down the hall, seeing two doors. From one, at the far end, another of Garcia's men leaned against the partially open doorway. From the other, a woman's legs, on her hands and knees, extended into the hallway. The woman sat back on her heels and dunked a scrub brush into a bucket. She paused and turned toward Wynn, revealing a girl of maybe eighteen or nineteen. She wiped the sweat from her brow, her eyes briefly meeting Wynn's.

Garcia's man tapped her on the back of the head. She leaned forward and quickly resumed her work.

Wynn turned to Delgado. She held his gaze for a moment, then nodded to the blindfold in his hand. "Put that back on when you get to the other end."

"I thought you said I was one of you."

"We're still allowed to keep some secrets."

Wynn tried to keep the frustration out of his face. He stuffed the blindfold into the back pocket of his jeans. "You got a bathroom down here?"

She pointed toward the hall. "Down there."

Garcia's man pushed off the doorframe, spread his feet and stood tall as Wynn shuffled toward him. He extended a hand to the first room, where the girl was cleaning. Wynn stopped outside the door and glanced in the bucket. The soapy water was dark and smelled heavily of bleach.

Inside, the lights were off, and the room was dim, lit only by the ambient light from the hallway. "*Perdóneme,*" Wynn said softly.

The woman stood and backed out.

Wynn stepped inside and looked for a wall switch. There was none. He glanced around the small room, maybe eight feet by ten feet, with a toilet and sink. Dark splotches stained the concrete floor.

He grabbed the doorknob. Smooth. No lock. A heavy deadbolt was fastened about chest high. On the outside.

This isn't a bathroom. It's a cell. Probably where they held Terrance. But where is he now?

Wynn stepped out and nodded at Garcia's man, then went back to Delgado in the main room. "She's cleaning. Got anything upstairs?" *Maybe I can catch a glimpse outside. Find a landmark.*

Delgado rolled her eyes. "Here or nowhere, Mr. Wynn."

"I'll wait."

"Your choice." She motioned him toward the tunnel entrance. A three-foot-square section of concrete lay beside the opening.

"There's only one way out, so you won't get lost," Delgado said. "Just follow it back. When you get to the ladder, put on the blindfold and hood, then climb up and knock on the door. My guy will be waiting for you."

Wynn took one last look around, then climbed into the hole. Garcia's man had come out of the hallway and leaned against the wall a few feet away. Wynn nodded to him and then descended until his shoulders came level with the floor. His gaze drifted to the man's feet.

He was wearing cowboy boots.

Rattlesnake skin wrapped around the base. Swirls and curlicues snuck out from beneath the bottom hem of his jeans.

That's him.

Wynn glanced up at the guy's face, committing it to memory. The man stared back.

Wynn nodded again and continued down, his feet finding solid ground after twenty-one rungs, exactly as expected. *No doubt. This is the place. These are the guys. But where exactly is this?*

He took one last useless look up the ladder, hoping to see something that would help him identify the place. There was nothing. He turned, his eyes skimming across the wooden boxes stacked against the wall. There were three, all of them labeled, "Danger: Explosives." A dwindling spool of electrical wire sat on top of the stack.

He lifted the lid of the top box and peered inside. Thin sticks of dynamite, eight inches long and an inch in diameter, filled over half of the box. He recalled the turn in the tunnel, the drill marks in the rock wall.

This is the dynamite they used.

Worse, if the labels were to be believed, the dynamite sat on top of a box of blasting caps.

Assuming it hadn't aged too much, dynamite alone was fairly stable, the risk of an unintended detonation relatively low. The same could not be said for blasting caps. Their job was to take a small electric charge, sometimes no more than a spark of static electricity, and ignite, creating a concussive blast that by itself was relatively minor. But when that blast occurred next to a stick of dynamite, well, he needed no explanation of what happened next.

Wynn lowered the lid on the box and heard a slight click. The string of lights that extended into the tunnel went out, surrounding him in darkness. The only light came from the top of the chute he had just climbed down, and even that was fading as the slab was pushed back into place.

He looked into the dim light above and called up, "Hey! The lights!"

The face of Garcia's man appeared in the partially covered opening. "Have a nice trip, Cabrón." Then he was gone, and the slab slid the rest of the way over the entrance, plunging Wynn into darkness.

Shit.

He didn't even have his phone for a flashlight; left it in Vegas per Delgado's instructions. He waited a few moments, allowing his eyes to adjust, hoping there was some small amount of light to adjust to.

There wasn't.

Maybe the guy just flipped a switch.

Wynn tried to recall how the lights were wired. There was a bare bulb in the cavern where he now stood, but was there one at the top of the ladder? Might there also be a switch up there?

He ran his hands across the ceiling until he found the wire that linked the row of bare light bulbs, then followed it to the back corner of the shaft where it snaked upward, opposite the ladder.

Keeping one hand on the cable, he climbed, bracing himself against the back wall each time he reached for the next rung. Climbing slowly, he reached the nineteenth rung before his hand bumped into a small box attached to the cable. He felt for a switch, found it, and flipped it.

Nothing.

Damn. The guy must have flipped the circuit breaker.

He felt around the top of the box, looking for an exit wire. There was none.

This is the end of the circuit. Power supply must be on the other end, meaning this is coordinated.

With his head inches beneath the concrete slab cover, he ran his hand across the slab and found a small loop of rope with both ends embedded in the concrete.

Used to pull the slab into place. Is there a way to move it?

He climbed two more rungs, hunched himself over, then adjusted the cinch sack and placed his shoulder against the slab above. He straightened his legs, pressing down on the wooden rungs of the ladder, forcing his shoulder up.

The slab didn't move.

He repositioned himself, tried to gain more leverage, then pushed again. Still nothing.

Only one way out, Delgado had said. *You won't get lost.*

Shit.

Wynn wasn't afraid of the dark, nor was he particularly claustrophobic, but combine the two thirty feet below ground? It was one of the reasons cavemen created fire. A fear as primal as ancient man himself. One every human could understand: *Is there something here in the dark with me?*

An uncontrollable shiver coursed down his spine.

He climbed down the ladder and paused at the mouth of the tunnel. It was a couple hundred steps to the turn, then close to a thousand, sloping upward to the other end. Roughly three thousand feet. A little over a half mile.

Pitch black.

With his heartbeat pounding in his ears, Wynn steadied his breathing and strained to listen. He drew the SIG from its holster, the sound of metal sliding against leather seemed amplified in the darkness. He held the gun out in front, kept his left hand on the dirt wall, then set off down the tunnel.

He crept slowly, crouched over so as not to hit his head on the wooden beams that braced the ceiling. The feel of the rough dirt walls sliding past his fingers became strangely comforting in the otherwise sensory-deprived environment. Compared to the walls, the floor felt smooth. Sandy, even. As if its rough edges had been smoothed by thousands of trampling feet.

Three minutes in, the left wall angled away as the tunnel made its turn. His left foot snagged, sending him toppling forward, landing on something instantly recognizable.

Not something. Someone.

Wynn quelled the panic that threatened to erupt. He fired two quick shots that burst like lightning through the darkness, the massive explosions echoing in the cramped space. He pushed himself up and scrambled backward on his ass, tangling his legs with whoever—whatever—was there.

He fired again, hoping the flash would reveal the additional presence, but there was nothing. As the darkness resettled, he paused in the slight corner, realizing that now, even his hearing was useless. Neither his own heavy breathing nor racing heartbeat were audible over the ringing in his ears.

Taking a deep breath, he forced himself to calm down, willed his heart to slow, and remained motionless, waiting.

For two long minutes.

Then three.

And four.

After five minutes, the ringing stopped. He could hear his heartbeat. He could hear his fingers as he rubbed them together.

But there was nothing else. No other sound at all.

Getting his feet beneath him, Wynn crouched low. Holding the Sig in his right hand, he reached out with his left, and shuffled forward. Within a couple of steps, his hand brushed against something. He immediately jerked it back, then reached out again, this time resting it on something solid.

Jeans. Covering a shin.

He moved his hand down the shin to the ankle, then the foot. It was bare. And cool. He moved his fingers to the toes, felt a slick wetness, and snatched his hand back.

His pulse spiked again.

Reaching out, he found the foot and ran his fingers along the four small toes.

The big toe was gone, only a jagged stump of bone remaining.

No...

He ran his hands up the body, found the right hand. The pinky finger was missing. Ran his hands toward the left ear, crossing the face. Unshaven. A man.

No...

The left ear was fine, but there was an empty, wet hole where the right ear should have been.

He didn't need to, but he wanted to be sure. He gently moved his hands across the man's eyes. One missing.

Wynn sat back, a sick feeling growing in his stomach.

No doubt about it.

Terrance.

CHAPTER 37

Wynn backed away and sat in the darkness, his mind racing.

Was it one of my shots that killed him? Or was he already dead?

He felt the body again and took one of Terrance's arms, moved it. Pliable, but stiffening. Rigor mortis was beginning. He put his hand beneath Terrance's shirt. Maybe not cold, but definitely cool.

Already dead. At least an hour or two, maybe more. The bleach smell from the basement suddenly made sense. *I wasn't fast enough.*

Wynn sat against the wall, exhausted as the adrenaline spike faded. The cinch sack jammed into his back as he thought of Krista. He'd failed her. No matter what happened between them in the future, Terrance's ghost would always be there, reminding them both of his failure. A sick feeling rose in his stomach. He lurched forward and retched, emptying his stomach.

He leaned back against the wall and shook his head. *Snap out of it, Wynn. Unless you want to join him.* Terrance's death, and this way of discovering it, created pressing new questions. Was his cover blown? Would they be waiting for him when he emerged from the tunnel? Would they kill him immediately or torture him, just as they had Terrance?

Slow down, Wynn. Think it out logically.

If Delgado intended to kill him, why had she waited this long? Why had she given him his gun back? And why would Garcia have insisted Wynn work for him?

No. Whoever is behind this, it's not Carmen Delgado or Ruben Garcia.

Which left Kovacs. He followed the trail. Kovacs could have given the order to Vaz, who passed it on to Eddie, who passed it on to the guards here. *That makes sense. Would Kovacs have also ordered the guards to kill me? Maybe, but they wouldn't do it if Garcia or Delgado didn't approve.*

Wynn felt a little better. Maybe his own life was safe. For now. *Maybe.*

So what's the point? Why did Kovacs give up? Did he realize his ransom would never be met, and therefore decide to move on? Does he actually know I'm working for the Feds, or is this another of his damn tests? Wynn racked his brain. He hated to admit it, but there were several ways Kovacs could have found out. *Most likely is that Chad got back and squealed. They could have found the burner in my motel room. Or maybe someone saw me leave with the Marshals the night this whole thing started.* Except for Chad, the other options, while possible, seemed unlikely.

Which left the other possibility.

Let's say Kovacs doesn't know anything but thinks the timing of my showing up is too coincidental. Maybe he's devising one more test to see how I'll react.

The realization of what that meant rushed into his brain. *I can't let on that I know who this was. Running at this point would be as good as a confession, basically confirming that rescuing Terrance is why I was here. I have to stick around and act like it's either a bad joke or a warning.*

Assuming they don't kill me the moment I pop up.

He ejected the magazine from the Sig and counted the remaining rounds as he unloaded them into his lap. In his panic, he wasn't sure how many shots he'd fired. He counted seven left. *Not enough if I need to shoot my way out.* He reloaded the mag and slipped it back into the grip.

Sliding the SIG back into its holster, he pushed off the wall, stepped around the body, and started walking. He was no longer concerned about finding something in the tunnel. He'd found what they wanted him to. Now he had to worry about what was waiting for him at the other end.

Ten minutes later, the tunnel opened into the small chamber. He ran his hands across the dirt ceiling, found the electric cable that linked the light bulbs, and followed it with his hands. He climbed the ladder until he found a box with a switch near the top, then flipped the switch. The lights came on.

Assholes.

There was no point in going back just because the lights were on. It wouldn't change a thing. *And I'm sure as hell not dragging him out of here.*

He paused and considered the door in front of him. It was small, maybe three feet square. Plywood, with a two-by-four wood frame. Unlike the tunnel entrance on the Mexican side that opened into the floor, this one opened into a wall. He remembered Delgado positioning herself between his legs as he jumped into a pit of some kind. He had then gotten down onto his knees and crawled backward into the tunnel. Presumably from the other side of this very door.

Which gave him a slight advantage. He could hold on to the ladder and duck down beneath the opening. If someone wanted to shoot him, they'd have to at least stick their arm into the shaft.

It might also provide the setting for a litmus test of their intentions.

He tapped his back pocket, felt for the blindfold and hood, then flipped off the light switch, plunging himself back into darkness. Once his eyes adjusted, he pounded on the door, then scrambled down several rungs and pushed himself into a corner. He drew the Sig with his right hand as a scraping sound came from above. A thin sliver of light appeared in the wall, growing as the door slid away.

The deep voice of Delgado's bodyguard came from outside. "Hey, what took you so long, Cabrón? Did you run into something?"

"Based on his personality, I thought it was you."

The bodyguard laughed. "Fuck off." His head appeared through the opening. "Unless you want to stay down there, get your ass up here."

Wynn lowered the gun to his side, confident the darkness hid it. "Wanted to make sure you don't have any more surprises for me." He leaned against the wall and climbed a couple of rungs.

"Stop." The bodyguard's expression turned grim. "You're not wearing the hood."

"Didn't know I'd need it."

"You need it, Cabrón. Do you have it?"

"Right here. Give me a second." *If they were going to kill me, he wouldn't care what I saw.* He holstered the Sig and put on the blindfold and hood. *Here goes nothing.*

He climbed to the top of the ladder and crawled out onto the floor. The bodyguard led him through all the same steps, in reverse, that Delgado had put him through on the way in. Eventually he was led to a waiting car.

He got in the back seat, wriggled himself down onto the floor, then waited while two guys drove him out of the garage. Small pebbles once again battered against the wheel wells as they rolled over the undulating gravel road, taking lefts and rights, hitting the gas and the brakes.

After ten minutes, the car stopped.

"You can take that off now," the bodyguard said.

Wynn took off the blindfold and hood, pausing a moment to wipe Terrance's blood from his hands. He climbed onto the back seat and looked out the window at a strip mall parking lot.

"Get out." Delgado's bodyguard was behind the wheel, while a second man he hadn't seen before sat shotgun.

Wynn got out and closed the door, expecting the car to take off. Instead, the driver's window eased down. The bodyguard's arm came out the window.

"Ms. Delgado wants you to have this." He handed Wynn a key fob.

"What's this for?"

The guy pointed across the parking lot. Two rows away, beneath an ornamental maple tree, sat a brand-new Indian Challenger motorcycle.

"She said you'd know what to do."

The two bodyguards pulled out of the parking lot, leaving Wynn standing alone. A weight lifted off his shoulders, but was immediately replaced by another. He was safe for now, but soon, he would have to tell Krista and Ruiz that he had failed to save Terrance.

He strolled over to the bike. It was a beauty. A Dark Horse. Ruby Smoke tank, bags, and fairing; black seat and dash; matte black engine, forks, and pipes. On any normal day, he'd have been able to truly appreciate the craftsmanship of the bike. Today, it reminded him of failure.

Still, it was the fastest way back to Vegas.

He popped open the saddlebags. Nothing in the right. Inside the left were a helmet, gloves, sunglasses, and a bill of sale. A name Wynn didn't recognize was listed as the seller. The buyer information was blank. He unslung the cinch sack from off his back and put it in the bag, followed by his gun and holster. He put on the gloves and sunglasses, then shoved the bill of sale and helmet into the other bag and threw his leg over the seat. He lit up the dashboard. All kinds of lights, gauges, and a touchscreen navigation system burst to life.

He thumbed the starter and the engine rumbled awake, then settled into a steady rhythm, like a horse trotting down the track. He checked the odometer; less than a hundred miles. The gas, full. He checked the time. 2:38 p.m.

He'd wait until he hit Tucson to call Ruiz and update him on Terrance. From there, it was another seven hours to Vegas. He should be there by eleven. Maybe by then they'd have a plan to get out of this mess.

CHAPTER 38

ON THE OUTSKIRTS OF Tucson, Wynn found a burger place sitting next to a chain drug store about a half mile off the freeway. Delgado's Indian rode like a charm, but he didn't know if it might carry a GPS tracker. He'd had enough experience with those over the last year not to take any chances.

He parked in the burger joint's lot, then hustled over to the drug store and purchased a prepaid cell phone. He took it back to the burger joint and went into the restroom, where he scrubbed the rest of Terrance's blood off his hands. When finished, he went out to the restaurant where he activated the phone while wolfing down a quick lunch.

Outside, he stepped to the rear of the building, away from the traffic noise of the busy street. He tapped in Ruiz's number from memory.

Ruiz's voice was cautious when he picked up the call. "Hello?"

"Hey. It's me," Wynn said.

"I didn't recognize the number."

"This couldn't wait." Wynn took a deep breath. "Terrance is dead. I found his body this afternoon."

"What? Where?"

Wynn explained where he was, how he'd gotten there, and how he had found the body in the tunnel.

"Shit," Ruiz said. "You're sure it was him?"

Wynn thought about the missing eye, ear, fingers, and toes. "Yeah, it was him."

"Okay," Ruiz said. His voice turned serious. He was all business now. "We'll mourn him later. Now we've got to get you out. We'll initiate the exit plan tonight."

"Negative," Wynn said. "If I disappear too quickly that'll all but confirm for Kovacs that Terrance was the reason I was here. I need to stick around at least a week or two before you take me out. Besides, I won't even be back there until close to midnight. You take me out tonight you might as well put up a sign."

Ruiz hesitated. "Alright. But let's not wait too long. I don't want you there when Chad resurfaces."

Wynn let out a deep breath. "Agreed. But we still need to wait a while."

"Let's increase those check-ins to twice daily."

"When I can," Wynn said. "Kovacs still wants me to be a driver and those could easily turn into twelve-to-fourteen-hour trips. I'm not gonna act suspicious just to check-in."

"Continue at least once a day, then," Ruiz said. "Twice when you can."

Wynn agreed, then disconnected. He placed the phone on the concrete curb, then smashed his heel onto it, shattering it into dozens of small pieces. He picked up the largest and tossed them into the restaurant's dumpster.

He strolled back over to the bike, put on his gloves and sunglasses, then threw a leg over the seat. It was still over six hours and four hundred miles back to Vegas.

It was nearly eight o'clock in the evening by the time Chad made it to the designated sports bar in Henderson. He sat in a corner booth, trying to ignore the disapproving glances from the other customers. He'd become nose blind to himself, but their reactions as he walked by made it clear he hadn't showered in a couple of days.

Even his waitress, a pretty young thing he might've hit on a week ago, had come by only once, just long enough for him to say he'd wait to order until the party he was meeting showed up.

A trickle of sweat slid from his armpit down his right side.

The party I'm meeting.

Arturo Murano was no party. More like a desperate Pitbull, backed into a corner.

After seeing the cops pick up the AirTag in Wickenburg on Saturday morning, Chad had hitchhiked up to Kingman. He spent the night breaking into cars, trying to find enough money to get something to eat, and figuring out who he could contact for help. Everyone in Kovacs' organization was off limits, but there was still one guy, Tommy, with connections to Murano's team, whom he might be able to trust.

Chad had never met Arturo Murano, let alone spied on Kovacs for him. But for some reason, Vaz thought he had been spying, and had ordered Wynn to kill him.

But Wynn didn't. Instead, he put a tracker in his pocket and told him to disappear. And then the cops showed up. Which could only mean Wynn was working with the cops. And that Kovacs was compromised. Which created a perfect opportunity to request a meeting with Arturo Murano. Maybe provide a bit of information that Murano could use in his battle with Kovacs. *And in the process, hopefully, be well-rewarded. Maybe even given a place in his organization.*

Still, it was a risky move. But by Sunday morning, Chad was tired, hungry, and desperate enough that he'd convinced himself that Tommy could be trusted. He put together a plan, found a phone, and tried to remember the number. It took four tries, but he eventually dialed the right one.

"Yeah?"

"Tommy?"

"Who's this?"

"It's me. Chad."

There was a short pause, then, "What the fuck? You're supposed to be dead."

"Yeah, well, not yet."

"What are you doing, man?"

"I need help. Are you still connected to Arturo Murano?"

Tommy hesitated. "I can be. Why?"

"I've got some information I think he'll be interested in."

"Like what?"

"Uh-uh. I need some help first."

"Now ain't the time to be asking for favors, man."

"Why not?" Chad asked.

"People are coming after him. They say he was behind a failed kidnapping attempt of Carmen Delgado. He says he had nothing to do with it. Says he's being set up. But they're coming after him, regardless."

"Then he's gonna want to hear what I've got to say. It has to do with Kovacs and his new guy, Wynn."

That was enough to pique Tommy's interest, who agreed to take Chad's meeting request to Murano.

Now, Chad glanced at the clock on the wall. Murano was ten minutes late. A twinge of anxiety shot through him. He hoped Murano wouldn't blow him off. He was hungry and didn't have enough money in his pocket to cover even a cheap plate.

Minutes later, Tommy appeared near the front of the bar. Chad made eye contact and gave a small nod, which Tommy ignored as he scanned the rest of the room, then left. After another minute, the heavy-set form of Arturo Murano rounded the corner. Chad rose, extending his hand, but Murano disregarded it and slid into the booth opposite.

"Mr. Murano, thanks for coming."

Murano's face was cold, his voice deep and flat. "When only the second person in known history rises from the dead and requests a meeting, a wise man takes it."

Chad wasn't sure how to respond to that. He paused. "Uh...Thank you. I appreciate that. It's been a rough couple of days."

Murano wrinkled his nose. "I can tell."

"Yeah, sorry about that."

The waitress appeared alongside the booth. "Can I get you something to drink?"

Before Chad could say yes, Murano cut him off. "Give us a few minutes."

Chad's face fell slightly as she left. He could hear his stomach rumbling.

When she was out of earshot, Murano asked, "You have information for me?"

"Yes, sir." Chad hesitated. "But like I said, it's been a rough few days."

Murano waved dismissively. "If the information is good, you'll be taken care of."

"Thank you, sir."

Chad told him what had transpired in Wickenburg. How Vaz had instructed Wynn to kill him, and how Wynn purposefully missed the point-blank shot. How when he woke up, he found the AirTag, and when he planted the AirTag at the Subway, cops had shown up. He didn't need to explain what it meant.

The waitress re-appeared as Chad finished his story. "Ready to order?"

"Unfortunately, I can't stay," Murano said as he climbed out of the booth. He dug into his wallet and dropped several hundred-dollar bills on the table. "But get my friend whatever he wants."

CHAPTER 39

IT WAS A LITTLE past eleven p.m. when Wynn got back to his room at the All-Nighter. He tossed the cinch sack full of Garcia's money into the box spring, then took a few minutes to wash the dirt and grime from the road off his face before heading over to Pink. He thought about calling Krista—Ruiz was sure to have given her the news by now—but couldn't bring himself to do it.

A little before midnight, he strolled through Pink's back door, doing his best to act calm and natural. Inside, his heart hammered against his ribs. He'd done a lot of acting in the past week, but this next performance needed to be Oscar-worthy. If dumping Terrance in the tunnel had been a test, Wynn needed to act as if it were just another body. If it wasn't a test, if Kovacs really knew what Wynn was up to, it wouldn't matter.

Kovacs was sitting alone in his office when he strode up the hall. Wynn kept his right hand near the Sig on his hip as he stopped at the open door.

Kovacs leaned back in his chair when he saw Wynn. "Come on in. Sit. Tell me about it."

Wynn glanced at Kovacs' empty hands. He was relieved when Kovacs steepled them in front of his face, waiting to hear the story.

Wynn pulled out a chair and sat. "We flew down to Nogales, met with Ruben Garcia. He thanked me for helping Delgado, then she gave me a bike, and I rode back."

"You met Ruben?" Kovacs' voice sparked with interest.

"Yeah."

"Where?"

"In a house across the border."

"How'd you get there?" Kovacs asked.

"They've got a tunnel."

"Did you see it?"

Wynn shrugged, as if it was no big deal. "The inside, yes. But not the entrances. They kept me blindfolded at either end."

Kovacs nodded thoughtfully. "Did he try to buy you?"

"Yeah, actually he did."

Kovacs arched an eyebrow. "How much?"

"No idea. The bag was big enough, but I didn't look inside or ask."

"Why not?" Kovacs said.

"You said it yourself; we've got each other's backs." Wynn allowed a slight smile to curl his lips. "Besides, if I'm going into business with the devil, I'd rather it be the one I know."

Kovacs sat silently for a moment, his eyes fixed on Wynn, then burst out laughing. He reached down and unlocked one of the desk drawers, pulled out another stack of bundled hundred-dollar bills and tossed it to him. Another ten grand.

"You did good. Don't think I don't appreciate it."

Wynn held up the bundle. "Likewise."

"Anything else interesting?"

Wynn shrugged. *Time to sell it.* "Garcia—or maybe it was Delgado—sent me a warning." Wynn had thought long and hard on the ride back how he'd tell Kovacs about what he'd found. "They had me come back through the tunnel alone and turned out the lights. They put a body down there for me to run into."

"A body?" Kovacs sounded surprised.

Hell. He's the actor, Wynn thought. "Practically still warm."

"Who was it?"

"No idea," Wynn lied. "But it wasn't pretty. It was dark so I couldn't see anything, but I felt around a little. I think he'd been tortured."

"Tortured?"

Wynn shrugged. "He was missing some parts."

Kovacs nodded and paused. "A warning for what?"

"Either to keep my mouth shut about the tunnel, or not to turn Garcia down the next time he wants to buy me."

Kovacs nodded again. "What'd you do?"

"I left it there. The message was delivered. Not my job to move their bodies."

Kovacs sat silently, his expression unreadable. Wynn hoped he was buying it. After several awkward moments, Kovacs said, "And after all that, Carmen gave you a new bike?"

"An Indian Challenger. Pretty sweet ride. You should get one. We'll go riding together."

"Maybe I will," Kovacs said. "You ready for another road trip?"

"You're shitting me, right? You realize I just did five hundred miles?"

"Relax. Not tomorrow. Tuesday night. You and Marcus."

"Sure," Wynn said. *One or two more runs and then Ruiz can get me out of here.*

"Good," Kovacs said.

Wynn waited for Kovacs to say something more. When he didn't, Wynn asked, "Is Deborah here?"

"Over at the Deuce. Why?"

"She's got my phone. If you're good here, I'll run over and grab it."

"We're good," Kovacs said, dismissing him. "You've had a busy day. Take the night off, get out of here."

Wynn got up and eased to the door. "Don't mind if I do."

———

Vaz waited until Wynn left Kovacs' office, then entered and closed the door. "Well?"

Kovacs shrugged. "He obviously hasn't run. Admits to finding the body, but claims he doesn't know who it was."

He wouldn't, Vaz thought. *Eddie says it was one of the girls' dads. One who was asking too many questions.* "Did he see the mutilations?"

"Yeah," Kovacs replied. "He thinks it was a warning from Garcia."

"Or he could just be telling you that."

Kovacs slapped his hands on the desk. "For fuck's sake, Vaz. Wynn's done everything we've asked. He's solid. Let it go."

Vaz fumed silently, slowly counting to ten to allow his contempt for his boss to dissipate. When he finally trusted himself to speak, he said, "Consider it gone."

"Good."

The two men sat in silence a few moments, until Kovacs finally asked, "So how is our guest?"

Vaz sighed heavily. "As you requested. He's still alive."

———

Chad stumbled over the curb as he left the sports bar. After Murano left, he'd spent a couple of hours gorging himself and getting properly hammered. He'd used a couple of those hundred-dollar bills to try to entice the pretty waitress to invite him home.

She hadn't.

Bitch.

He startled when two guys appeared on either side of him and grabbed his arms. "What the..."

"Mr. Murano would like you to come with us."

———

Twenty minutes after leaving Kovacs office, Wynn rumbled the new Indian into the Deuce's parking lot. He went in the front door and sat at the bar while Deborah finished making a couple of drinks. She nodded when she saw him, then grabbed his phone from under the other end of the bar.

"You made it," she said, handing him the phone.

"Yeah. Thanks."

"Nice ride?"

"Perfect. I assume you're the one who told Delgado?"

"Guilty."

Wynn smiled. "Don't get in a habit of saying *that.*"

Deborah laughed. "Can I get you something?"

"Corona." He turned so he could see both Deborah and the rest of the club. He was surprised to see Jenna dancing on one of the satellite stages. "Looks like you brought the A-team tonight. What's up?"

"We're short on dancers." Deborah popped the top off a bottle and set it in front of Wynn. "I needed to bring a few over from the other club."

Wynn nodded. Something about that didn't sound right, but he let it go. He had more pressing concerns.

CHAPTER 40

RUIZ HAD JUST SAT down with his Monday morning coffee when his desk phone buzzed. He reached across the piles of files and punched the button next to the flashing light.

A female voice came over the speaker. "You've got a couple of visitors. FBI and DEA."

Ruiz looked at the time. Barely a few minutes after eight a.m. "What do they want?"

There was a pause, and then a male voice, one Ruiz vaguely recognized, came over the line. "Ruben Garcia, Special Agent Ruiz. We need to talk about Ruben Garcia."

"Come on back." Ruiz cleared his desk, placing a stack of files on the credenza behind him. He turned around as two men appeared in the doorway.

The first man was tall and slender, with dark hair. "Agent Parker?" Ruiz asked.

"I was wondering if you'd recognize me," Parker said with a slight smile.

Ruiz had spoken to FBI Special Agent Will Parker on a Zoom call about a week before he recruited Wynn. As someone who had worked with Wynn—although Parker would probably say that was too strong a term to accurately describe their past interactions—Parker's assessment weighed heavily on Ruiz's decision.

"Nice to finally meet you in person," Ruiz said.

"Likewise," Parker said, as the two men shook hands. "This is Agent Tim Hodges, with the DEA."

Ruiz shook Hodges' hand, then motioned to the chairs in front of his desk. "How can I help you?"

"By explaining your interest in Ruben Garcia," Parker said.

"I could ask the same thing," Ruiz shot back.

Parker and Hodges exchanged a look. "Ruben Garcia," Hodges said, "is a person of interest in a joint FBI-DEA investigation."

"A person of interest, or a subject?" Ruiz asked.

Hodges smiled.

"It just seems awfully coincidental," Parker said, "that two weeks after you and I have a conversation about Sean Wynn, you then make an inquiry regarding Ruben Garcia. I have to wonder if the two are related?"

"And if they are?" Ruiz asked.

"Then we have a problem," Hodges said. The warmth and friendliness had evaporated from his voice.

"How's that?" Ruiz asked.

Parker leaned forward. "Tell you what. How about we all put our cards on the table? Tell each other what we're doing."

Ruiz hesitated. Normally, he wouldn't be willing to easily share the details of an undercover operation. But since Terrance was dead, and the only thing left was to pull Wynn out, he didn't want to make a career-ending mistake as he wrapped this thing up. If he and Wynn had somehow stumbled into a joint FBI-DEA investigation, he needed to know. He nodded his agreement.

"Okay," Parker said. "You go first."

Ruiz spent the next ten minutes explaining the situation with Bennie and Danny Kovacs, Krista Hampson, her brother Terrance, and now Sean Wynn. He explained how it all tied into Ruben Garcia, ending on how none of it mattered anyway, now that Wynn had found Terrance dead.

"Now we're waiting for a little time to pass so that Wynn's extraction doesn't align too closely to Terrance's murder," Ruiz said. "For Wynn's future, we need these to look like two separate events."

Parker nodded while Hodges remained silent.

"Your turn," Ruiz said. "What kind of investigation have we stumbled into?"

"Don't feel too bad," Parker said. "This didn't start as a joint operation. It only turned into one when one of my cases stumbled into Ruben Garcia also." He turned to Hodges. "You tell him."

Hodges cleared his throat. "It started like a hundred others. We put a person undercover to stop the local dealing in L.A., but we always want to move up the ladder. Get the supplier. You know the drill. That eventually led us to Arturo Murano and Ruben Garcia, both of whom you've asked about, as well as Carmen Delgado."

Hodges paused. "But shortly after your boy Danny Kovacs took over, Garcia expanded his product line. Did Wynn tell you about these fashion shows that Kovacs hosts?"

"Yeah," Ruiz said. "There was one the other night."

"They aren't selling clothing at those shows," Parker said. "They're selling the girls."

Ruiz closed his eyes. He wasn't sure he wanted to hear this.

"I've been working sex trafficking for four years now," Parker said. "Including that case in Wyoming last summer that Wynn witnessed. That case led us to Vegas and Kovacs, and then to Garcia. Like you, when I started asking questions about Ruben Garcia, Hodges and the DEA here stepped up. We compared notes and decided a joint investigation was appropriate."

Ruiz paused, thinking about his conversations with Wynn. "This all makes sense. Wynn's been on one of those 'supply runs' where they bring the drugs and the girls up from Mexico. What I don't get is how they're doing it. Wynn said these girls seemed excited about coming here."

"It's all in the recruiting," Parker said. "They pose as photographers and talent agents. Take a girl's picture, tell her she could be a model in the U.S. Then they take 'em to Garcia's compound outside of Nogales, teach 'em to dance and how to walk a runway. They treat 'em like goddesses and tell 'em that dancing at the Deuce is the audition for being selected to participate in the fashion show."

"That's why they're eager to come up and dance," Ruiz said, the realization dawning across his face.

"It's the first step," Parker said with a shake of his head. "They fill these girls' heads with dreams, but the reality is the Deuce is a way for buyers to preview the merchandise. Then they put 'em on the runway at those fashion shows and sell 'em to the highest bidder. The girls have no idea until it's too late."

"These girls can't be that naïve," Ruiz said.

"Not all of 'em," Parker said. "Those that figure it out or want to leave get shipped off to rings like the one Wynn helped us bust in Wyoming last summer."

"What about their families? Don't they say anything?"

"Some do, but Garcia's men take care of the loudest. The rest learn to stay quiet."

Ruiz shook his head. "I can't believe it's that simple."

"Unfortunately, it is," Parker said grimly. "The girls are smuggled in, so there's no record they were ever in the U.S. Once they sell, they're told they're being taken to New York to start a modeling career. Instead, they're taken out on private planes to South America, Saudi Arabia, Russia, all over. That's when the dream turns into a nightmare. Their families are either killed or threatened to stay quiet, and to the rest of the world, it's like they never existed."

Ruiz let out a heavy sigh. "What do you need from me?"

Parker leaned forward. "I've seen the chaos Sean Wynn can create when he sets his mind to something. Our op with Garcia is in a very delicate phase. We need him out of the way."

Ruiz nodded. "How soon?"

"Real soon," Parker said. "Tonight, if possible."

CHAPTER 41

WYNN WOKE WITH A frantic start. The dream was back, with a twist.

Dinner at the restaurant on his last night with Nicole. He heard the gunshots, saw the stray bullet pierce her chest. Only this time, when he pushed up from the floor, slipping on the blood, it wasn't Nicole staring up at him.

It was Krista.

He didn't need a psychologist to tell him what it meant. *I've failed them both.*

He took a moment to let his heart rate calm and gather his bearings. Before going to sleep, he had moved the dresser and television to block the door and window. He'd also moved the bed to the opposite side of the room, where the dresser had been. He wanted to make sure if someone shot through the window, he wouldn't be sleeping where they expected him to be.

Paranoia makes you do strange things.

He had also reviewed every move he'd made in the last week. Focused on things he might have done differently to press harder or move faster, anything that might've saved Terrance. Only when he was convinced none of it would have made a difference, had he finally drifted off into a restless sleep.

The clock on the nightstand read a little after nine a.m. A sense of dreadful purpose filled the void as the adrenaline faded away. He knew what he had to do, but had little desire to do it.

He rolled out of bed, pushed the mattress away, and dug out the burner. He'd memorized the number Krista had slipped him more than a week ago in San Diego, had even punched it into the phone a couple of times, but this was the first time he hit send.

U there? he texted.

The reply was immediate. *S?*

She was confirming it was really him. *Yes,* he typed.

Prove it.

Wynn thought for a moment, then replied. *I should've asked you to the Brig's Ball.*

Within a minute, the phone rang in his hand. The screen indicated an "unknown caller," but he recognized Krista's number. "Hey," he said when he picked up.

"Are you okay?" Krista asked.

"Yeah, I'm fine," Wynn replied. "I assume Ruiz told you?"

"Yeah." Her voice cracked.

"I'm so sorry, Krista. I didn't work fast enough."

She took a deep breath, fighting back tears. "It's not your fault. We knew it was a long shot."

"Still, I wish I could have done more."

"You've done more than any of us had a right to expect," Krista said.

"Where are you?" Wynn asked.

"At a safehouse. Not far from Vegas. Ruiz and Todd don't like it, but I insisted. I wanted to be close."

Wynn nodded to himself, but stayed silent.

"Tell me what happened," Krista said. "How did you find him?"

Wynn repeated the story he'd told Ruiz, how he'd wound up in the tunnel, then stumbled over the body.

"If it was dark, how do you know it was him?"

"The injuries. I felt the body. It was missing a right pinky finger, left big toe, and right ear. It was him."

"I had hoped all of this was behind me," Krista said. "But it seems some mistakes stay with you forever." She sighed heavily. "The important thing now is to get you out."

"*One* of the important things," Wynn said. "I told Ruiz we can't do it too soon. It'll look suspicious. So if I'm staying, I'm gonna see if I can find something to tie Kovacs to it. Put him in a cell next to his old man."

"Let Ruiz handle that. Don't do anything that'll raise Danny's suspicions."

"I'll be careful," Wynn said.

"Good," Krista said. She paused a long moment. "Did you mean it?"

"Mean what?"

"That you should've asked me to the Brigadier's Ball?"

Now it was Wynn's turn to pause. "Yeah. I meant it."

She laughed humorlessly. "I suppose it doesn't matter now, but back then, I was hoping you would."

"I should have," Wynn said. "Would have saved a lot of trouble."

"Coulda, shoulda, woulda."

"Yeah."

They were both quiet.

Krista finally broke the silence. "When this thing's all over, I'd like to see you again."

"Ruiz will never allow it. Even if we put Danny away, he and his dad still have connections. They could still come after you."

Krista sighed. "Not exactly what I meant when I said, 'til death do us part."

"No. I suppose not."

The silence returned, this time awkwardly. "I should let you go," Krista said.

They said goodbye and disconnected.

Wynn spent the next hour going through his morning kata, something he hadn't done for more than a week. Usually the kata left him refreshed, but today his muscles were stiff, his movements clumsy and jerky. As he warmed up, his fluidity returned, but his mind never eased. Constant thoughts of Terrance, Krista, and Nicole clouded his mind. He moved from one form to the next, incorporating both yoga and the various martial arts in a choreographed exercise that soon had the sweat flowing from his pores, but today, left his mind as foggy as ever.

CHAPTER 42

It had taken Arturo Murano less than eighteen hours to arrange the meeting. Now, sitting at a table overlooking the fountains of Bellagio, he hoped he'd calculated correctly. A three-way meeting where the other two didn't know the third would be there was always risky. Even more so when the other two both wanted to kill you. But after being blamed for the attempted kidnapping of Carmen Delgado, something he had nothing to do with, he needed to make a big move. And Chad had given it to him.

He didn't trust that little shit, Eddie, with his stupid pencil-thin mustache. Eddie had proven himself dangerous by setting up the meeting at the speedway, costing four men. Murano would prefer to kill him. And he would, if Eddie wasn't Ruben Garcia's nephew. But Eddie was the only one who could prove to Delgado that what Murano was about to tell her was true.

He took a sip of his bourbon, its rich warmth a small comfort, then let out a deep breath as the maître d' led Eddie over to his table. The guy was cocky and brash, swaggering through the restaurant like he owned it, with no idea of just how out of place he looked.

Suck it up and remember the goal. Murano hit the "record" button on his phone and set it face down on the table before standing. He pulled out a chair to the side of where he was sitting. "The view of the fountains is better from here."

Eddie paused to look out the windows, then sank into the chair. The maître d' unfolded the linen napkin from the table and laid it across Eddie's lap as a waiter appeared. "Can I get you a beverage, sir?"

"Scotch on the rocks. The good stuff. None of that cheap crap," Eddie said.

The waiter glanced at Murano, who nodded slightly.

"Of course, sir. Right away." The waiter hurried away.

Eddie leaned back and laced his fingers across his stomach. "Big news, huh?"

Murano shrugged.

"After the setbacks you've had," Eddie said, "I'd think your biggest news is that you're leaving town. Permanently."

Murano glanced over Eddie's shoulder. "I have the feeling my luck is about to change."

Eddie opened his mouth to respond, but closed it when Murano rose to his feet. The maître d' re-appeared alongside the table and pulled out a chair.

"My lady," the maître d' said as he bowed his head.

Carmen Delgado paused as she locked eyes with Murano, then sat directly opposite. She was warm and pleasant as she exchanged niceties with the waiter and maître d', then turned icy when they were left alone.

"Tell me why I shouldn't have you killed right now," she said to Murano.

"Because I had nothing to do with what happened the other night," he said calmly.

"They were your men."

"No, they weren't. I knew nothing about it."

Eddie let out a short laugh.

Delgado tilted her head toward him. "Even the village idiot knows that's a lie."

Eddie opened his mouth to protest, but apparently thought better of it.

Murano flashed his eyebrows and shrugged. "The truth," he mused, "can sometimes be hard to spot."

"I don't have time for innuendo, Arturo. Nor do I enjoy either of your company. You said you had information that would be valuable to Mr. Garcia. What is it?"

Murano leaned back and crossed his legs. "How well do you know Sean Wynn?"

"What about him?" Delgado said, her tone carrying a note of impatience.

"He seems to be Kovacs' new boy wonder. I'm curious how well you know him."

"Well enough."

Murano paused and nodded, then addressed Eddie. "I hear Kovacs likes to test his men's loyalty, is that right?"

"Yeah. So?" Eddie said.

"I hear he recently gave Wynn a test."

Eddie smiled. "Several."

"One in particular involved a hired gun named Chad. Does that ring a bell?"

"Yeah. So?" Eddie repeated.

"What exactly was the test?" Murano asked.

"To eliminate a problem."

"Permanently?"

Eddie smiled. "No other way."

Delgado had a puzzled look on her face as Murano continued. "And Wynn completed this task?"

"Permanently," Eddie said.

Murano nodded, then uncrossed his legs and turned in his seat. He gestured subtly into the restaurant, forcing Eddie to turn and look over his shoulder. Delgado simply turned her head slightly to the right. "So then, who's that?" Murano asked.

Several tables away, within direct line of sight, Chad lowered a menu from in front of his face and stared back at Eddie.

Eddie mumbled. "What the..."

"I'm sorry, Eddie," Murano said. "What was that?"

Eddie slouched back in his chair but remained silent.

"Who is that?" Delgado asked.

Murano paused, waiting for Eddie to answer. When he didn't, Murano said, "That's Chad, the problem Wynn was supposed to eliminate."

Delgado and Eddie remained silent as Murano relished the moment.

"But wait," Murano said as he leaned forward and lowered his voice. "Lest you think Wynn is simply a compassionate soul, or perhaps a very bad shot, there's more." He paused, savoring their discomfort. "Your buddy Vaz and Wynn did indeed take Chad into the desert, and Vaz did instruct Wynn to kill him. But rather than put a bullet in his head, Wynn knocked him out and planted a tracker on him."

"A tracker?" Delgado asked.

"So Wynn would know where Chad was. But the best part..." Murano raised his eyebrows, "was who showed up to find the tracker."

Murano paused again, enjoying the suspense.

"Who?" Delgado asked.

Murano's face turned serious, his voice a whisper. "The cops."

Eddie, who had kept his eyes down this whole time, glanced up as a silence fell across the table.

"Wynn's a plant," Murano said. "Working for the cops."

The silence resettled over the group until Eddie said, "I'm going to kill the bastard."

"You'll do nothing!" Delgado said sharply, addressing Eddie directly for the first time since they'd sat down. Turning to Murano, she said, "You didn't tell us this out of the kindness of your heart. I assume you want something?"

Murano leaned back and smiled at Eddie. "That's why she's in charge." Locking eyes with Delgado, he said, "Three things. First, I want to be the one to tell Ruben. I want you to set up a meeting with him to include the three of us along with Kovacs, Wynn, and Vaz. And I want it soon. Tomorrow."

Delgado nodded. "I'll see if Mr. Garcia is available."

"Good. Second, I want to add the Rocky Mountain region to my distribution area. I'll take over Kovacs' position and you, Eddie, will function for me just as Vaz does for Kovacs. Rather than being deceived by Wynn and Kovacs, we'll position ourselves to Ruben as a team who has proactively uncovered a mole, and is ready to step in and take over with no disruption to his distribution."

Eddie's eyes darted up and to the left.

Murano picked up his phone and tapped the screen several times. "And before you get any ideas of going to your uncle and trying to take credit for all this yourself, you should consider how he would react, if he found out you lied to him, and were so blind that you didn't see this."

Murano paused and glanced at Delgado. "That goes for both of you. You should also know that I just sent a recording of this conversation to one of my men. If something happens to me, or I find out either of you told Ruben first, this recording will find its way to his inbox, and you can explain it." He smiled smugly. "I'm sure he'll be understanding."

Delgado nodded and exhaled deeply. "And the third thing?"

"Kovacs and Wynn are mine."

CHAPTER 43

WYNN SHOWERED AND WENT out for a late lunch, then returned to his room at the All-Nighter. He slid his phone onto the dresser, where it came to rest next to his Harley keys. *The bike's still over at Kovacs' from Saturday night.*

With a little time to kill, he called for an Uber. Forty-five minutes later, he stood in front of the gate at the entrance of Kovacs' driveway.

He stabbed the button on the call box and waited. A female voice came over the speaker. "Yes?"

"Hi. It's Sean Wynn. I left my bike here from the party the other night. I came to pick it up."

He waited again, a full minute, before the gate clicked open and rolled to the side. As he strolled up the driveway, Kovacs descended the stairs from the house to meet him.

"I was kind of hoping you'd leave it here," Kovacs said, "considering Carmen bought you a new one."

Wynn smiled as they turned and strolled toward the garage. "Why would you want my second-hand junk? I'm sure you could have something brand-new, exactly what you want, delivered within the hour."

Kovacs grinned. "It might take a little longer than that, but you're probably right."

Wynn paused. "I was thinking. I'm surprised Delgado doesn't have us make the pickup right there in Nogales. Why take the risk of having her guys drive 250 miles into Arizona? Not to mention the stop and transfer time."

"Not her call. Garcia insists on it."

Protecting the tunnel location. He thumbed the keys in his pocket. Felt the empty AirTag case. "What about the trucks?"

"What about 'em?"

"Why not swap trucks instead of transferring the cargo? That would reduce the stop time to less than a minute."

Kovacs nodded. "Maybe." He paused. "Why the sudden concern?"

Because I want to find something to nail your ass with. "Nothing sudden about it. I've only done it once, but the stop felt the most exposed. If I'm going to be doing this a lot, I want it as tight as possible. Self-preservation, remember?"

"Yeah." Kovacs smiled grimly. "I get it. I'll mention it to Carmen next time I see her."

Kovacs' phone chirped in his pocket. He pulled it out and looked at the screen. "Speaking of..." He tapped the screen and put the phone to his ear. "Carmen. What a pleasant surprise. What can I do for you?"

Wynn couldn't make out whatever Delgado was saying. Kovacs' face revealed nothing.

"We'll be there," Kovacs said. He disconnected the call and turned toward Wynn. "You can ask her yourself. Ruben wants both of us, and Vaz, to meet him in Nogales tomorrow."

Wynn's spider-sense spiked. "What about?"

"She didn't say. If I had to guess, he might want to talk about Murano. I can't imagine there won't be some blowback from that botched kidnap attempt."

Wynn paused. Something about that theory seemed too neat. Too clean. "Remind me why we think Murano was behind it?"

"They were his guys, according to Vaz and Eddie."

"And you trust them?"

Kovacs shook his head disgustedly. "You two are getting to be a real pain in the ass. Maybe I should let you fight it out. I wouldn't have to listen to this shit anymore."

Wynn shrugged. "I'm just saying, from Murano's perspective, it seems like a high-risk move when he had no need to be that desperate."

"So who did it?" Kovacs asked.

Wynn shrugged again.

Kovacs turned and walked toward the house. "Let me know when you figure it out."

Wynn watched him go. *That's the million-dollar question, isn't it?*

———

Two hours after leaving the Bellagio, Eddie sat with Vaz in the back office at the Deuce. Vaz used it as his own when Kovacs wasn't around. The door was closed, even though there was no one else in the building.

"You saw him?" Vaz asked skeptically.

"Alive and well. And apparently now on Murano's payroll."

Vaz had seen Chad's body lying in the sand outside Wickenburg. There had been blood. But it was dark. And he hadn't looked closely. *Damnit! I knew Wynn was gonna fuck us.*

"But this can be a good thing," Eddie continued. "Murano's asking for a meeting with all of us. Uncle Ruben, Delgado, Kovacs,

Wynn, you, and me. All in one place." He stopped and looked at Vaz, then raised his eyebrows. "All in one place."

Vaz sat motionless, staring back. Slowly his right lip curled upward.

CHAPTER 44

WYNN RODE THE HARLEY back to the All-Nighter and parked in the lot next to Delgado's Indian. As nice as the new bike was, he didn't want to get too attached. He knew Ruiz wouldn't let him keep it. It was sure to get impounded and used as evidence, then sold off at some government auction.

He removed the seat from the Harley and pulled out the second AirTag, then fitted it into the leather case attached to his keys. He hadn't liked the feeling of being off the grid without his phone or an AirTag when he'd gone to Nogales yesterday.

And now, with the plan to go back tomorrow, Ruiz could use this new AirTag to track Wynn, and maybe find the entrance to the tunnel.

He replaced the seat on the Harley and hustled up the stairs to his room, which was still a mess, exactly the way he'd left it. As a weekly tenant, he didn't get daily housekeeping. Which was just as well. After rearranging the furniture, he was sure they wouldn't be pleased.

He pushed the mattress off the box spring and retrieved the burner. There were several text messages from Krista. They started with a simple *call me,* and became more insistent as the afternoon wore on.

Frowning, he punched her number and waited for the call to connect. She picked up on the first ring.

"Which ear?" she said immediately.

"What?"

"Terrance. The body you found. Which ear was missing?" Tension filled her voice.

Wynn paused and closed his eyes. He recreated the scene in his mind. Crouching in the dark. His right hand holding the Sig, his left rummaging over the body. How he had reached across the victim's face toward the left ear because that's the one he subconsciously believed to be missing. When he found it in place, he had moved to the right side of the victim's head, careful to go across the top so as not to accidentally brush across an eyeless socket. "His right," Wynn said.

"Did he have the other?"

"His other ear? Yeah, he did. We knew that."

"It wasn't him," Krista said.

"What?"

"It wasn't him! It was his left ear that was mailed to Mom and Dad."

"How do you know?"

"Terrance was homophobic. He wanted an earring but didn't want people to think he was gay. And yes, I know, left or right doesn't matter much today. But fifteen years ago, when he got it done, there was this saying, 'left is right, and right is wrong.' For straight guys, the left ear was the one you got pierced, because the right meant you were gay."

"So?"

"Terrance had this stupid iron cross stud he wore all the time. When Mom and Dad received the package, they knew it came from Terrance because they recognized the stud. In his *left* ear."

Wynn thought back again. Remembered the slick wetness of the hole, and on the foot; remembered washing the blood off his hands when he stopped at the burger joint in Tucson. *Terrance's injuries were two-to-three weeks old. They'd have scabbed over. These were still fresh. That means...*

"Shit," Wynn said. "You're right. They did this to someone else to make me think it was Terrance. To see how I would react. Another of Kovacs' damn tests."

"Terrance is still alive," Krista said.

Wynn thought back to the basement in Nogales. To the second door at the end of the hall. The one that was partially open but blocked by Garcia's man. *He wanted me to think the room was empty, but...*

"I know where they're keeping him," Wynn said. "I couldn't have been more than ten feet away from him."

"Where?"

"In the basement of the house on the Mexican side of the tunnel."

"Do you know where that house is?" Krista's voice rose. "Could you find it again?"

Wynn shook his head. "Not now. They kept me blindfolded. But Garcia's called a meeting. I'm heading back there tomorrow."

"You've got to tell Ruiz. Have him track you and get some people down there."

"I'm on it."

———

Ruiz and Todd were reviewing the case file in Ruiz's office when Wynn's burner buzzed.

Ruiz put it on speaker so Todd could hear. "Hey—"

Wynn interrupted, getting straight to the point. "Tell me again, which ear did they cut off?"

"What?" Ruiz asked.

"Terrance. Which ear?"

"His left. Why?"

"Because the body I found had its *right* ear missing. It wasn't Terrance."

Ruiz paused, briefly exchanging a look with Todd. "Are you sure?"

"Yeah. I recreated the scene in my mind. Went through all the motions. It was definitely his right ear."

Ruiz paused as he considered the implications. "You're telling me these sick bastards killed and mutilated someone just to make you *think* it was Terrance?"

Wynn hesitated. "Yeah, that's exactly what they did."

Ruiz's stomach turned. "Shit. I've already told the family."

"Call 'em back. Tell 'em I was wrong."

Ruiz paused. Didn't say anything.

"What?" Wynn asked.

"You may be wrong now, but that doesn't mean you won't be. I don't know if I want to give them hope only to have to tell them again."

"Then don't tell 'em," Wynn said quickly, his voice growing urgent. "Garcia's called a meeting. Kovacs and I are both going to Nogales tomorrow. I've got that second AirTag. Track me. If I find him, you can go in and get him. And *then* you can call 'em with the good news."

Ruiz hesitated, his mind going to his earlier conversation with Parker and Hodges. They wanted Wynn out. Now.

"Okay, Sean. Go do your thing. We'll track you. But don't expect the cavalry to come running as soon as you find him. We'll have to coordinate with the Mexican authorities and that'll take time. Get down there, find him, and get your ass back. Then you're coming out." Ruiz paused. "And do not, I repeat, do not, try to save him. Got it?"

"Got it." Wynn disconnected; the line went dead.

Ruiz and Todd looked at each other. "Do you really think he's still alive?" Todd asked.

Ruiz sighed. "I don't know. Maybe. But if this is one of Kovacs' tests, that means he's suspicious. Between that and this guy Chad still floating around, Wynn's cover could be blown any minute."

"Assuming it hasn't already," Todd added grimly.

"The Hampson's already think Terrance is dead. And for all we really know, he is. If Wynn goes down there, there's a good chance he won't come back."

"What do you want to do?" Todd asked.

"Pull him," Ruiz said. "Tonight."

CHAPTER 45

Wynn rolled into Pink a little before eight o'clock that evening. Early, but he was too amped up, the adrenaline flowing a little too freely to just sit around his motel room.

Apparently, everyone else in town was amped up, too. The lot was nearly full.

He came in the front, passing Marcus, who was stationed inside the front door.

"Your new friend is here," Marcus said, nodding to the semi-circular booth left of the main stage.

Carmen Delgado sat in the booth with one of her bodyguards. Wynn caught her eye, but she quickly looked away.

Strange. I just left her in Nogales yesterday.

Curious, and with nothing else to do, Wynn strolled over. He recognized the bodyguard. It was the one who'd let him out of the tunnel and gave him the new bike. The guy showed no sign of recognition or acknowledgement as Wynn approached.

Delgado looked up at him but remained silent.

"Ms. Delgado," Wynn said, "I never got a chance to thank you for the new bike. It's a beauty."

"It's nothing," Delgado said, her voice flat. "A token of my appreciation."

"Consider us even," Wynn said. He paused. "I thought I was going to be on your security team when you came to town."

"This is a quick trip. There was no time. Besides, I overreacted. The request was impractical. Consider yourself free from that obligation."

"Are you sure?" Wynn asked. His spider-sense tingled. Something was off. The friendliness was gone. She was being way too cool, too standoffish.

Delgado took a sip from her drink, then set the glass on the table. "When someone releases you from an obligation, or provides a way out of an impossible situation, the smart man takes it, Mr. Wynn."

Wynn didn't know what to say to that, so he replied with a simple, "Yes, ma'am."

"Good luck, Mr. Wynn."

Dismissed, Wynn returned to the bar, his mind racing as he tried to unravel Delgado's cryptic message. He barely noticed two guys wearing dark sport coats blocking the entrance to the area behind the counter. He pushed past them and stepped up next to Deborah.

"What happened to being on her security team?" Deborah asked.

Wynn shrugged. "Says she overreacted. Told me to forget it."

"Just as well," Deborah said. "New convention in town today. A lot of first night partiers. We can use your help back here."

"You got it," Wynn said, turning his attention to the crowd. Two more guys in dark suits forced their way through the packed bodies and leaned their elbows on the bar directly in front of him.

"What can I get you?" Wynn said.

"Sean Wynn?" the guy on the right asked.

Wynn's spider-sense leaped. "Who's asking?"

The guy flipped open the wallet in his hand to reveal a badge. "Clark County Sheriff. Are you Sean Wynn?"

Wynn knew what was happening; the exit plan was being execut-
ed. It just wasn't supposed to happen yet.

From day one, he'd agreed to Ruiz's exit plan. Not that he liked
it, but it made sense. Ruiz would have deputies of the Clark County
Sheriff arrest Wynn publicly, in front of Kovacs and as many wit-
nesses as possible, on charges of tax evasion and fraud. They would
then whisk him away to a federal, low-security penitentiary for the
next eighteen-to-twenty-four months, or however long it took for
Kovacs to either be imprisoned or forget about him.

At least that's what they wanted Kovacs to believe.

In reality, Wynn too, like Krista and Joshua, would be given a
new identity and a healthy bank account. He'd then be relocated to
someplace small and quiet, until it was deemed safe for him to be
"released" and resume his former life.

But with the prospect of Terrance still alive, and an opportunity
to find him in Nogales tomorrow, there was no way Wynn could pull
out now. He needed to stay in. Needed to see this thing through.

And he couldn't do that from inside a jail cell, or on the run.

Wynn looked the guy directly in the eye; shook his head
ever-so-slightly.

The guy stared right back. "I'll take that as a yes."

Quickly, Wynn reached into the cooler and grabbed two bottles
of beer and held them up. "Be right back."

He glanced left to the end of the bar where the two guys he'd
noticed moments ago looked back at him, blocking the only exit.

What the hell, Ruiz. You said I had a few more days.

He turned to his right and carried the two beers to the enclosed
end of the bar. He set the bottles down, then planted his hands on
the counter and launched himself up, leaping across.

With the four men and the back hallway behind him, Wynn
sprinted for the front door as two more suits appeared directly in
front of him.

Veering slightly, Wynn raised his arms and charged at the guy on the left, barreling into him and shoving him out of the way. The guy flew into the crowd, tumbling over a table.

With his momentum slowed, a pair of hands grabbed onto Wynn's shoulders. Wynn ducked and twisted away, then slammed a fist into the second guy's jaw, sending him crumpling to the floor.

The four guys from the bar pushed their way through the crowd, shouts of "Stop! Police! Stay back!" sounding throughout the club. Marcus rushed forward from his spot next to the door and threw himself into the guy who'd badged Wynn. They went down in a heap, forcing the other three to squeeze through the maze of tables in pursuit.

Wynn shot through the double doors leading to the foyer, then grabbed the podium sitting in front of the doorman. "Tell Vaz to pick me up at the warehouse," he said to the doorman.

The guy stared back at him, blankly.

"The warehouse!"

The guy nodded, and Wynn flung the podium to the floor, blocking the doors.

He burst through the glass front doors and sprinted across the street, turning left into an alley a half block away. He continued to run, zigzagging left and right through deserted streets and dark alleys as he made his way generally north. His goal was the warehouse where he and Vaz had delivered the girls and drugs after their run to Wickenburg three nights ago. After half a mile, he paused at the exit of an alley and glanced both ways.

A pair of headlights three blocks away were headed his direction.

Shit! How'd they— He remembered the AirTag attached to his keys.

An internal debate flared through his mind. He'd hated being off the grid when Delgado took him to Nogales yesterday, but he couldn't hardly broadcast his every move to Ruiz if he wanted any chance of finding Terrance.

Pulling the AirTag from its leather holder, he popped the cover off and removed the battery, then slipped the disassembled pieces back into his pocket and powered off his cell phone. He glanced around the corner.

The car stopped.

Satisfied, Wynn backtracked a half block into the alley, then darted between two buildings, making his way west several blocks, before finally turning north and resuming his path to the warehouse.

Within minutes, he stood in the shelter of a building across the street. The chain and padlock he'd tended a few days ago secured the gate, preventing him from going inside. He stayed hidden in the shadows, watching as various cars drove by, until more than an hour later, the familiar shape of Kovacs' Lincoln approached.

It slowed as it neared the gate. The passenger window buzzed down, revealing Vaz behind the wheel. Wynn gave a short whistle and the Lincoln stopped. The rear passenger door opened, and Wynn darted out from the sidewalk, leaping in as the Navigator slowly accelerated away.

Wynn glanced at Kovacs in the seat next to him. "Thanks." Vaz was behind the wheel, the shotgun seat empty.

"Fuck that," Kovacs said. "What the hell was that about?"

If he played this right, this little episode might further convince Kovacs he wasn't a plant. "I told you. I've got a problem with the IRS," Wynn lied.

"Bullshit. The IRS doesn't send six guys into a strip club for someone who's a little behind on their taxes."

Wynn followed the story Ruiz had come up with. "There might have been a little more to it. Money laundering. Fraud. They seem to think there may have been some Fentanyl involved."

Kovacs laughed disgustedly. "And you didn't think to tell me that?"

"Would you have hired me if I had?"

Kovacs shook his head unbelievingly. "You're full of surprises, Sean."

"I could say the same about you," Wynn said. "You got a place a guy could hang out until the heat cools down?"

"Mr. Garcia still wants us in Nogales tomorrow," Kovacs replied. "I've arranged for you to spend the night in Wickenburg. We'll figure it out after that."

Vaz pulled into a deserted parking lot where the old Ford cargo truck waited. Eddie sat behind the wheel, the driver's window down.

"I don't have all the details on when or where Garcia wants to meet, only that he wants us there tomorrow." Kovacs handed Wynn a small burner phone. "Eddie will set you up in a hotel. I'll be in touch in the morning. If you really don't want those guys to find you, ditch your old phone and keep this handy. Stay low and keep out of sight. Got it?"

"Got it."

"Any more surprises you want to tell me about?" Kovacs asked.

"No, that's all of it."

"Then get your ass out of here."

Wynn slid out of the Lincoln, then jumped into the cargo truck.

"Well, well, well," Eddie said as Wynn settled in. "Maybe you're more of a badass than I gave you credit for."

Wynn nodded. "Whatever." He wasn't in the mood for conversation. Especially with Eddie.

"Kovacs said to get you to Wickenburg."

"Yeah."

"You also need to ditch your phone."

Wynn's ears perked up. He felt his phone in his rear pocket. Ditching it was the last thing he wanted to do. He held up the burner

Kovacs had given him. "Already done. Traded it to Kovacs for this one."

Eddie eyed him suspiciously. "Good."

They settled into an uncomfortable silence. After a short while, Wynn sank down in his seat and pretended to sleep. He was both surprised and grateful that Eddie didn't ask a bunch of questions. His story, the lies, Ruiz's unexpected extraction attempt, and Carmen Delgado's cryptic warning, had his mind reeling as he tried to figure out what it all meant.

Three-and-a-half hours later, they pulled into a cheap motel on the outskirts of Wickenburg. The old Nissan he'd ridden in from the airport into Nogales sat in the lot. Wynn's spider-sense, which had been tingling almost constantly for the past week, kicked up a notch as Eddie pulled the truck to a stop beside it.

The driver's window of the old Nissan buzzed down next to Wynn, revealing two of Garcia's men inside. Wynn recognized the driver as the one with the cowboy boots. The guy's arm extended out the window, holding an old-fashioned room key.

"I had Hector get you a room," Eddie said. "Gotta keep you hidden."

"Great. Thanks." Wynn stepped out of the truck and took the key.

"One-oh-nine," Hector said, pointing at a door directly in front of him.

"Stay put until you hear from Kovacs, got it?" Eddie said.

Wynn nodded, then watched as Eddie backed up the truck and drove away.

Wynn waited, expecting the old Nissan to do the same. When it didn't move, he ambled over to his room and went inside. He set the key on the dresser, then pulled back the curtain and peeked through the window.

The old Nissan sat directly in front of his room. The guy in the passenger seat looked fast asleep, while Hector stared straight back, looking directly at Wynn.

————

Eddie dialed Vaz's number as he left the parking lot.

"Is it done?" Vaz asked.

"I've got two of my guys watching him. He's not going anywhere until we say so."

"You sure?" Vaz asked.

"Don't worry about it," Eddie said. "I've got this. I've got a couple more guys on the way. Wynn's locked up tighter than Fort Knox and doesn't even know it."

CHAPTER 46

SEEING TWO OF GARCIA's men outside his motel room did nothing to ease Wynn's spider-sense from tingling. There was something else going on. While it finally felt as if he'd gained Kovacs' trust, Delgado's coolness, Garcia's call for a meeting, the men outside his room, all indicated that something had changed.

Normally he'd call Ruiz, but that was no longer an option. The man had lied to him. Told Wynn he could stay in, only to pull the trigger on the exit plan without telling him. Clearly Ruiz wanted him out, but he was too close. He couldn't leave now.

But without Ruiz, Wynn was out on a limb. On his own. No backup. No help if things went sideways.

With maybe one exception.

Wynn took his phone into the bathroom. The burner Ruiz had given him was still back in his room at the All-Nighter. And there was no way he'd use the one Kovacs had given him. Can't hardly use the boss's phone to call his supposedly dead wife. The landline in the room was out of the question, leaving Wynn's cell as the only option.

He pulled up information on the AirTag, confirming what he already suspected. When he had removed the battery earlier, the

AirTag lost all connection with its previous setup. Reinstalling the battery wouldn't reconnect the previous devices. His connection to Ruiz was permanently severed.

Wynn reassembled the AirTag, then powered up his phone. Using it was a risk, but at this point, everything was. He reconnected the tag to the phone, then pulled up the messaging app. At almost two in the morning, he hoped Krista would hear his text. He punched in a short phrase: *U up?*

He waited thirty long seconds before a reply popped up. *S?*

Yeah.

Proof?

He thought about what to type. Eventually he decided on *BB*. The Brigadiers Ball. He hoped he wasn't being too cryptic.

Seconds later, the phone vibrated in his hand as the call came through. "Hey," he said.

"Where are you?" Krista whispered urgently. "Are you okay?"

"I'm fine. I'm in Wickenburg. A little north of Phoenix."

"What are you doing there? Why didn't you come out with Ruiz?"

"We're too close. I told you, I'm sure I know where Terrance is, I just need another day or two. Ruiz promised he wouldn't pull me out, but he tried. I ran."

"You ran to Wickenburg?"

Wynn shook his head. "Garcia called a meeting in Nogales tomorrow. Garcia's nephew, a guy named Eddie, drove me down. I'm hoping I can use this to confirm Terrance and the location, then I'm out."

"Ruiz is pissed you didn't come out tonight."

"Well, the feeling's mutual."

"I don't like it," Krista said. "You're going to be in there completely on your own."

"That's why I'm calling. Are you still near Vegas?"

"Yeah."

"Is Joshua with you?"

"He's at a safehouse with my parents," Krista said. "We're good on this end. What do you need?"

"I need you to lose Ruiz and his marshals."

———————

Krista hadn't climbed out of a bathroom window since she was a teenager, but tonight, it was the first of three tasks she'd need to complete if she had any hope of helping Wynn. The second task, transportation, she'd have to solve on her own. The third, weapons, Sean had told her exactly what to do.

The safehouse was a 1960s-era adobe-style ranch in Whitney, on the outskirts of Vegas. A few days ago, she'd been skeptical when she was told there was no alarm system in the old house. Now, she was grateful. It meant the only real obstacle was the night-duty agent watching TV in the living room.

Putting her ear to the bedroom door, she heard the unmistakable laughter of a 1980s sitcom echoing down the hall. She gently cracked the door open. The hallway and living room were dark, lit only by the flashing of the TV. The agent sat in the middle of a sofa facing the television, but with a turn of his head, would have a clear line of sight down the hallway.

Leaving the door slightly ajar, Krista gathered her clothes into a small, tight bundle, then peeked toward the living room. The agent's head drooped. Grabbing her phone, she slipped into the dark hallway and scurried to the bathroom.

Inside, she dressed quickly, then stepped to the window at the back wall. Unlatching the levers at the top of the frame, she pushed the window up, then slipped outside, landing gently in a bed of pea gravel.

She was several blocks away before she pulled out her phone and called for an Uber. She knew she was leaving a trail, but it didn't matter. Her hope now was to get out of town as quickly as possible. To do that, she needed a ride.

"Going into Vegas?" the driver asked when he pulled up beside her ten minutes later. The guy was mid-forties, Caucasian, with greasy hair that looked wet in the moonlight. He drove a shiny but several years old Toyota Corolla. On a normal night, she'd never get into a car with this guy. But compared to Danny Kovacs and Ruben Garcia, this guy was nothing.

"If you can make it," she said, eyeing the car skeptically.

"We'll make it," he said.

Krista rode in silence most of the way. The guy made a couple of attempts at conversation, but she shut him down each time. When they arrived at the All-Nighter, per Wynn's instructions, she caught the driver staring at her in the rearview mirror.

He thinks he's delivering me to a booty call. Or that I'm a pro. Whatever.

Eager to get away from the guy, Krista jumped out and went into the office. The night attendant, lounging in the back room, lowered his feet and came out when she stopped at the front counter.

"I lost my room key," she said. "Number 217. Sean Wynn." She was suddenly glad Sean's name was unisex.

"Got some ID?" the guy said.

"Lost that, too. With the key."

"Not supposed to give out a room key without ID."

"C'mon, man. It's been a really bad night. Give me a break."

The guy rolled his eyes. "Not like I give a crap." He grabbed a blank key card, stuck it in a machine, and tapped a few keystrokes on his computer. "Here ya' go."

Krista grabbed the card and rushed out of the office. The old Corolla with the creepy driver was still sitting out front. She was keenly aware of his eyes on her as she crossed the parking lot and climbed the concrete stairs to the second floor.

She found Wynn's room and ducked inside, bumping her knee against the dresser that had been moved in front of the window. She turned on the light and rushed to the bed, where she pushed the mattress off the box spring. Finding the loose staples, she pulled the fabric back and retrieved the spare Glock, holster, and ammunition Wynn had stuffed in there.

Strapping the holster to her waist, she marveled at how natural it felt on her hip. Four years in the Corps, five years married to Danny, and now six years of looking over her shoulder, meant she had spent plenty of time on the range. If it came to a gunfight, she'd know what to do.

Glancing back into the box spring, she saw the burner phone Ruiz had given Wynn, and a black cinch sack. She stuffed the phone into her pocket, and then, curious, pulled out the cinch sack.

Her eyes popped wide as she retrieved a neat bundle of hundred-dollar bills. Inside the cinch sack were at least another dozen bundles. Giving it only a moment's thought, she swung the cinch sack over her shoulder and rushed out the door.

The creepy guy in the Corolla was still there.

She waved to him as she rushed down the stairs, and over to his car.

"Your John's not there, huh?" the guy said. "Or maybe he's uglier than you can stand?"

"Shut up," Krista snapped. "Can this piece of shit handle a road trip?"

"Sure. Where do you want to go?"

"None of your business. I just need to know if it'll get me down the road?"

"Well, sure, but I kind of need to know—"

"Get out," Krista interrupted. "I'm buying it from you."

"What?"

Krista slung the cinch sack off her shoulder, pulled out a bundle of bills, and tossed it at the guy. "I'm buying your car from you."

The guy looked startled as he caught the cash, then paused as he flipped through the stack. "I don't know..."

Krista tossed the guy another bundle. "I guarantee that's twice what this piece of shit is worth. Now get out."

The guy eyed the cinch sack. A greedy look flashed across his face.

Krista drew the Glock and leveled it at him. "Don't even think about it. Now get. Out."

The look of greed turned to fear as the guy unbuckled his seat belt and stumbled from the car, dropping one of the bundles. As he bent to retrieve it, Krista pushed him out of the way, sending him sprawling to the pavement. She jumped behind the wheel, grabbed his phone from the dash, and threw it at him, then turned the ignition and sped away.

She checked the second task—transportation—mentally off her list.

The third task, weapons, wasn't quite complete yet.

The night was still dark as she drove northeast on Highway 604, toward the speedway. In the short amount of time they'd been on the phone earlier, Wynn had done his best to pinpoint exactly where he had buried the TAC. Now, she followed the map in hopes of finding the proverbial needle in a haystack.

Once past the speedway, several dirt roads split off to the north. Most were blocked by concrete barricades.

Eventually, she found a road where one of the barricades had been moved, creating an opening wide enough to drive through. She briefly debated leaving the car and walking in, but quickly dismissed the idea. Speed was of the essence. Instead, she dimmed the headlights, leaving only the parking lights to illuminate the way.

She zoomed in on the map app, following the route Wynn had indicated, eventually coming to the large circular quarry dug into the desert floor. She circled to the east, scanning for the patch of bushes Wynn had described.

She immediately had a problem.

There wasn't just one thicket, but literally dozens.

Hoping to hide the car, she parked next to a large limestone mound. She lined herself up with the southern edge of the quarry and, using the flashlight on her phone, set off due east. Luckily, the bushes were concentrated around a thirty-foot rain wash that stretched from north to south.

Using a grid pattern, Krista traversed back and forth across the gully, slowly making her way northward. She stopped and dug in two promising locations, before finally hitting paydirt on the third.

The TAC lay exactly as Wynn had indicated, a piece of cloth stuffed in the barrel, and an armament vest wrapped around the midsection. She unwrapped the vest and brushed the sand off the rifle. It looked to be in good shape. Digging into the vest's pockets, she found the three magazines, two full, and one missing two rounds.

Lucky thirteen. Hope that's enough.

She ran her hand through the sand, making sure she hadn't missed anything. Satisfied, she stood, acutely aware of the cars streaming by on Interstate 15 barely a quarter mile away. She kept the rifle next to her leg as she hustled back to the Corolla, then tossed it in the back seat.

With her three tasks complete, she followed the dirt road back to the highway and paused as the first hints of daybreak glowed on the eastern horizon. She launched the map app on her phone and searched for Wickenburg.

Four hours away.

Slamming the car into gear, she punched the gas and sped onto the highway.

CHAPTER 47

WYNN MANAGED ONLY A few hours of restless sleep before finally getting up around seven a.m. He pulled the curtain aside and glanced out the window. Garcia's two goons were still sitting in the car directly in front of his room. Although now, the driver had his head back and eyes closed, clearly sleeping. The other guy was awake, but his head was tilted down, probably looking at his phone.

Letting the curtain fall back into place, Wynn grabbed his phone and went into the bathroom. He powered it on and checked for messages. There was only one. From Krista: *On my way.* It had come in more than an hour ago.

Wynn texted back: *Where now?*

Krista's reply took a few moments: *Near Kingman*

She was making good time. Could be to Wickenburg in two hours. Maybe less. Hopefully the two goons, or whomever was supposed to take him to Nogales, wouldn't be in any hurry. He wanted her close today.

He powered off the phone and jumped in the shower, more to waste time than anything else. When he came out, his stomach growled, giving him an idea.

He dressed, then went outside. The two goons in the car out front straightened up in their seats. Wynn gave a friendly wave, then moseyed around and tapped on the driver's window. The window buzzed down.

"You guys hungry?" Wynn asked. He pointed to a Denny's across the parking lot. "I'm buying if you want to join me."

The two goons looked at each other, then the driver shook his head.

"You sure?" Wynn asked. "We've still got a long drive ahead."

The driver shook his head again.

"Suit yourself." Wynn shrugged and strolled toward the Dennys. He didn't really care one way or the other. A table of three would likely take longer, thereby wasting more time and allowing Krista to get closer, but he could linger by himself. Waste as much time as he needed. What were they gonna do? Physically pull him out in front of a restaurant full of people?

A half hour later, the burner Kovacs had given him buzzed on the table.

Wynn picked it up. "Yeah?"

"Eddie will be there in twenty minutes," Kovacs said. "He'll drive you to Nogales. Vaz and I will meet you there."

"Okay."

"Be ready." Kovacs disconnected.

Wynn looked at the time. Unless she'd run into some kind of trouble, Krista should be no more than an hour out by now.

He finished his coffee, went to the restroom, then casually made his way to the cashier in the front lobby. There was a short line of people waiting to pay. He didn't mind. Just stepped in line and waited his turn. He checked the name tag of the cashier. Carol. He pulled out his personal cell, powered it on, and sent a short text, then powered it off.

When he reached the cashier, he presented his bill, along with a hundred-dollar bill. "Give the change to the server."

The cashier's—Carol's—eyebrows shot upward.

Wynn pulled another hundred-dollar bill from his wallet and wrapped it around his cell. "I was wondering if you could do me a favor. This phone belongs to a friend of mine. She's on her way and should be here within an hour, but I have to leave. Could you hang onto this and give it to her when she gets here?"

Carol smiled widely. "Sure. What's her name?"

Wynn hesitated. He realized that in all this time, he'd never bothered to ask what name Krista was going by now that she was in witness protection. He smiled in a *forgive-me-for-being-stupid* kind of way. "She got married recently, and she always used her middle name as a first name, so I'm not sure what she goes by these days. She'll ask if Sean left anything for her."

"And you're Sean?"

"I am." He handed her the phone, and the cash.

"I'll make sure she gets it," Carol said.

"Thanks."

She winked at him. "Come back anytime, Sean."

He nodded and smiled back, then turned and walked out.

Outside, the two goons had repositioned the old Nissan to keep watch through the diner windows. The old cargo truck was parked alongside. Eddie stood between the two.

Wynn strode straight to the truck, tapping the hood of the Nissan as he went past. "Should've joined me, fellas. It was great." Then to Eddie, he said, "You ready?"

Eddie tossed him the keys. "You drive."

"Fine by me." Wynn climbed in behind the wheel, pulling out the burner phone Kovacs had given him and making a show of looking at it. "This piece of shit. You got a decent phone?"

"Why?" Eddie asked, clearly annoyed.

"Check traffic. See what the best route is."

Eddie didn't bother. "Traffic's fine. Let's go."

"Until it isn't," Wynn said. "Phoenix traffic is a bitch. And you don't know until you're stuck in it. I don't want to be late, so check it."

Eddie sighed and pulled out a fairly recent model iPhone. It wasn't the latest generation, but new enough. He pulled up the maps app and checked the route through Phoenix. "Traffic is fine. Let's go."

That'll work, Wynn thought, not referring to the traffic at all.

———

The old Corolla wasn't the nicest car Krista had ever driven, but it was far from the worst. Most importantly, it was getting the job done, running smooth and steady as she pushed down the highway.

She arrived at the Denny's forty-five minutes after Wynn left. She had no trouble getting the phone from Carol and picked up a muffin and coffee to go. Back in the car, she powered up Wynn's phone and opened the tracker app. It worked. Wynn's AirTag showed him to be on the 303 approaching Interstate 10 on the west side of Phoenix, roughly fifty miles ahead.

Krista stopped for fuel, then jumped back onto the highway and jammed the accelerator to the floor.

CHAPTER 48

THE DRIVE TO NOGALES was long and uneventful. Wynn stopped outside of Tucson for gas and a sandwich, but otherwise maintained a steady pace right at the speed limit. As they approached Nogales, Wynn asked, "You know where we're going?"

Eddie's reply was predictable. "Shut up."

"Do we need to pick up Vaz and Kovacs?"

"Don't worry about it."

Five minutes later, Eddie said, "Exit here."

Wynn followed Eddie's directions through town and eventually onto a gravel road that undulated over several small hills. Wynn recognized the feel of the road and the sound of the gravel being thrown against the wheel wells.

We're going to the tunnel. He's gonna let me see it.

Wynn wasn't sure if that was a good thing or not. Maybe it meant they trusted him, or maybe it meant they didn't plan on him coming back.

Small houses lined the road on either side. Eventually Eddie directed him into a driveway largely hidden by overgrown acacia and oak trees. Once past the initial thicket, the driveway opened to a large clearing.

To his far left, two men with AR-15's sat on the porch of a small ranch-style home. The place was made of gray cinderblock, turned a mucky tan near the ground by the sand and dirt of the surrounding area. Immediately in front of him, two more men stood in front of a three-bay service garage. A small entry door sat between the second and third bays.

The area to the right of the garage had been cleared of trees and sloped away to the south, giving view of the rusted steel border fence a third of a mile away. The fence snaked through the center of a shallow valley, then rose across rolling hills in either direction. Small and medium-sized houses packed the rising hillside on the other side.

One of the men pressed a button, and the garage door on the far right slid up. Wynn glanced at Eddie, who nodded, then eased the truck into the service bay, feeling the familiar bump as the tires crawled up onto the concrete floor. A second man motioned Wynn forward until the truck was all the way in.

The harsh grating of metal on metal echoed as the door slid closed behind them. Eddie jumped out to greet the guards, while Wynn took his time climbing out of the truck, pausing to tie his shoe. *The tag won't work underground. And doesn't give history. Krista needs to see me now.*

Standing, Wynn roamed around the truck. Eddie and one of the guards watched while the second guard held a light switch next to the door. A motor whined as a large concrete slab, elevated by a fourteen-inch hydraulic lift, rose from the first bay, revealing a four-foot-deep, six-by-eight-foot pit in the concrete floor.

As soon as the slab was clear, one of the guards slung his AR-15 onto his back, then jumped into the pit. The concrete appeared smooth and unbroken. The guard worked his fingers into a tiny crack at the bottom of the far wall, then slowly pulled a panel away, revealing a dark opening. Cool, stale air wafted up. The guard got down on his hands and knees and disappeared down the ladder.

"After you," Eddie said.

Wynn jumped down and stepped to the opening. While appearing from the outside like solid concrete, the removable wall was in fact just a framed piece of plywood covered with a thin layer of cement. Wynn got down on his hands and knees and backed into the tunnel.

Gripping the familiar rebar ladder, Wynn leaned back and looked down. *At least the lights are on.* He counted the twenty-six rungs until he once again stood in the small chamber at the bottom of the ladder. The first guard was already making his way down the gently sloping tunnel. Glancing up, the light from above faded as a second guard, and then Eddie backed through the opening and descended the ladder.

"Let's go," Eddie said when he reached the bottom. Wynn gave one last glance to the surface as the light faded, and the plywood door slid back into place.

———

Krista pulled over to the side of the gravel road. She'd sped like hell all the way from Wickenburg trying to make up the forty-five minutes she was behind Wynn. Now, barely a mile ahead, the red dot that represented Wynn's AirTag stopped.

She zoomed in on the map, trying to decipher the lines and rectangles that represented roads and buildings, then looked up as she attempted to match those with the real world outside. Her heart stopped when she glanced back down at her phone.

The red dot was gone.

———

Wynn crouched in the low tunnel as he counted his steps, pausing to take a deep breath each time he felt the warm, fresh air that flowed down from the ventilation shafts. He slowed at the bend where he'd found the body, quickly examining the dirt for stains. Seeing none, he made the turn and continued on.

When he reached the chamber at the other end, the first guard had already scrambled up the wooden ladder and was gone. Wynn paused, his gaze drawn to the wheeled garden carts and crates of dynamite. Turning to Eddie, he said, "Last time I needed a blindfold to go up."

Eddie's smile was thin. "Last time we didn't know if we could trust you." He nodded to the ladder. "Head on up."

Wynn grabbed a rung and climbed, emerging a few moments later in the dingy basement. He scrambled to his feet, thinking, *If I'm right, Terrance is down that hall. Need to confirm, then pinpoint where the hell this place is.*

He stepped to the side as Eddie popped out of the tunnel.

"Your piece?" Eddie held out his hand.

"I thought you trusted me," Wynn said.

"Not that much." He kept his hand out.

Wynn rolled his eyes in exaggerated disgust and handed his Glock to Eddie, who placed it on the workbench beneath the stairs. Wynn was once again grateful for the knife strapped to his ankle.

"The party's upstairs," Eddie said, motioning Wynn to lead the way.

Wynn took the stairs two at a time, then followed voices to the small dining room where Garcia, Delgado, Kovacs, and Murano all sat around the small dining table. Vaz leaned against a kitchen counter while two of Garcia's goons stood on each side of the archway. A third propped himself against the back of a couch in the adjoining room.

Carmen Delgado caught Wynn's eye and gave the slightest of nods, before Garcia said, "Now that we're all here, Arturo, perhaps you can tell us why."

CHAPTER 49

Krista inched the car along the gravel road, crawling at a snail's pace, her eyes darting back and forth between the map on her phone and the world outside.

After a brief moment of panic when the dot had disappeared, she'd snapped a screenshot of the map where it had last shown Wynn's AirTag. Now, as she zoomed in, she compared the image to her surroundings as she eased ahead.

For whatever reason, she'd expected the entrance to the tunnel to be in a remote, isolated area. What she saw around her was anything but. Driveways marked by mailboxes mounted on thick posts led off from the main road every forty yards or so. Dense trees and brush made it hard to see the houses beyond, but moving slowly, she was able to make out in the real world what showed on her screen.

A thicket of overgrown acacias blocked her view of the next property. She pressed the brake and stopped next to a dirt drive practically hidden by trees.

No mailbox. They wouldn't want one.

Reversing slightly, she backed up a few feet, then turned onto the dirt track, her right hand going instinctively to her side and tapping the reassuring bulk of the Glock at her waist.

Beyond the trees, a clearing opened in front of two buildings. One man stepped off the porch of a small house on her left, while another leaned against the corner of a three-bay garage directly ahead. The man who approached wore a loose shirt, untucked, his hands held up, motioning her to stop. The left arm of the other man was hidden behind the corner of the building.

Glancing at the screenshot once more, she rolled forward and eased to a stop, then buzzed the window down.

Showtime.

"Private property, *senora*. You need to leave."

She shut down the engine and popped the hood. "I wish I could." She opened the door and stepped out. The man leaning against the garage stood straighter, his left arm still out of sight. "I'm overheating." Krista nodded toward the garage. "You don't sell any coolant in there, do you?"

The first man hurried to the front of the car and pushed the hood down, locking it back into place. "No. You need to leave."

"Maybe some water? For the radiator?"

"No, *senora*. We cannot help you." He stepped close to Krista, herding her back toward the open car door. "*Por favor,* you need to go."

Krista took a step back, giving the man a cross look. "Geez. Thanks for nothing. Are all your neighbors this helpful?"

The man stared back.

She climbed in behind the wheel. "Maybe those cops up the road can help. There's enough of 'em."

The color drained from the man's face. "Go!"

Krista started the car and backed up, then turned and headed out the driveway. A glance in the rearview mirror showed the man hustling to his friend near the garage.

Hope this works.

She turned right and proceeded up the main road to the next driveway, where she eased in and parked beneath a large oak. Quickly, she slipped out of the car, drew the Glock from her hip, and struck out into the trees.

Moments later, the backside of the small house appeared through the brush. She stooped low and crept to the back wall, then slipped along the side to the front. Crouching down, she peeked around the corner.

Neither guy was in sight, but the door to the middle garage bay was open. An old Nissan pickup sat nose out. Behind it, an old Ford cargo truck sat in the third bay. A hydraulic humming came from the open door.

Moments later, the humming stopped, and the two guys jumped into the old SUV and roared out of the garage. The door closed behind them as the Nissan raced down the driveway and disappeared.

Unsure if anyone else was in either the house or the garage, Krista circled the back of the house, glancing in the few windows for any sign of life. Seeing nothing, she peeked through the glass panes of the back door into a deserted kitchen.

Her heart raced as she tried the knob. Locked. She surveyed the brush behind the house. With a quick exhale, she psyched herself up and smashed one of the small glass panes with the barrel of the Glock, then raced into the brush, hiding behind a thick bush.

After a couple of minutes and no reaction, Krista's heartbeat slowed sufficiently, allowing her to creep back toward the house and let herself in. Keeping the Glock raised in a two-handed grip, she swept the small house until she was sure it was empty.

One down.

She exited via the back door and snuck down the rear of the house until the garage became visible around the corner. The side of the garage was solid, void of either windows or doors. From her vantage, neither the front nor back was visible. She took a deep breath and raced across the twenty yards of open space between the buildings and sucked herself to the side of the garage.

Moving toward the back, she glanced around the corner and saw nothing but bushes growing close to the back wall. She slipped around to the rear, again finding only a blank wall, and another on the far side.

Feeling more confident the garage was also deserted, she took a few steps away from the building and examined the front. The guys in the Nissan had closed the bay door behind them, leaving the place closed up tight. A personnel door between the second and third bays contained a small rectangular window with reinforced webbing integrated into the glass.

Not breaking that one out.

With a quick glance back at the house, she took a step back and aimed the Glock at the lock, then hesitated. Lowering the gun, she reached for the doorknob.

It turned.

CHAPTER 50

The small kitchen was crowded.

Wynn stood next to Vaz, both of them behind Kovacs, who sat at the grown-up table with Garcia, Delgado, and Murano. Eddie circled the table and stood behind Murano.

Wynn's spider-sense jumped. He'd misread the situation. Garcia hadn't called the meeting; Murano had requested it. The symbolism of where Eddie stood was unmistakable. Kovacs had said Murano was going to strike back. *Maybe this is it.* The first hints of worry knotted his stomach.

Unable to see Kovacs' face, Wynn glanced at Delgado. Apprehension, as opposed to impatience, etched subtly across her face.

She knows why we're here. And doesn't like it.

"We're here, Mr. Garcia," Murano said, "because I'm afraid you may have put your trust in the wrong people."

"And why would you think that?" Garcia replied.

"Mr. Kovacs has a police informant on his team," Murano said, looking directly at Kovacs as he spoke.

Wynn's stomach dropped.

Kovacs gave a short, derisive laugh. He opened his mouth to speak, but Garcia held up a hand, silencing him.

Garcia looked curiously at Murano. "And who would that be?"

Murano slowly nodded toward Wynn. "The man right behind him. Sean Wynn."

"Fuck you," Wynn spat. "That's bullshit." He lunged forward, but Vaz grabbed him and held him back.

Kovacs smiled and shook his head, alternating his gaze between Garcia and Delgado, ignoring Murano. "He's pissed because Wynn's taken out half his guys. Hell, Wynn saved you, Carmen," Kovacs turned to Murano, "from *his* guys."

Murano shook his head. "Those were not my guys. I had nothing to do with Carmen's attempted kidnapping. What reason would I have? And if I did, would I really be stupid enough to request a meeting with all of you? No, whoever was behind that, it wasn't me."

Wynn glanced at Eddie, a slight smirk curling the corners of his mouth. Eddie's eyes darted behind Wynn. To Vaz. A knowing glance passed between the two.

Eddie and Vaz?

"But I do have proof that Wynn is working with the cops," Murano continued.

"I'd love to see that," Kovacs said.

Murano nodded to one of Garcia's men who stood in the archway. He disappeared around the corner and came back a moment later.

With Chad.

Kovacs' eyes widened briefly. He glanced at Vaz, but Vaz looked away.

"Who's this?" Garcia asked, a slight frown creasing his forehead.

"Why don't you tell him," Murano said. He nodded toward Kovacs, who closed his eyes, as if not wanting to believe what he was seeing. Kovacs remained silent, so Murano continued. "This is a man Wynn was supposed to have killed. But instead, Wynn put a tracker on him. A few hours later, the cops showed up. How could that happen if he weren't working with them?"

"He's lying," Wynn said. "I felt sorry for the asshole, so I let him live. But I don't know shit about a tracker."

The room exploded in a chorus of angry voices, everyone shouting to be heard. Garcia nodded to one of his men who pulled a Sig from his waistband and pointed it first at Chad, who fell silent, then at Wynn, who did the same. By the time the man pointed it at Kovacs and Murano, the room was quiet.

Garcia addressed his man with the gun, then nodded at Wynn. "Take him downstairs—"

"Let me," Eddie interrupted.

Garcia stopped, then stared at Eddie for a long moment. Finally, he nodded, and said, "Put him with Danny's other guest."

————

Vaz shoved Wynn toward the hall. "Move."

With Eddie using his gun to prod Wynn down the stairs, Vaz risked a quick look back. Carmen Delgado was watching them, but no one followed.

When they reached the basement, Vaz stopped and turned toward Wynn, then sucker-punched him in the gut. "Big mistake, asshole. I knew you were a plant all along, but you convinced Kovacs. Now that that's over, you're mine."

Vaz stepped to the first doorway, grabbed a key off a hook next to the door. "There's someone I want you to meet." He swung the door open and glanced inside. Kovacs' guest sat huddled on a small mattress against the side wall. He stepped back as Eddie used his pistol to prompt Wynn toward the door.

"Who the fuck is this?" Wynn asked.

Vaz smiled "Nice try."

"Whoever the fuck this is or however you think I know him, you're wrong," Wynn said.

"Then you are one of the unluckiest bastards on the planet." Vaz grabbed Wynn by the arm and shoved him into the small room. "Sit tight," he said coldly. "This won't take long."

Vaz slammed the door closed, then locked it and hung the key back on its hook.

"How many others are in the house?" Eddie whispered. He ducked beneath the stairs, hauled out a crate, and opened it. Reaching inside, he handed Vaz a Kevlar vest.

"None. Everyone I saw was in the kitchen," Vaz said. "Your uncle may have one or two more outside, but if we do this right, they won't matter." He put on the vest and pulled a spare magazine from one of its pockets. Full. He stuffed it back and grabbed a Glock from the crate.

"Good," Eddie said. "We need to take out everybody. Make it a bloodbath. Just like fucking Scarface."

Vaz ejected the mag from the Glock and checked it. Satisfied, he stuffed it into a holster on his right hip. "And do it quick. Hit anyone around the perimeter first. Make sure no one gets out. Those in the middle will have no place to go."

Vaz reached into the crate again, pulled out an AR-15 assault rifle. He checked its mag and slammed it home, while Eddie got similarly geared up.

When they were both fully locked and loaded, Eddie stepped toward the stairs. "Let's do this."

"Aren't you forgetting something?" Vaz asked.

"What?"

Vaz nodded toward the hallway that held Wynn and Terrance. "We need our shields."

———

Wynn was surprised to see Terrance Hampson in better shape than he'd expected. He was sitting on a thin mattress with a pillow and blanket behind him. Bandages covered his eye, ear, hands, and feet. His clothes were relatively clean, and he looked—and smelled—like he'd been recently bathed. An empty plate sat on the floor beneath the sink.

"Terrance?" Wynn asked.

Hampson nodded cautiously.

Wynn crouched down next to him. "My name's Sean Wynn. Krista and the U.S. Marshals sent me to find you."

Terrance began to sob, shaking uncontrollably.

"Hey. It's okay." Wynn reached out and put a hand on Terrance's shoulder, pulled him into a loose embrace. "We're gonna get you out of here."

Although at the moment, he had no idea how.

CHAPTER 51

KOVACS TRIED NOT TO fidget. Tried not to show his nervousness. He wasn't sure what was going on with Wynn, but it didn't matter. The only thing that mattered was what Garcia believed. And Murano was doing a good job convincing him.

No one had said a word since Vaz and Eddie had taken Wynn to the basement. Garcia and Delgado sat stoically, while the corners of Murano's mouth ticked up in a satisfied smile.

I've got to get out of here.

Kovacs couldn't help himself. The words slipped out. "What's taking so long?"

Delgado let out an exaggerated sigh. "I'll go check." She strode through the kitchen toward the stairs.

"I'll go with you." Kovacs rose from his chair but was stopped when one of Garcia's men put a hand on his shoulder.

"Why don't you stay here," Garcia said.

————

Wynn had gotten Terrance calmed down, even gotten him to his feet and tested his strength and balance. He wasn't about to win any races, but he could stand and walk. *They started treating me better a few days ago,* Terrance had said. *Had a doctor come in and treat my wounds, gave me some antibiotics. They even started feeding me.* Wynn wasn't sure what to make of that, but he was glad Terrance could move on his own. If an opportunity to escape did present itself, Terrance's mobility might be the key to both their survival.

Wynn heard the deadbolt slide back. He stood and turned toward the door, curling his fingers to hold the knife hidden up his sleeve. "Stay back," he told Terrance. He squinted his eyes, hoping to reduce the temporary blindness from the incoming light before his pupils adjusted.

The door swung open to reveal Vaz and Eddie, decked out in bulletproof vests and armed with AR-15s. Both guns pointed straight at him.

"Time to party, hero," Eddie said.

Wynn hesitated.

Eddie lowered his weapon and stepped into the small room. As Wynn prepared to strike, there was movement behind Vaz.

"Hold on, Eddie," Carmen Delgado said.

Wynn glanced beyond Eddie and saw Delgado holding a Glock to the base of Vaz's skull. It was a bit of a reach considering their difference in size, but there was no doubt what she was doing.

One brief thought flashed through Wynn's mind. *Why?* But when Eddie turned his head toward Delgado's voice, the time for thinking was over. Wynn flicked his wrist, dropping the knife into his hand, and lunged at Eddie, aiming for his throat. Eddie raised his shoulder, not much, but enough to cause the blade to bounce off his Kevlar vest and slice him across the cheek.

Wynn's momentum carried him into Eddie, the two of them crashing into Vaz and Delgado. Feet tangled in the cramped hallway and Wynn felt himself falling, landing in a heap on top of Eddie and Vaz. Delgado scrambled away. Wynn brought the knife up and slashed again, this time catching Eddie on the tricep. Better than nothing, but not by much.

As Vaz pushed off the floor, Wynn kicked out a leg to pin him down. If either man had the space to raise their rifles, the fight would be over.

Terrance, apparently realizing the same thing, leaped forward, landing on top of Vaz, struggling to take the AR-15. He was no match for the larger man. Vaz brushed him away like a flea and rolled free as Eddie squirmed beneath Wynn.

Gotta keep Eddie between us.

Locking the fingers of his free hand beneath Eddie's vest, Wynn rolled onto his back, pulling Eddie with him. It wasn't the optimal position for hand-to-hand combat, but he needed Eddie and his vest between Vaz and himself.

Eddie sneered down at Wynn, his face a mask of rage.

Wynn swung the blade again, this time opening a two-inch gash above Eddie's ear.

Eddie cursed in pain as blood streamed down the side of his head and dripped into Wynn's eyes. With a speed that surprised Wynn, Eddie lunged for Wynn's wrist. He slammed his hand to the floor. Once, twice, three times. Wynn held tight, gripping the knife with all his might.

For a brief moment, Eddie backed off. Wynn sensed Eddie's hand moving toward his waist. *He's got another gun!*

Wynn grabbed Eddie's wrist, then wrenched his other hand violently, breaking Eddie's grip and burying the five-inch blade into his shoulder. Wynn pulled the knife out, twisting as he went. Eddie grunted as his left arm went limp. Wynn drew the blade back, preparing to thrust it toward Eddie's throat, when Eddie jerked his good hand free and lunged for the blade.

He caught Wynn's wrist an inch before the knife reached his neck. Wynn raised his hips and tilted to the right, exposing the Glock at

Eddie's waist. Wynn grabbed it, slipped it beneath the Kevlar vest, and pulled the trigger.

A muffled pop sounded throughout the room, followed by silence.

Wynn felt the resistance drain from Eddie's body. His thoughts immediately turning to the next threat.

Where's Vaz?

Wynn pushed Eddie's body off him and wiped the blood from his eyes, then looked up the short hallway to the main room. Terrance sat leaning against the wall, his head swiveling back and forth as if watching a tennis match between Wynn on one side, Delgado and Vaz on the other.

Beyond Terrance, Vaz was on one knee. Perfectly aligned behind him was Delgado, with a Glock in her outstretched hands.

Pointed directly at Wynn.

————

Kovacs froze at the sound of the gunshot. Muffled, but unmistakable. He glanced around the table to Garcia and Murano. Murano scraped his chair back, but on a look from Garcia, remained seated. All three guards drew their weapons.

Garcia withdrew a Colt Commander from his jacket, then sneered at Kovacs. "You wanted to see what was happening. Go check it out."

Garcia nodded to the guard next to Kovacs. "Go with him."

Kovacs got up and crept down the hallway with the guard following. He drew the Sig still strapped to his waist.

From behind, the guard said, "Hold it."

Kovacs raised his hands and turned back to the guard. He held the gun loosely, his fingers extended, not on the trigger. "What?"

"I'll take that."

"Then you go first," Kovacs said.

The guard looked indecisive.

"I don't know what the hell's going on here today," Kovacs said. "But if you want me to go down there, I'm taking this with me. You want my gun? No problem. But you go first."

The guard paused, debating.

"Fuck it. Come on." Kovacs turned and stepped toward the basement door.

––––––––

"Move!" Delgado barked at Vaz. She motioned the gun in Wynn's direction. "Quickly!"

Terrance gingerly picked up the AR-15 that Vaz had dropped to the floor. With his bandaged hands, he could barely lift it, let alone fire it.

"Careful with that, Hampson," Delgado said. "I'm a good guy."

Wynn jumped to his feet and pushed the rifle in Terrance's hand down. He pulled him deeper into the hallway as Delgado forced Vaz to stumble toward them. Blood covered Delgado's hands and dripped from Vaz's upper arm.

What the hell is she doing?

The sound of feet shuffling across the floor came from above. Wynn reached down and picked up the knife that he'd dropped during the fight and slipped it back into its sheath on his ankle.

"In there." Delgado motioned to the small room where Wynn and Terrance had been held. "All the way back," she said as Vaz went inside. When he was in, she swung the door closed and slammed the deadbolt into place. Turning to Wynn and Terrance, she said, "Let's get you out of here."

"Are you hurt?" Wynn asked, nodding at Delgado's bloody hands.

"I'm fine. It's his," Delgado said, nodding toward Vaz.

Wynn nodded, then ran over to the shelves beneath the stairs and grabbed his Glock. "Who are you?"

"Doesn't matter. Get to the tunnel." Delgado grabbed Terrance by the shoulder and pushed him forward.

Movement on the stairs caused Wynn to glance up.

Kovacs stood three steps from the bottom. "What the fuck?"

Wynn looked back, tried to understand the source of Kovacs' confusion. Delgado was herding Terrance out of the hallway. With a gun. Exactly as it should be.

Except Terrance also has a gun.

As if in slow motion, Terrance raised the rifle toward Kovacs and started firing, his shots missing wildly, spraying across the room.

Wynn leaped toward Terrance and pushed the rifle down, forcing him back into the hallway as Kovacs dove toward the tunnel and returned fire. From the top of the stairs, the barrel of an AR-15 peeked from beneath the ceiling and strafed bullets throughout the room.

Wynn pressed Terrance to the floor while Delgado snapped off several rounds with her Glock. The telltale smack of a bullet hitting flesh came from next to him, and Delgado sank to the floor. Wynn ripped the AR-15 from Terrance and sent a volley of bullets toward the top of the stairs. The gunfire from above stopped, then one of Garcia's men tumbled down the steps.

Scanning for Kovacs, Wynn realized he must've gone down the tunnel. Turning, he found Delgado slumped against the wall, her left shoulder bright with blood.

"Will said you had a real problem following orders," she said.

Wynn stared back at her, perplexed. "Who?"

"Will... Parker."

Wynn's face was blank. He knew Parker from his time in Sturgis last summer but couldn't see how Delgado connected.

"*Agent* Will Parker. He said you were a wild card. And now, thanks to you, I've just wasted the last two years."

"You're FBI?"

"DEA. You're not the first to go undercover."

A glimmer of hope flared in Wynn's chest. "Are they close? Can you call 'em in?"

Chairs scraped across the floor on the ceiling above.

"We're in Mexico. Doesn't work that way here."

Wynn grabbed her beneath her good arm. "C'mon. We gotta get out of here."

Delgado winced in pain. "You go. I'll tell Ruben you shot me. Maybe I can still salvage this thing."

"No way. It's too dangerous," Wynn said.

Multiple pairs of feet scrambled across the floor above, stopping near the basement door.

"If I run, I'm dead," Delgado said.

Wynn knew she was right. Knew too, that time was running out.

Delgado nodded. "I'll be okay. Go."

He gave her one last look, then grabbed Terrance and shoved him toward the tunnel. After a quick glance down the ladder to make sure Kovacs wasn't waiting below, he slung the rifle over Terrance's head and pushed him to the opening in the floor. "Go!"

CHAPTER 52

KRISTA ENTERED THE GARAGE with the Glock up and ready, her heart pounding. The only light came from the window in the door, creating large, dark shadows throughout the room. The possibility of a tunnel entrance kept her on high alert, knowing anyone could appear at any time, from anywhere.

After a few moments her eyes adjusted, allowing her to make out cluttered shelves along the back wall and several large tool chests in the aisles between the bays.

To her right was the old Ford cargo truck she'd seen earlier. She crept around it, glancing through the tinted windows into the cab. Seeing no one, she crouched to examine the floor beneath the truck, looking for anything that might indicate a tunnel opening. Nothing.

Lowering her weapon, she scanned the garage. A hydraulic lift sat embedded in the floor of the first bay. She went back to the small door and flipped a switch, turning on the overhead fluorescent lights, then hustled back to the lift.

At first glance, the lift appeared like any other in-ground system. Two long steel plates sat parallel to one another exactly a car's width apart. They were connected by an iron beam, making an "H" shape. Beneath the middle beam, presumably, would be a foot-wide steel lift that would raise the assembly, allowing the mechanics to work beneath whatever vehicle sat atop it.

A switch hung from a cable against the wall. She stepped over and flipped it. Nothing happened.

Frustrated, Krista flipped the switch back and forth several times, eventually pressing it harder in the up position. The switch moved a fraction of an inch further, and the lift began to rise, a gleaming silver cylinder emerging from the floor. She held the switch until the metal "H" was above her head, six feet in the air, where it stopped with a heavy clunk.

Krista ducked beneath the lift and examined the floor around the cylinder. The concrete was smooth and perfect. A six-by-eight-foot rectangular joint line was pressed into the floor. Perfectly straight on all four sides. Used by masons all over the world to prevent slabs from cracking. She glanced at the floor of the second bay. No joint lines. Nor in the first bay where the cargo truck sat.

Returning to the switch, she examined the box that hung from the cable. No other toggles or buttons. She flipped the switch the other way, then pushed it beyond its first stop. The heavy lift descended back to the floor. When it was all the way down, she pushed the switches again, harder, but they didn't go any further. She toggled the switch back and forth, watching the lift rise and fall as she pushed.

Puzzled, she glanced around the room, looking for any other cables or switches, then cursed to herself. She hustled over to the light switch by the door. It was already in the up position, the fluorescent lights shining brightly. She pushed it further.

The slab around the lift began to rise.

———

Kovacs paused when he reached the turn in the tunnel. He ejected the magazine from his Glock and counted the remaining bullets. Eleven.

From the south end of the tunnel, he could hear the muffled sounds of automatic gunfire. The gradual bend prevented him from seeing that part of the tunnel. He wasn't sure what had happened to Vaz or Eddie, but had to assume that with Terrance holding an AR-15, he and Wynn had somehow overpowered them and were about to escape.

But what the hell was Carmen doing? Was she trying to stop them?

It didn't look like it. But things had happened so quickly he wasn't sure what the hell he saw. But he was sure of one thing. *Vaz was right. Wynn's a plant.*

Whatever was going on back there, Kovacs knew he had to get out before Garcia's men caught up. He could figure out the details when he was safely away.

Wynn's voice echoed from the chamber. "Go! Hurry!"

Shit. They're coming.

He snapped the magazine back in place and fired two quick shots that ricocheted off the walls, then turned and scrambled away.

————

Wynn cringed as he held onto the top rung of the wooden ladder, praying Kovacs' bullets wouldn't ricochet up. He glanced down at Terrance, who clung to the ladder several feet below. Terrance was pulling off the AR-15 that Wynn had slung onto his back moments ago.

Beyond Terrance, at the base of the ladder, sat the crates of dynamite and blasting caps.

"Don't shoot!" Wynn pointed at the crates. "Those are explosives. Don't shoot."

Terrance looked up, fear in his eyes.

Wynn glanced up. A few inches of the square concrete cover hung over the opening. The rope loop embedded in the slab dangled a few inches above his head. He tugged on it, but the slab didn't move. Voices yelled from the room above.

"Terrance! Look at me. Climb down. Make sure no one comes out of that tunnel."

Terrance nodded, looped the rifle over his shoulder, and climbed down, stumbling and falling the last few feet. Wynn exhaled in relief when he sat up, scooted against the wall, and pointed the rifle down the tunnel.

Knowing he had only moments before Garcia's men flooded into the basement, Wynn climbed to the top of the ladder and grabbed the rope loop set in the slab. With both feet on the ladder, he pulled.

The slab moved a fraction then stopped. Wynn climbed up one more rung and heard the stairs creak. Confused calls of "Vaz? Eddie? What's going on?" came from above. He heard Delgado's voice, faint and weak, but couldn't make out what she said.

Wynn leaned back, pushed his ass into the wall, then braced his feet on the dirt behind the ladder. He wrapped the rope around his wrists and pulled.

The slab slid halfway over the opening.

Footsteps and angry voices crashed down the stairs above. He adjusted his grip and pulled again, the slab moving once more and tipping into the shaft, leaving a two-inch gap. Shouts of "Where is he?" echoed from above.

A shadow fell over the opening just as Wynn pulled a third time, but this time his effort met resistance.

The muzzle of an AR-15 appeared in the crack and fired a short burst, the rounds burying themselves into the dirt wall next to Wynn's head.

Wynn grabbed the Glock from his hip and jammed it in the crack, pulling the trigger three times. The blast was deafening. He could no longer hear what was happening above, but the shadows fell away. He yanked on the rope one more time, and the slab thunked into place.

Bought a few minutes, but this won't stop 'em.

Wynn eased himself back onto the ladder, then scrambled down to where Terrance sat at the bottom.

"You alright?" Wynn asked over the ringing in his ears.

Terrance nodded but said nothing, his eyes wide.

"You're doing great," Wynn said. "Hang on a little longer and we'll get moving."

Terrance nodded again, his breath growing fast and shallow.

He's panicking. About to lose it. Wynn reached out and grabbed Terrance's arm. "Hey. Hey. Look at me." Wynn got up close into Terrance's face. "I need you to calm down. We'll be alright. I need you to keep it together, okay?"

Terrance nodded.

"Let me hear you say it."

"We'll... we'll be okay."

"Again."

Terrance's voice came back stronger. "We'll be okay."

Wynn pulled him to his feet. "Good. Get ready to move, okay?"

"Alright."

Wynn found the roll of electrical wire sitting on top of the crates. Unspooling the few feet that were left, he clambered back up the ladder and strung the wire through the rope loop, then around the ladder's top rung, twisting the ends together and securing the slab in place.

Wynn flew down the ladder, dropping the last few feet and crashing hard onto the dirt floor.

"You okay?" Terrance asked.

"Yeah, I'm..." Wynn's voice trailed away as he pushed himself off the floor, his gaze lingering on the crates of dynamite and blasting caps.

Maybe there's a way to permanently close this end.

"What are you doing?" Terrance said. "Shouldn't we go?"

Wynn opened the box of caps. At least two dozen, each about four inches long, a little thicker than a pencil, with two wire leads coming from one end. Wynn looked down the tunnel at its gentle curve. *No direct line of sight. Can't just stand back and shoot the dynamite, the force of the blast would shoot straight through the tunnel. I'd be too close.*

Wynn glanced around the small chamber, his eyes landing on the light gray Romex electrical cable strung between the lights.

An idea flashed through his mind.

Maybe... "Terrance. Come here and help me."

CHAPTER 53

KRISTA WARILY EYED THE concrete slab floating inches above her head. The fourteen-inch hydraulic cylinder holding it aloft appeared solid and well-maintained. She tucked the Glock into the back of her jeans and draped her shirt loosely over it, then jumped into the pit. Like above, this area was solid and smooth, no cracks or joints anywhere. She ran her fingers along the edges, searching for any crevice or indentation, anything that might indicate a tunnel entrance.

A muffled pop came from behind her. Twice. Like the sound of a Glock, faint and far away. She wasn't truly sure if she'd heard or imagined it. She listened intently, the sound of her own pulse pounding in her ears. Turning to the opposite wall, she eased around the gleaming silver post and ran her fingers down the right corner, then across the floor, stopping at a small indentation, barely large enough to get the tips of three fingers into.

Her adrenaline spiked as she crouched low and wedged her fingers into the crevice.

As she adjusted her stance, a shadow fell across her vision. Krista looked up into the faces of the two guards, each holding an AR-15 pointed straight at her.

"I told you to go, *senora*."

———

Wynn grabbed a cart from the wall and loaded one of the boxes of dynamite and the blasting caps into it. He tapped the flashlight button on his phone and handed it to Terrance. "Hold this."

Angry voices came from above as Wynn scrambled up the ladder. The loop of rope strained against the wire he'd attached to it as the men above tried to remove the concrete cover. Wynn checked the wire to make sure it was holding, then flipped the light switch at the top, dropping the tunnel into darkness.

Hurrying back to where Terrance stood bathed in the glow of the phone, Wynn reached up and grabbed the electrical cable that strung the lights together. He yanked hard, creating a small bit of slack in the line, then used his knife to cut the wire.

With Terrance holding the light, Wynn peeled back the insulation on one end of the wire, revealing the two copper strands inside. He touched the two ends together. A spark flared as the lights flashed.

Damn. This is gonna hurt.

Wynn was screwing up the courage to twist the live wires together when Terrance, his voice meek and quiet, said, "Wait. Your sheath."

Wynn looked at him questioningly.

"Your knife sheath. Is it leather?"

"Damn. Thanks." *This guy might be an asset yet.* Wynn bent down and removed the sheath from his ankle, then used it to insulate his fingers as he pinched the two bare wires and twisted them together. The lights came back on.

"So... what's the plan?" Terrance asked tentatively as he handed the phone back to Wynn.

"At the other end of the tunnel, there's another switch at the top of the ladder. I need you to go there, turn the lights off, then use that," Wynn nodded to the AR-15, "to make sure nobody turns it on until I get there."

Terrance nodded.

"Repeat it back to me," Wynn said.

Terrance did.

"Good. You can do this."

Terrance nodded. "Yeah. I can do it."

"Hurry," Wynn said.

———

"Go ahead, *senora*. Open it." The guard motioned his AR-15 toward the wall panel.

Sitting back on her haunches, Krista looked up at the two men. She suddenly had zero desire to open the tunnel.

"You no longer wish to find our little secret?" the guard asked. "We'll show it to you anyway." He motioned her away from the wall.

Krista stepped backward to the far end of the pit, facing the two men directly, hiding the bulge of the Glock tucked in the waistband beneath her shirt. The guard who'd spoken remained on the garage floor, four feet above her, while the other jumped into the pit, crouched down, and slid the side panel back, revealing a dark hole in the wall.

When the panel was clear, the man tentatively peeked his head into the shaft. "*Nada*," he said to his companion.

The guard above replied in Spanish with a phrase Krista didn't recognize. To Krista, he motioned down with the barrel of his gun. "Sit."

Krista wedged herself into the corner as the guard in the pit came back and crouched next to her. He kept his gun on her, while the other stood above the opening.

Shit. They're waiting to ambush Sean. "Aren't we going in?" she asked.

"In a moment, *senora*. There's someone coming to us first."

———

Carmen Delgado was going into shock. She sat against the wall, holding a dirty rag to her shoulder to staunch the flow of blood, staring at Eddie's lifeless body, trying to make sense of what she was seeing.

He and Vaz weren't wearing that tactical gear when they came down. Why would they? Wynn wasn't armed, and yet they geared up like they were going into battle. Who did they think they were about to fight?

It had taken Garcia's men a few minutes to gather themselves, precious time that hopefully allowed Wynn and Hampson to get through the tunnel before Garcia ordered his men to seal off the other side.

Time also, that allowed her adrenaline rush to wear off. She could feel herself crashing, her energy dissipating, her thought process slowing.

She was only vaguely aware of Garcia's men rushing down the stairs, voices yelling, fists pounding on doors, Vaz's cell being opened, someone calling her name...

The sharp smell of ammonia startled her awake.

"There you go." Ruben Garcia's bearded face came into focus. He was crouched in front of her. "Stay with me, Carmen." He waved the smelling salts beneath her nose; she twisted her head away.

"That's good," Garcia said.

Delgado glanced over Garcia's shoulder as Vaz rushed up.

"She's a fucking plant!" Vaz said. "She's working with Wynn. Helped him get away."

Garcia turned and looked at Vaz. He paused and slowly swiveled his gaze back to Delgado.

She shook her head, her voice slow and breathy. "No... It was Vaz... and Eddie. They were going to kill you... Look at what they're wearing."

Garcia glanced up the hall toward Eddie, then over his shoulder.

"I'm telling you," Vaz yelled. "She pulled a gun on us. Helped Wynn and Hampson escape."

Garcia ignored Vaz's comment. He stood and addressed one of his men. "Do they have the other end covered?"

"Yes, sir. They caught a woman and are waiting for anyone who pops up."

"Good." Garcia turned toward Vaz. "Then get in there and stop 'em."

Vaz nodded, then rushed over to the tunnel where two men were working with a crowbar to remove the slab covering.

Garcia turned to the man beside him. He spoke quietly. "I'm going to take Carmen upstairs. You stay here. Make sure both ends are covered and keep an eye on Vaz. No one gets away. Kill 'em all if you have to."

———

Kovacs stopped, frozen in his tracks when the lights went out. His heart hammering wildly, he pressed himself against the side wall, doing his best to control his breathing. Silence was imperative.

There were switches at either end of the tunnel. With no way to know which had been thrown, he couldn't predict from which direction a threat might be approaching. *Wynn and Hampson are behind me, but Garcia is sure to have men on the other side.*

This place is going to get crowded. And I'm in the middle.

The lights flashed once, then, a minute later, came back on. He looked hard in both directions, relieved to find the tunnel still empty. He set off again, climbing the slight incline toward the U.S. side.

Four minutes later, the ladder loomed before him. He was about halfway up when the entrance panel slid back. Unsure of who was above, he scrambled back down and ducked into the tunnel.

A male voice drifted down from above. "*Nada.*"

Garcia's men. I can work with this.

He stuffed his gun into the back of his pants and began to climb.

CHAPTER 54

Krista's heart froze when a hand emerged from the tunnel. "Sean! Stop! It's a—"

The words died in her throat as the familiar face of her ex-husband appeared inside the opening. He didn't see her immediately, his attention instead drawn to the guard next to her. The one with the AR-15 pointed at him.

It took only a moment for Danny to register the sound of her voice. His eyes snapped to the side and found her. A thin smile curled his lips. He opened his mouth as if to speak.

But Krista didn't wait for it. Her outburst had diverted both guards' attention.

Sensing her chance, Krista whipped the Glock from behind her back and fired it point blank into the guard next to her. Bullets from the other guard's AR-15 ricocheted off the cylindrical lift in the center of the pit. Leaning around the steel column, she fired three times, sending the guard above sprawling backward against the wall and collapsing to the floor.

Glancing to the tunnel, Danny's face was gone, but a hand—with a gun—was rising from the opening. She fired twice more into the tunnel, then scrambled out of the pit and rolled away.

Of all the scenarios she'd envisioned, this was the last she expected. Conflicting emotions of fear and rage surged within her, threatening to overwhelm her. Part of her wanted to run away, to never see this man again. The other wanted revenge. Vengeance. For Terrance. Joshua. For the pain he'd caused her parents. For ruining her life.

Hoping it would take Danny a moment to climb out of the tunnel, Krista pressed herself to the floor and slithered beneath the cargo truck, hiding behind the rear wheel, where she had a clear view of the pit. Although she couldn't see down into it, she sure as hell would see anyone trying to jump out.

Danny's voice rang mockingly through the garage. "Well, honey," he said, in a sing-song voice imitating Ricky Ricardo. "You're home."

Krista raised the Glock and sighted down the barrel. It shook noticeably in her trembling hands. Whether from fear or anger, she wasn't sure.

The stock of an AR-15 rose from the end of the pit. Krista fired twice, uncontrollably. The first glanced off the concrete floor while the second went high, through the far wall.

"That's not very nice, sweetheart," Danny said. "Aren't you glad to see me?"

Get ahold of yourself, Krista! He's got an AR-15 from the guard and whatever else he brought with him. She tried to remember how many shots she'd already fired. *Nine, I think. Meaning I have six left. At best.*

Tactically, she was also at a disadvantage. To approach the pit, she would be completely exposed, while Danny could hide in the tunnel. *All day if he wants to. Or at least until more guards show up. Then I'm screwed.*

"Your brother wasn't real happy to see me either," Danny called out. "Come to think of it, he didn't see much of anything."

Memories of the horrific video of Terrance's eye being removed made Krista's vision blacken from rage, resolve hardening in her gut. She lined up the sights toward the pit. The gun barrel no longer trembled.

———

Wynn pushed the cart carrying the blasting caps and the box of dynamite to the mouth of the tunnel. He slid the second crate nearer to where he had spliced the wire, then glanced at the time on his phone.

It'll take Terrance at least seven or eight minutes to reach the other end, assuming he doesn't run into Kovacs or anyone else.

Opening the box of caps, he took one out and examined it more closely. The insulation on the two wire leads stopped short of the ends, leaving an inch of bare wire exposed. *Easy enough to attach to the Romex, but how the fuck am I gonna attach the dynamite to this?*

He rummaged through the box, hoping to find a roll of tape or zip ties—something, anything, he could use to tie it all together—but there was nothing.

Along with angry voices, a cloud of dust drifted down from above. He glanced up. While the rest of the lights in the tunnel were on, the shaft was dark. Unable to see anything, he placed his phone between his teeth, grabbed the wooden ladder, and climbed.

At the top, Wynn leaned back, bracing himself against the back wall. The wire he'd used to tie the slab cover in place still held, but a spot around the edge of the slab crumbled away as a large pry bar was repeatedly jammed into the crevice, slowly enlarging the tiny crack.

The frantic shouting had subsided, replaced by a steady pace of work—consistent and methodical. He glanced down at the chamber, still dimly lit from the bulbs strung through the tunnel.

They know we're trapped. As long as the lights are on, I have to assume they control the other end. So what's plan B?

He glanced down at the box of dynamite. *When their hole gets big enough, I could always stuff a stick in there. Hell of a boom when they hit it with that bar.*

He dismissed the idea. *No way I'd get away fast enough. Plus, the ladder would be destroyed. I'd be stuck.*

More dirt fell away as the pry bar finally burst through. Wynn's arm brushed the Glock still in his holster. *I could shoot 'em when they break through.* He quickly dismissed that idea also. *This little Glock against a roomful of AR-15s won't last long.*

He glanced down again. The chamber still glowed.

C'mon, Terrance.

The pry bar hammered down again and again, widening the narrow hole, and creating enough wiggle room for the bar to be wedged next to the slab. Grunts came from above as the bar was pushed against the side, attempting to lift the cover, but the angle was bad. Rather than lift the slab, the bar pushed it against the opposite wall.

The men above retracted the bar and then pounded it repeatedly back into the hole, continuing to widen it. Wynn gripped the ends of the wire securing the rope loop to the ladder and twisted the short tails tighter. After a few moments, the bar emerged again, this time at a lower angle.

Better leverage.

The grunts from the men above sounded again as they pushed on the pry bar. The slab lifted a fraction until the loop pulled tight, straining against the wire.

Hold on, baby. Wynn drew his gun, just in case.

The bar withdrew and the hole was attacked again, in a furious frenzy. Dirt and small concrete chips fell between Wynn's legs as a tiny shaft of light peeked through the widening gap.

The pole emerged again, now at a forty-five-degree angle, creating maximum leverage. The voices above were now clear, unmuffled. Vaz's dominating the rest. "Try it."

Wynn watched as the rope strained against the wire, the tails he'd just twisted quivering. A tiny squeak came from the wooden ladder in front of him. He watched in horror as the nails holding the rung in place slowly separated from the side rails.

———————

From her spot beneath the truck, Krista glanced at the body of the second guard, the AR-15 he'd been carrying still strapped around his shoulder.

Danny knows—generally—where I'm at. Gotta improve my position. And firepower.

His voice came from the pit. "I can't wait to see Joshua. Does he look like me? I'll bet he's grown like a weed."

Keeping her eyes on the pit, she slithered across the floor to the front wheels, then crawled out from beneath the truck and crouched near the front bumper.

"You know," Danny continued, "that wasn't very nice of you to take him away from me like that."

Hugging the back wall, Krista scampered silently across the second bay and dropped to her stomach a few feet from the pit. She raised her head a few inches and looked in. Only a couple of feet of the opposite end were visible, including the head of the first guard, blood drooling from his mouth as he leaned propped up in the corner. His eyes were open and vacant.

"We don't have to do it this way," Danny said. "All I ever wanted was for the three of us to be a family. And maybe add to the family. Give Josh some brothers and sisters."

A wave of disgust surged through Krista's stomach. From the corner of her eye, she sensed movement from above. Glancing up, she noticed for the first time a convex, circular mirror mounted above the garage door at the opposite end of the pit. Used, no doubt, to help people coming out of the tunnel see who might be in the garage before exiting.

Danny held the guard's AR-15 and was getting into a crouching position outside the tunnel entrance. He turned back and looked up into the mirror. Their eyes met.

Krista scrambled behind a large, wheeled metal tool chest as Danny rose up and sprayed the area she'd just vacated with a hail of bullets. The toolbox pushed into her as Danny's bullets punched into it from the opposite side.

This thing isn't gonna stop 'em forever...

She reached the Glock around the edge of the chest and fired blindly toward the pit, hoping one of the rounds might find its mark. The deafening roar intensified when a second AR-15 blasted from the pit. It's bullets tore into the concrete slab hovering above, causing debris to rain down. The shooting stopped.

Risking a glance to the mirror, Krista saw Danny crouching in the corner of the pit, a second figure now visible in the tunnel.

Terrance!

Danny had dropped the AR-15 and was drawing his Sig.

Crouching low, Krista placed her shoulder against the toolbox and heaved. The heavy chest rolled toward the pit, its wheels teetering over the edge before it crashed down on top of Danny.

Krista pointed the Glock into the pit. The heavy chest pinned Danny to the floor; his legs and torso trapped, his arms remained free. He struggled to transfer the Sig from his right hand to his left.

"Don't do it, Danny." She held the Glock in a two-handed grip.

Danny locked eyes with Krista, then pointed the gun toward Terrance.

Krista squeezed the trigger.

Click.

An evil smile curled Danny's lip.

"Terrance! Duck!"

The Glock in Danny's hand blasted at the tunnel entrance as Krista dove toward the second guard. She ripped the sling of the AR-15 over the dead man's head and turned, blasting down into the pit until the magazine emptied.

With the echo of the gunfire still ringing, Krista looked down onto the bloodied, barely recognizable face of Danny Kovacs. An already large and growing pool of blood seeped from beneath his body.

Terrance.

She jumped into the pit and wedged herself between the heavy tool chest and the wall, then used her legs to push the chest away, its bulk sliding across Danny's clothing. When clear, she rolled to her hands and knees and stuck her head in the tunnel.

"Terrance?"

He clung to the ladder a few feet below. "How you doing, sis?"

A wave of relief washed over Krista. "Where's Sean?"

"He's a ways behind me..." Terrance found the switch on the side of the tunnel wall and flipped it, plunging the tunnel into darkness. "About to do something stupid."

CHAPTER 55

WYNN READJUSTED HIS FEET, ready to place one on the wooden rung of the ladder that was slowly being pulled from the side rails, when the chamber below plunged into darkness.

Terrance did it!

Using the flashlight on his phone, he scrambled down the ladder and found the wire he'd spliced together. He yanked on it hard, pulling several feet loose from the ceiling, then twisted it apart and wired in one of the blasting caps. He dragged the second crate of dynamite close and buried the cap inside.

Terrance better hold that switch.

The high-pitch squeal of nails being pulled through wood echoed in the chamber. Using his phone to light the way, he grabbed the handle of the cart and set off down the tunnel.

On his previous trip, Wynn had thought the floor of the tunnel to be sandy and smooth, but as he hauled the cart, its rocky nature was revealed. Wynn cringed as the two boxes bounced over unseen bumps and the cart jolted into the side walls. To make matters worse, the cart was loud, its rusty axles and loose joints rattling and squealing as he moved.

Reaching the turn, Wynn slowed, carefully maneuvering the cart through the bend. A puff of warm air drifted across his face.

Ventilation shaft.

He pointed the light from the phone up, finding the four-inch hole in the ceiling. The gray Romex cable ran next to it a few inches away.

Using his knife, he peeled back the outer casing on the electrical wire and carefully separated the two wires within. Cutting one, he stripped back the insulation and twisted the two leads of a blasting cap into the line, then took several sticks of dynamite and stuffed them, along with the cap, into the ventilation shaft until they held tight.

When finished, he paused and listened intently. The passage was quiet except for the faint, mouse-like squeaking of the nails in the ladder.

That thing can't hold much longer.

Seizing the cart handle, he slipped away, moving as quickly as he could while still trying to minimize the jostling of the cart. The going became noticeably more difficult as the tunnel began to rise. Two hundred yards further, another warm blast of air drifted across his face. He stopped and listened. The tunnel was quiet.

They're either in and coming, or I'm too far away to hear it.

He covered the light from his phone and strained to see back down the tunnel.

They won't use a light.

He found the overhead electrical cable and within ninety seconds had another cap wired in, another shaft stuffed and loaded.

A tiny sound nudged the back of his brain. He froze, holding his breath. The sound, if there ever was one, was gone.

Wynn flipped off the light from his phone and delicately spilled the remaining sticks of dynamite into the cart, then placed the empty wooden crate on the floor.

That should make some noise when they run into it. He grabbed the cart and continued up the slope. A minute later he passed the next vent without stopping, his breathing heavy, his heart pounding in his ears. Two minutes later he came to yet another vent, paused, listened, and was in the process of wiring a third bundle when a muffled thump came from behind.

It wasn't much—no scream, no yell, no cursing—just a solid thump, exactly as expected.

They're here. A couple hundred yards back at most.

He stuffed the dynamite into the shaft, grabbed the cart, and shuffled through the low tunnel as fast as he could, no longer concerned about the noise.

———

Vaz froze, pressing his back against the wall. His arm throbbed. Somehow, it'd been cut in the scuffle with Wynn and Eddie. He'd been able to stop the bleeding when he was locked in the cell, but still felt winded and a little light-headed from the loss of blood. Luckily, he'd only tapped the wooden crate Wynn had set on the floor some hundred and fifty yards back. He'd gotten around it with barely a sound. Garcia's three guys who had accompanied him into the tunnel hadn't been so lucky.

Wynn's close.

He waited for the sounds of the squeaky cart before moving. As long as he heard the axles squealing, he could hustle ahead, knowing the sounds of his heavy breathing and footsteps were covered.

But then the cart stopped.

Wynn had either abandoned it or was waiting behind it to ambush whoever might come along.

Or is he doing something else?

When they'd finally gotten the entrance to the tunnel open, the chamber had been dark. In his hurry, he'd rushed headlong into the tunnel, quickly leaving Garcia's men behind.

Vaz reviewed his steps. *What am I missing?*

When he bumped into the crate, he paused long enough to run his hands over it. The realization of what it was—the only thing it could be—instilled a new sense of urgency. Had Wynn dumped the dynamite back in the chamber at the beginning of the tunnel? Or was it loose in the cart with him now? Vaz had run his hands across the floor of the tunnel but found no dynamite there.

Meaning Wynn had it with him.

Meaning also, he couldn't shoot at Wynn for fear of blowing up the tunnel, and himself along with it.

He'd hustled forward until the squeaks from the cart stopped, then moved slowly until the sound of someone stumbling over the crate came from behind.

Keep your lights off, assholes.

He inched ahead as the sounds of Wynn breathing and the rustling of cloth, along with some other noise he couldn't place, reached him out of the darkness.

He's close.

Real close.

Twenty or thirty feet away at most.

The cart squeaked again. Vaz hustled after it.

———

Within moments, a dim light illuminated the cavern at the base of the northern access shaft ahead. Pulling the cart behind him, Wynn hurried forward, pausing outside the chamber, straining to hear any sounds from above. A muffled voice floated down.

Terrance!

The cart rammed into the back of Wynn's legs, sending him sprawling to the floor, the knife still clenched tightly in his hand. A demonic scream filled the chamber as Vaz leaped onto his back, pushing Wynn's face into the dirt.

Fists rained down on the back of Wynn's head. He tried to roll and free his hand, but he was blocked by the cart, now jammed against the back wall beneath the ladder.

Suddenly, the pressure eased. Wynn felt Vaz trying to roll him onto his back.

He wants me face up. Can do more damage that way.

Wynn rolled with it, but his right arm remained trapped beneath his body. He used his left arm to cover his face while Vaz's fists resumed the assault. Wynn twisted and squirmed until he finally freed his right hand. He swiped upward with the knife, driving it toward Vaz's chest.

Normally, a solid kill strike.

But not against a man wearing Kevlar.

The knife bounced off Vaz's vest and twisted in Wynn's hand. Vaz grabbed Wynn's wrist and slammed it against the cart. Wynn dropped the knife as caps and dynamite spilled to the floor.

As they grappled, Vaz lifted Wynn's head and slammed it to the ground, once, then twice. Stars shot across Wynn's vision. Vaz readjusted his grip and pulled Wynn's torso up, then smashed him back to the ground. Wynn wheezed as the air flew from his lungs.

Both men flinched as the roar of an AR-15 exploded into the tunnel, causing small bits of dirt and dust rained down.

Instinctively, Vaz ducked low. Wynn flung his head forward, catching Vaz solidly on the nose. Stars burst again into Wynn's vision as Vaz's body relaxed on top of him. Dazed, Wynn pushed him off and reached for the first rung of the ladder. He pulled himself up, only to feel Vaz tugging on his shirt.

Wynn swatted the hand away and began to climb. Slowly, painfully.

Another hand grabbed his ankle. He kicked it away.

"C'mon, Sean! Hurry!" The voice was female.

Krista.

Wynn's head cleared. He climbed steadily.

Twelve rungs. Thirteen. Fourteen.

Vaz grabbed his ankle again. Wynn kicked, but Vaz held fast, his angry and bloody face glaring up at him. The little light from above reflected brightly off the whites of his eyes, which grew larger as a shadow fell across the shaft. Krista's head and shoulders appeared in the opening above. "Sean! Duck!"

Wynn squeezed himself against the ladder as the AR-15 exploded again, the rounds burying themselves in the dirt walls behind him.

Unfortunately, Vaz had done the same thing, still clinging tightly to Wynn's ankle, using him as a shield.

"Bring it to me!" Wynn yelled.

Krista disappeared for a moment until her feet reappeared and found the upper rungs of the ladder.

Feeling Vaz's grip loosen, Wynn quickly climbed a couple of rungs, only for Vaz to grab him again, higher, in the pocket of his jeans. Instead of descending, Vaz was climbing.

Wynn kicked out, but had no leverage, no momentum. Vaz's huge arm wrapped around his leg, leaving his foot dangling in the open air. The man's weight pushed against his leg, forcing Wynn's other foot from the ladder.

Wynn's knuckles turned white as he clung to the rebar. Looking up, he saw Krista in the shaft, a rung above him, the AR-15 dangling from a strap around her shoulder. "Now! Shoot him now!"

Wynn pulled himself as close to the ladder as he could, watching as Krista leaned back and aimed the AR-15 around him.

"Now!"

Click.

The AR dangled impotently in her hands.

Vaz laughed, and Wynn felt himself being pulled from the ladder. His eyes landed on the light switch at the top of the shaft.

"The switch! Krista, flip the light switch."

Wynn watched as Krista scrambled up the few remaining rungs, then braced himself as she reached to the back of the shaft and flipped the switch.

Somewhere far off, a deep rumbling echoed through the tunnel, punctuated by frightened screams. A massive cloud of dust belched from the opening below and rushed up the shaft. The ladder quaked in Wynn's hands as the explosions rumbled. Feeling Vaz's grip ease, Wynn kicked free and scrambled up the ladder.

"Go!" he shouted, coughing as the dust filled his mouth and lungs. Climbing as fast as he could, he followed Krista to the top of the ladder and flung his upper half through the opening, gasping for air.

He laid his cheek on the cement floor of the pit and sucked in a couple of large breaths before realizing he was laying in something wet and sticky.

Krista!

He jerked his head up. Krista sat with her back against the concrete wall next to the tunnel entrance. Coughing, but alive. He turned his head the other direction and saw Kovacs lying in a pool of blood next to a huge tool chest.

Wynn rolled onto his back, coughing, and greedily sucking in air as he scooted away from the opening, his legs still inside the shaft. He'd gotten one leg out when Vaz's hand grabbed onto the other, his face appearing in the tunnel entrance.

With a swift kick, Wynn planted his heel squarely on Vaz's already broken nose. The big man stopped, a vacant look in his eyes. He wavered for a moment, then fell backward.

Wynn watched him disappear from sight, when a realization flashed across his mind. *Oh shit.* He jerked upright and pushed Krista into the corner, covering her body with his own as a massive explosion erupted from the base of the shaft.

CHAPTER 56

As if spewed from a jet engine, rocks the size of bowling balls, along with another violent cloud of dirt and debris, exploded from the tunnel entrance, smashing into the tool chest and twisting the hydraulic lift with a sickening squeal. The slab teetered dangerously above Wynn and Krista, whose position next to the tunnel entrance put them to the side of the blast wave, not directly in its path.

The slab collapsed to the side, landing on the garage floor, and creating a makeshift roof above the pit, as the stone, steel, and concrete projectiles fell back to earth, landing with heavy thuds or loud crashes as they tore through the building.

Wynn shielded their heads with his arms until the onslaught ended. Dust hung heavy in the air.

"What the hell was that?" Krista asked, her voice shaky with shock.

"There were caps and dynamite at the base of the shaft." He shrugged. "Vaz must've landed on 'em."

She stared at him in disbelief.

Wynn shrugged. "Where's Terrance?"

Krista's face dropped as if suddenly remembering. "Terrance!"

He appeared at the pit's edge above them, from behind the blast. "You guys okay?" Using his good hand, Terrance helped them climb out, and together, the three of them picked their way through the rubble.

Outside, Wynn wove around the debris between the two buildings and gazed south, toward the border. A trail of dust clouds hung in the still air, as new depressions in the ground marked a slightly curving path toward the rusty border fence. On the other side, a heavy cloud of dust and smoke rose from one of the homes. There was activity around it.

Delgado.

"Did you bring the TAC?" Wynn asked, his tone urgent.

"It's in the car," Krista said.

"Get it. I need the scope."

Krista rushed into the trees while Wynn scoured the area for a better vantage point.

I need to be higher.

The roof of the garage was the highest point around. At least it used to be. With a hole blasted through a large part of it, he was afraid what remained may not hold his weight. He jogged over to the house and stepped up onto the porch, then jumped onto the railing, using one of the posts for balance.

"Terrance! C'mere! Give me a boost."

Using Terrance's shoulder as a step, Wynn climbed onto the roof as Krista emerged from the trees with the TAC. She reached it up to Wynn.

"I have no idea how well it's sighted," she said.

"Let's hope I don't have to find out."

"Take these just in case." Krista tossed a pair of magazines up to him.

Wynn took the rifle and scrambled to the peak of the low roof. He sat on the warm shingles and extended the bipods, using the tail of his shirt to clean the dust off the scope, then inserted one of the magazines. Settling in, he pointed the TAC toward the smoking house, and put his eye to the scope.

The angle was good, the view unobstructed. The house sat above the border fence on the opposite hillside, nestled in among several others.

Raising his head, he took in the broader area. The neighborhood was a couple of miles outside of town, and while there were a number of people standing in the street or on their porches watching what was happening, no police or fire services had yet arrived.

C'mon, Federales. Hurry up.

Wynn put his eye back to the scope and zoomed in. There was movement in the windows. One of Garcia's men swung open the front door and bounded down the porch steps, then jumped into a Mercedes sedan sitting in the driveway. He backed up and parked in the street immediately in front of the door.

Garcia himself appeared in the doorway, a gun in his hand. He scanned the street before stepping back and motioning to a third. Chad came out the front door, holding a gun to Delgado's side. She looked weak, her shoulder still bloody, bruises around her face and eyes.

They know. Can't let 'em take her away. She'll be dead in a day.

Wynn pulled back the bolt on the TAC, loading a round into the chamber. He estimated the distance. A thousand meters. *Can't shoot at Chad, Delgado's too close.*

He shifted his aim to the driver. Just like out in the desert with Kovacs, Wynn willed his heart rate to slow, let out a breath, and squeezed the trigger, hoping to hell the thing was sighted. The TAC boomed and the Mercedes' window shattered, six inches in front of the driver.

Wynn racked the bolt, ejecting the spent casing and loading a new round. He snuggled the stock into his shoulder and peered through the scope as Chad pulled Delgado behind the car. The driver scrambled across the center console, trying to get out the other side. With no more glass to obstruct his view, Wynn made a slight adjustment and pulled the trigger again.

The TAC boomed, and this time, the driver slumped over, lifeless.

Delgado appeared from behind the rear of the Mercedes, crawling to get away. Wynn focused on the area behind her, waiting, but Chad remained hidden. She made it around the car, collapsing against the driver-side rear wheel.

Good girl. I can cover you 'til the cops come.

The front door cracked open again, and a face appeared in the opening. Wynn zoomed in. *Murano.* His face was dirty, and his eyes wide. He yelled something at Chad. A moment later, the rear passenger door opened on the far side of the car. Wynn racked the TAC again and sent a round through the rear side window, shattering it and sending glass shards tinkling down next to Delgado. He saw movement inside the car as Chad scrambled back and disappeared behind the car, directly opposite the DEA agent.

Murano cracked the door and continued to yell at Chad, but nothing happened. There was no movement toward the rear of the car, nor any that he could see through the broken windows.

Wynn focused on Murano, whose face turned red as he continued to scream from inside the house. Soon, the front door opened a bit wider, and Murano extended an AR-15 through the door.

The muzzle of the AR-15 flashed. Not toward Wynn, but Chad. Three seconds later the sound of rapid gunfire reached Wynn from across the valley. Chad's body slumped from behind the Mercedes. Wynn racked the TAC and focused on Murano. Adjusting for the misaligned sights, he put the crosshairs a few inches to the side, then pulled the trigger.

Click.

Fuck! The mag from the speedway. Used two rounds there.

While Wynn changed magazines, Garcia emerged from the house and pushed Murano in front of him, onto the porch. Murano stumbled down the steps as Garcia raced around the car to where Delgado hid.

Murano was the first target Wynn acquired when he put his eye back to the scope. Without thinking, he aimed and fired.

The TAC boomed across the valley as Murano spun around and collapsed on the sidewalk.

Wynn moved the TAC, his world reduced to the circular, five-foot area shown inside the scope.

He found Garcia leaning against the car, his left arm wrapped around Delgado, lifting her up, using her as a shield. Garcia's right hand held a gun, but was down at his side, searching for the door handle.

Delgado struggled against Garcia's grip, blocking Wynn's view of his face.

C'mon, Carmen. Give me a shot.

Garcia finally opened the door and sank behind the wheel, pulling Delgado on top of him. Without bothering to shut the door, Garcia started the car, Delgado's body still blocking Wynn's view.

The car lurched forward, causing Delgado to fall from the open door. Garcia turned and leaned out, attempting to hold onto her. His head was clear.

The TAC boomed.

Garcia's head exploded on impact as the round slammed into it. Delgado dropped to the asphalt as the car rolled slowly forward, depositing Garcia's headless body onto the street.

CHAPTER 57

Two weeks later, Wynn sat inside a windowless surveillance van parked on the tarmac of the North Las Vegas Airport. It was crowded. FBI Special-Agent-in-Charge Will Parker and Carmen Delgado, whose real name was Elana Lopez, sat in the back with him. Two more agents sat in front.

Delgado-Lopez, he was glad to see, was healing well. She still moved slowly and stiffly, but her color—and her determination—had returned. Parker had told her she could sit this one out; she'd responded with an *over my dead body*. Wynn thought that might not be the best way to talk to your superiors, until she'd reminded him that Parker was FBI, while she was DEA. *Not in my chain of command,* she'd said.

Parker's phone dinged with an incoming text message. "Five minutes out," he said to the group.

Wynn's attention was fixed on a video monitor displaying the private jet sitting on the tarmac a hundred yards away, its engines running. The outline of one of the pilots in the cockpit was visible, but otherwise the scene was still. Normally, Wynn would never be allowed anywhere near this type of operation, but Jenna had insisted. *I'll do it on one condition,* she had said. *Sean needs to be there.*

Wynn had spent the past two weeks in Vegas, much of it at the Federal Building, under the watchful eye of Ruiz and Parker. Wynn had been pleasantly surprised to see Will Parker again. He thought, maybe, Parker was glad to see him, too. But that didn't prevent Parker from assigning two agents to stay with Wynn the whole time.

"Remember last summer?" Parker had said. "You promised to come in and give a full statement, but I never saw you again. I'd like to make sure you show up this time."

Which was no problem for Wynn.

It allowed him to spend time with Krista, who was still under Agent Todd's protection. Even with Danny dead, the threat—in the form of Danny's father, Bennie—remained.

After the mess in Nogales, the joint task force of FBI and DEA agents had descended on Pink and The Deuce. Deborah and several of the bouncers had been taken into custody, but she and Andre were the only ones still being held without bail two weeks later, largely based on Marcus's cooperation and willingness to testify.

Careful, Wynn thought of Marcus. *You'll end up in witness protection, too.*

Rumor had it that Bennie, from his prison cell, was trying to recruit some of the lesser bouncers to rebuild the organization. It was too early to know if he'd be successful.

With Kovacs, Murano, and Garcia dead, the flow of cocaine into the U.S. was seriously, albeit likely only temporarily, curtailed. DEA Agent Hodges was pleased with the outcome.

Publicly, we tend to prefer trials to funerals, but privately, well... this way there's no doubt as to the outcome, Hodges had said.

Parker was also pleased. The collapse of Kovacs' and Garcia's organizations shut down a major pipeline in the flow of human trafficking.

Delgado-Lopez, however, still had a problem. She had told Wynn about it when he'd visited her in the hospital.

"I'd been undercover in L.A. for eight months when I first met Arturo Murano," Delgado-Lopez had said. "He introduced me to Ruben Garcia, who hired me to help recruit girls for his new venture with Kovacs. Initially, I did it with the intent of stopping his drug business, but when we learned Parker was looking at Kovacs and Garcia too, it made sense to work both sides of the investigation.

"Early on, I had told Murano I was gay, so he wouldn't hit on me. Later, when I visited Kovacs' clubs, I used that as an excuse to get some of the girls alone. Of course, I couldn't come right out and tell them who I was, or what they were really into. Most of them were so brainwashed by the idea of becoming a supermodel that they didn't want to hear it.

"But some, maybe one in four, already sensed something wasn't right. If I felt they were open to it, I'd tell them what was about to happen to them and arrange for them to be taken out."

Wynn thought about Maria, the bleach-bottle-blonde two doors down from him at the All-Nighter. "Was a girl named Maria one of those?"

"Yeah. She even helped us transfer girls from time-to-time. They'd stay with her for a few hours until Parker could get someone there to take them out."

Wynn thought about the other girl he'd seen peeking out of Maria's window the morning after the speedway shooting. He hoped she was okay. "What about the guy?"

"Who?"

"When I first checked in to the All-Nighter, there was a guy in a rumpled suit coming out of Maria's room."

"That was one of our guys," Delgado-Lopez said. "Checking up on her."

Wynn nodded. *Good actors.*

"But there's still one loose end," Delgado-Lopez said. "The buyers. I can't tell you how sick I felt every time I went to one of Kovacs' damn fashion shows. All those mega-rich billionaires bidding on girls like they're buying a car, or a piece of art. It's disgusting. I'd like to bust just one of them to send a message to 'em all. Maybe that would slow 'em down."

"Is Nadeem one of those guys?" Wynn asked.

"The worst," Delgado-Lopez said. "When we saw him the morning after with that girl, about to board that plane, I tried to buy her from him. I knew that if she got on that plane, her life was over. He was having none of it. I hate to think where she is now."

Wynn didn't have an answer to that one. But he did know where Nadeem was.

Right now.

In a limo approaching the North Las Vegas Airport.

With Jenna.

As a dancer at Pink, Jenna was already on the joint task force's radar. They'd brought her in, and, with a little encouragement from Wynn, convinced her to use herself as bait to draw Nadeem out.

He likes you, Wynn had reminded her. *Asked you to go away with him. Now that Pink and The Deuce are closed, it's the perfect opportunity to tell him you've reconsidered. That you'd love to go away with him.*

Wynn watched the video monitor as the limo eased to a stop beside the small jet. The limo doors opened, and Nadeem stepped out, followed by Jenna. A female flight attendant appeared in the open doorway of the jet and descended the stairs.

"Go!" Parker said.

The van, along with two other FBI vehicles, sped across the tarmac toward the waiting plane, arriving just as the flight attendant, another FBI agent, stepped between Jenna and Nadeem and pulled her gun.

Parker, Delgado-Lopez, and a half dozen other agents spilled from their cars, guns drawn, encircling Nadeem and his driver. Within moments, both men were in custody on the ground.

Wynn stepped from the van, meeting Jenna's gaze across the tarmac. Relief flashed in her eyes, and she broke through the small crowd, rushing toward him. He wrapped his arms around her in a protective embrace.

Parker pulled Nadeem to his feet as Delgado-Lopez stepped in front of him.

"Where is she?" Delgado-Lopez demanded.

"Who do you mean?" Nadeem asked.

"The girl you took out of here two weeks ago."

Nadeem's smile was cold. "Way beyond your reach."

"It'll go easier on you if you help us get her back," Delgado-Lopez said, a hard edge of warning in her voice.

"That's funny," Nadeem scoffed. "With my resources, I'll be out of here within a week. I'll tell her you said hi when I see her."

Delgado-Lopez grimaced and turned away.

CHAPTER 58

THE NEXT DAY, WYNN stood in the living room of the safe house. The one Krista had snuck out of when she came to help him. Krista's father, John, and her son, Joshua, sat at the dining room table, assembling a Lego dinosaur. Wynn wasn't sure exactly what it was supposed to be. The picture on the box looked like some kind of T-Rex.

John's eyes were moist with unshed tears as he watched his grandson put the pieces together.

Joshua looked to be a great kid. He was a little over four feet tall, with dark hair and eyes. Cute. And most importantly, polite. When Krista had introduced Wynn, Joshua had shaken his hand, nice and firm, and said, *Nice to meet you, sir.*

He's met a lot of U.S. Marshals over the years, Krista had said. *He knows they're here to help.*

A bedroom door creaked softly as Krista and her mom emerged, Krista rolling a suitcase behind her. She stepped up next to Joshua as Agent Todd stuck his head through the front door.

"Two minutes," Todd said.

Krista's mom stopped next to Wynn as they watched Krista, Joshua, and John pack up the Legos.

Wynn turned to Krista's mom. "How's Terrance?"

"As well as can be expected, I guess," she said. "Physically, anyway. Mentally, emotionally, I think it's going to take a while."

Wynn nodded.

All told, Terrance had been held a little over four weeks. He'd lost the eye, an ear, two fingers and a toe. No one really knew why Kovacs had stopped cutting, and instead had started providing medical care, but they were grateful, regardless.

As grateful as you can be, given the circumstances, Wynn thought.

Terrance was to be released from the hospital in a few hours. He'd go live with his parents while Krista and Joshua would be taken away.

Back into witness protection.

With Danny dead, Krista, her parents, and Ruiz debated long and hard whether witness protection was still necessary. Krista had insisted Wynn be included in the conversation, but he'd stayed mostly silent. The outcome would affect him, but he didn't feel it was his place to affect it.

In the end, Ruiz's argument won the day. Danny wasn't the reason Krista and Joshua were being protected. Bennie was. And Bennie was still alive. His power and influence had been reduced, but not eliminated.

Marcus's murder a few days ago proved it.

It also put a target squarely on Wynn's back.

Krista had asked him to go into the program with her. Ruiz didn't like the idea, but he agreed. His contingent exit plan had been to put Wynn into the program for a year or two, anyway. Separately.

But knowing how easily Krista and Wynn had coordinated together right under his nose, Ruiz figured they would be easier to keep track of if they were together.

But Wynn had hesitated.

Not that he had a lot—really anything—tying him down.

He was single. No kids. No job. No obligations.

But did he really want to give up who he was, even if, at this point, he had little to show for it? His parents were in Colorado. Alive and doing okay. If he were to disappear, would that put a target on them, just as it had on Terrance?

No, he'd rather face whatever came head on. If there was a target on him, he'd rather keep it on him than risk it being refocused on his parents.

Krista had become angry when he told her of his decision.

Wynn watched as the family exchanged embraces all around. When they were finished, Krista stepped up to Wynn.

"You're sure you won't come with us?" Krista asked. Her voice was soft, hopeful, yet resigned. She knew what he was going to say.

Wynn's smile was sad. *Brigadier's Ball all over again.* He said nothing.

"I'll miss you," Krista said.

"You, too," Wynn said.

She reached up and kissed him on the cheek. "Thank you."

Wynn nodded. His voice suddenly nowhere to be found.

"They're here," Todd said.

Wynn watched as Todd escorted Krista and Joshua to a waiting SUV, then pulled away.

Still don't know her new name.

———

A week later, Wynn stood in the garage of his Ventura home, packing his duffle into the saddlebag of his Harley. A black Crown Victoria pulled into the driveway and eased to a stop. Lieutenant Lou Akins, of the Ventura Police Detectives, grunted his way out of the car.

Wynn strolled down the driveway to greet him. They clasped hands and embraced.

When they separated, Akins nodded at two men replacing the front window. "That's the second in barely a month."

"The first was my fault," Wynn said. "Not the second."

"What about the interior?"

"They were in yesterday," Wynn said. "Good as new."

Akins nodded.

Three days after Wynn had gotten home from Vegas, two men had broken into his house. To kill him, Wynn had assumed.

One had gone back out through the front window. One through the front door.

Both left in body bags.

Unfortunately, in addition to the broken window, they'd left behind several stains on the carpet and bullet holes in the walls. Those had already been repaired.

Their conversation paused as a second car pulled to stop at the end of the driveway. Linda Trilby, Wynn's attorney, stepped from the car and came up the drive.

"Wynn. Lieutenant." Trilby nodded to them both.

"Thanks for coming," Wynn said.

Trilby looked Wynn up and down. He was dressed in his riding gear. She pointed to his Harley, the saddlebag still open, the duffle visible inside. "Looks like you're going somewhere."

"I am," Wynn said.

"Where?" Trilby asked.

"No idea," Wynn said.

Akins looked at him, a concerned look on his face.

"Maybe Ruiz was right," Wynn said with a shrug. "Maybe I should've gone into witness protection. Clearly, based on what happened the other night, Bennie's still after me. I need to disappear for a while, until he cools off."

"That could be a while," Akins said.

Wynn turned to Trilby. "Which is why I asked you here. I want you to sell the place. Get whatever you can, but get rid of it." He shrugged. "I can't ever live here again." He turned to Akins. "You know what's in the closet, right?"

Akins gave a slow nod, understanding lighting his eyes.

Wynn's arsenal of guns. A lot of them.

"Can you find a place to store 'em?" Wynn asked.

Akins nodded again. "Yeah. I got a place."

"What do you want done with the furnishings and personal effects?" Trilby asked.

"Sell 'em," Wynn said. "And the Lexus." He glanced toward the bike. His wedding ring and the Topaz earrings he was going to give Nicole the night she died were packed in the duffle. She was buried with her wedding ring. "There's nothing personal in there."

"What about those two other bikes?" Trilby asked. She was referring to Wynn's Harley Davidson Sportster, and the Indian Challenger he'd gotten from Delgado, now parked in his garage.

Wynn looked at Akins.

"I've got room for 'em," Akins said. "I'll put 'em in my garage." His eyes glistened. "Maybe that way you'll swing back through here once in a while."

Wynn smiled. He was going to miss the old guy. "Count on it."

The End

For more Sean Wynn thrillers, including a free short story, visit
www.keithjweber.com

MAY I ASK A FAVOR?

IF YOU ENJOYED *NOGALES Pass,* I would ask you to please leave a review on Amazon.com. As an independent author/publisher, reader reviews are critical to helping others discover Sean Wynn, and allow me, a grateful author, to continue to tell his story.

Select reviewers may also be part of the Sean Wynn "Advance Team," with early access to unreleased novels as well as special content and events. If you would like to be part of the Advance Team, or if you have comments, ideas, suggestions, or would just like to talk about books, writing, or motorcycles, feel free to reach out. I always love to hear from readers. You can reach me via my website at keithjweber.com.

With Gratitude,

Keith

ALSO CURRENTLY AVAILABLE

NIGHT RULES, VOLUME 1 of the Sean Wynn series and a 2024 Grandmaster Award Finalist in the Clive Cussler Adventure Writers Competition. Former Marine Sean Wynn would prefer to mind his own business. Prefer he didn't see two men stalking a woman at a remote Wyoming rest area. But the last time he ignored something that didn't look right, his wife wound up dead.

Intentional, Volume 2 of the Sean Wynn series and a 2023 Grandmaster Award Finalist in the Clive Cussler Adventure Writers Competition, follows Sean Wynn as he discovers his wife's death may not have been an accident, and seeks answers—and vengeance—from those responsible.

The Interviews, a Sean Wynn short story. Special Agent Mark Ruiz needs help with a case—a bad one. Is Sean Wynn the right guy to help? Maybe talking with the people who know him best will shed some light on just who is Sean Wynn.

ACKNOWLEDGEMENTS

WRITING IS A SOLITARY activity, but creating a book cannot be done without the help of many others. In this case, that includes William Nuessle, Carly Stephens, Danny Raye, Dave Pasquantonio, Parisa Zolfaghari, Emily LeVault, Allison Pereslegin, Jack Savage, Thibault Heitz, and Kevin Chilvers. Special thanks to Kaitlin Weber for her keen eye on the cover design.

ABOUT THE AUTHOR

KEITH J. WEBER IS a long-time writer, short-time author. After starting his career as an advertising copywriter, he spent the next several decades writing everything from marketing copy to magazine articles and financial education. His debut fiction novel, *Night Rules,* and its sequel, *Intentional,* were both released in early 2024. An avid motorcyclist, Keith enjoys riding the majestic mountains of Colorado as well as the magical Black Hills of South Dakota. On a Friday or Saturday night, you may even find him strumming a guitar with his band at a local brewery.